Edison

PALLAVI SHARMA DIXIT

THIRD
STATE
BOOKS

SAN FRANCISCO

EDISON
by Pallavi Sharma Dixit

**THIRD
STATE
BOOKS**

Third State Books
93 Cumberland Street
San Francisco, CA 94110
Visit us at www.thirdstatebooks.com

First edition: June 2024
ISBN 979-8-89013-015-0 (hardcover)
979-8-89013-016-7 (e-book)

Library of Congress Control Number: 2024933123

Cover and text design by Kathryn E. Campbell
Printed in Canada by Friesens Corporation

For Amol, of course

phoolon mein, kaliyon mein, sapnon ki galiyon mein
tere bina kuch kahin naa
in flowers, in buds, in the streets of dreams
without you there is nothing anywhere at all

—Muqaddar Ka Sikandar (1978)

"Today, suburban areas like central
New Jersey serve as the backdrop
to both the beginning and end of the
search for the American Dream."

—S. Mitra Kalita, *Suburban Sahibs*

PROLOGUE

I ndians add "one" to things. When, for instance, Hemant Engineer attended the graduation party of his dear friend Sanjay Sapra's daughter at Moghul Fine Indian Cuisine, the most celebrated and formal restaurant in our town, he wrote a check for one hundred and one dollars, as opposed to simply one hundred, and tucked it into a mortar-boarded card. When Leena Engineer, daughter of Hemant, attended wedding after wedding of friends much younger than she was while being increasingly referred to as "still unmarried" and "that poor girl," she always brought with her a check for fifty-one dollars. Neither Hemant nor Leena, nor the recipients of these checks, nor the thousands of Indians in Edison, New Jersey—the Hindu ones, specifically—who give and receive such checks every week question the necessity of the extra dollar.

If pressed, a resident of Edison—this town brimming with Indians, where some joke there are more Indians than in India herself—might venture the opinion that perhaps it's a superstition, something you do "just in case." Such people who add one dollar out of fear of repercussions tend to add one to nonmonetary amounts as well. Several buildings over from the Engineers' in King's Court apartments, Beena Joshi adds one to the end of microwave-oven cooking times: 1:31 for leftover chana, 3:01 for popcorn. Her Seiko wristwatch is set one minute fast, and when she rewarded herself with diamond earrings after years of laboring as a cashier at Drug Fair and operating a catering business from her apartment on weekends, she insisted they each have precisely 1.1 carats, just in case.

Once, on a windless midsummer afternoon in 1988, a lively assortment of attendants at the Exxon gas station on Oak Tree Road attempted to answer their fellow attendant Abdul Rashid's question: "Why the one?"

Attendant #1, known for his quickness to point out the stupidity of those around him, said, "Why are Americans listening to a groundhog for a weather report?" His point, which he didn't state outright but which everyone understood, was that his parents in India added one, and their parents before them, and it was just another of the many inexplicable yet incontrovertible traditions lugged over to America, like cracking a coconut on momentous occasions.

"It is because zero has no meaning," Attendant #2 said with a confidence not regularly associated with him. "It is nothing. Not a good number."

Attendant #3, who was not scheduled to work that day but came to the gas station anyway for "time pass," for shooting the shit, added that no one affixed one to non-zero-ending numbers, like twenty-five or fifty-five.

A battered and apologetic-looking Buick pulled up and a man started to emerge from it, but the attendants kicked up a mild uproar, sending the man back into his car. "This is New Jersey, sir," Attendant #4 said at the rolled-down window, and after the requisite "Cash or charge?" exchange, amidst the heady bouquet of regular unleaded, he asked the customer to weigh in on the one-dollar discussion because, naturally, the man was Indian—what else would he be in this corner of our town?

"It is recommended in Hindu culture to stick to odd numbers," the customer said. "In our temples, there is always an odd number of priests; and for the head-shaving ceremony of young boys, the child must be an odd number of years old. In weddings, how many sacred steps do the bride and groom take? Seven." Before driving off, the customer, who was the chairman of public relations for the Sri Venkateswara Temple in Pittsburgh, handed Attendant #4 some flyers for the upcoming Janamashtami celebrations, stressing the importance of observing the birth of Krishna, who was, incidentally, seven years old when he lifted Govardhan mountain with one hand to shelter villagers from seven days and seven nights of cataclysmic rain.

Attendant #4 returned to his friends on the concrete stoops before the pumps.

"Really, it is one thing to add a one-rupee coin, but one whole dollar?" said Attendant #3, the only attendant without the ashy blue uniform. "For birthdays, on anniversaries, and I have four sisters I am having to give money to on Rakhi. It adds up, man. The exchange rate is not favorable for carrying over such a tradition."

They contemplated a silky black Mercedes as it glided into the station and up to a pump. Attendant #1 pulled out a handkerchief and wiped his forehead. Attendant #2 folded a temple flyer into a fan and waved it at his face. Then, in a move that Attendants #1–3 and Abdul Rashid would regret for years, they coaxed the ever-coaxable Attendant #4 into attending to the waiting Mercedes.

Attendant #4 still had the question of one dollar in his head when he walked over to the tinted-windowed car stopped at the farthest pump from where he'd been sitting. The driver, a jovial Indian who had dyed his hair to what some might argue was too jet a shade of black, made an enthusiastic attempt to explain the meaning of the extra dollar, but found himself stumbling on his answer. "Why don't we ask my good friend Bachchan here?"

For decades to come, Attendant #4, Prem Kumar, the hero of our story, would replay this scene again and again in his mind until the image became scratchy over time, just like the videotapes of his favorite movies, *Sholay*, *Don* and *Amar, Akbar, Anthony*, all of which starred the "The Big B"—Hindi cinema's first action hero, its "Angry Young Man," the brooding actor who performed his own stunts and sometimes even sang his own songs, the "one-man industry," the lanky king of what the world would one day refer to as "Bollywood," whose bouncy, graceful dance moves and romantic big-screen interludes with all the leading ladies caused millions to swoon, the erstwhile member of Parliament, who had by then achieved demigod status not just amongst Indians but also Kenyans, Fijians, the Thai, citizens of the Soviet Union, and residents of any nation that imported Hindi films, presumably pirated, which is to say in every corner of the globe. Amitabh Bachchan, the too dark, too gangly, entirely unlikely megastar whose poster had hung in Prem's childhood room, stepped out of the car.

"The question you ask," he said, in that baritone voice laden with gravitas that Prem knew so well, "is a good one." He folded his arms on the hood of the car. He turned his head and took in the crowd of riveted gas-station attendants at a distance. When he returned his gaze to Prem, whose thin, tall frame mirrored his own, the driver had also emerged from the car and was mopping his forehead with his sleeve. Amitabh Bachchan said, "I have wondered about this myself. The answer is this—"

For Prem it was a moment outside of reality, like a dream sequence from a Hindi movie. He tried, awestruck and trembling, to absorb the words of his idol on the other side of the car. Later, Prem would be grateful that Amitabh Bachchan was not interested that day in engaging in complicated conversation, but instead delivered a sort of monologue—not unlike his powerful monologues in *Sharaabi*—to which Prem was more witness than participant.

"One extra rupee, one extra dollar," Amitabh Bachchan began. "There are many who believe this is given for the purpose of avoiding something bad. They are mistaken; the extra one is for bringing something good. It is for luck. It means, 'May you add to this money I have given you. Here is one rupee for you to begin building on.' When we give an extra one on the occasion of a wedding, we are giving the couple a lift toward their journey to prosperity; when we give a young man an extra one on his birthday, we are wishing the same. It means keep going. It is one to grow upon."

The gas nozzle clip clicked, as if signaling the end of the speech. Amitabh Bachchan removed his arms from the hood of the car and turned and leaned against it, looking out at Oak Tree Road as though there were something there to see. Prem removed the nozzle, replaced the fuel cap, and brought the credit card slip to the driver. And when his work was properly completed, drenched in sweat and the scent of gasoline, he hurried around to Amitabh Bachchan's side of the car and uttered what was in his heart. "Sir, thank you, sir. I am hoping you will be winning a Filmfare award for *Shahenshah*."

The attendants, who had remained silent as if to keep from breaking a spell, erupted into pandemonium as the Mercedes pulled out of the station. In the din of his friends' cheers and the glare of the day's severe heat, Prem felt as though he were Vijay Verma from *Deewaar*—the role that established Amitabh as the preeminent tragic actor of his day—emerging from the warehouse after single-handedly defeating the bad guys, sunlight reflecting off his badge, a hero in the truest Indian sense. Attendant #2 and Abdul Rashid were approaching a state of agitation in their desire to learn what Amitabh Bachchan had spoken of, and when Prem related the facts of the encounter, that the most famous actor in the world, the man who would be declared the most popular movie star of the millennium by a 1999 BBC poll, spoke to him about the significance of adding "one," the attendants were stupefied.

"This is what you asked? Not 'Did you almost die during filming of *Coolie*?' or 'Who is prettier, Zeenat Aman or Parveen Babi?' You should have asked, 'Was it difficult to dance on a motorcycle in *Muqaddar ka Sikandar*?'" Attendant #1 said, then spat on the ground to remove the bitter taste of missed opportunity from his mouth.

Attendant #3 expressed a far more benign sentiment, saying simply, "It was God's intention that I come to the station on my off day so that I might behold Amitabh Bachchan." After the discussions about what was said and how it was said and what Amitabh Bachchan was wearing and how tall he looked were exhausted, Attendant #1 raised the possibility that it wasn't Amitabh Bachchan at all. After all, it was argued, what would he be doing in Edison, New Jersey? For this was before Edison had become what it is amongst us, before one Indian grocery store became ten, then twenty, and eventually all of Oak Tree Road was lined with Indian jewelry stores, grocery stores, video stores, and restaurants; before thousands of Indian people from surrounding areas flocked here to shop and eat on weekends, before Indian American brides from up and down the state and across the country began coming here to shop for their weddings, before a full-fledged India Day parade launched itself down Oak Tree Road every August, to the delight of some and the disgust of others. One day, Indian movie stars would be an unexceptional sight in the USA because they would appear at parades as guests of honor, and they would lip-synch and perform elaborately choreographed dances in colossal stage shows that packed Giants Stadium, and they would shoot *Kal Ho Naa Ho* and *Kabhi*

Alvida Naa Kehna and many others on location in New York, and Aamir Khan would attend the Academy Awards in support of *Lagaan*, and Anil Kapoor would join the cast of *24*, and Priyanka Chopra would star in *Quantico*, and power couple Abhishek Bachchan—the "Little B," as it were—and Aishwarya Rai would be guests on *Oprah*, and Madhuri Dixit would marry a doctor and move to Denver, and Continental Airlines would unveil a nonstop flight from Indira Gandhi International Airport to Newark Liberty, and the lines would blur between *there* and *here*. But these things had not yet come to pass.

As the years went on, the attendants would increasingly doubt whether they had really seen Amitabh Bachchan at the Exxon gas station. But Prem always knew it was real. And furthermore, he remembered every word just as Amitabh Bachchan had spoken it. The reason for this was that Prem was a man preoccupied by love. After Amitabh Bachchan talked to him about luck, Prem thought not about the miraculous fact of Amitabh Bachchan talking to him about anything, but rather of his *sapno ki rani*, his beloved, the queen of his dreams, and the way in which the wise words of the film icon related to her. He thought of all the extra dollars and rupees he'd been given in his twenty-five years and was struck by the enormity of the good wishes for prosperity that had been conferred upon him. Before leaving, Amitabh Bachchan pulled his wallet from the pocket of his impossibly long, white slacks. "For you to add upon," he said and presented Prem with a stiff dollar bill on which he scribbled his signature before handing it over. In that instant, with an Amitabh Bachchan dollar in his hand, Prem was overcome with the suddenly renewed possibility of building himself into someone in this country, a man worthy of Leena Engineer, a man of action, an entrepreneur, a success story, a viable suitor, an extraordinary immigrant in a town of immigrants, a visionary, a husband, a real American hero.

M uch earlier on in the story of his life, when Prem Kumar was a boy in Delhi enjoying a childhood ruled by self-doubt and the pressure to succeed, he began a lifelong, rapturous relationship with Hindi cinema. In the way of most children stricken at birth with shyness, Prem accumulated and hid behind a vast knowledge. His obsession kicked off with *Zanjeer* (1973) and went backward from there: *Chhalia, Jewel Thief, Pyaasa, Awaara*, all the way to *Kismet*. By the time he reached adolescence, he had made himself an expert and at the same time, a social outcast. True, he had a few similarly awkward friends, but no one he particularly liked, and he was too crippled by diffidence to make any new ones. He plodded through secondary school and university, finding escape in dream sequences and dance numbers and trying not to attract attention. But as is often the case with those who find difficulty in maneuvering the world, he longed secretly to break free of his nonspeaking role, to bask for a moment in the hero's spotlight.

The heroes with whom Prem grew up—Rajesh Khanna, Dharmendra, a bevy of Kapoors beginning with Raj—were debonair, confident, and popular with women. Prem was none of these things. He excelled as a student, but only because schoolwork came easy to him, not because of any special value he assigned to hard work, his lack of interest in his own progress staggering. He was quick-witted, but few people knew this, and from a young age he drank too much tea. At six-foot-one, he was taller than most people around him, and the flicker of confidence he possessed sparked from this fact. He feigned indifference but was flattered when people pointed out his resemblance to the milky-complexioned, absurdly handsome Shashi Kapoor, Hindi movie heart-throb of the 1960s to the early 1980s, and to bolster this comparison, he boldly adhered to prominent sideburns, even though the time for prominent sideburns had long passed. He longed to use his height and supposed good looks in service to his enduring hunger for romance but put forth no effort to speak with any girls, though more than one girl had put into circulation rumors of her interest. The youngest in a large family of great wealth, he bristled at the presumption that he would someday join the family business. Offices, presentations, meetings, people—these were not for him, he professed, citing an inclination toward a more creative and nebulous path. Even in the privacy of his own mind, he did not admit to an overpowering fear of his own future.

Essentially, even upon completing college with excellent marks, Prem was aimless. No one in May 1986 could have foreseen his future passage to America nor the meteoric rise of Superstar Entertainment, certainly not his father who entered the third-floor drawing room two years after Prem's college convocation, interrupting his movie to arrange his marriage. It was not often that Ashok Ratan Kumar, head of Kumar Group, a telecommunications, pharmaceuticals, and alcoholic-beverages conglomerate, was home on a Tuesday afternoon. There had to be an unsavory reason. So when Prem heard his father's footsteps approaching from the end of the hall, he pressed pause on the VCR and leaped behind the drapes.

This was not his first time behind the curtains. He had spent time there when he was supposed to be participating in team sports, and again on the occasion of his Class Eight speaking competition, and when he had wanted to skip a Kumar Group banquet for visiting heads of state. This time, it was for the purpose of avoiding a conversation, long overdue, about his future prospects. As Prem stood enveloped by his own hot breath, his father seemed to be surveying the room. A *dishoom!* then two *dishkiyaoons!* burst forth from the television, and it sounded like his father was settling into an armchair to watch *Muqaddar ka Sikandar*, which had resumed itself mid-fight. The door squeaked open and a tray clinked on the table. The servant exited. Two scenes later, there was a long, loud slurp of tea, and his father said, "Why this engagement party is so depressing?"

Prem smacked his teeth. "Because Vijay misses his mother who died, and though he has made a lot of money and has everything, he just wishes he still had her." He realized too late that his father had tricked him into revealing himself, but what else could he have done in the face of an affront to *Muqaddar Ka Sikandar*?

"Son, there is no need for hiding," Ashok said. Prem's father was not an unkind man, and Prem was not afraid of him, per se. He comported himself in a regal manner and had a flaccid, grandfatherly face with sympathetic eyes. He wore strictly business suits and was typically accompanied by two assistants and a secretary, yet was not as distant from his children as perhaps he could have been. When the demands of the Kumar empire compelled him to miss his children's milestone events—Prem's Class Three harmonium recital or his Class Seven Math Olympiad—he could be counted on to compensate with watches, electronics, the latest moped, or cash. Still, Prem did not wish to face his father's inevitable questions.

"I am not hiding."

"Then?"

"I am looking for something," Prem said with unwarranted indignation.

Ashok tried again with a more authoritative tone. "I have come to discuss your life plans."

"I don't really have time for that. I have to find this thing."

His father sighed. He had structured Kumar Group in such a way that Prem could not receive a salary unless he was an active and effective contributor to its success. Since his son contributed nothing, at most he would get an inheritance, but that might not be for decades, as Ashok was a sturdy man who walked regularly on a treadmill and stayed away from butter chicken. "We must think about your future," he said.

"That sounds fantastic, Papa, first-class." Prem knelt down and slapped around at the floor, making a great display of looking for something. "But now is not a good timing."

"You see," his father continued in his booming industrialist tone, "there is a time in a young man's life when he has to take the most important decision of all." He was pacing the room now, and Prem got the feeling he wasn't leaving. "When a young man must seize the opportunity before him and move boldly ahead."

"Can you pause the movie?"

"When he must take action and do what is right for himself and for his family."

"Is there tea for me?"

The curtain flung open. His father stood before him with a grim expression. He was wearing his typical uniform—black suit, no tie—but the top two buttons of his shirt were open instead of the usual one, which signaled to Prem that a miracle may have occurred. His father's frown underwent a slow and terrifying transformation into an enormous grin. "A marriage proposal has come for you," he said. "From the Aswani family!" He threw up his arms and wrapped them around Prem, thumping him on the back the way he'd once done to Prem's brother Akash after he won the Intercollege Table Tennis Tournament, Delhi branch.

"Wait, what?" Prem wriggled out of his father's embrace.

"Congratulations, Son! Many blessings!" The evergreen song "Salaam-e-Ishq" began just then, and father and son turned their heads to look at the TV, then swiveled back to each other. Prem slinked past his father and plopped down on the couch. His father's estimation of him stood in stark relief before his eyes: a dependent who would never be independent, a problem that needed fixing, a delicate flower bud that would probably never bloom, but would instead sit at home its whole life and watch movies. He would have preferred a job offer; at least there was some dignity in that. Yet—and this was what stung most—he knew it was his own fault. He stared at drunken Amitabh singing to a sex worker and descended into profound self-loathing.

In the course of the previous two years, Prem's father had periodically thus entered the drawing room as his son was mid-movie, dismissed his assistants and secretary, sat down, and exhaled loudly through his nose. He would proceed to question his inactivity and general lack of aspiration. It was always, "Look at Anshul, he was promoted," or "Look at Vanisha, she was in *India Today*." Later it became, "Look at Anmol and Anshul, transforming us from a supplier of pharmaceutical ingredients into a manufacturer of pharmaceutical products of our own with the launch of our ulcer and reflux esophagitis medication, Kumarizine," or "Look at Vanisha and Akash, selling so much of beer." His father never stated outright that Prem did not show the same promise as his well-spoken and aggressive siblings, but he felt it all the same. While watching *Parvarish*, he learned he was a huge disappointment. During the pivotal roti-feeding scene of *Yaarana*, he caught on that his entire family doubted he would ever do anything with his life. And during the interval of *Mashaal*, he understood at last that his father was embarrassed by him.

"Are you talking about Malveena Aswani?" Prem said.

"You know the girl?" Ashok said. "Wonderful!" In the realm of wealthy and offensive Indian industrial families, the Aswanis were the wealthiest and most offensive. The heiress in question was a mainstay of the over-the-top, too-much-money Delhi social scene and she was frequently found in Page 3, the gossip-and-glitterati section of the venerated *Times of India*, Delhi edition. At a jungle-themed extravaganza, the only poolside college soirée he had attended, Prem had come across her wearing a revealing zebra-print number and carrying a spear with which she poked alleged gatecrashers. He recalled her going on about her hairdresser's egg yolk hair treatment ("You *must* try it, Pramesh").

"She is horrible."

"She is well-educated and sophisticated."

"She smells like eggs."

Ashok grunted and leaned back in his chair, then sprung forward again with a forefinger raised to the air. "What if we invite film stars to the wedding?"

Prem had no intention of moving ahead with an engagement but wanted to hear more about the film stars. "Which ones?"

"Whichever ones you want. The best ones."

"Shabana Azmi and Jayaprada?"

"Of course!"

"Can we get Rajesh Khanna and Dimple in the same room?"

"We can try."

"Maybe Parveen Babi can perform a dance number?"

"Why not?" Ashok appeared jubilant upon making so much progress in the conversation, but then a shadow fell over his face and he shifted nervously. "Now, Son, they want, you see, after marriage . . . after marriage, what would be expected is . . . you would be staying in the Aswani house."

Prem was aghast. "What kind of arrangement is that?"

"What can I do? The girl is very attached to her family's cook, and the mother is also attached, so they want to keep her and her husband and the cook and the mother all there only." He went into complicated detail about potato subji. Prem was pained by the paucity of options before him.

"Son, you would never have to work in your life," Ashok said gently.

Prem wished he could vault back into the drapes. He didn't want to work but he didn't want to not work, and he definitely didn't want Malveena Aswani as a wife. He had always wanted to emulate the on-screen exploits of the ever-amorous film stars he revered, and as far as he knew, there was no Hindi movie in which the hero married rich and coasted through life alongside a miserable woman with buckets of cash.

His father was watching the movie while digging around with his finger for a lost piece of Parle-G in his tea. When the sex worker had fallen sufficiently in love and the song ended, he turned back to Prem. "So?"

"No," Prem said.

Ashok's face fell. "But, Son, you cannot just watch movies for your whole life."

"I am not just watching movies," Prem said. He realized he'd said this with unjustified conviction because what he had been doing for two years was, in fact, just watching movies. But from this place of unfounded outrage sprouted the kernel of an idea. "I was researching," he said. "Preparing. *Working*."

His father laughed, then noted the seriousness in his son's face and adjusted accordingly. "What kind of work is that?"

Prem sat up straight and spoke with confidence and an atypical tinge of defiance. "Making movies," he said. This was fiction, something that had come to Prem in the moment, at first as a way to save face, but then, wondrously, as a possible cure for all that had ailed him since he was ten.

What more appropriate career path? And who more qualified to pursue it, with his exhaustive understanding of Hindi filmdom and his utter neglect of everything else? As a boy, he tended to forgo outdoor play for the indoor pleasure of films, which he regarded as primers for life, though they often demonstrated a complete disregard for the rules of time and space. From *Sholay*, which he had viewed twenty-three times at the Plaza, he developed a strong belief in the good-versus-evilness of the world and a keen ear for iconic one-liners. His deep mistrust of the law as a means of exacting justice had its origin in the classics *Mother India*, *Awara*, and later *Deewaar*, although this impassioned standpoint had no relevance to his own life. Because of the cinematic pervasiveness of long-lost family members, Prem had throughout his childhood suspected the existence of a twin; and because of the longstanding onscreen link between lust and singing in the rain, he experienced an intense desire for female companionship during monsoons. Above all, Prem's filmic education instilled in him an abiding faith in heroes. He harbored a dream of becoming a real-life hero himself—not the angry-young-man kind popular in the 1970s, but a more lighthearted hero, the kind that had frolicked across screens in the 1960s and was resurfacing in the mid-1980s, someone who twirled around trees and ran through fields of tulips, who eventually achieved complete personal and professional success, oozing glory and macho virility.

In a multistoried joint-family home with armed guards and de-tached servants' quarters on Kumar Group Road, shy Prem had grown up wanting to do something big—bigger even than his father, sister, and three older brothers—yet he was scared of doing anything at all. So he hid himself in movies, studying them, reading anything he could find on the subject, and wound up with a head full of corresponding data, fervently gathered and hitherto useless. He became familiar with industry history reaching back to the patriotic, slightly communist, post-Independence days; read with great zeal about story sittings, narration, and dubbing; and gained a comprehensive understanding of the generally incomprehensible system of independent distribution. By the sixth standard, Prem could have written a dissertation on the relationship between narrative content in Hindi films and the national political climate, with a focus on Indira Gandhi's Emergency; a fairly technical book about lighting and camerawork; or a substantial report on the appeal of Indian movies in Eastern Bloc nations.

All of this unprescribed research did nothing to improve his social standing, which by the time he was twelve had hit rock bottom. His classmates viewed him as eccentric and hurled uninspired insults in his direction. More than once he bunked class to avoid being teased in front of a pretty girl, and on these occasions he caught a matinee. On the Plaza's fabled single screen that year, he watched *Mili* and *Julie*, enjoyed the low-budget piety of *Jai Santoshi Maa*, and witnessed the tragedy of star-crossed brothers in the groundbreaking *Deewaar*. On the opening day of the comedic and by-and-large incoherent blockbuster *Hera Pheri*, Prem brought a box of Frooti mango drink back to his cheap seat in the stalls, where he often sat to avoid being spotted. When three other truant classmates began flinging roasted pistachios at him from the balcony, Prem tried to focus on removing the straw from its plastic wrapper, but soon the pistachios were too much. He dropped the straw on the floor in the sticky darkness between seats and went home.

Home, at that time when his mother had not yet moved on to her next life, made everything bearable. Lavanya Kumar was the kind of nurturing mother about whom kids with unloving mothers dreamed. In those utopian fantasies of maternal perfection, the mother was lovely, with cascading waves of unfrizzy hair, a glowing complexion, an air of rosewater, and eyes that smiled. Prem's mother had possessed all these qualities. In the sixteen years he knew her, she was entirely blind to any flaws in her last-born's character. When his essay, "Challenges to Environment in the Modern Age," for the Class 9 writing competition was disqualified for relying entirely on Hindi movies for references, she explained it was ahead of its time and wrote "100%" at the top of the first page. When he came home brokenhearted because his few friends had all been absent and he'd sat alone at lunch, she held his hand as they watched *Junglee*. And on days when he feigned sickness, she let him stay home with her and play carrom and watch movies until he regained a degree of courage. She never acknowledged the fact of his debilitating shyness, always emphasizing how clever and charming she found him. And had she lived, she would never have said he was incapable of anything and therefore had to marry a shrew.

The illness appeared in her stomach when Prem was fifteen, and it was a negative prognosis from the start. She must have been in a great deal of pain, he recognized many years later, but at the time, he did not guess it as they enjoyed their afternoons together on the drawing room couch under a blanket. They watched picture after classic picture: *Shree 420*, *Chori Chori*, and other Raj Kapoor films; *Pyaasa*, *Mother India*, and *Baiju Bawra*; and the hits of Dev Anand, beginning with *Guide*. It was as though she had wanted to leave him with a thorough motion-picture education grounded in the golden age of Indian cinema. Some days he forgot she was even sick, but by his sixteenth birthday, the disease had spread. His father and siblings and various aunts and cousins were there as much as their schedules would allow, but it was Prem who spent the bulk of those last days by her side. Her final words to him were not melodramatic utterances about being good or moving on. Instead, and this he would remember until the end of his own life, after a marathon day of watching *Mughal-e-Azam* (run time: 3 hours, 11 minutes) and *Madhumati* (run time: 2 hours, 59 minutes), during which she was in and out of sleep, she said, "You know, Hindi movies can be quite long sometimes."

The years after Lavanya Kumar's passing were tough on the whole family but for none more so than Prem. He kept his sadness to himself. And by the time his father entered the drawing room and proposed marriage, he had very much learned how to be alone.

"You want to make movies?" his father said in a way that did not suggest rampant enthusiasm.

"Not movie*eeez*," Prem said. "Just a movie. One. I would try one and see." Not wanting to appear desperate, he leaned back and crossed his legs, but then uncrossed them and sat up straight again, then repeated the sequence two more times. Ashok wiped away a piece of soggy biscuit at the corner of his mouth and stood. He clasped one elbow behind his back and began again to pace. The strained jaw, the pulsating neck vein, the eye twitch, and occasional nose pick—all of this suggested to Prem that his father was thinking hard on the matter, sorting out the financing, mulling over the connections he had in the industry, and considering the potential return on investment.

At last, Ashok spoke: "What if we find another, more suitable girl?" he said.

Prem visibly deflated. For a quick second, the lights had finally come on in his life, and the next, they were extinguished by a procession of eligible socialites with spears. "I am not marrying Gauri Jindal or Bhumika Damani either."

"Those families said no already because you do not work."

"Oh," Prem said. There was a minute of silence between them, then Prem said, "I can make a film, Papa." He tried in earnest to convince him that he understood the production process as well as the tastes of today's movie-going crowds. "In fact," he said, "I have the story half-written"—he didn't—"and I have rung up Subhash Ghai to direct"—he hadn't. He talked at length about the role that advanced technologies would play in the industry in the coming years and the opportunities for innovation in film distribution, including the possibility of vast networks of multiscreen theaters (as opposed to the prevailing single-screen behemoths). This fount of ideas formed on the spot and spouted forth from within him, his excitement gaining momentum as the thoughts came tumbling out, mounting until he was breathless and hopeful.

"What about that round, happy girl from the Sharma family?" Ashok said.

"Papa!"

"Okay." Ashok cleared his throat. "Work just is not in your nature, Son. Also, movie halls with five screens? This will never work."

But when Ashok Ratan Kumar, Titan of Technology, Giant of Generics, Purveyor of Lite Lager, glimpsed his son's long face, he reconsidered. Prem, fighting back tears, had returned his gaze to the movie with a high-speed motorcycle chase now in progress. Ashok observed his son's profile, which echoed the angel features of his late wife. Prem watched too many movies and was distressingly timid, but he was a good boy, the most decent, in fact, of all his children. He had been left largely alone since his main supporter's departure from this world. Perhaps, Ashok thought, he could have spent more time with Prem and perhaps he could have guided his path somewhat. Here he was now, exhibiting signs of ambition and the inklings of a career, albeit in a ludicrous field. A wave of guilt-laden love came over the Titan of Technology. Eyes welling with tears, he resolved then to give his youngest child a chance.

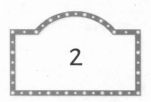

2

It was a transformative moment in the history of Hindi films: the destined-to-be-legendary Sridevi and Anil Kapoor were hitting the scene, displacing aging industry stalwarts; Govinda's gyrating hips had begun gyrating while Mithun Chakraborty had launched a decade-late but well-received disco revolution; fans in India and around the world welcomed the proliferation of romantic comedies, which were a departure from the serious "social" films that had reigned for so many years, and they embraced the tunes of Bappi Lahiri, that rotund music director who ushered in an era of synthesized Hindi film music (some of which bore a suspicious resemblance to certain Western tunes) while wearing fifty gold chains. All of this occurred without the benefit of bank loans or commercial financing, which is to say, with the help of sinister forces, shadowy underworld figures, and "black money" in need of laundering. It was a chaotic business, every man for himself, no place for the meek.

Into this entered the meek Prem, unimpressive in a T-shirt and jeans, armed only with an unwavering love of Indian cinema. On an oppressively humid morning at the end of May, he first set foot on the grounds of the storied Mehboob Studios, knees quivering under the weight of great responsibility, both to his father and, he realized after turning onto the tree-lined drive and spotting one of the grand old

soundstage buildings, to the studio itself. Mehboob was the setting
of the masterpiece *Mother India,* where Dev Anand became the Guide,
where Amitabh *Khaike Paan*-ed his way into history. Prem experienced
a kind of euphoria muddled with nausea as he entered Soundstage One.
The inside of the building, it turned out, was not as glamorous as the
movies filmed in it would suggest. The cavernous space was crammed
with stacks of crates, large coils of cable, wooden planks of all sizes. In
one corner was shattered glass and what looked like a pile of rubbish;
a cat wandered around in the shadows. Prem discerned the stale smell
of cigarettes mixed with tandoori fish. It would be a serious task to
transform this place and get the project off the ground. Historically, he
had not enjoyed a challenge. He kicked a hairspray can, nearly hitting
the cat, which screeched. He paced a cheerless, dirt-covered rug for
several minutes before accepting his limited options. So, like Amit in
Silsila when he marries his dead brother's pregnant fiancée, in classic
hero fashion, Prem decided to try rising to the occasion. He opened a
side door to let the cat out then got to work.

It did not go well. From the dining room of his family's flat in
Bandra, Prem attempted to coordinate the preproduction of his movie. From his years of casual study as well as a recent magazine article,
"So You Are Wanting to Make a Hindi Movie," he had some notion of
what needed to be done. With a script (written by him) and the money
(from his dad), he went in search of a top director. Subhash Ghai, of
Karz, Hero, etc., his top choice, had unfortunately established his own
production company and would not come to the phone. Others who
would not come to the phone included Ramesh Sippy, K. Balachander,
Govind Nihalani, both Ramsay brothers, and Gulzar. As Prem continued his search for a director, a hero and heroine, and a supporting cast
and crew, he was reminded that Hindi films were a family business.
Without deep roots and personal connections in the industry, you had

little chance of breaking into the talkies, even with a heap of cash. Prem felt betrayed by the thing he loved most, and the heavy weight of failure bore down on him as he sat at the dining table one morning next to a silent phone. At nine thirty, he asked Chandraprakash, an ancient and loyal servant of the Kumars, to make him a cup of tea. At ten, he asked Chandraprakash to teach him how to make the tea himself. He drew several doodles of a monkey in the margins of a diary and then spilled his tea on the floor, shattering the cup. He cleaned up the mess and then decided to clean the entire flat. At noon, he sat back down by the phone.

A month in Bombay and all he had was a studio space reserved for him by his father's University of Delhi batchmate's accountant who was vaguely related to Mehboob Khan. He would have to settle for a third-rate director and no-name actors. It could be good, he told himself, giving young newcomers with fresh ideas a chance. But the talent he ended up finding was neither young nor talented. The cameraman was blind in one eye, the music director uninspired, the remainder of the crew a motley assemblage of has-beens. For lead actors, the best Prem could do was Brijesh, whose teeth were alarmingly crooked, and Yashika, who, along with the director, smelled strongly of whiskey. Somehow, after several weeks and considerable bribing of city officials for the necessary permits, they were ready for production.

Three days before filming was to begin, Prem threw up in a giant ashtray. He had come down to Mehboob to see the renovated set, which was supposed to look like the interior of a gaudy mansion. It was an unbearably muggy Bombay afternoon, so when his car reached the end of the driveway he was surprised to find a malevolent-looking man withstanding the heat in the unattractive courtyard between sound-stage buildings. Prem got out and exchanged nods with the man, who upon closer inspection miraculously turned out to be Amrish Puri, the quintessential villain of Hindi films. He was ashing a cigarette into an enormous bowl. Prem stood slack-jawed and staring at the veteran actor until at last and somewhat inevitably Amrish Puri waved him over.

"Come," Amrish Puri said, "give me company."

Prem blinked several times and, heart pounding and dizzy with anxiety, walked across the courtyard; this was his first brush with a genuine movie star, and he had embarrassed himself with mangled words in the presence of far lesser individuals. He wiped his hand down his pant leg and extended it to the actor. "There are so many villains," Prem began, "you know, Goga Kapoor, Prem Chopra, Ranjeet, Amjad Khan, well, actually Amjad Khan is quite good, but, you know, I think you are the best one." Immediately, as always, Prem was horrified by his own ineloquence. Amrish Puri—who had made a recent Hollywood turn as the evil priest in *Indiana Jones and the Temple of Doom*, which was temporarily banned in India due to its insinuation that Hindus eat monkey brains—was physically daunting, just as in his films, but also a nice guy, and Prem soon found himself in easy conversation about *Samundar*, the Sunny Deol–starrer being shot on Stages Four and Five of whose largely respectable supporting cast Amrish Puri was a part. Then the conversation turned to Prem's own project.

"Wonderful to see young people joining the industry," Amrish Puri said. "Tell me, what is your movie about?"

Prem could hardly believe that the dreaded, wickedly mustachioed gangster from *Shakti* was asking about his film. He felt his palms growing damp again and he stuffed them in his pockets before relating the story of star-crossed BCom students. "There is this boy and this girl," he began. When he was done, Amrish Puri thwacked him on the back, which, as if dislodging a too big chunk of potato from his throat, caused Prem to spew forth all of his fears about entering Soundstage One that day. "I should have come sooner, but the art director and set designer make a hopeless team and I was scared to see the mess they made, and also, the whole production is in a sorry condition. What if my film is a flop? What if I never even finish it?" Breathless and embarrassed, Prem became aware that he was unburdening himself to a movie star who had not asked to be unburdened to. "Sorry, Amrish Puri," Prem said.

"Have a deep breath," the actor said. "Go in, look around, then come immediately out. This way, if it is bad, we can discuss the forward steps."

Prem took the suggested breath. So what if the set is a disaster? He would come back outside to the loving embrace of Amrish Puri and figure out a plan. He crossed the courtyard and entered the building.

It was a disaster. Instead of the mansion he had requested, the stage looked like a stage. An ornate purple couch stood in the center of the floor and some unmistakably fake flowers were arranged poorly in a vase on a brass coffee table. The crates, coils, planks, and rubbish had merely been shifted to the other end of the room; even the cat had returned and was napping on the couch. Some effort had been made to erect a sweeping staircase, but the job was apparently abandoned because the stairs ended halfway down, leaving a kind of cliffhanger in the middle of Soundstage One. Prem was dejected. The set was a disgrace to the memory of Nargis and Sunil Dutt, who fell in love while filming there even though she played his mother. The room was void of people; it seemed the construction workers had left for the day though it was barely two o'clock. Maybe they could make the scenery look nicer in editing, he thought, although, as of now, there was no editor. Still, Prem remained calm, hopeful even, until he went to a far corner of the stage to investigate a fetid odor and discovered, in a paint can, a heap of human excrement. He burst out into the courtyard where Amrish Puri handed him the giant bowl.

Three days later, Prem waited to begin. It was 9:00 a.m., and though they were all meant to report at six, the only crewmember present was a scrawny boy who helped with lighting. The lack of written contracts— no one in the industry seemed to sign anything—caused Prem to worry about the others turning up at all. They must want to be paid, he reasoned, so he paced and waited. The set showed slight improvement: the stairs had been completed and the can of feces removed, along with the cat. When, at last, the actors and crew trickled in, it was noon and they required lunch. Prem had not made arrangements for meals, so he ran out into the street in search of a bulk quantity of pav bhaji.

Once everyone was fed and substantially drowsy, Prem scraped together some courage and stepped up on a dirty tire. It was unclear to him what a dirty tire was doing on set, but that mystery would have to wait. "Listen," he said, almost to himself. "Listen. Listen! LISTEN! Okay, thanks." The ragtag assembly, out of a mixture of confusion and mild curiosity borne of boredom, decided to give their attention to their producer, who proceeded to read a speech: "Mehboob Khan," Prem began, "never fired his workers." Someone turned a page of a newspaper. Prem cleared his throat and began again louder. "Mehboob Khan never fired his workers. He came from a humble background and was aware of the struggles that the working people faced. He made the symbol for Mehboob Studios the hammer and sickle."

"Sir?" came a voice from the back.

"The symbol of Russia's communism," Prem said. "It means he cared about common people, little people." Prem shook a palm at his audience as if trying to erase his words from a chalkboard. "I do not mean you are little people," he said, struggling to maintain his balance on the tire. "You are big. What I am saying is, in his footsteps, I want to take care of my workers, all of you, so we become a family. And together we can make a super hit!" When no one reacted to the culmination of his inspirational address, Prem raised one fist in the air belatedly. Yashika yawned and the director batted at a fly. The head makeup artist examined something she had extracted from her teeth. Prem decided it was time to break a coconut.

He would have liked to break the coconut and perform the Hindu rites in a proper mahurat weeks ago, but he couldn't manage it. These days, he'd heard, mahurats were no longer simple inaugurations held on auspicious, priest-approved days, but rather lavish affairs at five-star hotels in which a token scene was enacted and filmed for potential distributors to consider. Without a major hero or a big-name director with which to showcase his project, however, there was no point. They would just have to perform a small aarti ceremony here and bless the camera and hope for the best. Afterward, the priest—an avid watcher of Hindi movies, particularly ones with excessive violence—decided to stay for the start of shooting.

The first scene in the schedule was a simple one that would figure toward the beginning of the film: The hero enters the drawing room and touches his father's feet. The father, played by a theater performer whose extravagant acting style caused Prem some concern, wearing an oversized, crumpled suit, no tie, pours himself a drink and proceeds to question his son about his plans for the future. The hero collapses onto the couch, puts his feet up on the table, hands behind his head, and says: "Aare, Papa, relax. No need for so much worrying!" It was a short but crucial scene, elucidating the father-son dynamic and, Prem thought, an uncomplicated one with which to ease into filming.

In the first take, the father collapsed onto the couch and put his feet up on the table instead of the son, who forgot to do this altogether. In takes two through nine, Brijesh went through a series of permutations of his two lines, and in the tenth take, when at last he recited his lines correctly, he kicked a vase off the table. At the end of the fourteenth take, the priest stood up. "I am going to watch the shooting in the other building," he said. "I think Amrish Puri is there."

It turned out Brijesh was not the only one who could not remember his lines. In the weeks that followed, Prem learned that the heroine, both of her parents, the hero's brother, the neighbor, and the college headmaster were all incapable of delivering their lines without multiple attempts. Additionally, nobody could dance. Not the hero and heroine, nor the supporting dancers; even the dance director seemed to lack grace and the essential elements of rhythm. On the day they were to shoot the climactic scene in which the young man defies his father and marries his love, the director arrived late and drunk. By the end of the second month, they were so far behind they had to throw the schedule in the garbage. Prem, utterly discouraged, tried to keep morale high on set, mostly through food. The camera crew enjoyed his frequent orders of samosa and chai, and the actors adored him for providing unlimited butter chicken. And everyone looked forward to the biweekly trays of steaming hot dhokla.

It was a terrible time for Prem but also a wonderful one. Though he was struck with terror whenever he considered that it would take him ten years to produce an awful movie, he was, nonetheless, producing a movie. So when this was disrupted by visits from gang members, Prem felt it like a punch, not just to his wallet but to his sense of well-being in the world. In retrospect, Prem would question how he did not recognize that they were goondas immediately; they could easily have been cast as such in a film, with their king-size aviators, their flashy rings, their showing-much-chest-hair fashions. Three weeks later, he was back in Delhi on the couch in front of the TV.

* * *

When he left the Kumar Group Towers on Barakhamba Road to meet Prem at home in the afternoon, Ashok was doubtful that his son had returned from Bombay mid-shooting to report that the project was going exceedingly well.

From the start, Ashok Ratan Kumar had been uneasy about financing Prem's passion project, a full-blown feature film about two university students who fall in love despite their families' rivalry, working title *Mein Apne Baap ko Chhod Sakta Hoon Tere Liye* (*I Could Leave My Father for You*). It just wasn't the sort of thing his company did. The Kumar Group was the ninth largest company in India and its market value was steadily rising. They were leading the way in taking advantage of recent governmental reforms in the telecom sector, at the same time becoming the first Indian company to export active ingredients for pharmaceuticals to Europe while also making beer. Ashok was a pioneer, revered among heads of prominent business families not only for his shrewd dealings and appalling wealth but also for the way he structured the management of his company. He delineated clear lines of succession within the family based on performance, he counted his daughter as equal to her brothers, and he left no question as to who was in charge of what. No room for infighting or feuds after he was gone. The whole configuration had an undeniable elegance, he felt, like atoms arranged in a rabeprazole sodium molecule as found in his new ulcer and reflux esophagitis medication, Kumarizine. The system would have been flawless but for the waywardness of his youngest son, who chose to forgo a spot at the helm of one of the most successful companies in the world in favor of producing a movie with too many songs and practically no murders.

His driver Baidyanath took his briefcase and opened the door of the Mercedes, the white one, and Ashok got in. He laid his head back and closed his eyes. The morning had been a long one and he could no

longer work the way he had as a young man building his empire. He
remained an imposing figure, though, which gave him solace, towering
and intimidating in business casual. The Delhi traffic was not especially Delhi-ish that day, and this served to improve his dismal outlook
on his meeting with Prem. Perhaps the abandoning-your-father movie
was ahead of schedule and turning out splendidly. Could he have been
wrong? he wondered. Could it become a smash hit and win one of
those movie prizes?

When he entered the main drawing room and caught sight of his
youngest offspring's appearance, however, he knew there would be no
prize. Slumped on the couch, unshaven and untidy, Prem was watching a movie. His jeans had a violent tear in one knee, and he looked
five kgs thinner. All of this could have been attributed to the rigors of
artistic production, but when his son looked up, his eyes gave it away:
the movie venture was a flop.

Prem leaped from his seat to touch his father's feet, and Ashok patted him on the shoulder as his son stood back up. Though Prem was
the only Kumar child who was as tall as Ashok, he seemed suddenly
little in Ashok's view, a frightened child, though he was twenty-three.

"Come, come, sit," Ashok said. "What news of your picture?"

"Ya, you know, it's good, it's good," Prem began, returning to his
place in front of the television. His mother had always said Prem was
the most beautiful of their children: puffy lips, long lashes, enviable
cheekbones, and a robust nose that kept him firmly in the category of
handsome rather than pretty. But it was a transparent face, she had
said, which couldn't hide a thing. "The dance numbers were fantastic,
Yashika and Brijesh learned the steps very fast, that's what the dance director said. Did I tell you we got the best dance director in the industry?
She said Yashika was quite graceful, even with no training. I tell you,
Yashika is going to be a megastar. The director is not bad. He is slightly

lazy and comes late every day, but once he is there he is quite good."

Prem was not telling him the whole story, avoiding eye contact through the entire bewildering speech, instead watching two men sipping tea on TV. He was leaning forward and his knee, the one with the tear, was bouncing uncontrollably.

"Prem Kumar," Ashok said, "tell me."

"I had to stop production because the mafia came."

"Oh." Ashok's heart sank, and he felt it would stop altogether if he did not have to stay alive to watch over Prem. "Which gang?"

"T-Company."

Ashok exhaled loudly from his nose. "That is the worst one."

"This goonda came to the studio one day during the shooting. He was small and had nice manners. He said his boss wants to invest four crores in my film. I thought, you know, that's a lot. But I don't need it, I told him. The next day he came again, this time with two other normal-size goondas. Again he said his boss wanted to invest, and I sent him away. Two more times he came, and finally I said, 'Who is your boss?' and he said, "'Tiger Nayak.'"

"Then?"

"Then I told him, 'Sorry, sorry, I did not know,' and gave him chai and made him sit. I explained nicely that I did not need more money."

"Good, you talked to him nicely. You do not want to make these thugs angry."

"The next day the goonda came and said Tiger was very angry. He said Tiger no longer wants to invest in a third-rate film and instead wanted the money I had for making the film or they would break Yashika's nose and jaw."

"So you gave him money to save Yashika's nose?"

"And jaw."

Ashok rose from his seat. He clasped an elbow behind his back and paced in front of the TV. The two men in the film had finished their tea, and suddenly one of them was on a dock talking to a buxom woman. "How much did you give?"

"Five crores."

"So all of it."

"Yes." Prem hung his head so only his rumpled hair was visible. "I could not let them hurt anyone, Papa."

Ashok perceived a crack in the boy's voice, a quiver he had not heard since his mother's passing. He sat next to Prem on the couch and patted his untorn knee. "No, beta," he said, "you could not."

A servant entered with a tray of tea and biscuits and began serving father and son. Prem blew on his tea and had a sip, then returned the cup to its saucer with a loud clink. He seemed to be trying to say something, but instead issued a series of small grunts.

"What is it?" Ashok said.

"Sorry," Prem said, "about the money."

Ashok was moved by Prem's illogical concern. "Nonsense," Ashok said. "Good you gave them the money. These crime networkwallas, they are ruthless. They think they own India. Never did any decent work in their lives. Thugs who can hardly read! How can you own India but not know basic mathematics?" He caught himself being overtaken by indignation over the scourge of underworld activity afflicting the nation and returned his thoughts to Prem. "Bombay is no place for you, Son. Stay here. Join Kumar Group. No one will break anyone's body parts."

"But the five crores," Prem said, "we can get it back. The police cannot help because they are scared of T-Company, but what if we call the home minister . . ."

Though Ashok felt the rage of a powerful man being toyed with, he had lived long enough to know the way things worked in this country and knew the harm that criminal organizations could inflict. They were a lawless, godless bunch. "There is no need for calling Hari. Do not think of the money. It was nothing," he said. "I expected to lose it."

"Huh." Prem pushed his tongue against the inside of his cheek and nodded slowly. During the entirety of his Bombay excursion, from the long, frustrating days on set to his unfortunate dealings with the mafia, Prem had been buoyed by his father's unprecedented faith in him. But now, to learn that his father had had no faith at all, Prem contemplated jumping behind the drapes.

The whole production had been abysmal, from the sluggish beginning to the blood-spattered, cruel-to-animals end. After multiple warnings—a smashed camera, a fire in a dressing room, a script that had been shredded and stuffed inside a broken mirror ball that was to appear in a discotheque scene—Prem had tried desperately to reason with the goons. The final threat came wrapped in a Marathi language newspaper left at the side door. Yashika found the package and, upon opening it, shrieked and fell to the floor. At first everyone assumed, naturally, that she was drunk again. But when Prem came closer he discovered the cat, its head severed from its body. Attached was a note: "The girl's nose is next."

That evening, Prem went to the market to purchase a large suitcase. The luggage shops were huddled in the middle of a lane congested by a slow-moving mass of people and an upsetting number of dogs. In a dreary hovel of a store, he found an orange hard-backed suitcase that he purchased without bargaining. That night he filled it with cash and the next morning gave it to the tiny gangster.

There was a long silence between the younger and the elder Kumar in the drawing room. They watched Rajesh Khanna try to convince his girlfriend Hema Malini to pursue her study of law in America despite the implicit three-year separation, unaware that it was part of her sinister, well-dressed father's plot to tear them apart. Prem and Ashok, at the same time, wondered about the usefulness of an American law degree in India. But Rajesh Khanna, all asparkle, felt it was a brilliant plan that would ensure her success and, somehow, her fame, and their future children would proudly proclaim that their mummy was "America return." Prem turned the odd phrase over in his head. *America return.* He'd heard it once before, in reference to a cousin who had gone to do something in Michigan and was today basking in steady employment and knee deep in respect at Maruti Suzuki, Delhi corporate offices. From there his thoughts darted to other America returns: their family friend's daughter who returned with an MBA, which she did not use but which her parents always mentioned when introducing her; the guy who came once a month to treat their koi pond, if Prem recalled correctly, held an advanced degree in marine biology from the United States. And didn't their head cook train under someone somewhere there?

"Now what will you do?" Ashok said as an Air India plane, presumably with Hema Malini on board and headed to America, took flight.

"I have some ideas," Prem said.

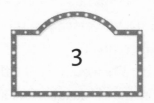

3

Hindi movie scripts in the mid-1980s did not often take America as their settings as they would in later years, and Prem would never have imagined that his life would. But in the days following his botched cinematic foray, he concocted a plan to run far away from his excessively successful family into the wide-open arms of the United States. The seed planted by Hema Malini took root in Prem's brain when during his usual study of *Stardust*—the *People* magazine of India before there was an actual *People* in India—he came across a sidebar describing a film project that was in its early stages in New York City. The director was an unknown, so it was all the more impressive that he should choose to be among the first to shoot on location in the US. But the movie—*Love in New York* it was called, in the *Love in Tokyo* and *Love in Simla* vein—seemed promising. Prem felt instinctively that he needed to be involved. He tracked down the number of a cousin of the director and spent two days battling anxiety and a general aversion to phone calls by scripting his side of a conversation and rehearsing it until it resembled something natural. The cousin, it turned out, knew nothing. But he registered Prem's information and his ardent desire to be part of the production and promised to look into the matter. The next day the cousin called back: "Bunty says, 'Yes, join us in the States.'"

Ashok was skeptical. "What really do you know about this project?

Who is this director you have not talked to? What is your position? What is the film's story?" Prem had few answers. But in the end, his father helped him obtain a work visa and purchased a ticket for him with an open-ended India return.

Prem didn't know what life would be like there, but he found reassurance in the fact that some of his favorite Hindi films had begun as American ones: *Chori Chori* had borrowed liberally from *It Happened One Night*, while *Ek Ruka Hua Faisla* was an Indian *Twelve Angry Men* and *Satte pe Satta* was unapologetically *Seven Brides for Seven Brothers*. This all seemed to bode well, he thought as he waited at the gate next to a family of four. The daughter was penciling answers into a math workbook, and the boy, in an all acid-wash ensemble, was nodding in agreement with his Walkman. In the next row sat a monk in saffron robes and glasses with thick lenses that made his eyes bulge. He seemed an unlikely candidate for overseas travel, and Prem felt a sudden concern for how he would be treated abroad. But upon further consideration, Prem decided the monk would be fine. What could go wrong in America? He boarded the plane and wedged himself into a middle seat.

He didn't sleep during the entire eighteen-hour (plus a brief Amsterdam stopover) Air India flight, instead migrating from cabin to cabin, finding an available seat in whichever cabin was showing the movie he preferred. Sometime in the fifth hour, he began questioning the prudence of his latest life choice. It wasn't that he doubted the merits of *Love in New York*, which would absolutely be a hit, what with its inevitable Statue of Liberty love scene; he doubted his own ability to thrive. He had never had a job before, never worked for anyone, and with his recent utter failure, there were legitimate reasons to panic. He felt suddenly suffocated in his middle seat, as if on the upward incline of a rollercoaster. It was too late to get off and marry an eggy heiress.

A flight attendant asked if anyone needed anything, but when Prem requested tea, she said no.

John F. Kennedy International Airport was a marvel of orderliness. The floors were shiny and void of debris, while Customs and Immigration was a series of tidy queues with nobody shoving anyone. Its lofty ceilings, functional water fountains, and adequate lighting were magnificent. After many cramped hours of anxiety and compulsive movie watching, he found the excitement for his American adventure swell again. On the walk to baggage claim, he envisioned a pivotal scene in which a hero chases a heroine through the terminal, dodging attendants, pilots, and a track team from Kenya, at last catching her as she is about to board the plane. After a breathless declaration of everlasting love, she says yes and they break into a dance number under a colorful display of international flags. He would have to mention the idea to the director. Maybe they could call the song "Tu Meri Aakhri Manzil" ("You Are My Final Destination"), Prem thought as he came to the end of the hall and two men threw their arms around him.

What followed was backslapping and shoulder squeezing, bolstered by empty syllables including, "Hey!" "Ho!" "Aare!" and "Vah!" then booming laughter and more backslaps. Both men wore slippery tracksuits, one red, one black, with white stripes down the legs and gold hoops in one ear. Prem had known someone would be picking him up, but he hardly expected such a joyous welcome. He was delighted until it occurred to him that maybe they had the wrong guy. "I am Prem," he said. "Kumar?"

More laughter ensued, particularly from the burlier, red-tracksuit man. They seemed confident in the accuracy of their airport pickup, so Prem relaxed and enjoyed the jubilation of his first American minutes. Feeling uncharacteristically comfortable, he even related the story of a sari that was nearly unraveled by the plane's catering trolley. When the black-tracksuit man tightened his grip on Prem's shoulder and steered him firmly in the direction of the Air India carousel, Prem realized neither man had actually said an actual word. "How is shooting going?" Prem said. "Is Directorji there now? Also, who are you?"

The question of who they were would plague Prem for years to come. Were they petty criminals or mafia goondas? Did the Bombay goondas know the American goondas, or were they unrelated goondas entirely? he would ask himself whenever he saw a man in Adidas pants. In reality, they were not goondas at all. They were brothers from Pune temporarily lodged at their uncle's in Queens. Getting by on the occasional odd job— unloading trucks, walking dogs for an elderly Colombian woman— they found themselves disenchanted by the US and wondered if they should have tried Canada instead. Their uncle, who operated a respect-able newsstand, was making frequent calls to their mother in India asking when her hopeless sons would decamp from his house. So when they got the call from their buddy in Pune that a foolish but wealthy boy would be coming to New York and they should "help" him at the airport, it reaffirmed just in time their faith in America as the land of opportunity.

"Pintu and Dinesh," the black-tracksuit one said in a way that sug-gested Prem should already have known this.

Prem did not recall a Pintu or a Dinesh coming up in conversation with the director's cousin. But he did not wish to appear forgetful or bad with names on his first day. "Oh, ya, ya, Pintu and Dinesh, okay," he said, wishing he knew which was which.

When he tugged his slim suitcase from the throng of bigger ones, the red-tracksuit guy looked at it and then at Prem. "That is it?" he said. "The son of Ashok Kumar, the chief of the Kumar Group Company, is having one lousy bag only?"

"It's European," Prem replied. They stepped out through the sliding glass doors into the brisk, shadowy, 4:00 p.m.-in-November American air. It smelled of bus fumes back home, Prem thought, but in a fresher, breezier way. He would certainly need a more appropriate coat, maybe one of those really fluffy-looking ones, especially for outdoor shootings.

Pintu and Dinesh were silent as they walked for a very long time through a sprawling, staggeringly neat parking lot. "Are we going first to the hotel or directly to the set?" Prem said. Neither man said a word. The red tracksuit looked up at a low plane coming in for a landing. "Maybe we can go for some chai first?" Prem said.

If he had been slightly less hopeful and entirely less trusting, Prem might have recognized the situation for what it was. But consumed by movie-making dreams and willfully ignoring the signs, he kept walking until they reached a Toyota at the deserted outer limit of the lot. The men demanded his wallet.

"But why?" Prem said. Though the disastrous, possibly life-threatening nature of his predicament was becoming evident, he still held on to the unlikely thread of hope that they wanted his wallet for safeguarding.

"Because we are robbing you, idiot."

Prem let go of the thread.

"Passport too," Pintu or Dinesh said.

When Prem handed over the items, he looked with total ingenuousness into his assailant's bloodshot eyes. "But what will the director say?"

The brothers had diverging reactions to this unparalleled display of innocence: Pintu, of the red tracksuit, responded as he often did to people he deemed stupid, which was with anger, while Dinesh found himself atypically moved.

"How can anyone be so dumb?" Pintu said, tucking the passport into the waistband of his pants. "The director does not know you exist."

"What?" The truth sunk slowly, miserably in. "Oh," Prem said. He dropped his head and looked for a long time at his shoes.

"Really, I want to know, how can anyone be so dumb?"

"Wait, wait," Dinesh said, holding a hand up at his brother. He turned to Prem and spoke as he might to a frightened toddler. "You need to be little smarter, man, that's all. Pay attention, ask questions, maybe do not come to the other side of the world and go to a parking lot with strangers."

"I know your father is not dumb," Pintu continued. "Is your mother dumb?"

Prem saw in the far distance the workbook girl and acid-wash boy getting into a car as their father arranged their luggage in the trunk. Prem wished he could climb into their unattractive van and go with them to whichever American village they were from. How could he let this happen? How, indeed, could he be so dumb? He wanted to be done with these deceitful, felonious, slightly misaligned brothers, but when the question of his mother came up, Prem found himself throwing a wild punch that didn't land entirely on Pintu's face, but didn't entirely miss either.

Pintu came back swinging. The fight, if it could be called that, was over quickly, with Prem kicking Pintu in the shin and Pintu being forcibly pulled away by his brother.

"What you are doing? You didn't see him hit me?"

"You called his mother dumb," Dinesh said. "Sit in the car."

Pintu retreated with a surprising lack of objection, and Dinesh returned to Prem. "I am worried about you, man. How will you survive here?"

It was difficult to follow this man's motivations, Prem thought. "You could give me my wallet and passport back?" he said.

Dinesh shook his head. "No, this is not the solution." He knelt to unzip the suitcase on the ground between them. As he rifled through its contents, which consisted chiefly of cassette tapes, he continued with his oddly timed life guidance. "Look, if I don't take your wallet, someone else will. Go back in the airport and tell the security what happened. They will help you call to your family and get home. Man, you have lot of cassettes."

Pintu rolled down his window. "Why you are sending him to the police? You want us to go in the jail?"

Dinesh held up a few cassettes to his brother. "We have these?"

"*Qurbani* yes, *Namak Haraam* yes, take *Saagar*."

"You want any T-shirts? The jeans will not fit until you stop eating so many Snickers." Turning to Prem, he said, "Snickers is good. Try it."

"But you took all my money," Prem said.

"Do we have *Laawaris* or *Janwar*?" Dinesh said.

"Take them both," Pintu said. "Is there a tongue scraper?"

"You are going to use his tongue scraper?"

"I am desperate, man. You cannot find them in America. It is a country of unscraped tongues."

Dinesh dug out a tongue scraper from a bag of toiletries and then found a pen and scribbled some numbers on the liner of *Qurbani*. "Call if you need anything," he said.

Prem took the liner. "Uh, thanks."

"Hang in, buddy," Dinesh said, and got in his car and drove away.

There is a moment in many Hindi films in which the hero finds himself virtually defeated by the forces of evil. They have taken away his birthright, separated him from his beloved, killed his family members, destroyed his father's construction business, temporarily blinded his mother, banished his wet nurse, poisoned his father's rice pudding, or fed his brother to a crocodile. The hero is brought to his knees. But something in him awakens. He stands up, vows revenge, and enacts it painstakingly through the second half of the film. Sometimes this takes months, sometimes years. In the case of the not-uncommon reincarnation-themed film, it takes an untimely death, rebirth, and almost instantaneous ascent to adulthood. Standing alone in a foreign parking lot, Prem wondered if he would ever even the score with the strange brothers. In any case, he would have to go home unsuccessful and humiliated, bearing nothing but a lifelong tracksuit aversion. He wished he could rise up as in the movies and beat them both with a tongue scraper, then interrogate the black-tracksuit man about his odd combination of compassion and criminality. Maybe someday, Prem thought, but probably not in this lifetime.

From a hidden pocket in his suitcase, he pulled out a polka-dotted pouch containing a large sum of money and tucked it into his jacket. He lugged the suitcase back across the lot, intending to return to India. But as he neared the arrivals building, he saw that the first cab in a long line of cabs was being driven by a Sikh man. For reasons that were a mystery even to himself, he threw his suitcase into the trunk and got in.

* * *

On the same plane as Prem, there had been a young Indian couple just starting out. They would eventually reach the sleepy former coal mining town of Uniontown, Pennsylvania, where the husband would join an internal medicine practice and often get paid in fresh eggs. They would find no one who looked like them in that small town and would troll the local Kmart and Laurel Mall for brown faces, leaving homesick and discouraged each time. One evening, the wife would suggest they look for Indian names in the phonebook, whereby they would become fast friends with two Patels, a Sood, and a Balasubramaniam.

This white-pages-as-friend-finder methodology has been employed by Indians across the country in such far-flung places as Bisbee, Arizona, and Chaska, Minnesota, but in Edison, New Jersey, no such desperate measures are required. "I just tumbled out from the airplane and fell on a pile of Indians," one man said to another as they ate pistachios in front of Building 18 of King's Court Estates.

They had been discussing an article from that week's *India Abroad*, the chronicler of all things Indian in America, about Indians living miserable lives in transient hotels in New York City. "Happiness," the man continued, pitching a pistachio shell at a squirrel, "is a matter of wise decision-making."

"Wise decision-making," the second man said.

"You see, they *decided* to go where there is no good community, they *decided* to become alcoholics and to take the drugs."

"They decided, yes."

"Of course they will have the psychological problems then," the first man said.

"Of course, of course," the second man said. "Why?"

"Because when they come back in the night from their filthy jobs cleaning the toilets or cooking the meats, they come to a dirty room with rats and no friends." With his foot he swept the pile of shells on the pavement into the grass. "Someone just should collect them and bring them here."

"Collect them and bring them here, only," the second man said, nodding his head in agreement.

What they were agreeing on was that Edison, and King's Court specifically, was the right place for an Indian to start his American life. Where was the room for loneliness and immigrant despair when Beena Joshi was knocking on your door with a yogurt container full of vegetable biryani? Theirs was a complex crammed with the dreams of a generation of Indian immigrants who poured in when visa restrictions were relaxed in 1986 and the floodgates of opportunity opened wide. Word had reached the subcontinent that it was a miraculous place where young and middle-aged men gathered on warm weekends to play five-hour games of cricket on small patches of grass, and young and middle-aged sari- and salwar-clad women assembled on concrete steps with large steel platters to shell peas, and the din of at least three Hindi movies emanated from any given building on any given afternoon, their spangling soundtracks spilling out from beneath doors to give King's Court the air of the mother continent.

So, naturally, when Prem asked the Sikh driver to take him to a cheap, good place where he could stay for a while, the driver, Harbhajan Gill, thought immediately of Edison. He himself lived in a tall building in Irvington, where his four belligerent children and even more belligerent wife yelled at one another, at him, and at their majority Korean neighbors, who had stopped coming by with their cold pickled cabbage. His sister and her giant husband lived in King's Court and happened to be looking for a fifth paying guest to join the other four who slept on their drawing-room floor, so Harbhajan Gill pulled onto the Belt Parkway.

"I know a place you can stay for some time," he said, sizing him up in the rearview mirror. "Do you have money?"

Prem wanted to cry but also sleep for a long time. "I have a little," he told the driver.

"Good," Harbhajan said. "The apartment is close to the Metropark station, so lot of Indians live there and take the train for the jobs. Schools are good—but you do not have children, looks like." Prem found his judgmental tone unwarranted. "Crime rate is low," Harbhajan continued. "In bigger places there is so much of crime."

"Is that right?" Prem said. He took in the landscape of America as it flew past his window. The grass on the side of the highway was bright green and the traffic was comfortingly congested, with none of the overwhelming desolation his father had warned of.

"In Edison, small crimes happen, but not so much of murder."

"There is murder?" Prem said.

"Yes."

Prem dozed off, waking up when the driver rolled down his window at a stunningly well-ordered toll plaza. They crossed over a bridge that was under another bridge, which Prem found suffocating. He closed his eyes and tried to go back to sleep, but Harbhajan wanted to know, "Hey man, you going to look for the job?"

"Uh, I don't know, I guess, ya, of course," Prem said, remembering as the sentence went on that he might be staying with the man's sister.

"Good, good. You are married?"

"No."

"You want a wife, right?"

"Uh, of course, ya."

"Find a blonde-hair American wife, man. I'm telling you, your life will be set. Green card, citizenship. Less yelling, probably."

"Oh, okay, good idea. I'll try," Prem said, wanting to seem appreciative of the advice. "How do I do that?"

"Listen to me. First, buy lot of gold chains to wear." He glanced at Prem in the mirror. "Ya, you need chains."

Prem looked down at his clothing. "Uh, okay, gold chains. Then?"

"Then, get muscles. No American wife wants the skinny husband." He inspected Prem through the mirror again and confirmed, "Ya, muscles."

Prem crossed his arms, at once self-conscious and irritated. "Muscles, fine."

"Next, you will not believe, but the American girls, they like the man to be funny."

"Really?"

"Ya, man, I learned this on *The Three is Company* TV program," the driver said. "Are you funny?"

"Yes."

"Okay, good."

"Now, most important thing: act like you have the big plans."

For the past two years, everywhere he went, people had said he needed plans, work, ambition, a job. When he finally made a plan, it failed spectacularly. Twice. Now, on the other side of the world, away from his family, the cab driver was giving him the same lecture. "Plans? You know, really, I don't have any plans right now," he said.

Harbhajan stared at Prem in the mirror for what seemed like a little too much time for someone driving a car. "You can't tell the girl, 'I am thinking of maybe getting the job.' She will laugh in your face. You have to say you are having a job in engineering or joining the medical school. Then you should do one of those things."

Prem considered informing him that he was not actually interested in finding a wife but thought this news would not be well received. "What if I can't make a life plan or build muscles?"

This was too much for the driver. "Just do everything you can! What is your name?"

"Prem."

"Just do everything you can, Prem! And remember, find a blonde one."

"Why?"

"They seem nice."

Harbhajan's insistence was as fervent as his beard was thick, and all Prem could do was agree. After the bridge, they turned onto a dismal sort of expressway and Prem fell back asleep. He was again awakened by the driver: "Chh, chh. Hey, man."

Prem found they were stopped at a traffic light where, astoundingly, the cars waited in three quiet lanes. The light turned green and they moved forward in a systematic fashion up a long road with Drug Fair, Foodtown, and a "United Skates" sign on the left, which Prem concluded was a large-scale typographical error.

"This is Edison," the driver said.

At another light at the top of a slight hill, an intersection with two gas stations and a house with a neon-lit "Minerva the Psychic Reader" sign, they turned left. Prem watched a shoe store pass by, then a bank, then a vast sort of parking lot with a big screen at one end, and wondered what he was doing in this place.

"There are lot of Italians in New Jersey," Harbhajan said.

Prem wasn't sure what kind of response this required. "I would like to meet them," he said. They turned left and pulled into a parking lot in front of a plain-looking apartment complex. The two-story buildings were squat with faded, dull brown brick and ramshackle balconies with brown posts and white balusters, which created a mismatched, pieced-together effect, reminiscent of the village home in *Sholay* where Amitabh sat on a porch step in the evening and played a forlorn tune on a mouth organ. This was a livelier place, though, buzzing and bustling, with residents scurrying about and damp salwars hanging over balconies as from any ordinary Delhi flat. A circle of white-haired men in white kurtas sat in the grass and, upon seeing Harbhajan's taxi pull up, greeted him by name.

With the small amount of money he had exchanged at the airport, Prem paid the fare and stepped out onto the rutted pavement where some Indian children were whacking tennis balls with a cricket bat. "Is this New Jersey or New Delhi?" he said.

"Precisely!" Harbhajan said and patted him on the back approvingly. He pulled the suitcase from the trunk and heaved it at Prem's feet.

"Come, let us find my sister and her giant husband."

The hallway of King's Court Estates Building 3 had a single bald light bulb dangling from the ceiling. Harbhajan opened the door to apartment 3D without knocking. "Just do not say anything about the post office in India," he said before going in.

They seemed to have walked into a party in progress, to which only men had been invited or to which only men had shown up, Prem wasn't sure. The men, all of them young, were sprawled on mattresses laid out around the floor, palming plates piled high with cauliflower and facing a television that competed with a radio spouting "Hawa Hawai" from the upcoming *Mr. India* on the kitchen side of the room. The only decoration was a three-tiered woven basket of onions hanging from the ceiling near a ledge stuffed with packages of toilet paper, napkins, tea bags, batteries, cans of tomato sauce and chickpeas, an economy-size laundry detergent jug, and an unopened box of Corning plates. Though overcrowded, the place was clean. Harbhajan and Prem removed their shoes at the door.

"Come in, come in!" A gargantuan man was standing at the stove with tongs, preparing a mass quantity of roti. "What have you brought us this time?"

Harbhajan pushed Prem forward, causing him to trip into the kitchen. "Ya," he said, clearing his throat. "I am Prem."

"Can you pay?" the giant said.

"Uh, ya, I can pay," Prem said. He decided to omit specifics about his limited funds and recent history of disaster.

"Good! Welcome! Meet Amarleen. Amarleen!"

A tall, sturdy woman with a thick braid came rushing out from what Prem gathered to be the only bedroom. "What is this?" she said, looking back and forth between Prem and her brother.

"New paying guest," her husband said. He pointed at Prem with the hot roti tongs. "He is Prem and he can pay."

Amarleen studied Prem's face and attire, pausing at the hole in his jeans. "You can pay?" she said.

"Ya," Prem said. He dug his hands in his pockets and added, "I'm thinking of buying some gold chains too."

Amarleen's scowl mutated into the broadest, most frighteningly yellow smile he had ever seen. "Do you like gobi? Sit, have gobi. Iqbal!" she yelled at her husband who was standing right next to her. "Gobi for Prem."

She tugged Prem's sleeve, guiding him to an empty mattress. "This will be yours." She nudged him to sit and plopped down beside him. "Iqbal! Gobi!"

"Soft mattress." Prem pressed down on the mattress with his palm until, he was pretty sure, he felt the floor.

Iqbal handed Prem a plate of his spicy cauliflower then turned to his wife. "Are you sharing him or keeping him for yourself only?"

With unbridled apathy, Amarleen used her nose to point to her various boarders. "That is Gopal and that is Mohan. That one with no chin, he is Deepak. Sitting on that side with too much hair coming out from his shirt is Lucky." The four men, each with his own mattress, dispensed a series of nods, grunts, and hellos, neither particularly friendly nor particularly unfriendly. Amarleen's assessment of Deepak's chin was harsh in Prem's estimation, but her portrayal of Lucky's bountiful chest hair was unfortunately accurate. Prem nodded back.

"These other ones," Amarleen said, referring to a row of five men with varying dimensions of mustache sitting against a wall, "they are paying guests upstairs but come to eat the dinner here like a bunch of loafers."

"We give you money for the dinner," one of the loafers protested.

Harbhajan made a plate for himself and sank into a mattress next to Gopal. "Maybe I will sleep here tonight."

"No, no, you have to go home to your angry family," Amarleen said. She seemed to have shifted closer to Prem on the mattress, and he wondered when that had happened.

A very fair woman on TV was reporting a story about something serious in Paris, and a segment of the young men debated whether or not she was attractive. "What do you think?" Lucky—formerly Lakhvir—directed his question to Prem, and the entire room turned to look at him as if awaiting the verdict in the 1960 suspense thriller *Kanoon*, in which Kailash, played affectingly by Rajendra Kumar, defends an innocent man in the murder of a moneylender who was actually killed by the judge presiding over the trial, who was, coincidentally, also Kailash's prospective father-in-law.

Prem adjusted his position on the mattress several times. He wasn't sure why the issue had become so heated or what kind of answer would be regarded as favorable, so he stated his actual opinion. "You know, I don't know, she's okay, but maybe she has big teeth?"

The room burst into inexplicable anarchy. Mohan punched a pillow and Iqbal brandished his tongs.

"This is what I said!" Deepak, who sported a gold incisor, waved a roti in the air. "Monstrous teeth!"

"But the golden hair!" Lucky was impassioned on this point. "You would not touch her hair because you are scared of her teeth?"

"She seems nice," Harbhajan said.

"You look like Shashi Kapoor!" Amarleen blurted out to Prem.

"Wife, control yourself!" Iqbal said.

"The teeth I am finding tolerable, but the nose!" an upstairs paying guest said. "The nose is too small, it is like a bug."

"Shashi Kapoor has a blonde wife," Harbhajan said.

"Jessica!" another upstairs paying guest said.

"Jennifer," Prem said, glad to contribute something.

When the majority had regained their composure, Mohan asked Prem, "Hey, man, where you from? What you are doing here?"

Prem rubbed the back of his neck. He did not want to go into the distressing details of how he came to be in Edison. He was, himself, still confounded by the turn of events. Sitting there in King's Court on a mattress with Amarleen, he could not in actual fact say what he was doing here. "Delhi," he said finally, "but there was nothing for me to do there, so."

Much of the room nodded silently. Prem was relieved that the less than upbeat topic of unemployment in the homeland brought to an abrupt end the discussion of his background, but Mohan, chewing on a pinky fingernail, eyed Prem. He was wearing a grayish-blue one-piece uniform with "Exxon" emblazoned on the front, and his hair was rather straight and shaggy for an Indian person. Prem couldn't tell if his expression was one of curiosity, puzzlement, or antagonism. "So?" Mohan said.

"So, you know, everything is, you know, such a mess there. Roads, schools, hospitals," Prem said. Before adding the thing he hoped would divert the conversation altogether, he looked tentatively from Harbhajan to Iqbal, then said, "Even the post office." As if opening the gates of the Bhakra Nangal Dam, Prem's words unleashed a torrent of tears from Amarleen, who seemed to harbor a hatred of the Indian Department of Posts. She began to wail and her giant husband knelt in front of her so she could cry on his shoulder. He handed Prem his tongs.

"Nothing reaches!" Amarleen said. "They open your boxes and keep what they want like it is a shopping bazaar!"

Deepak stuffed most of a roti in his mouth and slid over to Prem's mattress. Still chewing, he whispered to Prem the traumatic story of a toaster oven and power adapter that Amarleen had parceled to her sister Simarleen as a wedding gift. The oven, a General Electric Ultra, was a wildly extravagant token meant to demonstrate to the sister their profound sorrow at being unable to attend the marriage festivities. Tragically, it never reached its destination. Though Amarleen insisted during several costly, static-ridden phone calls that she had sent it and could not afford to send a replacement, Simarleen and her new husband stopped speaking to Amarleen and Iqbal and, according to Harbhajan, had no intention of resuming relations until another toaster was sent.

"My sister's oven is warming the postal director's chutney veg toast right now," Amarleen said before resuming her sobbing.

"No, no," Iqbal comforted. "It is four a.m. in Ludhiana."

Deepak concluded his account in the same muffled tones, though everyone could hear him plainly. "And she cannot send another oven even if they find the cash because what if the post-wallas take it again?" he said. "They cannot allow the Indian post office to destroy her will to live."

This let loose a new wave of anguish from Amarleen, and by now, Iqbal was bawling as well. Prem felt terrible, but he hadn't been able to come up with another way to divert attention from himself. He stood and brought his plate and the tongs to the sink. Harbhajan, who was about to leave, blocked Prem's path. "What kind of move was that, man?" He narrowed his eyes. "I am watching you."

That night, after Iqbal and Amarleen, with their unique variety of volume, flirtation, and lament, had retired to their room and the up-stairs paying guests had dispersed, Prem was left to make the acquaintance of his new roommates Mohan, Lucky, Deepak, and one whose name he couldn't remember. It was the exact scenario that had crippled him his entire life, being left alone with peers to make a positive impression and be cool and normal. On the many occasions in which he failed to do this, well-meaning and not-so-well-meaning people had urged him to "have confidence" and "don't be shy." Well-adjusted people said the stupidest, most unhelpful things.

"They are crazy, but decent," Deepak said of their landlords while peeling a banana.

Prem looked around at the mattresses, the onions, the small windows, and the Zenith TV. "So you guys like it here?"

The one whose name he didn't remember shrugged. "Is okay."

"Okay only?" Mohan, who had been fully reclined under his blanket, sat up, visibly angered. "You get the cheap place for sleeping, warm food, you can walk to the job. What more you need, huh?"

"You are right, it is very good," the nameless one whom Prem remembered was named Gopal said, sounding cheerful and convinced. Prem wondered about the jobs they walked to. The prospect of having to find employment to secure his place on the mattress provoked in him a flash of dread.

"What kind of work do you do?"

Lucky, the lascivious-looking one with the corner mattress, laid it out for him. "Mohan and Gopal are at the petrol pump, Deepak is at Drug Fair, and me? I am busy with the ladies," he said and popped his extra-wide collar.

"He also works at Drug Fair," Mohan said.

"You need the job?" Gopal said. "I can get you the job at Exxon."

"No, man, he should come to Drug Fair. He can get the discount on the razor blades." Lucky smoothed his thin mustache. "You need to keep things trimmed for the ladies."

Prem was depressed by his choices. A petrol pump or some kind of store where they sell drugs and razor blades. He sighed. "Exxon, I guess. Not now, but maybe later. Thanks."

Mohan assumed an air of smug triumph, as though he and Gopal had won Prem in a custody battle.

"What, the Drug Fair is not good enough for you? You are too good for the Drug Fair?" Lucky said.

"Yes, no, I am worse than the Drug Fair," Prem said, "I mean, I like petrol."

The others looked at him blankly.

"The smell of it." Prem cleared his throat. "So, where can I exchange more rupees?"

"You didn't exchange them all in the airport? Don't worry. Beena Joshi in 11G exchanges the money. She is giving the best rate. Why the nickels are five cents and the dimes are ten cents when the dime is the small one?" Gopal said. Prem looked to the other three, who seemed not to have registered Gopal's question.

"You look like my dog in Jaipur," Mohan said, studying Prem's face.

"Your dog looks like Shashi Kapoor?" Deepak said.

"He does not look like Shashi Kapoor. What makes you think you look like Shashi Kapoor? Who do you think you are?" Lucky said.

"Nobody, no, I don't look like Shashi Kapoor." Prem dropped his head in his hands and gave up.

"Good. Now let me show you the toilet."

It was a tiny, spotless bathroom with no windows and a horde of toothbrushes and tongue scrapers jammed into a steel cup next to the sink. A stack of Archie Comics was piled on the toilet tank. Prem returned to the drawing room and rummaged around in his suitcase, which was apparently too big for the apartment and would have to be downgraded to something called a duffel bag as soon as possible. In the bathroom, he added his brush to the group and grabbed a Double Digest, emerging after ten minutes wearing his kurta pajama.

"Kurta pajama and all!" Mohan said. "Did you come from the village directly?"

"Man, leave him alone," Deepak said with a mouth full of banana. "This is his first time seeing electricity!"

"And the running water!" Lucky said.

"And plates!" Gopal said.

"There are plates in the village," Mohan said.

Prem looked around at the assortment of T-shirts and pajamas into which the others had changed. Mohan wore a Niagara Falls shirt and Lucky's matching top and bottom were silky and leopard-printed. In what he recognized as a pathetic attempt to regain some footing, Prem said, "I'm not from a village, your mothers are from a village."

Gopal, who failed to sense the tone, beamed. "Yes, my mother is from Derpur village, Birbhum district, West Bengal state. She grew up in a poor but happy hut there, then married and came to Calcutta. She knows sewing."

"Leave him alone!" Amarleen shouted from the bedroom.

When, after twenty more minutes of mocking his primitive night-clothes, they finally took turns in the bathroom and shut off the light and television and went to sleep, Prem stared at the basket of onions suspended above his head. When had he decided to stay? Or was it somehow decided for him? It occurred to him that he wasn't panicking. He should be, he thought, but instead, he felt that he could at last rest. He pulled the blanket to his chin, turned, and nestled his cheek into the pillow, closed his eyes, and slept.

Iqbal Singh rose at 3:00 a.m. to use the toilet, a habit that had arisen naturally as a constitutional adaptation to living with four men and a wife who occupied the bathroom for large swaths of the day. He peeked into the drawing room upon hearing something. It was the new boy, talking while sleeping. Prem said quite clearly and with a note of hostility the words, "But the egg smell is so strong!" then rolled to his side. Poor guy, Iqbal thought while reading for the fifty-second time about Veronica's rival for Archie's affections, the sassy redheaded Cheryl Blossom. He couldn't say exactly why, but he felt Prem would do all right here in America. Despite his awkward manner, his air of depression, and his outmoded sideburns, there was something compelling about him. The quiet ones—there was sometimes more to them than you thought.

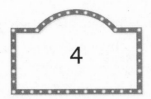

4

"See what you think of this idea: a store that sells sweets only."

"Sweets only. Ya, man, that is good!"

"Sandesh, cham-cham, besan laddu, some kaaju katli, and peda. Jalebi later, maybe."

"Can you have moti choor laddu? I am dying for moti choor laddu."

"He is not opening the store tomorrow, man, relax."

"It will do well here, no?"

"Very well. With so many of Indians?"

It did do very well, eight years later, when Gopal opened Gopal's Bengali Sweet House and sold hundreds of laddu each week, thousands around Diwali time. Even after several other sweets vendors set up shop along Oak Tree Road, Gopal's store continued to thrive because the burgeoning Indian population required an ever-increasing supply of sweets and because Gopal's kaaju katli was the best. It was only after Bengali Bob's Sweets Palace opened directly across the street that Gopal's Bengali Sweet House suffered a dip in sales. But he recouped by adding cross-country shipping to his offerings, which eventually necessitated the opening of a second location.

Gopal was not the only resident of King's Court with entrepreneurial tendencies; most people there harbored a ferocious dream. In 13A, Mrs. Mehra aspired to launch a jewelry store specializing in heavy twenty-four-carat gold, diamond-encrusted wedding sets to meet the needs of brides and their frazzled mothers throughout New Jersey. In 9D, Nitin "Nathan" Kothari, passionate in tight polo shirts that strained at the paunch, was cooking up a plot to start a travel agency, while in 16J, Raghava Sai Shankara Subramanya had plans for a Dosa Hut. None of this was idle woolgathering. Between 1982 and 1987, the number of Indian-owned businesses in America increased 120 percent, and the Indians flooding King's Court were gearing up to join the action. These were not the doctors or engineers who had come from India in previous waves. They were the waiters, the taxi drivers, the Burger King cashiers, and the jobless, who discovered that King's Court did not offer the glamorous American apartments about which they had dreamed. So they put up portraits of Laxmi, purveyor of wealth, and set out to make something of themselves. Their apartments became idea factories, hotbeds of ambition, and their dreams would eventually spill out onto Oak Tree Road, where they would transform an average American suburb into an extension of India.

In 3D, Lucky mulled over the possibility of a sari boutique catering to the "attractive and unattached," and the Singhs hoped to open an electronics store that carried top-of-the-line toasters. "Do I have to have a store?" Prem asked his crowd of roommates as they drank chai prepared in a sort of cauldron by Amarleen on his first morning in America. Already the TV was on, the cassette player was blaring Kishore Kumar, and Iqbal was first in the shower, singing a sad song loudly. "I don't really have any ideas for a store."

"You could open a bangle-and-bindi store," Gopal said.

"Or a sari store," Deepak said.

"No, I am already doing that, man," Lucky said.

"Okay, a music store," Gopal said.

"Okay, he can do that," Lucky said.

Prem was feeling suffocated by the bizarre and specific pressure to open a store and annoyed at having woken up to the very questions of plans and career that he was trying to escape. "You know, I don't think I . . . maybe I won't open a store."

"Oh, sorry, sorry, you must be more into computers," Deepak said. He dipped three biscuits into his tea at the same time. "Very good, this is the future. Are you into computers?"

"No, you know, that is not—" Prem began.

"Does he look like he is into computers?" Mohan said, gesturing at Prem with an open palm.

"Then let me see. I am thinking engineering," Deepak said.

"How engineering is so different from computers? Do you know even what is engineering?" Mohan said.

"Bathroom is free." Iqbal appeared in the drawing room with a thin towel at his waist.

Despite the eyeful of Iqbal's hirsute body, Prem was relieved by the interruption. "Who is going next? Should I go?"

"Sit down, man, relax. Gopal goes next because he has to be at the job first," Deepak said. "So, engineering? No? Then what will you do?"

"Why you are after his life?" Amarleen flung herself onto Prem's mattress as she had often flung herself onto the mattresses of the others. They whispered that she regularly added a splash of bourbon to her chai despite the strict injunctions of her religion, which loosened her inhibitions and explained her flinging. "He just came yesterday. Does he have to tell you his all plans today? Come, Prem, let me make you comfortable," she said, moving over as close to Prem as she could with impunity.

Her husband, still half-naked in the drawing room, asked, "What schooling did you do? What line your father is in?"

Prem jumped up. "You know, really, I have to, I should exchange my rupees. Which apartment did you say? What was her name?" He tripped on the end of Mohan's bedsheet and lost his footing, hurling himself into his suitcase. He fumbled around for his jacket, eventually emerging with his pouch of cash. When he stood back up and did a cursory smoothing of his kurta, he found all eyes in the room staring at him in bewildered silence. He tucked the pouch under his arm and brought his cup to the sink. "Where am I going?"

"11G, Beena Joshi," Deepak said, dunking another three biscuits. "Water drips from the ceiling in the hall there. Maybe take a hat." Prem ducked out as quickly as he could, just barely catching Amarleen's part- ing advice—"Do not let her touch you!"—and exited the building. He stood for a long time on the steps, watching men with briefcases head- ing toward the main road. Once again, he had behaved oddly. But there was no need, he felt, for these new people to know anything about his family. If they did, they would assume things: that he had spent his formative years boozing and partying, that he drove a Mercedes and had a private jet on which he flew down to Goa on a whim, that his life was without struggle. They would make him pay for everything when they went out and expect lavish gifts on their birthdays. Maybe his rent would be raised. Maybe they would try to get their sisters married to him. But could he have deflected their questions in a more normal manner? The parking lot across the street was lined with a disturbing number of cars in front of Quicker Liquor for 7:00 a.m. He had to get on with things, he thought, so he kicked himself for his unrivaled awkwardness and went in search of 11G.

"The main thing you must know is that Uttam Jindal wears a wig and tried to kill his wife." Prem was enjoying his second cup of chai that morning, sitting on Beena Joshi's plastic-covered sofa and wondering why she kept a second fridge in the drawing room. "You see, he was carrying on with a Gujarati girl from Hidden Valley apartments who works in the underwear section of Bamberger's. Who knows what the underwear worker wanted with Uttam and his wig, but after one year, she convinced him to put poison in Mrs. Jindal's Bournvita malted chocolate beverage."

Beena spoke in a Bombay accent with vaguely English inflections she had picked up at a boarding school run by nuns. Prem learned this as well as the other essential details of her life within the first ten minutes of entering her apartment and asking her to exchange his rupees. She had come to America in 1978 with seven dollars in her husband's pocket; they settled in Edison after staying in Parsippany with her maternal aunt's brother-in-law for a month. Although they had arranged their own love marriage, which their parents grudgingly accepted though the star charts indicated it was an inauspicious match, the pair was only mildly happy together. Almost immediately, the husband revealed an addiction to gambling, at which he was, unfortunately, extraordinarily mediocre. He journeyed frequently to Atlantic City and accumulated a massive debt just two years after immigrating. Beena divorced him and sent him back to India while she stayed on in America and began cooking on a large scale. Prem couldn't decide if she was a youngish old lady or an oldish young lady. He was just appreciative that, unlike Amarleen, she did not seem at all interested in touching him. "Then what?" he said.

"You won't believe it, he put the poison in, but she didn't die!" Beena laughed and laughed and slapped the table several times. "Constitution like a horse," she said. After she was done laughing, she slid a pair of scissors across the coffee table and motioned to Prem to help her cut coupons from an array of papers strewn before them. He found he quite enjoyed the task, resting his concentration on something outside of himself while Beena related the rest of the poison story. It turned out the wife figured out the whole plot, and instead of reporting the incident to the police, she forced her husband to stay with her for the rest of their lives as punishment. The underwear seller married a doctor and moved to Miami.

"So, ya, not much else happening here. Oh, Kailash Mistry in 3G was fired from his chemistry job in the Revlon factory for harassing female colleagues with perfume, and the Yadhavs' unmarried daughter is pregnant. They will be forcing her engagement shortly. Now, what about you, Mr. Prem?" As he would many times in the coming weeks, Prem wondered what he was doing in this place. He couldn't say how long he was staying or where he would go next, but he was comfortable and relaxed here with this large, lively woman in her sunny apartment that smelled of potatoes. So he told her his whole story, beginning with his lonely upbringing, his mother's death, his incompetence in the eyes of his father, and ending with the tracksuit brothers making off with his tongue scraper.

Beena Joshi was a practical woman, perhaps the most practical of all the many practical women in King's Court. After her divorce, she tripled her hours at Drug Fair and began cooking mountains of food for various clients. This underground catering business was a marvelous feat. When Indians from miles around arrived at her doorstep to collect their ordered stacks of parathas and vats of dal that would provide dinner for the week, the men of King's Court would turn to their wives in frustration for not applying their own cooking skills to any useful purpose except feeding their own families. After hearing about his struggles, she gave him a tip: "Do not tell anyone anything."

Her point was not, she clarified, that he should be embarrassed by his shortcomings and myriad failures, but that the people of King's Court would at best treat him differently and at worst resent him for his wealth. They would make him pay for everything when they went out and they would expect lavish gifts on their birthdays. The Singhs would raise his rent, and the paying guests would try to get their sisters married to him. "Ya, I was thinking the same thing," Prem said.

They talked for a while more, Beena getting up periodically to stir some chana, until it was time for her to begin the walk to Drug Fair. She pulled out a colossal calculator and figured out the numbers for the currency exchange, pausing briefly to call a mysterious bank teller to confirm the 12.8-rupees-to-dollar rate while Prem collected the clipped coupons into a neat pile.

Beena handed him a brown paper bag of cash. "Okay, come back and see me anytime, just come." She patted him vigorously on the cheek as if trying to imprint the invitation on his face. Prem agreed and took the bag, alarmed at how light it was.

* * *

Prem woke up the following morning bewildered anew by where he was and how he had gotten there. He longed for a servant to bring him a hot cup of tea with biscuits while he lay in bed watching movie news. Instead, five men took turns telling off-color jokes while waiting for the bathroom.

"And the woman says, 'You've been eating grass for past ten minutes!' " Lucky said to a highly receptive room.

"Wow, man, good one," Deepak said, trying to lick some jelly that had fallen from his toast onto his shirt. "I think I know her!"

"Here's one, here's one," Mohan began. "A guy goes to the store to buy the condoms . . ."

At some point, Prem wasn't sure when, Amarleen had slid onto his mattress and was blowing on a cup of tea with great fervor. "First chai is for you," she said, handing it over to him, then staying to adore the side of his face.

". . . he is not *that* ugly!" Mohan finished, unleashing another round of knee slapping and guffaws. "Village boy, your turn," he said to Prem.

"Don't talk nonsense," Amarleen said, admiring her new paying guest with awe and wonder. "Prem is too pure and clean for nonveg jokes."

Prem proceeded to tell the dirtiest, smuttiest, most vulgar joke any of them had ever heard in their lives. He had acquired the joke and many similarly obscene ones in the movie halls of his youth, not knowing that the filth he was gleaning would be so useful. When he delivered the foul punchline, there was a brief silence before the crowd erupted into mayhem. There was hooting and backslapping as Prem had never before seen and it was all directed at celebrating his surprising vulgarity. Even Amarleen seemed delighted and proud. He had never commanded attention or regaled a room before. It felt good.

For the next hour, they exchanged crass jokes, and Prem continued to offer up the choicest ones. At times, he wasn't even sure what they meant or to what they were referring, but he kept going. Some of the upstairs tenants heard the hoopla and wandered in, throwing their own bits of filth into the mix and adding to the general salute of Prem's lewdness. It was the most shining moment of his life to that point. He wished his mother could see him, though perhaps not hear him, making friends of his own age, having fun, being applauded and accepted by his peers.

"Who is this skinny kurta pajama boy anyway?" Keshav Rathod from upstairs said. Bitter about the tepid response to his joke about Bengali sex workers versus Punjabi ones, he lashed out at Prem, whom he recognized as an easy target. "Did he just come from the village? Does he know what is a toilet? Does he wash himself outside with the bucket and mug?"

Prem was thrust right back to his school days, singled out and ridiculed, ready to die of discomfort, with no one on his side. "We already made those same jokes yesterday about the village," Gopal said. "Find something new to joke."

"Or even better, just go," Deepak said, waving his toast in the direction of the door.

"Maybe he is a skinny kurta villager," Lucky said, "but he is our skinny kurta villager."

The joke session soon simmered down and slowly the men went home or got ready and filtered out of the apartment to start their days. Prem was the last in the bathroom as he had nowhere to be. The remainder of the morning, he wandered around the unkempt apartment grounds, perplexed by how much he liked it here. He took a long afternoon nap; in the evening, he distributed some of his remaining cassette tapes to his new friends.

"I love this filthy villager!" many of them said.

During the next three weeks, Prem settled into an unexpected life in which he slept on a mattress near four men and Beena Joshi became his best friend. Although he still had no bearings on where his life was going, he fell into a kind of happy routine. In the mornings, he lounged on his mattress and enjoyed his tea as everyone got ready around him. Amarleen often settled herself onto his mattress, and he would spend the rest of the morning trying to get her off of it. He would lie down again before taking his shower, waiting for the hot water to replenish itself after his roommates were done, which it never fully did. Then he would stay in the shower until the water ran cold again. Early afternoons were spent wandering the scraggly grounds of the apartment complex until he found some similarly idle person on a porch step to have a chat with. For the first time in his life, he felt his natural reticence receding, discovering that people liked to tell him things. One time an outwardly strict Jain vegetarian accountant divulged a love of Kentucky Fried Chicken, while another time a very old woman in sneakers and a sari told him she had a priceless Mughal miniature painting hidden in her sock drawer. Some days he would join the circle of white-haired men he'd seen on his first day there as they sat in the yard and talked or just sat. Later in the afternoons, he would nap, have more tea, and visit Beena either in her apartment or at the Drug Fair. After he discovered that Tun-Tun and Tony Gupta in 12D had a VCR and three Hindi movie videos (*Awara*, *Don*, and a shaky copy of the underrated *Jaane Bhi Do Yaaro*), he stopped in regularly to watch for an hour or two. And in the evenings, after the roommates trickled in from their various jobs and the upstairs neighbors came down, they would eat the feast that Amarleen made them. No one questioned him again about his background, and Prem was relieved he didn't have to recite the story he had concocted about being the son of a toothpaste sales-man. Once a week, he made a call to India from Beena's apartment to assure his father that filming was going well, and once a week, he felt bad about himself for an hour.

And so Prem became an integral part of the block-printed raw silk fabric of King's Court. He made himself readily available to anyone who wanted to waste some time before or after or sometimes even during work, and he felt at last the freedom to do nothing. Yet he was not ignorant of the hard work going on around him. Everyone was trying to be someone; no one sat still. The three paying guests in 20A woke up at 4:30 a.m. to walk to their jobs as line cooks two miles away. Tony held two jobs, one as a power equipment operator at a department store distribution center and another in the stockroom at Kmart, while Tun-Tun gave hours of exacting Kathak dance lessons in their drawing room to mostly unenthusiastic second-generation girls. Prem witnessed with admiration the opening of Ashoka, the first Indian restaurant on Oak Tree Road, and when it was vandalized—its decorations destroyed, its entrance egged, the police reportedly unconcerned—just one day after the Grand Opening sign had been taped up on the window, Prem helped the owner tape his sign back up and pluck the eggshells from the pavement. King's Court's would-be shop owners steeled themselves and worked twice as hard, leaving Prem astounded and guilty once again for his lack of striving. Lazing while his friends toiled, Prem eventually felt the pressure to act, and at the end of November, still living out of the nearly depleted polka-dotted pouch of his father's money, he was told by his best friend that he needed to get a job.

* * *

The snaps on the Exxon jumpsuit took a long time to button all the way up, and on his first morning stepping into it, Prem had misaligned them. He stood alone in the drawing room, unsnapping and start-ing over. Everyone had already left, even Amarleen, who was helping Urmila Sahu in 12A wax her arms. When he was done getting dressed, he looked down at his spotless uniform and considered the possibil-ity of catching the next flight back to India. He had maybe gone too far with this charade. What would his family say if they saw him? But, then again, how would they?

He walked up Oak Tree Road as though strolling alongside a river, enjoying the largely concrete scenery, feeling relaxed and free under the mild New Jersey sun. It was an unseasonably warm day for late November, perfect for starting a gas station job. He pondered the abandoned-looking parking lot with the screen, which he had learned was a defunct drive-in theater, and couldn't understand how such an excellent concept had failed. Probably it would fail in India too, he thought, on account of the excessive honking and total disregard for traffic rules. He remembered there was such a theater in Ahmedabad and wondered how that had worked. He passed Oakwood Pizza—where he had tried American pizza for the first time two nights before, finding its cheese rubbery—and across the street was Exxon's rival, BP, whose employment opportunities the Indians in Edison had so far resisted for the obvious British reasons.

Mohan and Gopal were already at work when Prem reported to a real job for the first time in his life. The other attendant working that morning was Abdul Rashid, a professorial man with perfectly round wire-rimmed glasses and tasseled shoes. Mohan and Gopal had warned Prem that Abdul Rashid tried to match his personality to his accessories by cornering people and lecturing them on obscure subjects such as farm subsidies in the Deccan or the Indic origins of chess. He had aspired to be a historian or scholar and harbored the hope still, but wound up in America where he could theoretically earn enough to finance his higher education. At times he went on and on, deeper and deeper into a topic until his audience wanted to run into the street screaming. But in the end, he was a good person, Mohan and Gopal explained, thoughtful and harmless.

It was a physically grueling, very pleasant morning, with a bump in customers around lunchtime followed by a lull. Prem had learned the basics of pumping gas and collecting payment the day before, but everyone agreed he was the worst Exxon employee to ever wield a squeegee. He never gave customers the correct credit card slip and showed a remarkable lack of dexterity with American coins. At noon, he soaked one leg of his uniform with gas. By 2:00 p.m., Abdul Rashid lured him into a lopsided conversation about kites. Yet it was a good day.

"You see, many people believe kites were invented in India, which is a logical supposition, of course, because of the intense nature of kite festivals and kite fighting there." Prem marveled at the accuracy of Mohan and Gopal's description of their coworker. They were idling near the pumps, pitching pebbles into a greasy puddle. A warm petrol-laden breeze passed, and Prem closed his eyes and tilted his head back to feel the sun on his face. As if this wasn't gratifying enough, when he opened his eyes, he found that a wild-haired woman was undressing on Minerva the Psychic Reader's lawn across the street.

"But in actuality, kites originated in China in the fifth century BC, where materials for making kites—silk and bamboo—were readily available."

The woman, whom Prem decided must be Minerva, had stripped down to her undergarments or maybe a bathing suit. She was, as far as Prem could tell, not planning to remove any more clothing and preparing to lie in the sun. With great care, she spread a towel out on the grass and arranged herself on top of it, propping up under her chin some sort of collapsible board with aluminum on one side. By now, Mohan and Gopal were also transfixed, but Abdul Rashid persisted with his kites.

"Yet, it was in India that the fighter kite evolved. We are the ones who began to coat the line with crushed glass."

Minerva put aside her reflector and rubbed her body with oil until it glistened. Passing cars began to slow down, and one honked. Mohan swallowed hard. If this was work, Prem thought, he could endure it for some time.

Gopal's interest in Abdul Rashid's seminar was briefly aroused by a tangentially related question: "If d-o spells 'do' and t-o spells 'to,' then why g-o doesn't spell 'goo?' "

Abdul Rashid continued, "And kites were used not just in play fighting. The *Air Service Journal* describes the military use of kites in trench warfare." He went on to delineate the three uses of kites in World War I.

Minerva put her board aside and fully reclined on the towel. Her complexion seemed already two shades browner, and Prem couldn't understand why she would do this to herself.

"Two: suspending illuminating devices over the field of combat—"

Then a most outstanding thing happened: Minerva flipped onto her stomach and unclasped her top.

"And three: raising photographic apparatus."

There was a long silence as the three men watched Minerva. Abdul Rashid became engrossed in a book that had materialized out of nowhere. After some time it appeared that Minerva had fallen asleep, and Prem suspended his hope that she would suddenly stand up and face the Exxon. Gopal said, "That kite camera would be of great use today."

In the next hour, the attendants periodically pumped gas and chatted. Upon learning that Prem was a Hindi movie aficionado, Abdul Rashid began a discourse on the evolution of gender roles in the films of Rajesh Khanna. Eventually the discussion reached the 1970 hit *Kati Patang*—the "kite that has been cut"—and Abdul Rashid began again to lecture about kites. After Minerva's skin was sufficiently burned, she reclasped her top and stood by the side of the road with her board. The nonshiny side had a message scrawled in marker:

Communication
with the Dead
2-for-1 Special

Such an unusual woman, Prem thought. She shook her sign and lifted it above her head at times. Prem wondered if the special meant one person could talk to two dead people, or if two people, for the price of one, could each talk to their own dead person. Could she really converse with the dead? Didn't she notice that it wasn't *so* warm? And why couldn't this guy stop talking about kites?

Minerva held up her sign straight through rush hour, with no one turning into her driveway the whole time. When traffic slowed and the day began to dim, she folded it up and went inside. She had left her sun-burning accessories—the towel and oil—on the grass. Prem immediately identified this as a moment in which a certain boldness might be rewarded. "Should I, maybe, I don't know, collect them and knock on her door?"

"And then what?" Mohan said. "She will invite you to her bed?"

"Maybe?" Prem said.

"I already tried that," Abdul Rashid said. "No luck."

Lying under his onions that night, Prem thought of Minerva. Her arms must have gotten tired holding that sign. And she never sat down. How hard she worked, standing nearly naked by the road all day to bring in customers for her talking-to-the-dead business.

In the month that followed, Prem was confounded by the joy that Exxon brought him. Despite the daily exhaustion, aching feet, and more than a few condescending customers, he took as many hours as they would give him and came to love his comfortable one-piece uniform. During the slow afternoon hours, huddled together in the Tiger Mart on the coldest days of winter, the attendants carried on a never-ending game of teen pati with a ragged deck of cards. Minerva stood by the side of the road on a regular basis with her sign, regrettably fully clothed, and one time Prem thought she maybe winked at him, but the other guys said there was no chance. It wasn't long before it became widely known that Prem had no ambition beyond working at Exxon, for which he took some regular ribbing and which he didn't mind. His peers gave him an assemblage of nicknames—Pumpwalla! Petrol!—rooted in his apparent contentment with pumping gas for a living. And when he held his first paycheck, an off-the-books check from the owner's personal account—a paltry sum, peanuts, really—he was proud.

On the walk home in the evening after his thirty-ninth day of work, Prem decided he would stay a few more months, maybe even a year. He could let his family think the movie was being made, and then, when it never came out, he could say there was a problem with distribution. He would take this time to figure out a plan, something that would dazzle everyone, including himself. This was a chance to take a break, gain some life experience, regroup, breathe. When Prem walked in, Iqbal was at the stove flipping rotis. He used his tongs to pick up an aerogram from the counter and toss it to Prem. In Ashok Kumar's inimitable handwriting was a one-sentence message:

I know there is no movie.

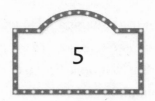

5

Prem spent the entirety of the following morning pacing Beena Joshi's apartment, which was difficult to manage because of all the papad drying on the floor. Beena had been up at five grinding and kneading two pounds of urad dal, then flattening it into one hundred thin lentil pancakes which she would like to have dried in the sun. Instead, she laid them out on a series of overlapping blue floral bedsheets, where they would remain for two days. It was Saturday, so naturally, *Cinema Cinema*—the TV show of Hindi movie song clips, some brand new and bouncy, some black and white and evergreen, all entrancing their viewers like siren songs from their abandoned homeland—was turned on, as it was in every apartment in King's Court in possession of a set. Today they were counting down the top ten songs involving the moon.

"Give it here." Beena snatched the letter from Prem. "This is it? No nothing about you-must-come-back-or-you-are-in-the-big-trouble-mister?"

"It is understood from the tone," Prem said, rubbing his eyes with the heels of his palms. He felt the way he had in the seventh standard when he was caught bunking class to see the below-average *Dharam Karam*. "So if you could, you know, tell me what to do, that would be helpful."

Beena ran the blender.

"Should I go home? How can I go back with nothing to show!"

Beena ran a second blender.

"Or should I stay and disrespect my father?" It was all too much for him to decide, there among the papad. He was enjoying his carefree American lifestyle and wanted to enjoy it a bit more before he returned to India. But he wasn't one to ignore his father.

Beena stopped the blenders and fished some green chutney out of one of them with a spoon. She tasted it and threw several palmfuls of salt into the mixture. Prem waited for her to offer some advice while a number from *Pakeezah*, a pillar of the tormented-courtesan genre, rang from the television, from the hallway, and through the ceiling. "How can I face my family when they know I lied?" Prem flopped down on the plastic couch and rested his head on an armrest. "This song should not be number five. Maybe eight or nine, but not five."

"Uh-oh," Beena said, slapping her forehead with her palm. She walked across the room and turned off the song mid-mujra. "Listen, this type of loafing will not do. So, you don't want to go back and work in the company."

"No."

"And you don't want to do anything here."

"I'm working in Exxon."

"You are hanging around to pass time."

"Ya, okay."

"You cannot hide here forever."

"I'm not hiding. Okay, yes, I am hiding. But not forever. Just until I am ready."

Beena examined Prem's face and decided he was sincere. "Okay then, let's have chai."

They sipped their tea and together composed a note on a US aerogram, which was a more vibrant shade of light blue than the Indian:

I am staying. Just a few more months.
With your permission, I have decided.
Okay, bye. Please send a tongue scraper.

After the letter was folded and sealed and the matter was settled and Prem spent twenty minutes in the throes of self-doubt and panic, they heard through the ceiling that "Dam Bhar Jo Udhar Munh Phere" was the number-one moon song, and they discussed for a while why this was right. In the subsequent months, Prem waited but did not get a response from his father. After a while, he stopped expecting one.

During that time, it came to Prem's attention that King's Court was crawling with eligible Indian women. They were everywhere: hanging laundry on balcony clotheslines, peeling potatoes in the courtyard, performing aarti at the Shree Ram temple, which used to be the First Baptist Church. At first, Prem was characteristically hesitant, but then they started to notice him back, waving him over to talk. He gained confidence with each encounter, developing a kind of awkwardly charming manner, which he learned to deploy at a moment's notice. When he was ready to move beyond flirting and into actual real relationship territory, however, things did not go so well. First, he tried courting the obvious beauty of King's Court, but she was holding out hope for a doctor. Next, he went after a somewhat nice-looking pharmacy student, which was all right for a few days before she declared he smelled too much of gasoline. He pursued a deep-voiced bank teller and a large divorcée, and although they were initially interested, both ultimately decided their parents would not approve so what was the point. Faced with the grim reality that no woman in King's Court would attach herself to a seemingly penniless, ostensibly rootless gas-station attendant, Prem wondered if it might be time to go home. Increasingly, his time was spent with senior citizens, and he had been suffering from backaches, most likely due to his hopeless mattress. He was beginning to miss things he didn't realize he liked, such as his Mysore Sandal soap and his Neem toothpaste because American toothpastes were far too tasty to be effective. He hadn't seen any new movies in the five months since leaving India, and Exxon was losing its luster. Unable to decide what to do, he remained in Edison by default, biding his time, enjoying the American holiday season, hoping he would have a vocational epiphany and head home soon. But not just yet.

It was in those fancy-free days of 1987 that the course of his life took a sensational Hindi movie twist. On a dewy spring morning, he had a hankering for Gold Spot. Since he'd heard from Amarleen that India America Grocers carried this drink, he had not been able to shake a yearning tinged with nostalgia for his mother country's orange soda. India America Grocers was owned by Hemant Engineer, a fleshy and short-even-for-an-Indian man, whose multiple chins cascading from his face underlined a permanent frown. His always-put-off expression combined with his impeccable grooming—his pressed shirts and shiny ties, his precisely coifed hair suffused with Brylcreem—lent him an air of importance. On the Saturday morning when Prem was about to walk in, Hemant was practicing an economic tactic that entailed exploiting the young men who loitered in his store.

"Nothing doing," Hemant said, inserting a broom and dustpan into Gopal's hands. Gopal began sweeping in front of the checkout counter next to Deepak, already on his knees wiping the floor with a rag.

"In one small corner, how about?" Gopal said. He was attempting for the third time that week to convince Hemant to carry some of his home-made sweets in the store. "Three, four types, just?" he said, sweeping the patch of floor just cleaned by Deepak. His deep desire to sell sweets in America came from his parents—good, modest civil servants with the Indian Railways—who saved their whole lives to send their only child to America where he could open a sweets shop and bring them over as well. No one had any idea this goal would take years to reach.

"Not here, donkey, not here!" said Hemant. "Sweep at the back!" He shooed Gopal in the direction of the packaged spices, then took a turn about his store, looking for tasks for the other two useless young men who were standing around, wasting their lives and distracting Deepak from his wiping. Worthless, all of them, he thought. It irked him that these boys who should have been the toppers, the best of the best, striving to elevate the name of India in this country, showed such little potential for growth. At least he could teach them what it meant to work hard. If any one of them ever made anything of himself, Hemant believed, he will think back to the work he did here for me and thank me for the lesson. "You there, donkey, the canned foods are covered in dust," he said and threw a threadbare undershirt at the boy. "Other donkey, listen carefully." Hemant lowered his voice. "Take this pen and change the expiry date on the achaar bottles from 1986 to 1988, got it? No messiness, very important job I am giving to you."

"How about sandesh only!" Gopal yelled from the back. "How about laddu and cham-cham!"

Hemant smoothed his already smooth hair and made his way back to his place behind the counter, nodding hello along the way to a woman squeezing an eggplant in either hand. He was satisfied; things were getting done this morning. His store, wedged in though it was between Quicker Liquor and a sinister sort of hardware store, was a glorious addition to Oak Tree Road. He was, he felt, a man who had given the people what they wanted: Parle-G biscuits, canned lychees, unlimited low-priced cumin, all of it neatly crammed into three aisles of shelves, two fridges, and a freezer which he maintained at the highest possible temperature. No point wasting money on overfreezing.

Hemant was correct in his assessment of his store's significance.

The advent of an Indian grocery store in Edison was akin to the arrival of the light bulb in America's homes; it lit up the neighborhood and no one could remember how they'd managed without it. In a dingy strip mall with a crumbling parking lot, India America Grocers was the first store in town to bank on the mushrooming Indian American population's ardent desire for basmati rice, canned ghee, and a wide selection of bottled pickles. Because it was directly across the street from King's Court, the store was wildly successful from the moment it opened its doors just one week and three days earlier.

It was barely 9:15 and a boisterous line had already formed at the counter. Two women were talking loudly about the cut-rate price of the coriander, and another woman was reprimanding her husband for God-knows-what, who cares, they both clutched baskets heaping with canned this and bottled that, the big-money items, to Hemant's great delight. The morning carried on in this manner, music to his ears—the ringing and slamming of the cash register drawer and the constant tinkle of the bell above the door signaling the arrival of more customers, which was barely audible above the hubbub of people and the Hindi movie soundtrack but which Hemant heard every time. But all of this came to a grinding halt, in his head at least, when the door to the back room opened at the far end of the store and Leena Engineer emerged.

"I need you to sign here and here, and then also here," she said, coming rapidly at him. In a phenomenal feat of vision, Hemant was at once aware of the movements of all four young men who were meant to be busy at their assigned tasks. These boys were not here for the pleasure of his company or the wisdom of his teachings; they were here to ogle his daughter, whom he therefore put in charge of accounts, at which she was exceptionally adroit and which kept her toiling away in the back room for extended periods of time. He was thus able to put off hiring help for the store while keeping the leering eyes of such rubbish boys away from her. But Hemant knew, as did the boys, that Leena had to come out some time.

"And I do not understand why we are ordering so little Hot Mix," she said. She was behind the counter now with Hemant, who was simultaneously ringing up a bag of okra and giving Deepak, paused midwipe in aisle one, an admonishing look.

"Really, Papa, everyone likes Hot Mix," Leena said, leaning her head on his shoulder and squeezing his arm. She turned to Hemant's customer then: "You are liking it, aren't you, Auntie?" There was no disagreeing with Leena Engineer and her aggressively effervescent air. It wasn't that she was pushy or difficult; it was that she was so passionate and so vivacious that no one could help but be swept up in whatever she wanted them to be swept up in.

"Because of economics, you see," Hemant whispered, "supply and demanding, you will be learning this when you go to the university—"

"Hot Mix?" the woman said. "Hot Mix, yes, I will have two bags."

From the back, Gopal yelled: "I am liking Hot Mix!"

Leena was pleased. "So, I will be ordering three more cases for next month, Papa. You're so sweet," she said, pinching his cheek.

Hemant could contend with unreliable packaged food distributors, hammer out a rental agreement that was just barely profitable for his landlord, wrangle the lowest possible prices for fresh vegetables short of getting them for free, and build a life in a foreign land, but when faced with the charm and iron resolve of his only child, he was defenseless. What he could do in that moment, however, was scream at the boys. "Gopal! Two bags of Hot Mix! Who takes the whole day in sweeping?" He gave Leena the signatures she required so she could head back to the office and then yelled in the direction of aisle two: "Dustingwalla! There is still dust! I am seeing it from here!"

The bell on the door tinkled and Hemant was disgusted to find yet another young man come to gawk at Leena. This one seemed particularly brainless, in an Exxon jumpsuit and blue winter hat with a pompom though it was warm and April. Hemant's exact thought was, No future, but tall, so he can stock the top shelves. His suspicions about the boy's exceptional patheticness were confirmed when the others addressed him:

"Petrol pumpwalla!"

"Pumpwalla has come? Pumpwalla!"

And from the achaar bottles section: "Petrol is here!"

Thus Hemant's first impression of Prem was an overwhelmingly negative one. He heard these pump-related nicknames and concluded that Prem was a joke among jokers, a buffoon in a gang of fools, at the bottom of the success barrel.

Hemant continued to ring up his customer while his daughter flitted down aisle three, pausing once to tidy the mango pulp cans on her way back to her accounting. He inspected Prem up and down. "Something you are looking for?"

Prem tugged at the pompom on his head and pulled off his hat. A fluffy mop of hair emerged, which he swatted from his eyes but which promptly fell back in an avalanche onto his face. It seemed to Hemant that he had not heard the question or, like an inexcusable barbarian, opted not to respond.

Hemant's irritation ascended as the boy closed his eyes and took a deep breath of his store's masala air. The thought crossed Hemant's mind that he should find a way to charge for this nasal pleasure, but it quickly passed when Deepak, chewing noisily on something and still wiping the same spot of floor in aisle one, called to Gopal in what he thought was a discreet voice: "Hey, how can we make her come out again?"

"That's it, OUT!" Hemant roared, slamming the cash drawer and startling a customer into dropping several bars of Ayurvedic soap. "Go, out, let's go!" he yelled, his hands fervidly shooing, his angered expression making his jowls appear even more jowly. The startled boys, not knowing what to do with their various cleaning implements, hesitated before dropping everything and scrambling for the door. Several confused shoppers also began heading in that direction before Hemant stopped them ("No, no, not you, Mrs. Verma. Please stay, Mrs. Parekh . . ."). To the boys he was about to add, "And do not come back," but he remembered the large shipment that had to be unloaded from the truck the next day and sighed. "Come tomorrow," he said.

A thunderous crash accompanied by the clatter of breaking glass erupted from the lentils section to Hemant's great horror. He presumed one of the boys, in a fit of unjustified fury, must have toppled a shelf, but when he hurried to the scene he found the petrol pumpwalla on his back, doused in Gold Spot. Lentils were strewn across the floor and orange soda mingled with glass everywhere. Most upsetting of all, the boy's pompom hat lay in a pool of orange next to him. This did it for Hemant. "No-good, worthless bevakoof from Exxon with the pompom—who is cleaning this mess, who is paying? What is the answer for this? I will tell you the answer, the answer is YOU."

The boy began uttering something about so sorry and all that, but Hemant was already on his way to fetch a rag and mop. "Where do these duffers come from, and why do they all find me?" he asked an assortment of customers along the way. "What is wrong with their brains?" And to the woman at the head of the line: "Give me two, three minutes, I will be just there, ginger is on sale, did you see?"

When he returned, the ridiculous boy was still lying on his back ridiculously, a dazed expression on his face. It occurred to Hemant that the boy may have suffered some sort of head injury and could threaten to sue. Then it occurred to him that the boy probably did not know the meaning of "sue." Still, someone could put the idea in his broken head, and then what would happen? Better to be nice, Hemant conceded. "Let me tell you what," he said to Prem. "Clean this mess and go. No payment necessary." He flung the mop and rag at him, but then thought this did not convey the desired tone, so he forced an unnatural and somewhat frightening smile onto his face. "First-rate deal, no?" he said. In this way, Hemant got Prem to clean up every sticky orange drop and, while he was at it, the entire store. Prem spent much of the rest of the day mopping and scrubbing in places where no Gold Spot could possibly have reached: on the tops of the highest shelves, inside the cabinets, both sides of the front door, inside the refrigerators. He gave the checkout counter a thorough cleaning and then, under Hemant's careful supervision, polished the cash register. The only part of the store untouched by Prem's hand was the back office.

By five o'clock, Hemant had to admit the boy was an above-average cleaner. He walked over to where Prem was straightening the shelf of divine supplies—ghee, sandalwood powder, cotton wicks, and whatnot. "You can go," he said, patting him on the back and taking a box of camphor from his hand. But he was sorry to see the boy go, with his gas station attendant's window-wiping expertise and his no-nonsense approach to mopping. Then Hemant had what he thought at the time was a light-bulb moment, a brilliant flash of genius, though in later years he would consider it to be the principal mistake of his life. "Your lucky day, Pumpy," he said. "Come four times this week, four times next week, and your debt will be erased, just like that. Free education I am giving you, my boy!"

Dripping with sweat and orange soda, his sleeves sopping wet from cleaning the inside of the horizontal freezer, Prem agreed to the plan wholeheartedly. Hemant rubbed his palm against the grain of his evening stubble. He wasn't certain, but he thought the boy might have glanced at the door to the back office before agreeing to his offer. But in the end Hemant chose to ignore this. Instead, he congratulated himself for another great coup in the realm of procuring free labor and thought of Prem's considerable height and the bags of atta he could easily place on the top shelves.

* * *

It had been five months since Prem held the long, skinny, somewhat grimy neck of a Gold Spot bottle in his hand. At the end of a disheartening week, he entered India America Grocers in search of this drink and was greeted by a whiff of India and an assortment of his roommates and gas-station colleagues curiously employed at various modes of cleaning.

Prem lingered at the door because conversations with these friends of his could be taxing, and he felt taxed enough. He held his pompom hat and took a moment to compose himself near a "we stock large variety rices" sign. A strong smell of cardamom came from someplace close, and "I am a Disco Dancer," the super hit song from the super hit film *Disco Dancer* of five years prior, was in the air. A tower of Frooti boxed mango drink rose up in a far corner, and at the back there appeared to be a section of Hot Mix. It was not a bad place to spend a little time. A miniature, more orderly India, Prem thought, but he didn't get how cleaning fitted into the agenda.

The fridge of beverages was located next to Lucky, who appeared to be wiping bottles of Hajmola Digestive Tablets with a man's undershirt. Prem was vaguely curious about the motivation behind this choice of pastime, but he also just wanted to find his drink.

"Not now, Pumpwalla," Lucky said, though Prem was quite sure he hadn't said anything.

"Just getting a Gold Spot and going," he said. He plunged his arm into a horizontal fridge that seemed to contain only Limcas and Thums Ups.

"Because I am busy," Lucky said, then looked over his shoulder and lowered his voice, "with a girl."

"Oh," Prem said, scanning the aisle in search of any girls, "because it looked like you were busy cleaning Hajmola with an undershirt."

Lucky stopped his wiping. From his unauthoritative squatted position he looked up at Prem gravely and said: "There is much you can learn from me, man, about the romance." This, Prem knew, was something Lucky believed absolutely. Just last week, he came across Lucky standing on the lawn of Building 19, yelling Urdu poetry up to the balcony of an irate seamstress. Later, after Prem would come to know him well, Lucky would regularly reference this as a fine example of his stately courtship style. "*Esh*tyle, man," he would say, "you are needing *esh*tyle for impressing the ladies, Pumpwalla!" He would also, Prem noticed, regularly omit the end of that story, the part when the seamstress dumped a pot of rice on his head. Generally, whenever Lucky stood beneath a balcony, a pot of something was flung upon him. Still, he gelled his hair vigorously and donned his signature white sunglasses, applied too much cologne, and carried on entreating women with his overly aggressive poetry. By the end of his first month in America, Prem had heard, Lucky had already been thus rejected by more than a dozen of King's Court's maidens, including a Neeta, a Geeta, a Sita, two Ritas, and a Praneeta. How he counted himself a ladies' man, Prem would never understand.

"So where is she?" From where he stood, elbow deep in the wrong sodas, Prem could see only a very frail woman in a sari sniffing a cabbage.

"Shhhhh," Lucky said, waving the undershirt at him. "He will hear you."

"Who will hear what?" Prem said. Just then, a distinctly movie-villain snarl commanded everyone out of the store and widespread pandemonium ensued. "What is happening?" Prem asked, at the same time triumphantly yanking a Gold Spot from the fridge. But in the midst of his moment of glory, the only remotely glorious moment he'd had that week, a panicked Lucky shoved him, causing him to lose his footing and fall spectacularly to the floor.

On his back in a pool of his favorite drink, amongst an alarming number of lentils packages, he propped himself up on his sopping elbows. "Man," he said, flicking some glass from his pant leg, "that was the last one." Lucky loomed above, still in a panic but offering Prem a hand, while at the end of the aisle a sizable gawking crowd gathered. "I am okay, no need for alarm," Prem called out, though no one was showing any sign of alarm. One of them, a disturbingly old man, snickered then recommended investigating a bag of onions. Suddenly, the store's owner barreled toward them from the head of the aisle. Lucky dropped Prem's hand, causing him to fall back with a thud into the orange puddle.

"Sorry, Pumpwalla. Okay, see you, bye." With that, Prem's friend stepped over him and ran for the door. Prem wrung orange soda from the sleeve of his only Exxon jumpsuit. "I am needing better friends," he muttered.

When Hemant reached him, Prem attempted ardently to apologize for the accident. "Uncle, so sorry, let me—" But he didn't get very far with this, as the thickset, incongruously dapper man launched into his own, considerably more wrathful speech. Prem gave up and gathered the packages of lentils into a soggy pile.

The week was not going well. Five days earlier, he had donned his Exxon jumpsuit and with an air of mild enthusiasm headed up Oak Tree Road to Shoe Town, where Sushila Mukherjee, his latest love interest, was a saleswoman.

The manager of Shoe Town, a heavy-set Punjabi woman with very long earlobes, fluffed up her hair when he walked in. "Oh, my love of my life," she said with a flourish of dramatic Hindi movie anguish which Prem quite enjoyed. "Just marry me already so I do not have to kill myself." He had been in three times that week to try on a pair of fairly impractical loafers, and she had conveyed a similar sentiment each time.

He pulled off his hat and grinned a half grin that never worked on anyone in his age range, but which older ladies seemed to welcome. "Auntie," he said, resting his arms up on the counter before her, "you know I would marry you today, but what would Uncle say?"

"He would not notice."

When Sushila emerged from the stockroom, she looked less like the woman of his dreams and more like a woman he might pass on a footpath without noticing. She wore a brown blouse with brown slacks, and he thought, but wasn't certain, that maybe her eyebrows had connected to each other in the past few days. Nonetheless, he remained undeterred, knowing that in other, more flattering, less fluorescent lighting, she was pretty. And she seemed generally to be a good person who was particularly kind to dogs and the elderly.

"I will try those same shoes," Prem said to the manager, who was holding his hand on the counter now.

"Sushila, those same loafers." The manager squeezed his hand. "Size eleven."

Prem found a bench on the other end of the store and sat down and took off his shoes. He looked up at the shelves of overpriced footwear and wondered if someday he would marry Sushila, and if so, whether she would continue to work at Shoe Town so they could enjoy many years of discounted shoes. He hadn't quite worked out whether they would eventually return to India or remain in America forever; nonetheless, he was envisioning the variety of sneakers he might own when Sushila reappeared and thrust a shoebox at him.

"I told you that do not come to my work. I am busy." Instead of kneeling down and helping him as she had done on his prior visits, she remained standing.

Prem looked to his left then his right. "But there are no customers," he said.

"Look," Sushila said, "you are nice. Also, you have a good height. But this is not enough. Look at Roopesh, he just got the promotion in the bank. And Urmila's friend Kishan, he is studying engineering in the night. The thing which I am trying to tell you is," she said, plopping down next to him on the bench, a familiar, leathery smell emanating from her skin, "you are a petrol pumpwalla only."

A petrol pumpwalla only. She was a salesperson in the Shoe Town. Prem opened the box and bent over to put on the loafers. Reluctant to face Sushila, he lingered at his feet for as long as he could and considered what had transpired before coming back up. He thought he understood but wanted to leave no room for misapprehension of what she was saying. "What are you saying?"

"We are finished."

Prem had heard the same story many times since coming to America: you are lazy, you have no future, you only talk about movies, you smell like gas. Amitabh never seemed to have this problem in any of his films, nor Rajesh Khanna, nor any of the Kapoors. He had spent many adolescent hours studying their demeanors, memorizing their suave dialogues, yet the Indian women of America were immune to these charms. There seemed to be widespread agreement that he was handsome, yet there was also agreement that he was good-for-nothing. After rejection upon rejection, Prem began seriously to worry that he might be a mere sidey in the motion picture of life. As such, he would forever be relegated to flanking the more virile and important hero, dancing unattractively alongside him and contributing inane dialogue that served only to elevate him, never breaking free of his sidey-ness and taking center stage. He turned to face Sushila, who was extracting something from beneath a fingernail. "So why did you wait so long?" he said. "From the beginning you knew I work in Exxon."

Sushila sprang up from the bench and stood in front of him, her arms crossed in a manner that Prem thought more stern than the situation required. "I was thinking that maybe you were having a plan."

"Plan for what?"

"Doing some better thing."

He had never noticed Sushila's large hands before, but now they were all he could think about as she laid out the usual reasons why he was not suitable: his lack of ambition, his lack of a bedroom, his limited funds. When she was done, she put her large hands on her hips, annoyed at having to explain the obvious. But then, her eyes brightened as something seemed suddenly to occur to her.

"Do you think you maybe will buy the Exxon one day?" she said.

"Uh, no?"

"Then ya, we are finished."

Prem removed the loafers and placed them back in the box. He stuffed the balled-up tissue paper back into each one and covered them with the lid.

"If you want to buy them I can give you the discount," Sushila offered, with the sympathetic tone of voice he'd once heard her take with a puppy.

He stood up and handed her the box. "Like me," he said, "they are not very useful."

On his way out, he stopped by the manager, who again fluffed her hair for him. He took her hand and held it to his chest. "I know you belong to someone else," he said, "but even so, from time to time, the thought of you will cross my mind."

The manager tilted her head and sighed. Then a look of sudden recognition registered across her face. "Is that a line from *Kabhi Kabhie?*" she said.

Prem nodded and returned the pompom hat to his head, then exited the Shoe Town. For the remainder of that week, the matter of Sushila weighed upon him. He felt, again, the contradictory urges to no longer remain in Edison and to not return home. At the end of several alternately self-loathing and self-pitying days, Prem went in search of Gold Spot only to find himself instead on the floor covered in it and scolded by an unpleasant, albeit nicely put-together man.

As Hemant left to fetch cleaning supplies, the defining moment of Prem Kumar's life occurred: The door to the back room opened, and the most beautiful head he had ever seen—on the big screen or off—peeped out.

Even as a lifelong lover of Hindi movies, Prem had never fully accepted the idea of falling in love at first glance. How really could Raj have loved Bobby and Dharam loved Rajkumari Pallavi immediately, without a word spoken between them? Surely it was a dangerous thing to devote oneself to someone based on appearance alone. But in that split second, he came to know that every Hindi movie, including *Bobby* and *Dharam Veer*, had been right. True love really could be so sudden.

His breath caught in his chest and he thought he might vomit. It was love-induced Hindi movie nausea, and he instantly diagnosed it as such. He became acutely aware of his Exxon jumpsuit and his Gold Spotted state but found himself paralyzed in the position he was in. In that frozen moment, he forgot about the bellicose dating landscape he had faced in America. He let go of the nice-looking pharmacy student, the recent divorcée, the deep-voiced bank teller, the slightly angry ice-cream shop manager, and even Sushila.

The woman had a full face punctuated by a heavy brow and puffy mouth. Her slightly crooked nose was dangerously close to belonging in the category of outsized but somehow fit her face perfectly. Her lush mane fell in waves past her shoulders. She bore no resemblance to any of the movie heroines he had spent his life dreaming about, yet she possessed a star quality, a decided unsideyness that provoked in him a tremor of excitement that would not end until his life did.

They stared at each other, he from a puddle of soda, she with eyes narrowed. Prem's heart pounded in his chest. The bustle of the store—the customers, the cash register, the bell on the door—became muted, and the movie soundtrack was the only sound left for Prem as he looked at her. Suddenly, she was wearing a sky-blue sari and running toward him on a snowy mountaintop, the end of her skirt billowing behind her. And he, too, was running in a matching leisure suit. When they reached each other, they stopped short of embracing and instead sang a song. She circled shyly around him, and when he leaned in for a kiss, she turned her face and he settled for her cheek. Then her father threw a mop at him.

Prem did not see Leena again that day as he cleaned the whole of India America Grocers. She had slammed the door almost immediately upon seeing him sprawled on the floor. There was nothing that suggested to Prem that she was thinking about him as much as he was thinking about her. Furthermore, he had no reason to believe she would not reject him as others had before her. But on that clear spring evening, the stars dazzling in the sky, as he walked the third of a mile up Oak Tree Road to the gas station for his shift, he thought of *Chori Chori* and *An Evening in Paris, Namak Halaal* and *Betaab*, and the dozens of other films in which the heroine doesn't initially but does eventually fall for the hero, and he was heartened by the possibility that so far things were going according to script.

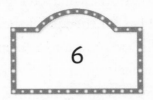

6

On the bright April day after Prem spilled Gold Spot and saw Leena for the first time, Tun-Tun and Tony Gupta were having a party in their apartment for no reason except just because. A jovial couple happy to celebrate anything and spend time with friends, the Guptas were almost always laughing—hers a deep, throaty laugh, his a high-pitched giggle. Some thought the buxom and round Tun-Tun and lanky Tony an odd couple, but that was before they understood the couple was bonded by the love of a good time. If they had fewer than three parties to attend or throw on a given weekend, they considered it a failure. Tony would pick out the perfect earring and trim his very neat beard, Tun-Tun would yank her hair up into a teetering bun, and they would be off. Though not often found together at these parties, the pair was also never without each other.

"We are keeping a get-together for this Saturday. Come down," they told everyone in Buildings 1–10 plus an assortment of people from 11–20. In preparation, four of the five young men of 3D vied for space in front of the bathroom mirror, elbowing and jockeying for position while the fifth took a hot shower.

Prem did and undid and redid the top few buttons of his white, slightly shiny shirt. He didn't know for sure but spent the entire day hoping she would be there. His recent decision to hang out and essentially not worry about anything for a while was replaced by a new resolution to see the store owner's daughter again and perhaps drink orange soda with her for the rest of their lives. He had learned that father and daughter had moved to Edison from Houston, where they had operated a convenience store for five years. It was unclear why they had uprooted themselves; it was rumored it had something to do with her mother, whom nobody seemed to know anything about. The daughter, who planned to apply to Rutgers next year, would continue to live at home to save money and help manage the business. Her name was Leena.

Prem was nearly on the verge of a decision about his buttons when he was struck, and simultaneously revolted, by the lengths to which men would go to attract the attention of a pretty girl, specifically in the realm of hair maintenance and removal. Would Leena really be swayed by the careful dishevelment of Mohan's hair? Or the meticulously plucked expanse between Deepak's eyebrows, which in truth was just one long eyebrow?

"Yuck, yaar, go outside and do that," Mohan said to Lucky, at once acknowledging their brotherhood and friendship while also berating him. Lucky was at work tweezing his nose hairs one at a time. He was hopeful that he might attract a lady that night, whether it was Leena or someone else, because it had been too long since he was alone. In India, he had grown up happily and comfortably in an upper-middle-class family, but when his parents passed away in quick succession when he was just nineteen, his uncles refused to give him his share of the properties and businesses. A lawsuit ensued; he was too inexperienced and uncunning to get very far and abruptly lost everything. In America, he hoped to forget his greedy relatives and begin anew. For him, this meant finding a caring mate who could be his new family and help him bear the burden he'd been carrying all these years, someone whose shoulder he could finally rest his head upon. Unfortunately, he had not yet found this woman and in the process of looking had garnered a reputation as a lecherous sari-chaser.

"Who is doing what!" Deepak called from behind the curtain.

"You don't worry what is happening out here," Lucky said just as he ripped out a hair and a tear plopped down one cheek. "What are *you* doing in *there?*"

"Ya, man, how long is it taking you to shower?" Prem said. He said this not out of annoyance or amusement or any of the other reasons why five young men crammed in a bathroom might harass one another, but rather out of self-defense, out of a desire to deflect attention from himself, out of sheer better-him-than-me, because as repelled as Prem was by the sight of the tiny hairs littering the sink, he recognized that he was not faultless in this regard. Just an hour earlier, he had stood in the shower and made an impulsive move from which he feared there was no turning back. He had shaved his chest.

Prem was not a chest-shaving sort of guy, but as he stood under the shower, engulfed in steam, and looked down at his patch of curly, not-terribly-thick-but-still chest hair, he had the sinking realization that all of his roommates shared the same goal for that evening. And even if he succeeded in beating out the others and attracting Leena with his sideburns and shiny shirt, what hope did he have of holding her interest? Why would she run across a field into his open arms when she could run into Mohan's or Gopal's, or better yet, the embrace of someone who did not work at Exxon? Weighed down by pessimism, Prem continued to lather when an image from the 1985 knock-off sleeper hit *Adventures of Tarzan*—much discussed for its racy content and frequent wet sari sequences—appeared in his head, its titular hero bare-chested and glistening. In a split second of desperation and flickering hope, he applied razor to chest.

Mohan gave Gopal a shove that propelled him out of the bathroom. "Why do you have to be in front of the mirror to spray cologne, yaar?"

"What kind is that?" Iqbal called from his bedroom. "It is smelling like my foot!"

Amid the commotion over Gopal's foul cologne, Prem tried to slip away from the bathroom.

"Petrol, wait," Mohan said. "Something is looking different here."

"Different? Nothing is different. Your mother is different," Prem said, turning away from Mohan and bumping into Lucky, still at work on his nasal grooming.

"Easy, man!" Lucky said after his tweezers were shoved a little too far into his nose.

Mohan wiped away the steam on the mirror and peered into Prem's reflected face. "Something is different . . ."

"What is different!" Deepak called from behind the curtain.

An alarming feeling of inevitability washed over Prem. These guys, who had become his good friends, were vicious. If they detected something was amiss in the region of his collar and then discovered his hairless torso, there would be no end to the taunting. "Come on, yaar," Prem said and smiled uneasily.

"No, no," Mohan said, directly facing him now. "Something definitely is there . . ."

Gopal, now returned to the bathroom, said, "Prem, yaar, you shaved your chest!"

What ensued was nothing short of a mauling. Mohan lunged at Prem's neck while Lucky went for his waist. Prem twisted and writhed as he clutched the neck of his shirt. He was plunged into the drawing room and wrestled to the floor, where Mohan climbed on top of him while Gopal and Lucky grappled with his flailing arms. Even Deepak jumped out of the shower and was on the sidelines with a towel and somehow a slice of cold pizza, dripping and cheering. In a moment of singular clarity and overwhelming calm, Prem recalled a dozen or more times he had watched his big-screen heroes barehandedly overpower a gang of swarthy villains. He stopped struggling and his roommates, surprised and suspicious, paused as well. Prem gathered his strength and when he was ready, with an eruption of pent-up energy— dishoom!—he burst forth. When Amitabh Bachchan cocked his fingers in *Sholay* and uttered, "Dishoom," he did not know he was launching a sound effect that would accompany all manner of movie combat: bullets, jabs, karate chops, uppercuts. But Prem's dishoom accompanied nothing. Instead, his head fell back to the floor with a thump. Mohan ripped open Prem's shirt, sending buttons skating across the floor in all directions and exposing his smooth chest.

Mohan shook his head. "Petrol, Petrol. You really were thinking this will improve your chances?"

Prem attempted in earnest to explain. "You know that hair at the top of the shirt, how it comes up?" But in the face of his roommates' smirks and looks of amusement, he hung his head and conceded defeat. "Fine," he said.

Mohan, Gopal, Deepak, and Lucky took turns passing comments in the vein of "Who do you think you are, Tarzan?" and "What kind of a skinny Tarzan are you?" then disbanded and resumed getting ready for the party.

Prem picked himself up from the floor for the second time in two days. "I am needing better friends," he said, collecting his buttons from around the room.

* * *

When the five roommates, preened to perfection but still as a group smelling vaguely of gasoline, stepped outside to head to Tun-Tun and Tony's party, the tilting streetlamps in the parking lot had already come on. It was a crescent-mooned night, clear and with a warm breeze, unusual for that time and place but harkening back to something familiar for the tenants of King's Court. Prem, feeling rather hopeful, was humming the tune of a long-ago film song while Deepak kicked along a can of soda. Lucky pointed out Shanta Bhatt's gigantic underwear fluttering on a balcony clothesline above them and they all had a pleasant laugh, as they always did when Shanta Bhatt's gigantic underwear was above them.

"Why is this here even?" Mohan said when they arrived at Building 12. The defunct intercom buzzer next to the door hadn't, to anyone's knowledge, ever buzzed. Much of King's Court similarly had not buzzed in years. Bald light bulbs had long since gone out in windowless halls, and thin white walls had faded to yellow. Banisters were rickety and wall-to-wall carpeting seldom reached from one wall to the other. Yet King's Court had become an Ellis Island of sorts, a first stop, sheltering the tired and poor masses from across the ocean yearning to breathe free and sleep on a mattress in the drawing room of a one-bedroom apartment with eight other people for sixty-seven dollars a month.

"So your mom can call me when she gets here," Lucky said.

"Your joke is not possible," Mohan said.

Prem pushed open the unlocked door, and immediately they found themselves in the midst of a very large pile of shoes. They added theirs to the heap and made their way into the apartment where, even above the roar of the packed-in crowd, the grating voice of Kailash Mistry attempting to sing a ghazal rose from one corner. As at every party Prem had attended at King's Court, bedsheets were spread across the floor; along one wall was a designated area for the elderly, whose longevity was rewarded with folding lawn chairs. Prem's roommates melded into the raucous crowd that included a bevy of women who had recently rejected him, huddled together somewhat nefariously, to Prem's mind. He squeezed past a flock of children and an uncle demonstrating bowling techniques with a fictional cricket ball. Tun-Tun was reliably drunk again and the customary buffet with its customary tinfoil trays had already been picked clean. Every window in 12D had been thrown open, yet the air in the apartment was laden with egg curry and heavy perfume, mingling with the distant strain of music issuing from a crackling cassette.

"Prem, really." Beena was forcing herself through a slim gap between two men's backs. "I have been waiting for you since two hours."

"Sorry, you see, in the bathroom—" Prem began.

"No time for that." She licked her hand and slapped down Prem's hair, which she maintained was too fluffy and feathery for someone who was not a 1970s movie hero. "I have inquired few places," she said in a conspiratorial voice. "Leena Engineer is coming tonight."

Prem ran his fingers through his hair, restoring it to its previous fluffiness. It was unclear how Beena knew about this latest development in his life. "What Leena?" he said. He scanned the room, pretending nonchalance while at the same time searching for her face in the crowd. "I don't care if any Leena is coming, or any Reena, Tina, Meena, or Veena."

"Yes, yes, they all will be here soon too," she said, batting away his hand.

Prem gave up defending his hair. Digging his hands into his back pockets, he slumped over slightly. "I have no chance with her anyway."

"Stop talking nonsense or I will hit you with my rolling pin," Beena said. She seemed always to be threatening him with her rolling pin, even when it was in a drawer four buildings away. She licked her hand again, this time using it to rub at one of Prem's sideburns as though trying to shorten its length. "Just stand straight and try not to look lazy."

Prem unslouched himself. "So, how long has this been going on?" he asked, gesturing with his chin in the direction of the unmelodic Mistry uncle struggling to carry a tune.

"From the start, Prem, from the start." She extracted two small tinfoil triangles from her purse and slipped one to Prem. With no paanwallas on the corner of everywhere as they were in India, Beena had, of late, assumed the role herself.

Not wanting to risk leaving any unattractive flecks of betel leaf on his teeth, Prem resisted the lure of the refreshing carcinogenic digestive and tucked his paan in his pocket for the time being. Beena, whose teeth bore the terrible brown-orange stain of a veteran chewer, unwrapped hers, stuffed it in her mouth, and chomped.

"Really, did he have too much booze? Or maybe someone should give him more booze. Does he really think he can sing? He is ruining my party, just *ruining*." Prem recognized the flamboyant lamentation of Tony, the more dramatic of the Guptas. A nice guy, a little theatrical, but always generous with giving him a lift to Exxon on cold days, he pressed himself uncomfortably close to Prem. "Look, Prem, Beena Auntie, people are leaving."

Prem looked around and saw no one leaving.

"Please, stay. Have a dessert," Tony urged.

"We are not going anywhere," Prem said.

"Excellent!" Tony said. "It is settled then. But what about this singing, my *God* . . ."

A squirt of orange escaped from one corner of Beena's mouth and dribbled down her chin. She raised an eyebrow at Prem and went in search of tutti-frutti.

Tony pressed in even closer to Prem. "Now, what about the girls, hmm? I hear you were going around with some Asha or Usha?"

Prem was not much in the mood to discuss this with Tony, not because he was still feeling the sting of rejection but because he had moved so far past it. He considered bringing the conversation back around to the unwelcome singing, which had in the past minute increased in intensity and dreadfulness, but concluded this would just upset Tony all over again.

"Sushila," he said with reluctance.

Tony took this bit of information and ran with it straight into a five-minute discussion during which Prem said very little and shook his head a great deal.

"Girls these days," Tony bemoaned.

Prem shook his head.

"Too, too Westernized," Tony argued.

Prem nodded.

"The drinking, the gambling . . ."

Prem shook his head, then nodded, though he wasn't quite sure anymore what Tony was talking about. He was glad, though, to be in this low-participation conversation because it allowed him to search the room and monitor the door. There were rumblings of a dance party from a small contingency of ladies, while the cricket uncles had moved into the hallway amongst the shoes. The garbage overflowed with Styrofoam bowls, and a framed poster of a red Ferrari tilted precariously on the wall above the elderly. Everyone, it seemed to Prem, was throwing their head back and enjoying. Someone in a sari cried, "Ediot!" and then laughed with a man standing scandalously close to her. Gopal was cackling wildly at something Lucky had said while Beena was handing someone a paan and leaning in carefully to listen.

Then, as if he'd willed her there, Leena appeared.

This time he could see all of her. She was in a bright pink salwar kameez that bared half of her slightly downy arms, of which he was immediately enamored. She was met at the door by an onslaught of young ladies—the large majority of whom Prem had tried to date and who seemed woefully sideyesque now—and was instantly the life of the group, a spectacular firework among soggy teabags.

"Want to go out for a fag?" Tony said. He appeared to be the only man in the room not distracted by Leena's arrival. Even the old ones were staring and Mistry Uncle paused midcroon. Prem knew Tony was waiting but allowed himself one more moment to look at her before she was engulfed by her friends and no longer in his sight.

"Outside? Ya, no," Prem started, but just then the electricity in King's Court went out and they were stuck in the dark.

The power company had been doing maintenance work, and this was the third outage that week. For this reason, and also because they were recent immigrants from India, there was no surprise or panic, just a collective "Uf!" that sounded of mild disappointment and inevitability. Tun-Tun and Tony sprang into action, lighting candles already positioned around the room. A few others groped their way back to their apartments, returning with assorted flashlights. Everyone else stayed put; it crossed nobody's mind that the party was over and they should go home. What was the point of sitting in the dark alone when they could sit in the dark together?

Prem peered through the dark for Leena's silhouette. As the candles and flashlights came on and joined the streetlamps and the neon sign of Quicker Liquor to imbue the room with a romantic glow, she came into focus across the room.

"Antakshari!" someone proposed. This was good news for Prem, who had grown up playing the parlor game in which two teams take turns singing verses of Hindi film songs beginning with the last consonant sound of the opposing team's previous song. A favorite subcontinental family pastime, it was liable to break out on bus rides and train rides, campouts and blackouts. Prem was roused every time he found himself in the midst of it, savoring the volley of hits and the late-round reaching for obscure ballads. It was a game at which he obviously excelled given his prodigious knowledge of film songs, so when someone seconded the motion, he was pleased at the chance to put his best self forward for Leena to see. He dug his hands into his front pockets and scanned the area to determine who was on his team. It turned out he was seated right in the middle of the most logical partition of the crowd.

"We have Pumpwalla this side!"

"Don't be crazy, yaar, Petrol is with us!"

"Look where the line is, yaar."

"Man, who cares? This is not the Line of Control we are deciding here!"

"Petrol knows every song!"

"Every song?"

"All of them!"

People sat down in place, and Prem sat down too as the debate about where to divide the room continued. He should have been basking in the limelight of being in demand, but instead he averted his eyes and tried to hide behind Tony. He had never before been bothered by the nicknames but now was acutely aware of how derogatory they must sound to Leena. Sweat began to issue from multiple quarters and dribble down Prem's chest, which lacked the hairs to stop them. Maybe she wouldn't have to know he was the Petrol in question.

"Petrol, what is your opinion?" Tony said, slapping him roughly on the shoulder.

Prem dropped his head and shook it with incredulity at the nature of his luck. He pushed his tongue against the inside of his cheek and considered his options. At last he lifted his head and said, "This side, I think."

There was uproar from both sides and the game began. He had placed himself on the team opposite Leena, and they started with "Mere Saamne Wali Khidki Mein" from the movie *Padosan*. Her team-mates clapped along with the song, swaying and falling over each other, becoming rowdy, but Leena remained vertical, enjoying herself within reasonable bounds. He could easily isolate her voice in the crowd as it turned out she was quite a loud person. She had the straightest, whitest teeth he'd ever seen, and they put him in such a trance he hardly no-ticed when the other team ended on H and his own team commenced with "Hai Apna Dil To Awara." There was whispering on the other side in anticipation of the last letter of the current song, followed by nod-ding as they settled on their next move, which turned out to be the romantic crowd-pleaser "Gaata Rahe Mera Dil." That sent both teams down a 1960s Dev Anand spiral that led to a Raj Kapoor spiral, fol-lowed by a songs-about-the-rain run, ending exultantly on S.

It was Prem's team's turn, and they were stuck. "Sab Kuch Seekha Humne" had been used, and so had "Sau Saal Pehle." Jarred from his reverie by the sudden silence, Prem noticed all eyes were on him.

"S, Petrol, S," Deepak said.

"Sawan ka Mahina?" Prem said.

"Sawan ka Mahina!" everyone on his side said.

He hoped Leena had noted his swift and celebrated contribution to his team's survival and that she had consequently attributed to him a short list of impressive qualities, including but not limited to depth of knowledge, quick-wittedness, affability, coolness under pressure, and the ability to think with the lights off. But probably she didn't register any of this, he thought, as his teammates sang on. Even if she did, it hardly meant that she was now ready to run off into the lukewarm

American sunset with him. Prem's team ended on R, and Leena's team countered with "Rasik Balma," an unbearably depressing ballad from *Chori Chori* that reminded Prem of the many appalling ways in which love can go wrong.

A waft of cool air through the front window caused all the candles to flicker. As the song was winding down, Prem noticed that Leena had stopped singing. She seemed to be trying to get her father's attention, possibly to assess whether he wanted to stay longer or go, and Prem was dejected by the thought of her leaving. He wanted her to stay and to notice him and to choose him from among the horde. He knew his chances to win her above all the more eligible, more suitably employed suitors were bleak, but when he watched her wiggling her head and eyebrows at her father as if to convey, *If you are tired, I am ready to go, but if you want to stay longer, I can do that too*, a feeling of longing welled up in him. His hands began to shake, and he took a deep breath. He had to make an impression before she left. It seemed the time for drastic action might be now. "Rasik Balma" would be ending on M, and he would think of a passionate song that would convey his emotions while showcasing his slightly above-average singing ability. As soon as the other team finished, he stood up.

There are moments in every life that bear the sheen of glory, that are recognized as unmistakably shining, vital points on a timeline. Prem didn't just sing "Mehbooba Mehbooba" that night in the dark, the room aglow in the warm light of flashlights and candles, mirroring the song's nighttime campfire setting in *Sholay*; he performed it. For her. He gesticulated dramatically in her direction, opening his arms wide, swaying and gyrating when appropriate. His nervousness fell away and he became the nimble and flexible rabab-playing Jalal Agha, bouncing around on his knees while warbling a soulful jingle, and at times he even became the sultry mononymous screen siren Helen and shimmied his hips. He sang well past the requisite two lines, and when Leena's eyes met his, it was the second time he fell in love with her that week.

Unfortunately for Prem, this was not one of those glorious, shiny moments. When he was breathless and done, the room was quiet. Prem looked around and found people staring. Beena Joshi's jaw was hanging open, and the elderly were shifting in their lawn chairs.

Finally, Gopal whispered to Prem: "The letter was Y, man. Maybe you should sit down now."

The power came back abruptly, and King's Court was plunged back into light. The children blew out the candles, Mistry Uncle resumed his solo concert, and Tony turned the cassette music up. Prem could not decide if this had been the most humiliating incident of his life; there were so many to choose from. Leena was standing now, exchanging goodbyes. Prem got up and headed outside to have his paan and hide near the bushes.

Outside was not as secluded as he had hoped. The party had leaked out past the hallway and onto the steps and into the yard, where on one side, an impassioned discussion of India's dismal Cricket World Cup chances was taking place, and on the other, a group of ten or so aunties—Prem's biggest fans—was lounging as though they were in Shalimar Gardens and not a scruffy bit of King's Court grass. As he unwrapped the foil, which was sticky and wet on the inside, Prem counted six of his country's twenty-two official languages being spoken, as well as two unofficial ones. Soon he was being summoned in three of these tongues by his dear older friends who would certainly not sit back and allow Prem to sulk in the bushes. He popped the paan in his mouth and walked over.

"Tell us, where is your chest hair?" Nalini Sen was a good-natured mother of unruly twin boys who came to Edison by way of Kenya and landed a conveniently located and therefore coveted job as a fabric-cutting associate at the Rag Shop. She regularly said the wrong thing at the wrong time without meaning any harm.

"Don't make him feel worse!" Shanta Bhatt said. "He already must be feeling like a fool. Right, Prem? Come, sit. Such good singing."

Prem scratched his forehead. "Was it really so embarrassing?"

"Yes," Nalini said.

Shanta gave Nalini a sidewise rebuke then turned to Prem. "You sang nicely. Wrong letter, but so what?"

"Ya!" Amarleen said. "Such dancing, such style. Absolute hero, hundred percent." With a flick of the back of her hand to the air, she considered the issue settled.

"Uh, okay, thanks," Prem said, trying to lean away from Amarleen's attempt to lean toward him.

"Now," the widow Urmila Sahu said, "let's have another song." The nearby rumble of a freight train caused someone to suggest they sing songs on the theme of trains, and after a brief discussion of the parameters—only songs in which the singer is on the train for the entire duration of the song; no train-station platform songs or songs in which the singer rides alongside the train in a jeep—Lucky, who had joined the camp along with the other roommates, began with "Apni Toh Har Aah Ek Toofaan Hai" from *Kala Bazaar*.

Prem wished he could sing to Leena on a train, but the chances were slim now. How could he come back from such a deficit? He felt inside him the familiar sinking and the usual threat of tears, though the tears never came. Beena Joshi came to sit with them and was hawking paan and soliciting gossip, which was a comfort. A few feet away, the talk was of Kapil Dev and India's pitiful test-series loss in March at the hands of Pakistan at M. Chinnaswamy Stadium in Bangalore and then, just that month, another wretched defeat to Pakistan at Sharjah Stadium in the UAE. Prem noticed Hemant still there on the lawn, mired in the cricket conversation. Leena could not be far, he thought, and when he turned, he saw her on the sidewalk chatting with a friend.

"Prem, what next?" Urmila said.

"Nothing, why would I do anything? There is no need for me to do something," Prem said.

"She meant what song should we sing next," Gopal said.

"Oh."

"Not what pathetic move will you inflict on that poor girl next," Mohan said.

"Got it. I think I'll go home to sleep now."

"Nothing doing," Shanta said. "We have at least seven more songs to sing."

Gitanjali Vora from 5B, diminutive and frail with a kind heart, joined them on the lawn, saying she was feeling suffocated inside the apartment, what with all the people and perfume and Styrofoam. Everyone welcomed her in the sensitive and supportive tone reserved for those who had recently been through something. The thing she had been through, about which all of King's Court was aware, was the illness and recent death of her father in India. She had longed to be by his side in his final days, but the ticket had been beyond her reach. Besides, she could only take two days off from her job at the A&S department store at Woodbridge Center Mall. She had called every night and spoken with her mother and the doctors in that loud and resonant voice universally reserved for talking on the phone to India, which meant that all the neighbors heard the call and the sobbing afterward. A group of them organized a collection to try to raise the money for the ticket, and though most people gave what they could, it wasn't enough. Gitanjali had walked around to each apartment to thank everyone and return the contributions. The next week, her father was no more.

Prem had been inordinately saddened by this sequence of events. He had spent hours holding Gitanjali's hand—which her husband found strange yet nonthreatening—and folding her laundry, even ironing her saris, and he had contributed the largest amount to the collection, causing a considerable dent in his savings. When she joined them that night in the yard, Prem did the only thing he could think to do to lighten the mood and cheer her up: he sang a song from the 1968 Jeetendra-Mala Sinha film *Mere Huzoor*, which takes place on a train.

By the refrain, he was on his feet and making grand flourishes with his arms. He circled the group with a silky glide and sang so beautifully in the light of the moon and the Quicker Liquor sign that even Mohan, Gopal, Lucky, and Deepak had to admit he was kind of dashing. And during the entire performance he looked only at one woman, Gitanjali Vora, serenading her right in front of the other women who didn't mind since they knew she was in need of a good serenade.

What happened next Prem would play over in his head again and again for the next sixteen years: From her place on the sidewalk, Leena Engineer called over in his direction. "Hey!" Everyone in the singing camp looked up. "Nice singing."

Prem opened his mouth but no words came out, just a guttural "Uhhhh" sound that impressed nobody. "Say something," Beena urged, but before he could, Leena turned away. He thought perhaps he'd seen a smile and, he wasn't sure, maybe even a slight wink, but that was hoping for too much.

"She wasn't talking to Pumpwalla, she was talking to me," Lucky said as Leena tried to extract her father from his cricket discussion.

"Why would she look at you?" Mohan said. "You weren't even singing."

"I sang the before song."

"Of course she was looking at Prem," Amarleen said to Lucky. "Why would she look at you when she can look at him?"

"Shall we go inquire?" Shanta said. "Find out if she likes him really?"

"No, no, that will ruin everything," Beena said. "Have you seen a Hindi movie in your life? She has to hit him with her bike now."

"Is her father unmarried?" Urmila said.

Prem didn't hear any of this as he was busy trying to decipher the tone in which Leena had said "Nice singing." It wasn't exuberant, and certainly not flirty; more matter-of-fact and casual, with a hint of play-fulness.

"Prem, yaar," Gopal said. "You going to make a move?"

Prem shrugged and watched as Leena tucked her father's hand in the crook of her elbow and walked him down the path to Building 5.

* * *

Prem spent the following afternoon unloading a truck and stock-ing shelves with bags of Swad-brand atta in Hemant's store. She was nowhere to be seen, but toward the end of the day, he heard her on a phone call in the backroom reprimanding a ginger paste vendor for a late delivery.

Mohan and Lucky were sweeping and dusting and laughing at Prem when he scratched his chest. They had conceded that, yes, Leena had indeed been speaking to Prem the previous night, but felt there wasn't enough evidence to suggest she was interested. "Maybe she was feeling bad for you because you don't understand the alphabet," Lucky said.

"Maybe your mother doesn't understand—" Prem began but quickly lost confidence in that strain of insult. After a while he moved to the last aisle in the back where he could scratch himself with abandon. He was deeply disappointed to not see her all day. The whole of his being, his entire notion of his future self, was tied to the question of whether he had a chance. He hoisted the last bag of atta onto the shelf and turned to look one last time at the backroom door.

7

It wasn't until the following weekend that he saw her again, and this time, she was reading palms. A sizable youthful subset of the previous party's crowd was gathered at apartment 3D Saturday afternoon while the Singhs were sightseeing with out-of-town relatives. Though Iqbal and Amarleen welcomed a full house, they did not permit alcohol to be consumed in their home. So, as if they were high schoolers whose parents were away, the young boarders seized the opportunity to throw a party.

"Are you sure they will be gone for a long time?" Mohan had asked.

"Yes," Deepak had said.

"They are going to Empire State Building, UN tour, the Times Square?"

"Yes."

"And Statue?"

"Naturally."

"Any Broadway show?"

"*Cats.*"

"Okay, call everyone."

Prem learned of the party when he walked in on it already underway.

"Did you bring beer?" Mohan asked. Behind him, a stranger was drinking water straight from the faucet while an assortment of tenants from Building 9 stood solemnly over a young man sprawled out on the kitchen floor.

"Why is everyone here?" Prem said. "Where are Iqbal, Amarleen? Did someone die?"

"Why would we need beer if someone died?"

"I don't know, I just . . ." Prem lost his train of thought as he spotted Leena across the crowded room, peering into someone's outstretched hand. Even as he was doing it, he recognized that he was staring at her in an aggressive and unsettling way, like Amitabh in *Namak Halaal* gawking at Smita Patil, he in a pink turban, she all in white, he serenading her with a subdued version of his previously boisterous song while the other guests looked on in confused silence.

"So," Mohan said, "you did not bring beer?"

Prem hoped to change out of his Exxon jumpsuit, but it soon became clear that both the bedroom and bathroom would be occupied indefinitely. He settled in a corner, leaning against a wall, trying to look engaged in a conversation with Tony and a guy called Sam about foreign versus domestic cars. When Sam shifted a certain way, Prem glimpsed Leena, who was now examining Deepak's palm, which vexed Prem greatly. He hoped she would look up and notice him, yet he also really didn't. He wouldn't know what to say or how to act or what to do with his hands. Sam had repositioned himself entirely, and Prem had an unobstructed view from which to study her. It wasn't just her one-sided dimple or her wide smile that vanquished him, it was the enormity of her personality. He envied the ease with which she talked to people, how she commanded attention without even wanting it. When she took an interest in someone, that person became the most fascinating person in the room. Everyone, women, men, the old, the young, wanted to melt into the delirious light surrounding her, none more so than he. She had everything he didn't. He was at her feet.

As she switched to reading Deepak's other hand, in a miraculous instant, she looked up and met Prem's eyes, causing his face to flush. He rubbed the back of his neck and looked down but couldn't stop himself from looking back at her. She glanced again at Prem, and he thought he discerned a slight smile before she looked away again, though it was just as likely he'd imagined it.

"Ya, Japanese, definitely, very, very efficient." He thought he was responding to Sam or Tony, but it was Gopal calling his name from across the room, waving him over frantically. Though he was reluctant to remove himself from the chance of further possibly suggestive eye contact, Prem squeezed and elbowed his way to his friend, who directed him to a crisis in the hallway. Apparently, a friend of Amarleen had come looking for her and was sobbing outside.

"Why are you telling this to me?" Prem said, though he was afraid he already knew why.

"Because, yaar, the auntie crowd loves you," Gopal said.

"Ya, man," a vaguely familiar person said, "they think you are Dilip Kumar combined with Dalai Lama."

The crisis that Archana Ambani from 2E was dealing with, poorly, in the hallway involved Stern's department store and an unreturnable Samsonite suitcase. She had forgotten to keep the receipt, without which they would not take it back, and this in turn had precipitated a major fight with her husband, who felt the purchase of the suitcase was a reckless mistake, the reverberations of which would be felt for years to come.

"Why do they give so much of trouble in America?" Archana asked between sobs. "In India, the suitcasewalla knows you, you argue for twenty minutes, he says he will give only half money back, you say you know he is having the affair with his neighbor, he takes the suitcase back and gives you full refund plus free neck pillow."

Prem was unsure what kind of response this required. He shook his head and tsked in a sort of show of solidarity.

"I feel scared of my husband," Archana said.

"What do you mean? Do you mean he will beat you? I will not let him, I will call everyone, Deepak, Gopal, everyone from Building 10, Tony, the police, also you should stay with Beena Joshi tonight—"

"No, no one is beating anyone," Archana said. She paused reflectively for a moment, then renewed her sobbing. "But he will give me crooked looks every time I ever use a suitcase again!"

Because he couldn't abide a woman's tears and also because he wanted to get back to staring at Leena longingly from a distance, Prem made a split-second decision to cover the cost of the suitcase himself. What was a little cash thrown here and there? he thought. He could always take on some extra Exxon shifts. If his little bit of prosperity could bring peace to the Ambani household plus allow him to extricate himself from the situation, how could he not?

"But why?" Archana said. She appeared to be examining his face, as if to determine whether he was a god or an idiot.

After a protracted silence Prem said, "Just come back in the evening. Good?"

Archana Ambani left elated, and Prem returned to the party.

"Mr. Prem Kumar, your palm, please." It was Leena, right there at the door, in front of him as if she'd been waiting, albeit with Lucky's hand outstretched in hers, which she abruptly dropped when Prem entered.

"You didn't finish my reading, but," Lucky protested. "What does my heart line say?"

Leena took a quick glance at it. "Oh, nothing, it looks like you prefer company of animals over people. You maybe should get a dog."

She turned to Prem then, who put out his hand. He was confused by this sudden attention, which, for lack of a better explanation, he attributed to his exceptional eye flirting. He could not have guessed that she had discreetly yet persistently asked his friends about him. Where did he come from? Was he going around with anyone? Why was he chosen to speak to the crying auntie in the hall? Nor could he have known that, despite some initial joking about his amazing way with middle-aged married women, his friends had said he was a decent fellow, a little quiet, a bit secretive, like we don't really know anything about him but that's okay, he is reliable, neat, and clean, with good habits, no tongue scraper, but still. The aunties like him because he listens and helps with the problems, makes them laugh, or they make him laugh, unclear who is laughing, and for no reason, they think he looks like Shashi Kapoor. The uncles do not mind because Prem is a mild kind of person, a bit sad, having no ambition, so when aunties are complaining to him about the neighbor's too loud music, they think, Better him than me, no?

Prem didn't know they'd said any of these things, nor that Leena had only heard "reliable, clean, listens, laughing, Shashi Kapoor," then rubbed her chin and said, "Huh." When he put out his hand for her and she stepped in closer and took it, he felt an overpowering desire to pull her in even closer, not to kiss her but to hold her there, their faces so close they could feel each other's breath, as in every Hindi movie he'd ever loved. "So, what does it say? That I am going to meet a beautiful grocery store owner soon?" he said.

"Are you kidding? Him?" someone said.

"Yuck. What a line, man," someone else said.

The woman of his dreams—who was taller than he'd realized and smelled even better than he'd imagined, like rosewater and Neem herbal toothpaste—rolled her eyes at the others then examined his palm closely, tracing one of its lines with her finger. "Let's see, Mr. Kumar. Your head line is showing a clear downward slope, then some upticks later."

"Naturally," Prem said.

"This shows you are logical and do not waste time in worrying," Leena said.

"Of course. Wait, really?"

"Then, if you look here at the fate line, oh, it starts very close to the life line, very close, almost touching."

Prem was so overcome by the thrill of what was transpiring that he forgot to consider until that moment that Leena might actually discern from his palm things about his life that he did not want her to discern. He yanked his hand out of hers abruptly. "Tell me, what do you do with the vegetables in the store when they become old?"

Taken aback, Leena didn't offer an immediate answer to the question of declining vegetables. She looked closely at his face as if trying to decipher him that way instead. "Where is your family?" she said.

"In Delhi," Prem said.

"Are you close to them?"

"No, actually, I am quite far."

She lifted her chin and narrowed her eyes, continuing to inspect his visage. "You don't want me to know something."

Even as she accused him and investigated his face with suspicion, a deep crease appearing between her brows, she was, he felt, altogether beautiful. Though he could not address her statement in earnest, it also seemed to him a moment for a bit of truth. "I like you," he said.

Leena cocked her head and blinked several times quickly. Her expression softened then to something resembling affection, but also rather too close to pity. "It's just that . . . are you trying to hide that you work at the gas station and maybe that you have a modest background? Because others have told me about how girls rejected you because of this, and I think it is very unfair. If a woman wants a rich lifestyle, she should put the burden on herself, not on anyone else, and why did they go around with you in the first place?" She paused for a breathless second, appearing suddenly self-conscious. "I know, really, it is not my place to say, but I just wanted to tell you that."

Shocked by her knowledge of his woeful dating history and in disbelief that someone like her could be embarrassed in front of someone like him, Prem opened his mouth, but no words came out. Meanwhile a crowd of assorted guests gathered in a loose circle began cheering at the young man supine on the floor. Other guests lost interest in their own conversations and joined the circle, which, it turned out, was spurring on Keshav Rathod from 3E as he shaved his unconscious friend's left eyebrow.

Leena and Prem moved closer to the tumult to have a look, and Leena took the opportunity to change the subject. "So," she sighed, "I have to go to the store soon to meet the cold-drinkwalla. But, you know, I don't know, maybe I can tell him to come another day . . ."

Prem stood incredulously as Leena continued this unexpected brand of wholesaler-related flirtation.

She turned to a nearby friend. "What do you think, should I go for my meeting?" she said, loudly enough for Prem to still hear. "There is so much of excitement going on here, but. I don't feel like leaving."

She glanced at him, then kept on. "Come on, yaar, help me, I can't decide."

Prem stepped around so he was squarely in front of her. "Listen," he said. "I know what you are doing. Go to your meeting. You have worked hard for the success of your family's store. I would never tell you to do anything that would endanger this."

Years later, at an uncomfortably ostentatious wedding, Leena would remember Prem's supportiveness and respect, his security in the face of female ambition, when a balding real-estate mogul would abruptly end their conversation when she noted the remarkable similarity in their career trajectories. "An overachiever," he would say, suddenly re-garding her as though she were a strange bug, then practically run to the bar.

"Go and come back," Prem said. "The party will be here still when you return."

"Will it really?" Leena dropped her apparently flimsy ruse and spoke plainly. "What time are Iqbal and Amarleen coming?"

"They are seeing *Cats*."

"Okay, I will be back."

While Leena was away, Prem found himself suddenly the object of seven different women's attentions. The eyebrow had been thoroughly removed and the mob dispersed when Roopa from 15H cornered him near the bathroom and asked if he knew where the bathroom was.

"Oh, it's just here," Prem said, to which Roopa responded with a nod and settled into a spot beside him. Neeta and Aparna from 17G joined them, and quickly thereafter four others elbowed their way in.

"Why I never noticed your good sideburns?"

"Are your parents living?"

"You look nice in the gas jumpsuit."

The barrage of comments and questions, the uncomfortable crowd-ing, the inordinate amount of laughter at his not-very-funny jokes—none of it seemed odd to Prem because he wasn't really there. His thoughts were still with Leena. Lucky and Gopal, however, were paying close attention to the strange turn of events.

"What is happening?" Gopal said.

"I am shaving my chest tomorrow," Lucky said.

"No, I got it!" Gopal said. "They are not interested in him."

"No?"

"No. They are interested in why Leena Engineer was interested in him."

And suddenly it seemed so obvious. The women weren't just talking to Prem, they were reevaluating him, taking a second look, as if he were a pair of shoes they had previously rejected as impractical. Lucky and Gopal continued to observe. Aparna was peppering Prem with questions while Neha and Latha from 19C seemed to be discussing his hair. Roopa played with the gold chain at her neck as she considered Prem's responses. When Neeta ran her hand down Prem's arm, Lucky sprang to life. "You know what we should do? We should talk to Leena Engineer sometime in front of everyone."

"Then the girls will talk to us?"

"Exactly."

Thus, when Leena returned to the party a half hour later, she was accosted by Lucky and Gopal, who took it as some sort of cosmic sign that she had reappeared. Gopal insisted that she read his palm, and Lucky talked a lot about saris. All three kept looking in the direction of Prem and the women. It wasn't long before everyone noticed everyone else, and Prem became jealous of his two roommates and Leena became jealous of the throng of women and Lucky and Gopal became jealous of Prem while Neha and Latha continued to discuss Prem's hair.

Although many people were enmeshed in the scene, Prem and Leena saw only each other. He shrugged and half-smiled, as if saying, *I don't know what all these women are doing here but I wish they would go away.* Leena giggled, and they held each other's gaze for a very long time.

Though Leena and Prem didn't speak again that evening—on account of Amarleen hating *Cats* and insisting they leave during the intermission—Prem was exuberant. He had confirmed Leena's interest in his existence. As he cleaned up with the others that evening, throwing out half-empty plastic cups, sweeping eyebrow hairs under the fridge, he marveled at the great luck written in his hands.

The next day, when he reported for duty at the grocery store, he

wanted to call her name to see if she was there. But that sort of thing—
screaming a girl's name, or even quietly saying it, right in front of her
father—just wasn't done in their corner of New Jersey. He kept his head
down and worked diligently all afternoon, dusting the Cadbury chocolate bars, rearranging the salty snacks, always hoping she'd appear. At
the end of the day, his patience was rewarded. The door to the back
room opened, just barely, and Leena's pretty hand passed him a note.

8

The note bore the refrain of a song from *Mili*, which she had watched in the theater when she was seven. She had liked the film and forever after liked its star, Jaya Bachchan née Bhadhuri, who many years later in an interview would describe her first impression of her husband, Amitabh. "He was very thin and his face was full of his eyes," Jaya would say. Leena would read this interview with astonishment at the similarity of their experiences. She would recall her first glimpses of Prem and how skinny and wide-eyed he was and how she'd liked him right away.

The morning after the party, Leena woke up at five and prepared the usual breakfast for her father: masala mung sprouts, two pieces of dry toast, and chai with no sugar, all of which he hated. Then she pushed him out the door to walk for at least twenty minutes at a rigorous pace while she prepared dal and rice for their lunch. When he returned and she was ready, they walked across the street together to their store, where she spent half her time looking after their accounts and the other half looking after Hemant.

At 10:00 a.m., the usual band of boys came in and she sequestered herself in back. She couldn't understand what it was they expected her to do. Would she look them over, choose one, and run into his arms? And even if she were the kind of girl to do such a thing, she wouldn't choose any of them. They were disrespectful to her father, thinking they were fooling him with their flattery and their tepid cleaning. The only reason she hadn't run them out of the store was that her father liked having them there. She heard him give them protracted lectures on self-discipline and the marvelous ethos of the hardworking local inventor Thomas Edison, and she knew in those moments her father was the erudite professor he had once dreamed of becoming.

At noon, Prem came in for his shift. Her father had him heaving heavy things onto high places. She watched him through a small hole she had discovered in the wall the previous week. He really was quite lanky. She liked the way his hair flopped about. And when the others—those duffers!—began to say things like "Hemant Engineer—Engineer of what? Groceries?" and "Why his hair looks like that?" and Prem didn't chime in but instead said, "I don't know, I think we maybe can learn some things from him," she wanted, it turned out, to run into his arms. At the end of the day she slipped him a scrap of paper with lyrics that ended on N.

Prem couldn't decide whether to respond with "Nakhrewali" or "Neela Aasman So Gaya." He sat on his mattress that evening, quietly trying to make the best choice while Amarleen clipped his toenails.

"Really, there is no need," he said, wrenching his foot from her grasp.

"There is need," Amarleen replied. "Now be still."

Her brother had stopped by again and was chewing on the end of a long stalk of sugar cane he had found in a Jamaican grocery store in the city. "Sister, get hold of yourself!" he said. Then shaking his head: "People will do the smelliest things just to come close to someone."

Prem didn't mind. It couldn't hurt to be well groomed, he thought, and then he wondered if his smooth chest had contributed to Leena's interest. If not the chest, then what? His awkward gyrating performance? His fluffy hair? And didn't she mind he worked at Exxon? What was the best response to her N, and where would he find paper and a pen, and how would he get the paper to her? All he wanted in life at that moment was to talk to her again, but he couldn't even find paper.

"Get up from there, woman!" Iqbal said from his place at the stove.

As Amarleen began to massage his calf, Prem decided to go with "Neela Aasman" for its more romantic, less offensive quality. The next morning, he went to Beena, who provided pen and paper and encouragement as well as an offer to deliver the note herself, at a moment when Hemant was looking the other way. It was unbearable to wait the entire day to learn whether the exchange had gone smoothly. But Beena returned in the evening with good news and a note from Leena ending in R. For several days, the antakshari continued like this, with Prem unable to think about anything other than Leena and the song she had just sent and what song he would send back. After a few exchanges, Beena removed herself from the equation to give them some privacy, though she was loathe to do so. She established a spot under a particular gallon container of canola oil for the two to leave their scraps going forward. The frequency increased to two, three, even four exchanges a day, with Prem's longing for the oily bits of paper—the shelf had never fully recovered from a prior Wesson leak—growing along with his profound desire to be in her presence again.

He kept every note in a cleaned-out mango pickle bottle that he hid in his bag. When they reached 121 total, he sat in the grass in front of the notoriously subdued Building 15 and read through them all. He searched for a pattern in her choices, a secret message she was trying to convey. When she wrote "babuji dheere chalna, pyar mein zara sambhalna," was she telling him to slow down and be careful? And when she responded to his T with "tere mere milan ki yeh raina," was she suggesting they have a night together? In the end, after reading the notes several dozen times, he decided there was no mystery in the words. But he also found that the accumulation of her side of their conversation was a pile of love songs; nothing about friendship, nothing about society or country or God, just romance and longing, rain-drenched desire, and moonlit avowals—a documentation of their sudden love, forever binding her in his heart with the pungent aroma of Priya brand pickle.

That same night, Prem wandered through Tun-Tun's open door hoping Leena might be there, but instead found twenty-one women wrapping peda in colored cellophane for an engagement party the next day. He sat on the floor and helped them pack the sweets, and when she never showed up, he returned to his apartment of men with the thought that he was cursed by the principal paradox of his country: an obsession with big-screen love stories matched only by the inordinate amount of time spent arranging marriages and forbidding dating. How could practically every Hindi movie ever made involve the subject of love when love was wholly prohibited by parents across the country and throughout the diaspora? How could the very people who had cried over the doomed affair between Prince Salim and the courtesan Anarkali in *Mughal-e-Azam* ask their daughters to wait until they were twenty-four to talk to any nonrelative of the opposite sex? It was virtually impossible to speak with Leena in person for her father was always watching. And in the rare moment he wasn't, others were there to watch for him, ready to start a rumor with the meagerest of pretexts. With the previous women Prem had tried to date, it was easier because they had emigrated without parents, but Leena was young—just nineteen—and had arrived with a traditional father who, though he was wrapped three times around her finger, was protective and watchful of her.

Prem kept a kind of vigil for Leena that night, vowing to remain awake until he conceived a way forward. At 3:00 a.m., Iqbal, who had risen for his nightly toilet ritual, spotted a scribbled note on the floor beside the sleeping Prem: "mere sapnon ki rani kab aayegi tu?" He was initially alarmed by this line—roughly "Queen of my dreams, when will you come?" from *Aradhana* (1969)—because he thought it was certain evidence of an illicit affair between his paying guest and his wife. But then he thought of Amarleen's brash manner and the frightening girth of her long braid and relaxed.

Prem planned to leave this in their canola-oil spot, but this time he would not rely on the lyrics alone. He added a question underneath, asking her to meet him on Tuesday at four behind the Dairy Queen. It was bold, he knew. Prem, not one for such moves, walked back and forth from the apartments to the store five times before going in for his final day of working to repay his lentil and Gold Spot debt to Hemant. Lucky and Gopal were already there, along with a hodgepodge of others from around King's Court. Together, they were trying to move a tall freezer stocked with packaged okra, packaged spinach, packaged peas, and several unmistakable pink tubs of Reena's Kesar Pista Ice Cream.

"More left," Hemant said, flicking his hand in a leftward direction. "Lefter!" He would have moved the fridge on his own, but he fancied himself an elderly and wise man who should have stopped carrying fridges long ago. Everyone looked up as a strange shuffling sound, like the skitter of carrom pieces, came from the ceiling. They stayed that way for a long time, craning their necks and listening, some of them still holding the fridge. The bell on the door tinkled and Prem entered.

"Perfect!" Hemant said, grinning wildly and marveling at the wonder of his good fortune. "There is a squirrel in the ceiling. Bring the ladder."

"Me?" Prem said, gaping widely and wondering at the marvel of his bad fortune. "You want me to bring the squirrel out of the ceiling?" He stared at Hemant, but then remembered whose father he was. "Yes, I will bring the squirrel out of the ceiling."

Prem had no idea how to do this but marched anyway up the ladder, the note heavy in his pocket. The others had gathered around and

Hemant had begun one of his lectures. With each rung, Prem felt a mounting pressure. The girl, the note, the father, the squirrel—it was all too much. He popped up a ceiling panel and stuck his head in.

"You see, boys," Hemant continued, "you must work harder than you think is possible."

"I don't see anything," Prem called down.

"Keep looking," Hemant said. Then to the others, "You must get your hands dirty. You must bargain hard with suppliers. And you must wait as long as possible to turn heat on in the winters."

The squirrel appeared and Prem nearly fell backward. "I see it," he said. "Back in one corner." Hemant handed Lucky a can of apple gourd and gestured for him to pass it up the ladder to Prem. "You want me to feed the squirrel some tinda?" Prem called down.

"No, no, Pumper, just throw the can on it," Hemant called up. "Injure it, then drag it out."

"Uh, that is not an easy thing to do."

"You should always do the things that are most difficult for you," Hemant said, nodding knowingly to his pupils.

Prem faced the squirrel. It sat still, cowering, and he thought he might actually be able to hit it with the can. But then he decided this was not the best course of action and purposely threw the can the wrong way.

When Prem descended without a squirrel, Hemant went next door to ask the hardware store owner, Mr. Settergren—whom he treated as an on-staff handyman, regularly coaxing him into performing odd jobs for no pay except the occasional bag of expired Bombay Mixture—for assistance. The crowd dispersed and Prem returned the ladder to its place against the wall. This was the right moment to place the note under the canola. He lobbed a silent prayer in the direction of the Ganesh and Lakshmi stickers on the cash register and hoped for the best.

After Mr. Settergren was firmly established in the ceiling, Hemant dusted off his hands as if he had removed the squirrel himself. Ever since the terrible incident some weeks back when the boys talked about Leena then destroyed the lentils aisle, he had been considering putting an end to the labor-in-exchange-for-life-lessons program he had instituted. But when he did some rudimentary calculations for how much it would cost to hire extra help and the number turned out to be too far above zero, he decided he could put up with the boys a little longer. He would have them stack the kidney beans cans in a neat pyramid then dismiss them for the day.

He headed to the backroom to tell Leena that the okra fridge had been shifted and they now had room for a Maggi Noodles display when something slimy caught his eye amongst the cooking oils. It was some sort of scrap of paper, a receipt or wrapper or something. He pulled it out from under a gallon jug and read it from the "mere sapnon ki rani" beginning to the Dairy Queen end, at which point he crushed the paper in his hand and yelled "Good for n—!" The phrase was meant to end with "nothing" and then move into a variety of insults and curses followed by threats, but Hemant caught himself. If I chuck them all out now, he thought, I will never get to the bottom of the mess. He smoothed out the wrinkled paper and placed it in his shirt pocket and waited a moment for his blood to simmer down before heading to the front of the store.

"What were you saying?" Mrs. Bhardwaj, the squat wife of a prominent pulmonologist, asked.

"I said something? I did not say anything," Hemant said. "Here, have these pistachios."

"No, no, you said, very loudly, 'Good for' and then you stopped."

"Oh, oh, yes, I was saying, 'Good for you!'" Hemant said. "For choosing the green peppers. Excellent quality, fresh from Mexico."

Mrs. Bhardwaj did not appear convinced, but Hemant moved on

to inspecting what the boys were up to. They seemed not to be doing much of anything, and when he approached them loitering near the bitter melon, they straightened themselves up as if he were a brigadier general of the Indian army. Prem was with them, standing at attention, looking reliably disheveled. It could not have been him, Hemant thought. He was too awkward and incapable of clandestine anything. Hemant motioned for Prem to come forward and follow him outside.

The previous days of sunshine and heat had given way to a gray, cool day that threatened rain. Prem, not yet understanding the unreliability of New Jersey weather, stood shivering in a shirt and torn jeans. "Listen," Hemant began, pulling out the note.

Prem recognized the scrap of paper instantly and contemplated which way he should run. If he ran toward King's Court, Hemant could easily corner him; if he ran the other way, he could get hit by a car, which, all things considered, was the more desirable option. He felt like a trapped mouse, akin to Amitabh's character Vijay in *Kaala Patthar* stuck in a coal mine, as sweat accumulated on his stubbly chest.

"One of these donkeys has written this and tried to leave it for my daughter to find," Hemant said. "I am thinking it is the donkey in the WrestleMania shirt, but who knows?" He peered inside between the herbal products window display and unique shopping experience sign. "I am giving to you the job of finding out which one it is."

Prem nearly cried from happiness, then agreed to do everything he could to ferret out the culprit and requested the day off so he could gather clues.

Back at King's court, he collapsed onto Beena's plastic couch and didn't do anything the rest of the day. When the fear wore off and the shaking stopped, he came to the realization that Leena would never get his note.

"This is good!" Beena said. She was kneading an enormous ball of dough at the kitchen counter. "You have already impressed her father with your . . . with your what?"

"Height," Prem said.

"Height, yes, very important. In *India Abroad* ads, everyone is looking for good height-body for the daughter's husband."

Prem rolled over on the couch, causing the plastic to whine. "I don't care about the father, I care about the daughter."

"Prem, Prem, father is always the key," Beena said. "Now, did Leena see what happened?"

"She maybe saw her father finding the note, but nothing else."

"Okay, first we must get her a note explaining that the other note was taken. Then we will write a new note and establish a new note place."

"No, that's it," Prem said, sitting up and waving his hands in objection. "No more notes. I need a plan where I actually can see her."

Beena slapped her big ball of dough and came over to the couch. "What if you tell Hemant who your father is?"

"What? Why? No, nuh-uh," Prem said.

"If he comes to know you are from the wealthy family, he will embrace you like a son and get his daughter married to you. You will not have to throw cans on a squirrel anymore."

"Out of the question."

"And you could stop this Exxon work."

"But I like it there."

"And move to Watchung!"

"Where?" Prem looked out the window at a child chasing a bird. "No one is telling anything to anyone," he said.

"Okay, do what you want, be alone, murder squirrels with Punjabi tinda," Beena said, returning to her dough.

There was a knock at the door, and an Americanly dressed woman entered without waiting for Beena to let her in. There was an exchange of cash for vindaloo and an ensuing discussion of next week's order, which included a disproportionate amount of peas. Prem rolled over on the couch and closed his eyes. He felt the stirring of a familiar sadness rooted in his continued dependence on his father's wealth and reputation. The pain of his failed attempts at autonomy came flooding back. The small victory of his employment at Exxon seemed suddenly slight. Leena's sweet, somewhat husky voice came into his head, and he considered the possibility of following Beena's advice after all. With this question spinning around in his mind, Prem fell asleep. After a while, Beena covered him with a blanket and made seventy-five rotis.

* * *

The next few weeks for Prem were like *Mera Naam Joker*—excruciatingly long and brimming with the loneliness of an aimless clown. He had decided not to say anything about his father to Hemant. While listening to his favorite compilation tape of Hindi movie love songs, *Romantic Duets Jukebox 2*, he was reminded that he wanted to be a hero, not a bad guy. Only a villain would use his family's wealth to attempt to win over a girl. A hero would remain patient and humble and try to find a way to be with his love while continuing to work at Exxon. So Prem quietly did his work, dropping in to the India America Grocers every few days to placate Hemant with reports of made-up leads—a guy with one eyebrow was loitering in front of the store with a pen and paper, Gopal had been looking dreamily into the distance a lot lately—and to catch a glimpse of Leena, which he never did. He attended the usual get-togethers and chuckled at the usual jokes, but all the time he was looking toward doors, hoping that Leena would walk through them.

In his fifth Leena-less week, nearly three months since he fell in Gold Spot, on a regular July Wednesday with staggering heat and Minerva

naked on the lawn, Prem was working a double shift. Mohan was standing at attention at the pumps, eager to make it clear to Mr. Khosla, the
gas-station owner who was there for a routine visit, that he was alert and
ready to meet his customers' most dire gasoline needs. Though Mohan
was often the first to pick on someone, ever ready to pounce with a sar-
castic comment, behind the bravado lurked a wounded soul, one who
had seen his father, a civil engineer, lose his job and, after years of unemployment and despair, take his own life. Mohan grew up determined
to get to America, a place where jobs were magically never scarce. He
had been angling for a managerial position at Exxon for weeks now and
hoped today was the day he would impress his boss with his superior
interpersonal and windshield-wiping skills. But Mr. Khosla was a tall,
oblivious man who was more interested in the arrangement of candy
bars in the Tiger Mart than in the yearnings of his gas attendants.

Mohan leaped over Prem to attend to a Pontiac, but the car veered
over to the pumps on the other side. He went around, but when he approached, it circled back until it came to a stop at the pump nearest Prem.
Again Mohan tried to attend to the car, and again it moved away as he
came close. Although Mr. Khosla was nowhere in sight, Prem knew this
was Mohan's day for impressing the boss, so he stayed where he was and
let Mohan come around again and handle the customer, who had rolled
down her window and was scowling. She was a pale Indian woman with
sharp features and too-bright lipstick, and even from a remove, Prem
could see she had deadly long fingernails, one of which was now pointing at him. "Not you!" she snapped at Mohan. "Him!"

Her name was Varsha Virani, and in eleven years she would be
thanking Prem profusely for his help in getting her pirated-video-and-
passport-photo store off the ground, but for now, she slipped him a
note between the dollar bills when paying for her half tank of unleaded
and drove away.

"What did your girlfriend want?" Mohan said. He didn't seem to be looking for a real answer. "Next time, tell her I can give it to her too," he said.

Prem unfolded the note, which turned out to be in Leena's handwriting:

I have given Papa the idea of taking some paying guests. He will post the ad in the store tomorrow only.

Prem did not immediately grasp the life-changing, prayer-answering nature of this message. He tucked it into his pocket and scratched his head. On more than one occasion during his childhood, Prem had been called "tube light," commonly used to describe someone who is slow on the uptake, who takes a few minutes to light up, like the fluorescent lamps found in many Indian kitchens and American basements and garage workshops, which flicker and fuss before they glow. He walked around the Exxon lot twice before he understood that his beloved had devised a solution to their problem.

The next day, he was the first to approach Hemant. Though the rent was higher than at Iqbal and Amarleen's and it was unclear what the meal situation would be, Prem secured a spot on the floor of the Engineers' apartment. Soon he would take up residence on a mattress even more unsubstantial than the last, wedged in among too many decorative whatnots, where his head would be situated under a swing—an improvement from the onions, to be sure—just a thin wall between himself and Leena.

9

When Prem broke the news to Iqbal and Amarleen and his room-mates back at the apartment, Amarleen threw a potato at a wall and began to wail.

"Looks like Prem is a gone case," Mohan said from a reclined position on his mattress.

"Gone case? Why?" a short man whom Prem had never seen before said.

"Because he will do anything to be near to that Leena Engineer," Mohan said. "Even share the bathroom with her hairy dad."

Amarleen let out an even bigger howl and ran to her room. Prem stepped into the bathroom and came out clutching his toothbrush. "It's not true," he said, trying to be casual, but appearing desperately uncasual. "I'm not, you know, I don't even, the reason I am shifting there is for more room on the floor."

"Who is Leena?" the short man said.

"The girl of Petrol's dreams," Lucky said.

"A masala bombshell."

"A firecracker with nice hair."

"Sridevi and Sharmila Tagore, mixed."

"Stop it, just stop," Prem said, waving his toothbrush in the air.

"Gone case," Mohan said.

Prem didn't care that everyone knew; he was going to live with Leena, sort of, and see her every day and smell her nice hair as much as he wanted. It was the single greatest piece of luck he had ever had.

"Is okay," Iqbal said to Prem. "I will tell Harbhajan to bring some new person from the airport."

"Why, Lord, why?" came a cry from Amarleen in the bedroom.

"Is maybe best for everyone," Iqbal said.

That evening, Gopal, Lucky, Deepak, and Mohan came home with a bottle of scotch. Because alcohol was not permitted in the Singh household, they kept it in its Quicker Liquor brown paper bag and gave Prem just a glimpse. "For tonight," Deepak whispered. Prem was moved. In India, he had never thought twice about the price of a bottle of anything, but here he was acutely aware of how much things cost and how hard people worked to pay for them. He imagined his four roommates bumbling around the liquor-store aisles searching for Johnnie Walker—the Indian gentleman's drink of choice—and then debating which color level to purchase. Prem decided in that moment that he wanted to be one of those people who never forgot a kindness, and indeed, he would always remember the gesture of his roommates wanting to make his last night with them a memorable one, though, it would turn out, he wouldn't remember much else.

Gopal would recall that the evening started off tame, with boozing outside on the steps, brown liquor in steel glasses. Mohan would remember an escalation in the drinking after the sun went down. Prem thought maybe Tony had joined them briefly, bearing a mysterious clear alcohol he had concocted at home. Deepak would vaguely recollect trying to talk to a cat, while Lucky seemed to remember amorously hugging a streetlamp. Apparently, Mohan argued with a tree, though he didn't remember it himself. They all agreed it was Lucky's suggestion for Prem to serenade Leena from under her balcony like an Indian

Romeo. Prem had a murky recollection of this happening, and then Beena and Shanta tackling him to the ground and dragging him away. Later, Deepak would recall that he did not try to talk to a cat but rather tried to eat it. The night ended back on the steps where Gopal declared his love for Prem. "We will miss you too too much, yaar," Lucky added. "He is just moving two buildings down, he is not dying," Mohan said. But later, after they all wished Prem luck in winning the girl, Mohan said, "I am happy you are not dying, yaar." They slept in various incorrect places that night: under Shanta's dining table, on Beena's plastic couch, beneath the Ferrari poster at Tony's place. In the morning, no one could remember how they'd each ended up where they did, but they walked home, got dressed, and went to work.

In the afternoon, Prem carried his few belongings across two courtyards and up one flight to apartment 5F. Father and daughter were at the store, but Hemant had given him a key and told him to come in and get settled. Prem had imagined the apartment to look like his previous one—spare with stockpiles of household supplies and a few stray onions—but this one was bursting with decorative items and overrun by a money tree. Widely known to be fiscally auspicious if it remained uncut, it was hanging in the southeast area of the room in a white plastic planter with a hook at its top, its vines thumbtacked in an intricate network across the ceiling so the entire surface was plastered with leaves, creating an unsettling rainforest effect. Baffled by the greenery, Prem found himself ducking his head as he wandered through the rest of the apartment. There were mirrored pillows at every turn and all manner of Hindu knickknacks, most significantly in brass: brass Ganeshas, brass Hanumans, brass Krishnas, brass Radha-Krishnas, brass Krishnas playing a flute, brass baby Krishnas stealing butter. In the hall closet was an altar featuring a large portrait of Laxmi surrounded by smaller portraits of other, less lucrative gods, as well as an old tile depicting a sacred fire—a nod to the Engineers' Parsi lineage that had taken a Hindu turn somewhere along the way. A garlanded portrait of a woman was displayed high and prominently. In the rows of blue Parachute coconut hair oil bottles lined up in the bathroom and the cassette tapes piled high on the radio, Prem saw the evidence of Leena, and he settled back on the ornate, oversized, carved wooden swing in the drawing room and waited for her.

The days that followed were the best of Prem's young life, and better than any in the sixteen years that would follow. The proximity to Leena, the thrill of being close to her, the tinkling sound of bangles at her wrists—it was almost too much for him to bear. He was surprised by how daringly she communicated with him right under her father's nose, which, in turn, made him daring too. He hummed the tunes of all the most romantic love songs when she passed him in the hall. He brought his plate to the sink at the same time she did and brushed her hand under the running water. When she cooked dinner, he stood beside her and stirred her dal.

In his second week there, through Urmila Sahu, who had just returned from Chicago, where she had been visiting her sister who owned a sari shop that was experimenting with carrying Hindi movie videos, he managed to get hold of a pirated copy of the recently released superhit film *Mr. India*. On the Engineers' state-of-the-art, two-part, top-loading VCR, the household, along with Leena's friends Varsha, Falguni, and Snigdha as well as Hemant's dear friend Sanjay Sapra, watched the movie and then immediately watched all of the songs again. Afterward, they had chai and discussed it all.

"How could he become invisible like that?" Snigdha said, her fluffy boy's haircut rustling in the slight breeze of the swing on which she was sandwiched with her friends. "It is just not real."

"I don't think it matters if it is real," Varsha said, smacking her gum while assessing a chipped nail. "It is a movie."

"And if it does not bother you when they show the couple suddenly singing on a mountain in Switzerland or at the pyramids in Egypt, why should this?" Leena said.

"I think in our movies we are meant to feel more and think less," Hemant said from his spot on the couch next to his dear friend.

"Yes, but come on, guys, he was *invisible*," Snigdha said.

"Prem, I hear you are the movie expert," Sanjay Sapra said, sweeping his silky, side-parted hair to the left.

Prem looked up from his uncomfortable place on a cushion against the wall. He scratched the nape of his neck and shrugged. "Here is the thing," he began, his chronic social anxiety muted by the prospect of a Hindi movie discussion. "The movie is fantastic. First-class. There is action, there is comedy, patriotism, orphan adoption, invisibility formula, terrifying villain with excellent catchphrase, and superb songs. But really, it should be called 'Miss India,' not 'Mr.'"

"Nonsense. Why?" Hemant said.

"That is stupid," Snigdha added.

"I do not understand," Varsha adjoined.

"God, you all, let him explain," Leena replied.

From his place on the floor, Prem looked up at Leena with love in his eyes, and everything he said next, he said only to her. "Because the heroine is the star. She steals all the scenes and dances in the rain. She mesmerizes. There is a certain quality about her. Who can look away? The silent, invisible hero has no chance. She is the serious reporter, the Charlie Chaplin imitator, the beautiful, the funny, the talented, the dazzling, the everything."

"Cool," Falguni said. The most numinous of Leena's friends, dabbling in astrology and numerology, harboring a firm belief in the power of a good gemstone, Falguni tended to go with the flow.

"Sounds like someone really likes Sridevi," Sanjay Sapra said. "She is not my type," he added. "Too funny nose."

Varsha agreed about the nose, and there was further discussion of the film's excellent qualities. Prem wanted to mention his brief but wholly positive run-in with Amrish Puri, who played the soon-to-be legendary villain Mogambo, but couldn't figure out how to work it in. The following weekend, they, minus Hemant and Sanjay, plus Abdul Rashid, watched it again. Prem thought of Leena, Leena thought of Prem, and Snigdha tried in earnest to suspend disbelief.

The third week after Prem's entry into the Engineer household, a second paying guest was introduced. "This is Viren Bhai," Hemant said. "He is chemical engineer."

An exceedingly slight and diminutive man, fifty-something Viren Bhai had been in America for quite some time. He was well respected at his job in Merck's Animal Health division for his contribution to the development of the first recombinant DNA vaccine against diarrhea in piglets, but his true passion was for ancient Vedantic teachings. He devoted himself utterly to understanding the principal Upanishads, particularly the Aitareya and Chandogya ones, and decided, as a result, to forgo marriage. As part of his ongoing austerity measures, he recently let go of his townhouse in favor of a mattress on Hemant's floor. Mild-mannered but with a core of confidence, Viren Bhai was quiet and kept to himself. Prem would often wonder how a man could be so noiseless, yet so strong. Because he rarely socialized, leaving the house only for work, groceries, and to lead a Bhagavad Gita discussion group, he seemed always to be in the apartment, wearing some variation of the same dress shirt and slacks, even during his morning yoga routine, which he performed in the middle of the drawing room.

The morning after Viren Bhai moved in, Prem tried to talk to Leena while Hemant was out for his involuntary morning constitutional.

Leena lolled on the swing, flipping through a pickles catalog, dog-earing the pages with the most popular kinds. The sun streamed in from the window behind her and through the swing's carvings, creating patterns on her golden arms. Prem watched her from the couch opposite while Viren Bhai contorted himself on the floor between them.

"You like pickles?" Prem said, immediately regretting this choice.

Leena smiled; Viren Bhai threw his legs in the air for Sarvangasana.

"I just, I mean," Prem said. What he really wanted to say was, *I want to know everything you like so I can one day buy it all for you and devote my life to giving you the things you like,* but he didn't know if they could trust Viren Bhai to keep their secret. So he had to confine his talk to pickles. "I like mango kind. You like mango?"

Viren Bhai began his Ujjayi breathing then, which could get quite loud, so Prem and Leena stopped trying to talk to each other about pickles and joined him on the floor. He taught them how to use their thumbs and forefingers for alternate nostril breathing, to calm the mind and cleanse the energy, which quickly became a daily ritual. The summer went on like this, with ancient yogic breathing exercises, Prem trying to be alone with Leena, and Viren Bhai getting in the way. Though he was a nice man, pious and peaceful, and together they learned a lot from him that would soon come in handy, he was also their kabab mein haddi, the bone in their meat skewer, their third wheel. Prem wished he could take Leena out somewhere for a secret dinner, but he had no money for that and had to content himself with the fact that he saw her every day, even though it was with her father and a spiritual chemical engineer.

He dedicated himself for the rest of July to gathering all the essential facts about Leena. She had finished school in India before moving to Houston and hoped to attend Rutgers. Her dear mother, like his own, had suffered an untimely death, the discussion of which immediately boosted their bond by two levels. Like her father, she passionately partook of the second of India's two national obsessions, the first being movies: cricket. She had amassed a vast knowledge of the finer points of the game—the importance of slip fielders being sure-handed, the need for India to pick up its run rate earlier in the innings, the line and length of the bowlers—and she ardently despised the Indian team's principal rivals, Pakistan and Australia, though she conceded a grudging respect for the latter. Together, she and her father cherished their 1983 Thums Up bottle top inners collection featuring images of the Indian and West Indian participants of that year's World Cup, along with their Kapil Dev flicker book, which they had earned by turning in a large number of inners and which they now considered their prize possession. In the absence of televised cricket matches, the thing she missed most about her original country, father and daughter contented themselves with reading recaps in *India Abroad* and admiring their collection, which was kept in the same closet as the gods, on a shelf just under Ganesha. In anyone else, Prem would have found such behavior strange, but in her it was endearing.

When she wasn't talking to her father about cricket or painstakingly controlling his diet, Leena was busy ironing hair. Prem was astonished when he first witnessed her dragging the ironing board from her bedroom to the space between the drawing room and kitchen, plugging in the iron, laying one side of her face down, spreading out her hair, and then ironing it. Hemant noticed the alarm on Prem's face. "Silkiness requires monumental effort," he said. It turned out that Leena spent considerable time ironing the hair of other women as well. They had learned of the secret to her perfect coif and begged her to similarly ease the frizzy quality of their waist-length tresses. At night, if Leena had left her equipment out, Prem collected broken pieces of her hair from the board and put them in the side pocket of his bag. He did this only on days when she had no clients and straightened only her own hair, because why would he want anyone else's hair?

It was when Leena was ironing Tun-Tun's hair that Prem first learned of the Dotbusters. "They won't rest until they kill us all," Tun-Tun said, her cheek flat on the board. "You must have heard, Hemant Bhai, they want to murder all Indians in America?" This account was somewhat of an exaggeration of something that did not require exaggeration, Hemant thought. "Not quite what they wrote, but yes," he said.

Prem went to Beena's to get his facts straight.

"Oh, ya, no, those Dot-kids are terrible," Beena said. She appeared to be simultaneously deep frying pakoras and chopping an alarming quantity of onions. "Where are their parents? They have been spitting on the Indians in Jersey City, smashing cars and houses and all, writing the graffiti on the businesses."

"Didn't they kill someone?" Prem said.

"Ya, and they killed someone," Beena said, wiping onion tears with the back of her hand. She pointed to a jumble of newspapers on the coffee table, among which there was a piece about a scribbled letter that had appeared at the offices of the *Jersey Journal*, ugly and shocking in its hatred of Indian Americans and its stated intent to harm them. "We will go to any extreme to get Indians to move out," it said. "If I'm walking down the street and I see a Hindu . . . I will hit him or her." The day after the letter, Bharat Kanubhai Patel was beaten in his home with a metal pipe after his name had been picked out of a telephone book.

"Do you think they know 'Joshi' is Indian?" Beena said. "Could be something else, no? But for Patel, there was no chance," she said, shaking her head.

"Are you not worried?" Prem said.

"Worried, no, but angry, yes. If we are such a weak race, why they are so jealous of us? And is this not a land of immigrants? Are their ancestors not from some other place? They are not Native Americans, are they? And doesn't their religion teach not to hurt people? What will their god say? Where are their parents?" Beena turned her attention to the oven, which seemed to be emitting smoke.

On his walk home, Prem wondered what kind of person would sit down to write such a letter. Did he think about what paper to use or the color of the ink? Did he compose multiple drafts and show it to a colleague for editing? Regardless, it would be fantastic to see one of them cross paths with Beena, who would surely thrash them with her rolling pin.

That evening, Hemant came home and announced that Sanjay Sapra and he had organized a meeting for the next night so the residents of King's Court could come together to formally discuss the racist incidents and come up with strategies to protect their community. The meeting would be held at Sanjay's apartment, would they like to come?

"Most certainly," Viren Bhai said from his one-legged inverted staff pose.

"Yes, of course, very important, I will be there," Prem said, then immediately took it back upon catching the sharp, eyebrow-raised look Leena was directing at him: "No, nuh-uh, not tomorrow, no, sorry, can't make it."

"Working in the Exxon?" Hemant said. He was using a black marker to make signs with information about the meeting to hang up around the complex.

"That's it, yes, working in the Exxon," Prem said. "Cannot miss work!" He realized belatedly that he sounded unnecessarily upbeat about this news.

"Very good, very good, sticking with the job, staying strong," Hemant said, nodding his head. "These good-for-nothings, they want to scare the Indians from the jobs. And then what? Are they going to do our jobs? Are they going to come here and order parval and karela for the store?" He continued on about how Indians were fleeing the state, and then something about Dotbuster identification cards found in a high school. Throughout Hemant's oration, Prem thought of how he would have an hour, maybe two, depending on the level of fury and disorder, alone with Leena. They could talk about everything openly: Where did she see this going? How long would they hide from her father? Were they in love? Maybe he could even hold her hand. Did she want to? He hoped she would be okay with it.

The next day was the longest day ever at the gas station. No one had anything interesting to talk about, so Abdul Rashid expounded upon the history of boredom. Prem tried to play cards with Mohan and Gopal, but his head wasn't in it, so then he threw pebbles at other pebbles for a while. He tried not to count the minutes until he could be with Leena. The hours dragged. Just when he felt like he couldn't listen to another word about ennui and the creative potential of the unengaged mind, it occurred to him that he should secure his alibi for that evening. He turned to Abdul Rashid. "Hey, at the meeting tonight, if Hemant asks, say I am working a late shift, okay?"

"Why you're asking Abdul Rashid when he is not even going to the meeting?" Mohan said.

"I am not going to the meeting?" Abdul Rashid said.

"You're going to the meeting?" Gopal said.

"They are trying to bust the Hindus," Mohan said. "There is no Hijabbusters."

Abdul Rashid removed his glasses and rubbed the lenses with a handkerchief. "You think these Dotbusters know the difference between a Hindu Indian and a Muslim Indian? You think they will stop and say, 'Sir, we know you are of Indian origin, but may we inquire about your religious affiliation?' before they beat me with their metal pipes? I am going to the meeting," he said. "And don't worry, Prem. I will lie to the grocer for you so you can have the romance with his daughter."

The pair had agreed to meet back at the apartment at 7:20, well after the start of the meeting. Hemant and Viren Bhai would be gone by then, and they could eat the dinner Leena had prepared earlier in the day. Walking down Oak Tree that evening, Prem relished the American summer, its luxurious, nonstifling warmth, the hiss of sprinklers over green grass. He breathed in deeply, trying to make the perfect air of that moment a permanent part of himself.

He entered Building 5 and reached the foot of the stairs and looked up. She was at the top, looking down with a funny smile. Her hair fell forward in two silky walls to frame her face, and her graceful arm was extended, her hand resting on the banister. She contained at once the radiance of a hundred movie heroines, and the hallway rang with the romantic songs of the fifties whose lyrics suddenly made beautiful sense.

"Flop plan," she said.

"What?" Prem walked up the stairs, coming as close to her as ever. He angled his head toward hers and took a breath of her coconut hair before turning the corner and discovering a pile of shoes.

The meeting had apparently been moved to the Engineers' apartment, and when Leena and Prem entered, the drawing room was crammed beyond capacity with people on the floor, on the couch, on mattresses, squeezed in on the swing which was perfectly still from the excessive weight, lounging on the dining table and kitchen counter, and perched on the windowsills, relegating poor Viren Bhai to a corner of the room, where he assumed the lotus posture.

That night Prem lay on his mattress across from Viren Bhai's, reflecting on how, instead of speaking with Leena at last about their future together, he had listened to various loud people of the community opining on how to battle an association of bigoted thugs. Someone had suggested penning a response in the *Jersey Journal*, while others proposed a protest march, meetings with congresspeople, education in the schools, meetings with local law enforcement, meetings with lawyers about the lack of response from local law enforcement, hunger strikes, taking up arms, and even buying a missile. In the end, it was decided to adopt a combination of all of these minus the artillery, and leadership roles were assigned. Prem was proud to see his fellow countrymen unite to take action. He wished he could be as impassioned as they were, but in the end, all he could think of was her in the next room, which seemed so far away.

By morning, he had decided he needed to figure out a new strategy for seeing her alone. It occurred to him that she had done all the scheming thus far to get them together. He resolved to become a more active schemer. When Hemant was in the shower, Prem dared to whisper something to Leena in the kitchen, with the hope that Viren Bhai wouldn't hear.

"Meet me behind the Dairy Queen at five," he said, leaning in next to her at the open fridge.

"Wow," Leena said, nearly toppling a spaghetti-sauce jar of coriander chutney. "Okay, ya, Dairy Queen, five."

"I won't tell anyone," Viren Bhai said.

10

Kissing has a glorious and convoluted history in Hindi films. Contrary to popular belief, there have been instances of lip-on-lip action on the Indian silver screen down through the ages, beginning in the surprisingly liberal era of colonialism and oppression, with a high spot in 1933's *Karma*, which featured a four-minute lip-lock. Soon after independence, the 1952 Cinematograph Act brought forth a unified and reconstituted Central Board of Film Censors and less kissing. Notable exceptions included Rishi Kapoor and Dimple Kapadia's 1973 kiss in *Bobby* and Shashi Kapoor's bold kissing spree of that same decade. Generally, however, making out was frowned upon, so directors had to get creative. Kissing, and indeed sex, became something alluded to with song and dance, bees drinking nectar, fish touching lips, closeups of flowers, rippling water, birds nuzzling, tipped umbrellas, turned cheeks, and wet sari choreography. By the 1980s, actually showing two people kissing was considered unimaginative. In this repressive climate, a generation learned to squirm awkwardly at the prospect of onscreen Indian kissing. By the time Aamir Khan embarked on a kissing rampage—*Qayamat Se Qayamat Tak, Love Love Love, Dil Hai Ki Manta Nahin, Jo Jeeta Wohi Sikandar, Raja Hindustani*—it was just uncomfortable. Much later, the norms relaxed again and kissing came back in full force, with even Shah Rukh Khan getting in on the action in *Jab Tak*

Hai Jaan. Youngsters these days grow up unfazed by rampant kissing in movies, but the older crowd still longs for the bygone days when a burning fire was good enough.

Behind the Dairy Queen, Leena licked her ice cream. It was melting fast on that hot day, and she ran her tongue along the perimeter of the cone's opening so the butter pecan wouldn't drip. They sat that way in the grass for a while, wordless, him watching her lick and then him licking too, until they were both done.

"That was good," Prem said.

"Mm-hmm," Leena said.

For almost an entire hour, they shared their likes and dislikes, hopes and dreams, though Prem had to concoct his answers somewhat to account for his lack of life plan and his hidden past. She said she wanted to open a salon specializing in Indian women's beauty needs. He said he wanted to buy an Exxon. He said they should go to a mountaintop in Switzerland, and she said they should attend the Filmfare Awards one year. They didn't overtly discuss spending their lives together, but that's what was implied when Prem took her hand and said, "I hope you like gas."

She did like it, the smell of it on his clothes when he came home at night, and emanating from his one pair of shoes placed carefully at the door. She liked that he worked hard and enthusiastically and that he was modest and meant what he said. Varsha pointed out that Prem was not very ambitious and kind of reserved, to which Leena replied, "Exactly." Their fates were sealed when Prem gave her a mixtape containing the songs from their oily note antakshari. She imagined him spending hours at a friend's apartment sitting on the floor next to abutting tape players, pressing rewind and stop and play and record over and over again until he got it just right, and she realized it was the best gift she had ever gotten.

Prem continued to collect her hair, which he found everywhere, though she still had so much of it on her head. They met again behind the Dairy Queen and also behind the Brunswick Lanes bowling alley, and, though they did not have a car, at the defunct Plainfield Edison drive-in. They stole glances in the apartment, and Prem soaked up the canorous tones of Leena arguing with her father about cricket matches whose outcomes had been written long ago. He found he wanted always to be in her presence. Around her, he was no longer nervous and awkward, but metamorphosed into someone charming and chivalrous. And to make matters more wonderful, she didn't care that he was only a pumpwalla and showed no signs of wanting to leave him like the rest. He understood now why there were so many Hindi and Urdu words for love—ishq, prem, chaahat, pyar, mohabbat, aashiqui, to name a few; one word cannot contain the breadth of the emotion. By the end of summer, Prem decided to find out if she wanted to marry him, but first he had to clear up a long-standing lie.

"Is your mind out of order?" Leena said.

They were in the dairy aisle of Foodtown, where they were picking up items as yet unavailable at India America Grocers: yogurt, aluminum foil, aspirin, tomato paste, laundry detergent, etc. Hemant had sent Prem to help his daughter with the bags on the walk home, and Prem took this as a sign that he should make his move.

Several weeks earlier, when Leena had asked Prem about his relationships with other girls in America, the lie had come easily to him—like, oh no, the truth will be too much trouble at this time, so dishoom! Lie! He thought he ought to come more clean. At Foodtown, he poured out to her the list of women he had attempted to woo, beginning with the somewhat nice-looking pharmacy student, moving to the deep-voiced bank teller, all the way to Shoe Town Sushila, enumerating the varied and creative ways he'd been dumped.

"So when I asked what was your dating history, you decided that lying would be fine?" Leena said with a shake of her head and an open-palmed gesture of disbelief.

"I did not want you to know I was so rejected." Prem scratched the back of his neck and wondered for a moment how the bit of information he was about to offer would affect his case. "But everyone else knows."

Leena threw her hands in the air. "Oh, I see, everyone else knows! Fantastic! Really, what is wrong with your brain?"

After a protracted discussion of what was wrong with Prem's brain in front of Roberta, the checkout lady with very high hair, they left Foodtown in bitter silence. Outside of Hit or Miss off-price women's clothing store, Prem broke the silence with an exasperated thump of the grocery bags on the pavement. "None of the others were anything next to you."

Leena looked wistfully beyond Prem at the cars stopped at the red light on Oak Tree. "But why not just say the truth? What else are you lying about? Are you secretly married? Do you have ten children? Do you really want to buy the Exxon? Do you even like the smell of gas?" she said.

He recognized that this was probably the correct juncture at which to talk to her about his true identity, about how he ended up in Edison, about his family's position and wealth, and how he tried to make a movie but ended up getting a cat murdered. Yet when he looked at her face, weary and annoyed, the frustration evident in her eyebrows, he couldn't do it.

"I'm going into Hit or Miss now," she said. "Don't follow me. And here, take the bags."

* * *

September unfolded as the worst month ever, owing not only to Leena's impenetrable barricade of silence against Prem though they continued to reside under the same roof, but also because of the renewed attacks against Indian Americans in New Jersey.

"I don't know, I just don't know," Hemant sighed. He was responding to Vilayat Hussain, a bulky, mustachioed anesthesiologist awaiting US medical licensing and meanwhile employed as a custodian at J. P. Stevens High School, who wanted to know how the police could possibly say the crimes were not racially motivated when the assailants were heard yelling "dothead." They were squeezed into the Engineers' apartment again for a meeting Hemant had quickly thrown together. It seemed he was becoming King's Court's unofficial community organizer, with his outrage in the face of injustice, his judicious proposals, and his excellent flyers.

"They beat him with a bat," Gitanjali Vora said.

"It was with bricks, eleven of them," Mohan said.

"Eleven bricks?" Gopal said.

"Eleven guys, you donkey," Mohan said.

"The way you said it, you made it sound that—"

"And it was in a busy area where anyone could see. Near to the Jersey City firehouse and a park also," Kailash Mistry said.

"And he was a doctor, can you believe?" Deepak said.

"Why does that matter?" Lucky said.

"It matters, yaar," Deepak said, biting into a nectarine.

"Okay, okay, you all are idiots," Uttam Jindal said. "There were two separate beatings. One was killed. They kept picking him back up after unconsciousness and beating him more with the bricks. Other guy was with the bat. He is in the coma now."

"Look," Hemant said, "we do not know as yet if this information is correct. But we do know some action must be taken. Now, who has ideas?"

"Maybe we can tell about this to the Prime Minister when he comes in a few weeks," Gopal suggested.

Mohan was visibly irked. "Okay, you will just walk into the White House and join Reagan and Rajiv Gandhi for tea. While you are there, please also solve this guns-for-hostages business."

Leena tried to refocus the discussion. "Who can help me to write the letters to the mayor and congress members tomorrow evening?"

Prem raised his hand to seize the opportunity; she couldn't snub him publicly without drawing attention to their curious dynamic. But it turned out Leena did not subscribe to this same view. "I do not need your help," she said, barely glancing at him.

Hemant cleared his throat and lowered his voice. "Then why did you ask, 'Who can help me?'"

Leena squiggled her mouth in annoyance. "I just meant—"

"Great, I'll be here at seven," Prem said.

"Don't you live here?" someone new asked.

The next evening, Prem was not alone with Leena, as Hemant convened his committee meeting in the apartment at the same time. Tun-Tun, Nalini Sen, Sanjay Sapra, and Hemant debated the merits of staging a peaceful protest march while Prem and Leena wrote letters from a preapproved template in silence. Prem tapped the end of his pen on the table, hoping to irritate her into talking to him, but she was resolute. He finished a letter and she slid him an envelope, which he took as a positive gesture, but after two more such exchanges, she shoved the entire stack of envelopes over so it sat squarely between them and he didn't have to ask for one again. Then she proceeded to churn out letters at breakneck speed. Seeing as she had the matter covered, Prem decided to focus his epistolary efforts in another direction:

Dear ~~Senator Lautenberg~~ Jaaneman, my Love, my life,

What a stupid idiot I am. I could fill 11 pages on this topic. You also, I know, could fill 11 pages on this topic. Please do not. I did not tell you everything about the other girls because I did not want you to think that maybe you should also reject me like they did. I did not want you to believe I was too poor or smelled too much like gasoline. I was scared. Now here is a poem:

Whenever life brings me to your presence,
This earth seems lovelier than the moon,
Your memories, sometimes knocking, sometimes whispering,
Wake me in the late hours of the night.
Whenever life brings me to your presence,
This earth seems lovelier than the moon.
Why does each meeting have to end in separation?

This thought torments me always.
Whenever life brings me to your presence,
This earth seems lovelier than the moon.

Of course, these lines are from Umrao Jaan, *the award-winning film of 1981. I do not know how to write a poem. But I know I only understood the meaning of these words after meeting you. I know you are not afraid of anything. I know you love your father and take care of him. I know you like to watch cricket and eat mango achaar directly from the bottle. You have a fire in you I cannot be without. I know I must be honest with you, forever.*

Your Prem Kumar

Prem folded the letter and tucked it into an envelope. He tried to slip it to her suavely under the table, but when she steadfastly refused to receive it, he ended up batting at her knee with it.

"Uf! What are you doing?" she said in an angry sort of whisper.

"Read it," Prem said. "Please. It's for you."

"It's not for Senator Lautenberg?"

"No, I wrote a letter to you."

"So you did not write the letter to Senator Lautenberg?"

"No, there is no letter for Senator Lautenberg."

"Fine," Leena said, snatching the letter from him. "But please, write the letter for Senator Lautenberg."

When Leena emerged from her room the following morning, she went about her routine, preparing her father's mung sprouts, packing their dal and rice lunch, and ignoring Prem, but when her father was safely out the door and Viren Bhai was mired in eight-angle pose, she plunked a cup of chai down on the table in front of Prem. "It was a good letter," she said.

Prem, who had been slouched over a piece of burned toast, straightened up. Leena continued to move around the kitchen, and he awaited her next words with the bright-eyed optimism of a terminally ill Rajesh Khanna in the 1971 classic *Anand*.

"Hold it," Leena said, quashing his hopefulness before it got out of hand. "I am not done with being mad yet."

As 1987 came to an end, Indian American women in New Jersey wore fewer saris and more jeans, and many stopped wearing bindis altogether, just in case. Legendary playback singer, actor, director, composer, and producer Kishore Kumar passed away, and Black Monday happened to the world's stock markets without much alarm from the residents of King's Court. Prem continued to apply himself at his job at Exxon, taking on extra shifts in the hopes of demonstrating his indomitable work ethic to Leena, who had barely spoken to him since the letter. She had softened a bit, making him the occasional chai and letting him help with the dishes again. Prem lived for these moments and hung all of his hopes on the word "yet."

In January, all of King's Court as well as Hidden Valley Manor and Brighton Village decided to go to the United Skates roller-skating rink. This epic outing of proximate apartment complexes had its beginnings in a heavy snowfall when three women, one from each complex, pushed their way forward, the accumulation already four inches at their ankles. "This is too too terrible," Rachna Bajaj of Brighton Village said, digging her hands further into the pockets of her puffy coat.

Shanta Bhatt concurred. "What sins did I commit in my previous life that I was sent to live in such weather?"

"I am cold," Priti Sinha, a no-nonsense dental hygienist, added.

They pressed on. They were coming from the Metro Park train station, having spent the day in New Brunswick assisting with preparing sweets for a wedding. When they reached Oakwood Plaza with the United Skates sign at a remove, Rachna had a thought. "We need something for making this winter go faster. Everyone is working so so hard in so much of cold. We need to try roller skating." Shanta and Priti got on board surprisingly quickly. In the next few weeks, the three women negotiated a discounted rate with Mr. Ramondi, the muscular rink manager, who gave them an extremely fair price for guaranteeing three hundred people, which was just one hundred above maximum capacity. Priti, who inexplicably had a certain rapport with Mr. Ramondi, got him to agree to play Hindi music that they would provide. Each woman spread the word in her respective complex, and soon, a sizable portion of Edison was looking forward to it.

"I don't see her," Prem said, hugging a carpeted pillar in the center of the rink, trying not to fall down, like most of the rink's patrons that day except Beena Joshi, who was bafflingly good at roller skating.

"She will be here," Beena said, executing a kind of grapevine move back and forth before him. "Don't you live with her? Was she getting ready to come here or no?"

Prem, still in his Exxon jumpsuit, attempted to turn around and lean casually against the pillar. "I am coming from the job," he said. "They are going to stop letting more people in when it gets too full. What if she does not come in time to get in? What if she decided she doesn't want to see me, I mean, more than she already sees me every day in the apartment? What if she found a new boy she likes?"

Beena did a quick spin and came to an abrupt stop. "Stop this nonsense before I hit you with my rolling pin."

Prem slid all the way down the pole and landed with a thump on the wood floor.

"There she is," Beena said.

In the midst of a horde of young women—sideys, all of them—there she sat, lacing up her skates, her silkier-than-ever hair cascading down her back in a luxurious torrent into which Prem longed to immerse himself headfirst. She wore a soft pink churidar while everyone around her wore varying shades of brown and gray. From his place on the floor, Beena moonwalking in the background, Prem openly stared at Leena until he willed her to look up. The meeting of their eyes, their aankh milana, set off a spark of renewed affection that erupted on the skating-rink floor.

He stood up easily and glided around the rink, gathering behind him a band of young men, some of them his friends but many whom he'd never before met. They were somehow all six inches shorter than him and fifteen to twenty pounds heavier, with unflattering, puffy hairstyles. Assuming a wedge formation with Prem at the apex, they skated toward the oncoming women's wedge helmed by Leena. As the groups approached each other, the playful, hopeful jukebox jingle "Papa Kehte Hain," from the soon-to-be-released *Qayamat Se Qayamat Tak*, kicked on, causing the crowd to go wild and the wedges to dance in perfect synchrony, with Prem and Leena clearly demonstrating the most talent and star quality. While it was not a love song, per se, for Prem and Leena, the upbeat number with its earnestness and undertones of rebellion embodied Prem's lifelong struggle to be something in the world other than what his father wanted him to be, which, though it caused him to lie prolifically, ultimately brought him to her. Leena was a vision, her dupatta fluttering behind her, and when the song came to an end, she fell into his arms and he dropped her back into a low dip. They remained frozen that way, like an ice sculpture from a lavish New Jersey Indian wedding from the near future, until one of Leena's sidey friends broke her wrist.

Varsha, in the coveted second row of the wedge, had performed her part well until the song came to what she felt was an abrupt stop, and she fell backward onto one hand and shrieked. Everyone in the rink came to a stop, or tried to, some rolling away involuntarily, while a few friends rushed over to her. Prem reluctantly pulled Leena up from their passionate and unnatural pose to a stable standing position, wishing the moment could've lasted longer, inwardly cursing Varsha's poor toe-stop management. But when he noticed Leena's expectant gaze, he skated over to help Varsha too. He and the others scooped her up and brought her to the concession stand, where a pale, pimply teenage boy called 911. The wedges disbanded and the spectators poured back into the rink, resuming their wobbly skating, except, of course, for Beena and, unexpectedly, Iqbal, who was also shockingly good. Leena skated to Prem's side, and together they comforted Varsha until an ambulance arrived and carried her away.

Prem took a deep, hopeful breath and turned to Leena standing next to him at the edge of the rink. "So?"

Leena tilted her head back slightly and looked up at him with the old tenderness in her eyes. "Okay, I'm finished now," she said.

Prem's heart leaped in his chest because he was pretty sure that the thing she was finished with was being mad. He tried to maintain his cool and restrained himself from picking her up and twirling her around. "Cool, that's cool," he said, then noticed her consternation. "What I mean is, is this moment real, or is it just a dream sequence?"

"This isn't a Hindi movie," Leena said.

"But maybe it is," Prem said.

After that, they resumed licking ice cream cones together behind the Dairy Queen, him sometimes licking hers, and vice versa. They continued blissfully for the next few months. Prem, flush with happiness, took to writing her frequent letters dripping with sentiment, adoration, and the scent of gasoline, which she accepted and read over and over before tucking them into a secret Gits idli mix box she kept under her bed and pulled out periodically to breathe in their aroma. At the beginning of April, when they were sitting out on the apartment's front stoop picking over lentils in large steel thalis, Prem said, "I think maybe, if it is okay with you, it might be time to take permission from your father."

11

If hung in the southeast corner of the home, the money plant, *Epipremnum aureum*, is said, according to Vaastu—the Hindu feng shui, as it is often mistakenly styled—to generate positive energy in the business and wealth arenas of homeowners' lives. It is believed a vast fortune is imminent once the plant's leaves reach the floor. Money plants are famously easy to care for, requiring no fertilizer or botanical knowledge, just a bit of light and water, which of course begs the question, If they are so easy to maintain, why isn't everyone rich?

This had occurred to Hemant, who was given his plant as a grand-opening gift when they launched their original store in Houston, but he chose to brush aside all doubt and instead take the lore of the money plant as fact. He applied himself very seriously to its upkeep, tending to it like it was his other child, even giving it a name—Hriyan, meaning "wealth." Leena's father had never been one to believe in free rides or easy money and always stressed the need to apply oneself. Hard work, he intoned, will always be rewarded in this land. So she was mystified with his fanatical dedication to the plant, spending hours fussing over the leaves, sometimes even taking the plant's side over hers, such as when she argued that it was making their apartment look like a jungle. "Don't talk about Hriyan like that," Hemant said to the plant's older sister.

On the day Prem and Leena were about to come home to crush his hopes and dreams, Hemant was working on his plant. Halfway up a ladder that he had purchased for the store but which spent equal time in the apartment for pruning purposes, Hemant was frustrated with the amount of yellow he'd been finding in Hriyan lately. Discolored leaves and dried-up ends of branches were the only pieces of his plant that Hemant ever cut away. The rest he tacked all over the ceiling, though Leena and anyone who visited told him that trimming the vines would not impact the plant's auspiciousness.

It had been drizzling all morning, which vexed Hemant because the store likely had fewer customers as a result. He would ask Leena when she came home for lunch. Strangely, she had asked if they could have lunch together that day at home instead of taking turns in the back office. It was Saturday, so Viren Bhai was also home, perched on the swing with a book about Vedic mathematics. What a simple, nice fellow he was, Hemant thought. No ego, no nothing. Just stretching and breathing, stretching and breathing, and occasional reading on incomprehensible subjects. Hemant commended himself on his choice of boarder. His other boarder had also proven to be a good choice. He helped with the dishes, paid the rent on time, and kept to himself. Hemant's only complaint was that the young man didn't seem to own a tongue scraper.

When Leena came in, Prem was right behind her, carrying a damp section of the *Star-Ledger* he had apparently used as an umbrella on his walk home. "Do not bring that in here," Hemant said without fully looking away from his plant.

Prem dropped the paper in the hallway. He ran his fingers through his hair, kicked himself for pre-angering the father, took a deep breath, and entered.

"Papa, I'm home!" Leena said in her lively way. "We have something to talk about with you." She put her account book down on the kitchen table and began filling a pot with water.

Viren Bhai got the sense very quickly, as meditative people often do, that something significant was about to happen in which he need not be involved. "I'll just go on the balcony, no problem."

"No, no, it is raining, Viren Bhai," Leena said.

"No worries, I'll do Kapinjalasana."

"Huh?" Hemant said.

"Bird-drinking-raindrops pose," Viren Bhai said, sliding open the flimsy screen door and exiting the room.

Hemant inspected Leena, then Prem. "You *both* have something to talk about with me? The same thing, or two separate things?"

"Just one thing, Papa," Leena said, smiling up at her father. "Come down from the ladder, be comfortable, I'm making tea."

Hemant remained on the ladder looking down at them. "Is it the store? What happened? Did those loafers knock down the Maggi Noodles display? Did the light go off again in the okra fridge?"

"Everything is okay in the store, sir," Prem said. He felt his legs tremble slightly and wished they could all sit down, but no one appeared to be moving. It would be odd if he alone took a seat, Prem thought, so it seemed he would have to remain standing and force himself to stop trembling.

"Nothing is wrong, silly Papa. But you see, we want to ask you," Leena said, adding milk masala to the pot. She cleared her throat. "The thing is that . . ." Her voice trailed off and she cleared her throat again. Prem had never seen her struggling like this to get words out, and it made him even more nervous to see that the least nervous person he had ever met was nervous.

"Do you remember the picture *Padosan*? When the people fall in love who live near each other?" she said.

Hemant used his clippers to remove an ailing leaf. "Never watched it."

"How about *Tere Ghar Ke Samne?*" Prem asked.

"Or *Mili?*" Leena said.

"Or *Ek Duuje Ke Liye?*" Prem and Leena both said, smiling at their synchronicity. Prem's anxiety lifted, and he was imbued with a sudden calm. She was with him. She was radiant, in an orange salwar with gold polka dots. But it wasn't just that she was pretty; she had confidence, self-assurance, work ethic, determination, a sense of herself in the world—things he didn't have, and that all the money in the world had never been able to buy.

"Why you are asking about movies?" Hemant said, looking back and forth between the two young people. Leena tilted her head to the side the way she did when convincing him that the store required more of something he didn't think it required, like crispy tea rusk or Hot Mix. In her gentlest voice, she said, "We have come to ask for your blessing."

Hemant made an unintentional snip and a long piece of Hriyan fell to the floor. The three of them looked down at it then back up at each other. "I am going to the store," Hemant said, climbing down from his ladder. "This loafer should be gone from here before I come back," and then, less forcefully, "which will be around six o'clock."

"Oh, Papa, don't be like that," Leena said. "Come, let's talk."

"Talk? Yes, talk. Tell me, how long you have been carrying on this disgusting romance under my nose? How many people have you told before telling your own father? Have you noticed he has no tongue scraper even?"

"I had a tongue scraper, but it was stolen," Prem offered.

"Really?" Leena said.

"Ya, I love tongue scrapers," Prem said.

"No, I mean, why would someone steal a tongue scraper?"

"Stop," Hemant said. "This is too much." He rubbed his eyes for a long time before continuing. "How can I marry you with this good-for-nothing bum? Why we have worked so hard in this country? So you can end up with a gas pumpwalla?"

"He is not a bum," Leena said in the firmest tone Prem had ever heard her use. "He is decent and good."

"And he looks like Shashi Kapoor, I know, I have heard. That is no reason to ruin your life."

Prem raised a finger in the air and attempted again to jump into the conversation. "Sir, actually, I do not think I look like Shashi Kapoor. Some people have mentioned it, but really, I don't think so. Maybe the hair and eyebrows, I don't know."

Hemant and Leena looked at Prem then continued on with their fight. "You always say good character is the most important thing," Leena said, dumping too much sugar into the chai. "Prem has that. Now you are saying you don't like him because he has no money?"

"I do not like him because he does not value the opportunity of America. He is not trying."

"He is not trying? Of course he is trying. He is even planning to buy a gas station one day, right, Prem?"

"Ya, someday, you know, maybe," Prem said, rubbing the back of his neck.

Hemant scrutinized Prem from head to toe, the wrinkle between his brows deepening as he made his way down. At last, he said, "You cannot marry him, you are marrying a doctor."

Prem looked at Leena, alarmed. She shrugged and seemed not to know. "What doctor?" Leena said.

"Any doctor!" Hemant said.

"What? No!" Leena said.

"Should I become a doctor? I can become a doctor," Prem said.

"Don't become a doctor," Leena said.

There was a lull in the argument, and Prem felt he could no longer remain standing. He crossed the room and sat on the couch, hanging his head and assuming a steeple-handed thinking position, which he soon abandoned after realizing it was a manner he'd inherited from his father. He had to find a way to make this situation better. Finally, heart pounding, he raised his head and spoke directly to Hemant. "Sir, please. Please. I can make a good life for your daughter. I can find a better job, I can find ten jobs. Even if we never become rich, we always will be happy. I always will want your daughter to be happy. Please, sir, I fall at your feet."

A clap of thunder caused the three of them to look outside, where the sky had turned dark in the middle of the day and Viren Bhai was doing complicated yoga. It was not yet pouring, but the threat was there, just like in so many Hindi movies when the pivotal moment of apparent doom—the rejection of the illegitimate child, the banishment of the wayward son, the orphan's revelation that his employer in a garment factory is actually his biological father, who had abandoned his pregnant, unwed biological mother, who subsequently died in childbirth—is portended by a perfectly timed flash of lightning or unrelenting torrential rain. The melodramatic movie weather signaled to Prem that something was coming, and it was worse than what had already come. There was a knock at the door.

Hemant opened it to find a young, well-groomed white man, jarring and conspicuous on a King's Court doorstep. "I'm sorry to trouble you," the young man began. "I'm from the Oak Wood Church, and we are trying to find what we can do as a group to serve the community."

"What you can do? You can remove this cockroach from my home," Hemant said, looking over his shoulder at Prem. He stepped out into the hallway and closed the door behind him. Leena let out a sort of growl of frustration.

"We're alone in the apartment, finally," Prem offered with a weak smile.

Leena's expression softened and she joined Prem on the couch, leaving adequate space between them. "I am so sorry for how my father is talking about you. You know he doesn't believe all what he is saying, right?"

"I think he believes it," Prem said. He felt no anger toward Hemant. Instead, he felt embarrassment for being an unsuccessful person, a failure. If he had been more capable, he might have had what he wanted in life, which was Leena. He looked around at the modest apartment teeming with knick-knacks, home décor, furniture, paper goods, fruit, the account book on the table. It was a life built on hard work in a foreign land, he thought, and felt deep shame.

Hemant came back in grumbling. "These young people, thinking they know better than me, telling me what I should think." He tossed a leaflet in the trash and took a seat on the swing, which creaked under his weight. Leena and Prem straightened up their posture as if this might help, but Hemant did not look at them. He rocked gently back and forth, looking at the ceiling, at the floor, around the room, into the distance—anywhere but at them. Finally, he planted his feet on the floor and stopped the swing's movement. "I have decided," he began. His nostrils flared wildly, and a flash of lightning briefly illuminated the room, revealing the silhouette of Viren Bhai in flying pigeon pose behind him. "You see, I want you to have a good life," he said, speaking only to Leena. "A life where you will not have to worry. If you think this gaswalla can give you this, then you can marry him—"

Prem and Leena gasped.

"*If*, only if"—Hemant paused for a sharp thunderclap to pass—"he first earns one million and one dollars."

There was a long, dumbfounded silence. Prem and Leena sat

slack-jawed and speechless, trying to understand what had just happened.

"Are you crazy?" Leena finally said. "You must be tired. Come, take rest and we will discuss more in the evening." She started to get up to help her father who was obviously in need of a nap, but Prem remained seated. He could see that Hemant was entirely lucid and serious.

"Go on," he said.

Hemant laid out the terms of his decree:

1) Prem and Leena must not communicate with each other until he has earned the money;

2) Leena must be open to meeting other suitable boys;

3) there is no calendar deadline for the completion of the task.

"And, of course, you must vacate this apartment immediately," Hemant said.

"Of course," Prem said. "Now, when I make the money, should I have it in cash or check?"

"Cashier's check, maybe?" Hemant said.

"Gold bars would be another option," Prem said.

"Yes, that might be nice," Hemant said.

"Stop this! No one is getting gold bars," Leena said, jumping up from the couch and throwing her hands in the air. "Papa, how can you sell me like some kind of biscuit from the store?"

"I am not selling you like a biscuit, I am ensuring that you marry someone who can take care of you."

"I do not need anyone to take care of me," she said, deadly serious.

"I know, my dear, but I do not want *you* to have to take care of *him*."

"That is fair," Prem said.

"I don't understand," Leena said, turning to Prem. "Are you agreeing to this crazy demand?"

The truth of what was occurring was settling in for Prem, and it was the culmination of everything he had ever feared. He had not succeeded in the world, had no talent, nothing to show for himself, and it was causing him to lose what he loved most. Panic began to take hold and he felt short of breath and dizzy. He clutched the arm of the couch and steadied himself. "Your father is right," Prem said. "I am a failure in life. How can he just give you to a failure? I have to prove I am worth something."

"No one is giving me to anyone," Leena said. She looked back and forth between them. "Who do you both think you are?" she said. "I can't look at either of you. You, make your money, and you, wait for your money. But I won't grow old waiting." With that she went to her room, slamming the door behind her just as the tea boiled over, creating a milky mess.

Prem and Hemant looked at the door and then at each other. "My family has money," Prem said.

Hemant did not respond or appear to have even heard what Prem said. Instead, he echoed the dreaded pronouncement of Hindi movie patriarchs down through the ages, who for one reason or another disapprove of their daughters' boyfriends. "Maine keh diya," he said. *I have spoken*, the final word of the father.

*   *   *

It rained the rest of that day and into the evening. Prem quietly packed up his few belongings and slipped out. Beena Joshi was working at Drug Fair until late, so he dropped his bag at her doorstep and wandered around in the cold drizzle for hours. The ugly scene in the

Engineers' apartment played over and over in his head, and the unanswerable questions kept coming: What could he have done differently? Should he have revealed that he came from a wealthy family? What should he do now? Could he make the money? Did it even matter?

In classic Hindi films, at dramatic junctures such as this, often a fakir or sadhu or some such wise and spiritual man appears and offers profound guidance that leads the hero out of darkness. Prem rested on the stoop of Building 8 and prayed for such a man to appear. Fat bulbs of water plopped down on his head periodically from the eaves. At three o'clock, the young man from the Oak Wood Church passed by carrying an umbrella. "Hey, man," he said, "you're getting wet."

After sitting there a while more, Prem decided to walk back to Beena's building and wait for her inside. He could have knocked on any number of doors and been welcomed in, but he did not want to have to explain his situation to anyone else. He could barely explain it to himself. "One million and one?" he could imagine them saying. "Is he crazy?" Prem wished he had not been in such a rush to approach Hemant. He wished they could just go back to how they had been before. If he could just talk to Leena, maybe they could rewind the tape back to where they had been. The rain was coming down harder now, and a fork of lightning flashed in the distance. He wished she would appear suddenly before him.

And then, there she was.

She shouted at him from across the yard. "You didn't ask what *I* wanted."

It took a moment for Prem to comprehend that she was really standing there, dripping wet and shivering in the flickering light of a nearby bulb. "I was respecting your father's wishes," he said.

"What about my wishes?" There was no anger in her words or in her eyes. Just anguish, which it pained him to see.

"Would you really go against your father?" Prem said as gently as he could from that distance in the rain.

"But you didn't have to agree like that," she replied, "about the plan to buy me like a cow."

"It is not buying, and why cow?"

"There is a middle road," she continued. "We can talk to him about our future plans, make him feel comfortable."

"What future plans? Your father is right, Leena. I am nothing. I don't want to ruin your life."

From a second-floor window of Building 7, a woman yelled, "Ya, definitely he will ruin your life, Leena!"

They ignored this and moved on, Leena's tone belying her mounting frustration. "This isn't a movie, we don't have to run away or sacrifice our lives."

"Are you talking about *Qayamat Se Qayamat Tak* or *Bobby*?"

"*Ek Duuje Ke Liye.*"

"Got it." Prem cleared his throat and spoke louder now, the rain having been joined by a harsh wind. "It's true," he said. "What do I have to show for myself?"

"Don't say that," Leena said.

"People will laugh at you for marrying me."

"Ya, hundred percent!" a family of six yelled from a balcony.

"You are young, you can do whatever you want in this life still," Leena said.

"It's cold, Leena, go in. You'll get sick."

"I want to be with you just how you are."

"But how I am is not very good."

"Why won't you talk about this with me even? Just, let's talk." She moved toward him, her expression softening.

Prem stepped back.

Leena stood silent, the rain tapping a rhythm on a wooden cricket bat abandoned in the grass. At last, she said, "Then go. Make your money, find some confidence. But don't think I'll be standing here waiting. I won't be."

Prem moved back toward her now and grasped her by the shoulders. "Listen to me. You don't understand, you don't know how the world is."

"And you do?" She pushed him away. "You know what? I think you are not even capable of making one million dollars."

"He is not!" a few people from different buildings yelled.

"You are right," she said. "You are a failure. You are nothing. I don't need you." She stopped struggling then and looked at him. In that moment, he recognized, he was the most adult he'd ever been, the most serious he'd ever made himself be. It was a role that didn't suit him and for which he should never have been cast.

"I'm sorry, Leena," he said.

She looked suddenly exhausted. "Don't think you are doing something great for me," she said. "You are not. You are ruining me." The flickering bulb above the nearby door sputtered and went dark. She began to walk away, but turned and looked back at him again. Prem imbued that tiny instant—despite all the words that had just passed between them—with an incalculable, improbable hope for their immediate reconciliation. Instead, she said, "If you see me in the yard or at the store, don't try to talk to me. If you make your million dollars, don't tell me. I won't care."

12

For days, Leena did not talk to her father. She continued to make his food and manage the apartment and work at the store but did not speak a word to him. This did not stop him, however, from speaking to her. "You see, it is entirely imprudent to marry for love," he explained one morning while taking his tea. He went on to lay out the particulars behind this line of reasoning, but Leena appeared to pay no attention and went about her kitchen work. Another day, while Leena was on hold with the dosa-batter distributor, Hemant tried to talk to her about the American dream, the land of opportunity, the drive and passion of Thomas Edison, and the words of the Founding Fathers, who declared, "We are a nation of self-made men." He concluded, "Immigration is about struggle and achievement, not love affairs."

None of this seemed to be well-received or received at all. Eventually he became frustrated with his daughter's cold shoulder and erupted one day at Cash, the affable old superintendent, who had come to the apartment to fix their fridge, which had been oozing a black syrup for three days.

"What kind of business are you running, coming after three days? This is unacceptable, inexcusable, unprofessional, irresponsible . . ."

Cash reached into the pocket of his overalls, pulled out a lollipop, and presented it to Leena. He always had a sweet for Leena and all the tenants' children, regardless of whether they were still children, and it made her feel precious every time. "Now, what seems to be the problem?" Cash said.

"The problem is that our problem started three days back!" Hemant barked.

Leena directed Cash to the fridge, where he began wiping up the syrupy substance with a rag.

"That's it, you are just going to clean the mess? I could have cleaned it. You have to fix the fridge. You know what a fridge is, no?"

"That's it, stop screaming at Cash!"

Hemant could not believe that his daughter had broken her silence. He threw his arms around Cash and started thumping him on the back and laughing, as if he were a defendant who had been pronounced not guilty by a judge and was now rejoicing with his lawyer.

"Thank you," Cash said, returning the thumps in a joyful yet bewildered way.

Hemant gave him a few parting thumps and said, "Okay, good work, keep working, good name, very auspicious." Then he turned to his daughter, who, he'd forgotten, was still angry.

"How could he possibly make that much money?" Leena burst out. "He is going to leave and go back to India."

"Cash?"

"Prem!"

"Would that be so bad?"

"Papa!"

"Were you not mad at him for agreeing to the idea? How could he do such a thing?" A leaf fell from the ceiling and landed on the floor between them. "Look, you have upset Hriyan," Hemant said.

Four buildings over and two back, the ugliness of that fateful day had plagued Prem every second of every day since he'd left the

Engineers' and moved in with Beena. When she arrived home that night and found him slumped at her doorstep, drenched, with his belongings and a long face, she immediately put on a huge pot of chai. The scent of lemon and asafetida from hours spent preparing her venerated pickles was still with her, which comforted Prem, though pickles and anything Indian grocery–related would forever remind him of Leena.

For two days, he remained tight-lipped, moping around the apartment, barely eating, never showering, drinking chai after chai, until Beena demanded at last to hear the whole story.

"He said what?" Beena cried when Prem related the details of Hemant's proclamation. "Is he crazy?"

Prem was on his knees working on the wobbly front doorknob though he had never held a screwdriver in his life. Beena regularly persuaded people who came over for one thing to help out with something entirely else, such as the plumber who routinely found himself rearranging furniture. "He is not crazy, he just wants a good life for his daughter."

"So what will you do?"

"It's hopeless. It is without hope. I should just jump from a bridge."

Beena threw a potato at him. "If you say that again, I will hit you with my rolling pin."

"Ya, fine," Prem said, continuing to fiddle with the knob.

"What you are needing is a list," Beena said. "To help you see better."

"Ya, good, okay. A list. What should go on the list?"

"First option, forget about her."

"That is the first option?"

"It is not in the order of importance."

"Uh, okay. What's next?"

"Get her to run away somewhere with you."

"What kind of option is that?"

"No? I thought you would like that one."

"I don't. Anyway, she is mad at me. She won't run even to Drug Fair with me."

"Okay, so you will not be running away."

"Correct."

"Next option is, talk to your father."

The doorknob fell off and landed with a clang on the floor. "There is nothing to talk about with him. He will say, 'Who does this grocerywalla think he is, demanding one million dollars?' Then he will order me to come home and leave behind this nonsense. Also, Leena would not like it at all if I showed up with one million dollars to her father's door."

"Is she crazy?"

Prem picked up the knob and shoved it back into the door. "Okay, what's the next option?"

"The final option is you tell Leena sorry, then find a way to show Hemant you are good enough for his daughter."

Prem was trying very hard to get the screws to tighten up and keep the knob in place, but when Beena listed this final option, he fumbled his screwdriver, causing everything to fall down again. "But I am not good enough," he said. "Not yet."

"Look," Beena said, placing the cover on a pot of dal with great emphasis. "Do you want to marry this girl or no?"

"Yes."

"Then you have to understand you are acting like an idiot." She went on to delineate the ways in which he was acting like an idiot, chiefly that he was not considering Leena's point of view or working on a solution together with her, but rather making a rash decision all on his own. "Are you trying to marry the girl or her father?" she asked.

"It's not that simple," Prem tried to explain, collecting the bits of hardware.

"Do you understand that it is not her father that is in your way, but your own ego?" Beena continued.

"Well, I don't—" Prem started.

"And that you drove her away with your own self-centeredness?"

"Uh, I think—"

"And at the end of your life, you'll be sitting on a big pile of money, all alone?"

"This is true," Kailash Mistry said passing by in the hallway on his way to his apartment.

"Okay, okay, fine," Prem said. "Let me think."

"Nothing to think about," Beena said, chopping up a large head of cabbage. "Find out if she will take you back, then make some money. Maybe you can negotiate the amount, I don't know."

The desperation he felt then was like a stranglehold leaving him unable to breathe or fix a doorknob. He feared she was already lost to him. He envisioned an empty future in which he would work forever at the gas station, without Leena, without joy, left only with a ball of hair. Or equally as catastrophic, a future in which he would work hard and make something of himself only to find that she had moved on. Yet he could not easily let go of Hemant's words or his own unworthiness.

For the next two weeks, he slept on Beena's plastic couch and barely functioned as a human. He cut down his hours at Exxon to the minimum amount required to still call it a job and hid inside the apartment all day, avoiding contact with everyone but Beena and Cash, who would occasionally stop in to fix a leaky faucet and end up shelling peas.

Prem made one major outing to the Service Merchandise electronics and appliance store to purchase a VCR with the money he had left in his polka-dotted pouch, and he purchased *Shree 420* from Urmila Sahu and watched it twice every day. The next time he ventured back into King's Court society was when Beena dragged him to the Holi celebration.

"It is for Lord Krishna," she said. "Or Vishnu. Or Shivji? I don't know, just come."

The celebration took place more than a month after the actual holi-day, when it was just warm enough in New Jersey for people to be out-side without shivering. It was the third year that King's Court hosted the event, which mimicked on a small scale the festivals of colors that took place throughout India each spring, leaving an entire nation mul-tihued and, in some regions, drunk. As in India, they played Holi in Edison with all manner of powders, pastes, colored water, water guns filled with colored water, and balloons filled with colored water, using supplies Nalini Sen had brought back from Pune. But unlike in India, where loved ones and strangers are equally fair game, in King's Court they limited themselves to coloring only each other, no ambushing stray passersby or the mail carriers. For Prem, and much of India, Holi was inextricably linked to the 1981 hit song "Rang Barse" from *Silsila*, sung by Amitabh himself, the entire picturization of which embodied all that was beloved about the holiday: graceful dancing by the lead performers, sideys dressed in white moving in perfect symmetry, the drumbeats of the dholak, the milky, refreshing, laced-with- marijuana thandai, the tossing of flower petals near a soothing backyard water feature, the buttons of Amitabh's kurta thrown wide open to highlight a gloriously hirsute chest gilded with chains, all in service to the im-mortal song sung playfully and soulfully as only Amitabh could. "Rang Barse" dramatized Amitabh's forbidden love for the sultry Rekha, and when someone at King's Court decided to blast it from his bedroom window to liven up the festivities, Prem was devastated anew, reminded of his own love who had forsaken him.

At that moment, Leena appeared across the yard, smeared in pink. She didn't look in his direction. He tried to talk to the people around him—Lucky, Gopal, Tun-Tun, Tony—and he let them throw colors on him, but didn't throw any of his own, encumbered as he was by sadness. She was right there. Option one, to forget about her, was impossible. Theirs was an honest-to-Ram love story, as bursting with romance and melodrama as any Hindi movie. The rich boy fell for the poor girl (as in *Devdas*) or the rich girl fell for the poor boy (as in *Ajnabee*), he wasn't sure which story this was, if he was the rich or the poor. There was the heroine's intractable father and the lovers who were forced apart. And then there was Prem himself, whose name meant the essence of who he was—love, but not casual love, pleasurable love, selfish love, but an elevated kind of love involving complete surrender and devotion, the kind of love for which a person is willing to give everything of himself, to lay it all on the line. Streaked with blue and drenched in red, a bucket of green water being cast upon him, Prem resolved to put aside his insecurities and beg her forgiveness.

The day after King's Court Holi, when the colors had been washed from people's faces but remained in the stained grass and sidewalks, Prem delivered a note to Varsha Virani to deliver to Leena.

13

The following weekend, apartment 3D was packed for the King's Court premiere of *Tezaab*, proudly billed on its posters, cinema hoardings, and cassette covers as "A Violent Love Story"—the violence, of course, not having to do with the love but a completely separate storyline—which naturally made it the most anticipated movie of the year. They were able to watch the film before its Indian release date thanks to a bootlegged copy obtained from Urmila Sahu, who was becoming quite an authority in the field of video piracy. *Tezaab* starred Anil Kapoor, the playful and not-so-angry young man with the baby face paradoxically overrun with facial hair, who had become a household name since his star turn in *Mr. India*; and virtual newcomer Madhuri Dixit, who would go on to star in over sixty movies, hold the record for most Filmfare Award nominations by an actress, be awarded a Padma Shri by the Indian government, and become a Hindi film icon, inspiring an adulatory movie, *Main Madhuri Dixit Banna Chahti Hoon* (*I Want to Become Madhuri Dixit*), as well as as well as paintings—and a creepy sort of admiration—from modern master M. F. Hussain. Trained as a traditional Kathak dancer, she elevated the song and dance aspect of films, bringing classical grace to the jhatka-matka, gyrating and titil-lating, spangling choreography of Indian movies, causing viewers to scramble for the rewind button before there were remotes.

"They should have taken Sridevi for the role instead," Uttam Jindal said. The immensely popular song "Ek Do Teen" was starting up, the flat-stomached heroine already front and center as the sideys, sporting their doughy tummies, poured onto the stage, and everyone was excited to see what the talented, destined-to-be-legendary dance director Saroj Khan had come up with.

"See the song first, then decide," Beena said.

"Damn good number," Lucky said, shaking his head as the catchy refrain began and the bass kicked in.

Madhuri sprang into action, all charm and vivacity in shiny hot pink. "Excellent dancer," Shanta Bhatt said.

"She is cheap," Uttam Jindal said, adjusting his hairpiece. "Sridevi would not behave in such a cheap way."

"Why you are in love with Sridevi?" Beena said.

"Stop passing comments and let me watch the song," Mohan said.

They didn't just watch the song, they got up and danced to it, cheered wildly, sang along, then rewound it and played it again. It wasn't until the intermission that Prem spotted Varsha in the crowd and leaped over four people and an end table to reach her.

"And?" he said, careful that no one else could hear.

"Ya, Prem, okay," Varsha said, pulling something from her purse. "Here is your letter."

Prem did not understand. "She wrote a letter back already?" he said.

"No, no, it is your letter, the one which you wrote," Varsha said.

"You have my letter still? You should not have my letter! Where is her letter, the one which she wrote?" Prem said.

"What letter?" Varsha said.

They went on like this until Prem was able to extract from her that Leena had left to spend two months in Minnesota with her father's sister and that Varsha had been unable to deliver the letter before her departure. Prem was dumbstruck. Leena would be gone for so long without having resolved anything with him. He didn't even know she had relatives in Minnesota.

"Isn't it like an icebox there?"

"Not so bad. Lot of lakes."

"Why did you bring the letter back?"

"I just told you."

"Keep it and give it to her when she returns. Do not lose it."

"What do you think, I am your mailman? You keep it."

Prem wished he had picked a less difficult friend of Leena's to work with. He stuffed the letter in his pocket and went in search of a second cup of Iqbal's chai. His roommates were debating the quality of the film so far.

Deepak: "The wordings of the song are so stupid—one, two, three, it is like a nursery poem."

Mohan: "Find the beauty in the simple things, or ullu ka patha."

Gopal: "Why son of an owl? 'Ullu ka patha' is used in India to say someone is stupid, but in America the owl is wise?"

But Prem's heart wasn't in it. Sullen and distracted, he returned to his spot to watch the second half of the two-hour-thirty-one-minute film, during which a gangster tried to avenge his brother's death by killing the hero in a showdown at the docks but was instead shot by an exceptionally helpful police inspector. It was entertaining, yet not enough to wrest Prem's mind away from Leena, Minnesota, and the million and one dollars. When the movie ended and they rewound the tape back to "Ek Do Teen" and watched the song again, Prem took to heart its refrain, which spoke of *intezaar*, the elegant Urdu word for awaiting, expecting, infused with heartache and yearning, often found in songs in which one lover is separated from the other and longs for their return. He considered how, like a Hindi movie trope, he was waiting for her return from Minnesota, and how, perhaps, she would wait for him as he built himself up and not so they could be together forever.

So in the coming days, Prem waited restlessly and began to mull over how to make money—a lot of it and quickly in this land of so much opportunity.

14

Everyone around Prem seemed already to be in hot pursuit of hap-piness. Despite the continued incidents of racism and harassment in northern New Jersey—vandalism of businesses, a letter bomb, ob-scenities spray-painted on apartment walls exhorting Hindus to "go home"—and the police's ongoing insistence that the occurrences could not be categorized as bias crimes, the Indian Americans in Edison pressed on, opening a jewelry store, a sweets shop, and a casual din-ing establishment specializing in South Indian cuisine that featured a small TV perched on a ledge playing Hindi movies on an endless loop. The shopping strips down at the Woodbridge Township end of Oak Tree Road had fallen into disrepair, losing their customers to those twin pillars of consumerism, the Woodbridge and Menlo Park Malls, and enterprising immigrants bought up the empty retail spaces at a premium. Leena's friend Falguni started giving singing lessons from her apartment, while Lucky began peddling prepaid international phone cards—a major boon for Indians in America—out of the trunk of Chotubhai "Charlie" Patel's Honda Accord. Prem felt the crushing pressure of the American dream closing in on him. He had to figure out a way to make some money himself.

But first, he decided to hang out on the front steps. The view right along Oak Tree Road, two buildings back from the parking lot, was different from the Singhs' and the Engineers'. The colorful, variously shaped cars of America zipped by while men in ties moved expeditiously toward Metropark. Shanta Bhatt was hanging her capacious underwear out on her clothesline, and Urmila Sahu was piling bulk quantities of laundry detergent and mixed nuts onto her balcony. The entire complex that morning buzzed with people going about their business, except for the white-haired, white-clad circle of men in the grass, who had presumably conducted a lifetime of business already and were now basking in their New Jersey retirement. Prem wished he were at their stage of life rather than his own.

After thinking about lying in the grass and doing nothing forever, he walked toward the parking lot, hoping to catch a glimpse of Leena in case she had come back. Lucky called to Prem from across the lot trying to sell him a phone card, and the Kotharis stood next to their brand-new Nissan Maxima with a coconut and a priest. Upon closer inspection, Prem found they were conducting a car pooja, procuring blessings of safety and prosperity for their vehicle and its drivers, with a special clause requesting excellent gas mileage. After the ceremony, the priest handed out his card to those nearby, including Prem, and added, "In inclement weather, we can perform car blessing inside the temple using car keys at devotees' shrine of choice, no problem."

The rest of the day, he worked at Exxon in a daze, wondering if he could possibly make a large sum of money by working extra hours there. At night, emptying his pockets before winding down on Beena's couch, he found the priest's card and had an idea.

The next morning, he borrowed Kailash Mistry's bicycle and set out to Krauszer's convenience store, where Darpan Singh Canadian—so called due to his years spent in British Columbia—was working the first shift. It had drizzled all night, but dawn brought a clear sky and the lingering petrichor smell of spring rain. Prem enjoyed the wind in his face, the first thing he had enjoyed in weeks. He had never been to Krauszer's and was impressed by the endless candy aisle and the partially obscured pornographic periodicals. After sufficient dawdling, he purchased the thing he had come for: a ticket for the Pick-6 lottery, whose jackpot was currently $2.7 million.

"You want to pick the numbers, eh, or let the machine pick, eh?" Darpan Singh Canadian said. He took great pride in his past and in his Great White Northern heritage, and tried to exhibit his Canadianness at every possible opportunity, though his use of "eh" was often incorrect and jarring.

"How do you like to do it?" Prem said.

"Me? No, no, I never buy lottery tickets. Colossal waste of money."

Prem rubbed the back of his neck, unsure how to proceed.

"But ya, good luck, you know, eh."

"I'll let the machine pick," Prem said. He tucked the ticket carefully into his wallet, which he shoved deep into his jeans pocket.

"You can see the lotto drawing tomorrow night before *Cosby Show*. A very tall, nice girl pulls the balls from the machine and reads them. I always watch."

"I thought you never buy lottery tickets."

"She wears small clothes."

Prem had a long bike ride from there to the Ram Mandir temple, but he was in no particular hurry. He admired the impossibly green lawns and violated several traffic rules, which elicited the comforting blare of car horns that reminded him of his original home. He passed under train tracks near the Metuchen train station and got slightly lost trying to find the correct tree-lined street. He arrived at the Ram Mandir at eleven, early enough to avoid the crowds at the noontime aarti service, which began at one. Once inside, he was overcome by a sudden calm. The onetime church had retained its innate churchiness, with lofty ceilings, stained-glass windows, and a massive wooden door that never opened. Prem entered through the side entrance, where he encountered, naturally, a pile of shoes. In their smelly midst, he felt hopeful. He had never been the most religiously inclined Hindu, but when the sandalwood and plumeria waft of nag champa incense hit him, he was brought back to the temple visits of his childhood and the innocent faith in something greater than himself. He removed his shoes and walked upstairs, where he found the priest from the King's Court parking lot and made his unusual request.

"You want a blessing on the lottery ticket?" the priest said, scratching something fervently under the many layers of fabric below his waist.

"Yes, Panditji, is it possible? I know it is irregular, but I would be very grateful."

"Not irregular. Just this year I have done archana for a dog, a medical license, a plane ticket, a motel, and a tree. Ten dollars, choose your god."

Prem chose Krishna, the most joyful, soulful, and eloquent representation, he felt, of the divine light. He stood before the altar, his spirit lifted by the realization that miracles can happen. While the priest chanted the pertinent mantras, Prem offered his own silent prayer, beginning with gratitude for everything in his life, especially Leena, and ending by pleading for a winning ticket. "I'll do anything," he implored. "I will give most of the money to the temple and to orphanages, I will do extensive pooja every day, I will even give up nonvegetarian food. Please, Lord. Thank you." After he was finished with his supplication and the priest offered him some blessed fruit, Prem went back outside into the radiant daylight feeling really rather optimistic. He hopped back onto the bike and set out for King's Court, eating his apple along the way.

For the next day and a half, he did nothing that would bring him closer to making any money. He played carrom with Gitanjali Vora on a scratched-up board until his striker finger began to develop a welt. Then he helped a new family, the Bajpais, move into Building 13. He ate scrambled eggs with tamarind chutney that Beena force-fed him. He watched *Shree 420*. His confidence in his consecrated ticket was so absolute that he sat down at Beena's dining table and wrote an aerogram to his father, explaining that he would not be returning to India as he had "significant matters" he was dealing with in the States, details to come. When it came time for the Pick-6 drawing, he watched it on the plastic-covered couch with Beena, who had bought into the potency of the priest's ticket pooja and was accordingly giddy.

"I always think of buying a ticket, but then I think, No, only dummies play the lottery, but look, you might become a crore-pati, a millionaire, only you would have to give almost half to that greedy grocerywalla. But what will you do with the remaining money? Let me see the numbers. You should have picked them yourself—more auspicious."

Prem was giddy too with these same thoughts about making so much money so soon. Would he collect his prize and then go to Hemant, or go directly there tonight and present him with the winning ticket? But how would Hemant know it was a winning ticket? It may be best to collect the money first, but who knows how long that might take? "I think I will let Leena decide what to do with the extra money," he said.

"Yes, but please also buy a Mercedes."

The lottery lady was indeed tall and wearing small clothing. She stood beside an overly elaborate contraption containing the numbered balls, which were sucked up through a tube and came to rest at the top. When the balls started to pop and circulate in their large plastic vessel, Prem's heart began to race. The lady's only job was to smile and turn the numbers so they faced the camera.

A male voice offscreen read the actual numbers aloud, which seemed to Prem like a waste of human resources. The first number came up, and the voice said, "19." He had a 19 on his ticket. Beena practically punched Prem in the face with excitement.

The next number was 41. Prem's ticket had a 41. Beena could not contain herself. She threw the entire weight of her body onto him during a badly executed hug, causing him to tip over on his side, his cheek pressing into plastic. He sat back up and kept a steady gaze on the TV, not wanting to break the spell. But when the third number was a match, he lost his senses and started strangling Beena's fleshy arm while bouncing up and down in his seat. This could be it, he thought. The one moment when something actually went right in his life.

The following number took a long time to pop into place, and the tall lady seemed to have some trouble straightening it out. When at last the faceless man announced the number, it was not a match. And neither were the next two. Prem released his grip on Beena's arm and folded the ticket into a tiny square.

"No, no, keep the ticket! Three numbers matched—you win one dollar!"

"Wow, great, one dollar," Prem said.

"One is good luck," Beena said. "I think you will need it."

Despite the overwhelming disappointment of that first time, Prem became addicted to the lottery. He continued with the Pick-6 and occasionally ventured into Pick-3 and Pick-4. A few times, he also tried 5 Card Lotto, but drew the line at scratch-card games, which he deemed amateur. As he moved forward with this form of gambling, Prem also took up more traditional modes, such as cards and dice, neither of which he was very good at. One Friday night, he even squeezed into Charlie Patel's Honda Accord with five other guys to drive down to Atlantic City, where after four hours of epic, nonstop blackjack, he broke even.

Prem started taking every opportunity he could to participate in all manner of get-rich-quick schemes: he paid a bank teller for bogus insider-trading tips, which he didn't know how to use anyway; upon the advice of Lucky, he went to Burger King and spilled hot coffee on himself but was not able to produce an adequate burn and was subsequently banned from that location; he purchased a crate of super vitamins which would supposedly "sell themselves" but which did not. In this way, he lost his money repeatedly, finally losing it all in a flimsy Ponzi scheme devised by a distant cousin of Tun-Tun in Queens.

At the end of two months of profligacy, down to his last couple of dollars, he stopped. With a deep sense of failure, he sat on the front steps with Beena. The setting sun to their left was dim, not like the burning one in India. She pulled out two tinfoil triangles and handed one to Prem. As they chewed their paan, slurping and slapping it against the roofs of their mouths, he thought about how difficult it was to make something of oneself, how hard it was to strive. The lottery and cards had taken hold of him not because of any special proclivity of his toward gambling, but rather because of his unwillingness to pursue any kind of legitimate enterprise. Beena didn't say anything. She eventually went inside and made fifty rotis, but Prem sat there for a very long time.

15

When he heard the news that Leena was returning in two days, Prem was holding up one end of a very heavy refrigerator. Bhaskar and Yogita Chhabra from 7A were moving to Hidden Valley Manor and gathered together an eclectic mix of King's Court's most able-bodied and eligible bachelors to help move their belongings and possibly marry their daughter. The Chhabras were tiny people, good-humored and good-natured, always smiling, and, Prem thought, the most harmonious couple he'd ever come across. Unfortunately, the daughter Chanchal's disposition was the exact opposite of that of the parents. Taciturn and unpleasant, Chanchal resented her parents for immigrating her to America, where she worked as a salesgirl at Fashion Bug. On that dewy June morning, birds chirping optimistically nearby, Chanchal opted not to assist her parents, though she was sturdy and somehow a foot and a half taller than both. Instead, she sat on the front stoop with a knife and apple, feeding herself slivers and scowling.

"Isn't Chanchal looking so nice today?" Yogita said to the bachelors as she struggled with the fridge's heft. As a courtesy to the sweet-tempered mother, they strained their necks to look over at the daughter, who glared back at them, rage simmering beneath the surface.

"Ya," Lucky said, clearing his throat, "very clean."

They shuffled in the direction of the small rental van double-parked in the lot. "Prem, what do you say?" Bhaskar asked. "Nice, no?"

Prem began searching for an apt adjective—cryptic, capable, brave—but the celebrated chartered accountant Yuvraj Bhatacharjee saved him before he had to speak.

"Pumpwalla is in love," Yuvraj said.

"With Chanchal?" Yogita said hopefully.

"With Leena Engineer," Yuvraj said.

Prem felt the blood rush to his face. "What? How do you know?"

"Everyone knows," Lucky said.

"Oh, right." Prem said. "I forgot."

"Ya, sorry, I also forgot," Yogita said, crestfallen. "Oh, but you must be so happy as she is coming back today."

Prem was caught off guard. When he woke up that morning and headed out to move a fridge, he had not expected anything to happen regarding Leena and was unprepared for it. "Ya, you know, so happy. What time is she coming?"

Just then, Tony Gupta yelled over from the India America Grocers parking lot across the street. "You are not supposed to take the fridge with you!"

"What?" Bhaskar called back.

"Fridge stays here!"

"Okay!"

The group reversed course, shuffling back toward the apartment. Prem felt at once anxious and overjoyed. His knees began quivering, though he wasn't sure if this was a result of the unexpected news or the bulkiness of the refrigerator. He tried to look around and scan the apartment grounds without calling too much attention to himself.

"She is not here as yet, Pumpy," Lucky said.

"Ya, don't drop the fridge on us," Yuvraj said.

Yogita turned her efforts to Lucky. "Did you know they are making

Chanchal the manager of the Fashion Bug?"

The group turned again to have a look at Chanchal, who had finished her apple and was hurling the core at a rabbit on the lawn.

* * *

Prem spent the remainder of that morning and much of the afternoon lurking behind a bush. He didn't know what time Leena would be arriving and couldn't just sit and wait on Beena's squeaky couch. There was no guarantee she would try to contact him upon her return—though he had a good feeling about it—so he would have to keep a look out without being too conspicuous. Thus, in a move reminiscent of his jumping-behind-the-drapes days, he settled into the Building 4 shrubbery, one building over from the Engineers'.

He ended up seeing everyone but Leena. First, Gitanjali Vora waved to him while hauling a sack of rice up the fire escape; and Shanta Bhatt, who was taking underwear down from her clothesline, called down to inquire if Prem had seen the blockbuster wife-possessed-by-an-unsettled-spirit flick *Woh Phir Aayegi* yet, which he hadn't. The circle of white-haired, white-kurta uncles set up camp as usual at eleven, their conversation about the weather in full swing by 11:05 a.m., and soon after that, Kailash Mistry strolled by, singing a ghazal poorly. At noon, Prem thought perhaps he was in luck when an airport taxi pulled into the lot, but it was only Harbhajan visiting his sister again to avoid spending time with his angry family. Gopal came by shortly after to ask why the nickname for John was Jack when both had the same number of letters. Around one, Prem considered giving up, the pitifulness of his endeavor not lost upon him, but Nalini Sen came by with a cup of chai, which he took as divine indication that he should stay put.

It occurred to him that his hiding place was not very hidden, so he shifted farther back into the bushes where he made himself so comfortable that he fell asleep. At two-thirty, he awoke to find a blanket on top of him and a pillow under his head, so he closed his eyes and slept a little more. Finally, after another half hour of surprisingly peaceful sleep, he was kicked in the leg by Beena Joshi looking down at him in the bushes.

"Why kicking?" he said, propping himself up on his elbows.

"Everyone is asking, Why Prem is in the bushes, why he is waiting like that?" Beena said.

"It's fine, I don't care if everyone knows," Prem said in what he felt was a bold, romantic Hindi-movie-hero tone. He fully expected her to kick him again and even adjusted to avoid the blow, but instead, with great effort, she kneeled down to talk to him at his level.

"Prem," she said softly. "There is some news."

It was in this tone of voice that he was informed of the first great tragedy of his life, his mother's passing. So it was fitting that it be used to inform him of the second: Leena Engineer was returning from Minnesota engaged to another man. Beena had heard from Sujata Mehra, who had heard from her brother-in-law, who was well acquainted with Sanjay Sapra. The boy's name was Mikesh Aneja and he was a doctor, the son of Sanjay Sapra's cousin Sanjana of Minnesota. He and Leena had been inseparable the past two months, and both families were ecstatic. No wedding date was set as yet.

Obviously there had been a mistake, Prem decided. "Thank you for worrying about me always," he said. "Really, you are such a nice friend. But you must have heard wrong. Nothing to worry about."

"Prem—"

"Now, either you should come in here closer so she does not see you, or you should just go from here and do your things for the day."

"If you do not believe me," Beena said, this time less gently, "then go ask Sanjay or Sujata. Ask Hemant himself. Just, at least get out from the bushes." With that, she went away, and he was left to consider what she'd said. Sanjana to Sanjay to nameless brother-in-law to Sujata to Beena to him. What kind of disjointed, unreliable chain of communication was that? So many chances for mistakes. The engagement, if there even was one, could have been for any number of other King's Court women—Reena, Tina, Meena, Veena, Nina, or one of the two Kareenas. The rhyming name possibilities were endless. Still, he would go to Varsha Virani's to confirm the mistake.

When he reached her apartment, her roommate directed him to find her at Falguni's apartment. At Falguni's, where a classical singing lesson for three very shrill girls was mid-raag, he was sent to Tun-Tun and Tony's. At Tun-Tun and Tony's, they made him sit for chai. After some light gossip, they released him to look for Varsha at the Rag Shop, where she was looking for buttons. She was crouched at the end of the cotton fabrics aisle when he found her, packets of plastic buttons, cloth buttons, snaps, and studs strewn about.

"It is true," she said before he could even ask.

A saleslady lingered nearby, so Prem pretended to inspect a bolt of plaid. "But she has not even read my letter," he said. "It says sorry and I understand and all."

"Ya, maybe you should have mailed that," Varsha said and gave the display rack an aggressive spin. "Oh, come on, yaar, there are so many other choices for you here. Yesterday only, Aditi Yadhav said you are damn cute."

"The unmarried girl who is having a baby?" Prem said.

"Maybe she is not a perfect example," Varsha said, clicking her deadly nails on her teeth.

"Just, please, give Leena this," he said, pulling out the letter, now somewhat rumpled, from his pants pocket.

"Prem, seriously, you are being a social embarrassment." She collected the button packets into a messy pile and stood. "Come, let me make you meet Manaswini Bandyopadhyay. She has three cats."

Prem sighed and said a sad thank-you, patting her on the hand before walking out of the store. Varsha called behind him, "What should I tell Manaswini?" as he went.

Prem didn't register her words, nor those of the fast-walking Raghava Sai Shankara Subramanya, who passed him on the way to Drug Fair, nor Nathan Kothari's who yelled something enthusiastically from the window of his blessed car, nor anyone else's as he made his way to the Engineers' apartment. Everyone was acting crazy, he thought. There was a rational explanation, he was sure. He would straighten it out and all would be as it was. End of story. Maybe he would watch *Woh Phir Aayegi* tonight. These were the things he was telling himself when Lucky, Gopal, Deepak, and Mohan tackled him to the ground.

"Man, what did you think, you were going to knock on the door and tell Hemant that Leena should marry you, a petrol pumpwalla, instead of a handsome doctor?" Mohan said. Prem's face was pressed into the grass as Lucky sat on top of him and the others pinned down his limbs.

"Hold it together, man," Gopal said.

"It is over, man," Mohan said.

"They say he looks like Chunky Pandey," Lucky said.

"Should we go for pizza?" Deepak said.

"Chunky Pandey? What a third-rate actor, man," Mohan said.

"Don't say such things about Chunky," Lucky said.

"Chunky is just okay," Deepak said, pulling a samosa from his pocket.

"A samosa was in your pocket?" Lucky said.

"I like Chunky," Gopal said.

"We are losing focus," Mohan said.

The roommates noticed then that Prem had stopped struggling; he was watching something behind them. From his wounded expression, they could tell it was pertinent to the reason they were on top of him. Leena and a tall, Chunky Pandey–looking man had exited a taxi and were walking up the path to Building 5. They paused when they spotted the strange pile of men who appeared to be staring at them. Leena whispered to the man, who looked directly at Prem. They disappeared together into the building.

Prem was utterly defeated. More so than when his movie production failed or when he was robbed by the brothers in tracksuits. More so even than when his father had no faith in him. Seared by her coldness, in disbelief of her perfidy and complete dearth of feeling, he gave up.

The roommates released him and tried to coax him back to their apartment, ultimately leaving him alone in the grass. He stayed there for a long time. Eventually, he walked in the direction of Beena's, all the time asking, "How could she?"

* * *

Two weeks later, the engagement of Leena Engineer and Mikesh Aneja, MD, was celebrated in grand fashion in the side yard of Building 5. Hemant broke from his traditional tightfistedness and put on a refulgent display—a multicolored tent of overlapping Indian fabrics encircled by torches and lit from within by Christmas lights, erected by unpaid King's Court residents—evoking on a small scale the luminous functions of India's glitterati. Three long folding tables disguised by block-printed sheets held a buttery feast prepared by Beena Joshi, who had chopped, fried, simmered, and kneaded for two weeks without rest.

"I will absolutely no way help you with this," Prem had said when she came home bearing three overstuffed Foodtown bags.

"What a prince you are," Beena said, dumping the bags in the kitchen.

Prem huddled under a blanket on the couch as he had for much of the previous day and the day before that. "And I will not eat any of the food you are making for them."

"Good, who asked you to?" Beena replied, unpacking vegetables and stuffing them into her second fridge. "What did you want me to do, say no to so much of money? Who are you thinking I am, the Queen of England? The now one, not the ruler of India one," she specified. "If you give me how much Hemant is paying, I will gladly stop all this cooking. You think I want to make chicken makhani, chana, okra, two types roti, mattar paneer, malai kofta, and lasagna with no help, is it?"

"Sorry," Prem said.

He retreated deeper under the blanket to ponder the meaning of his life—whether there even was one—for days, leaving the cover only as needed. His emotions followed the expected cycle, moving from denial through anger to pain, but then took a jarring detour to fear. He had tried to make himself into something in India and failed. He tried in America and failed. He had finally found purpose—Leena—but lost her too. What was left? What was the point of him? Who would even care if he left this life? And how could he be in this world without her? He wasn't considering ending his life, per se, but couldn't see a motive for carrying on with it either.

Beena boiled and sautéed in the midst of Prem's misery, her own feelings vacillating between empathy and resentment. One day, when she came home from Drug Fair to find him peeling potatoes, her heart softened. "Good. You're feeling better," she said and ruffled his hair like he was the son she never had.

"What should I say to her?" he said.

She took out a shiny, razor-edged knife he hadn't ever seen before and began vigorously slicing chicken thighs. "What do you mean,

'What should I say to her?' You should not say anything! She is engaged, it is done. You cannot go around harassing an engaged woman. It is not in our culture."

"I don't think it is in anyone's culture."

"Exactly."

With that, Prem crawled back under the blanket.

The night of the engagement party, the tent aglow at the end of the row of apartments, he purposely worked a double shift at Exxon. He had thought the festivities, the dancing, the laughter, the overly loud music and meandering speeches, everyone donning their Indian best, would be done by the time he came home, but the revelry was still carrying on, and it annihilated him. He thought he caught a glimpse of her in purple, but quickly remembered she hated purple. Then again, maybe she didn't.

Two weeks later, he saw her at Chi-Chi's Mexican restaurant, on Route 1 near Woodbridge Mall, which Edisonians frequented in droves. It was a logical attraction, Indian immigrants to Tex-Mex, with its vegetarian options, beans and rice, adequate spices, and tortillas akin to roti. The principal difference from Indian cuisine, that everything was doused in cheese, was a welcome one. For these reasons, many were willing to wait over an hour for a Tampico—three cheese enchiladas, the vegetarians' dish of choice.

He was there with the gang to celebrate Deepak's twenty-fifth birthday, for which he wanted to try a margarita. The others were surprised to learn that Deepak had never before had one, but then, he had always been a vague sort of character. No one really knew anything about him—where he was from in India, what shape his immigration story took—and though they liked him and guessed he was probably just a regular guy, they also agreed they wouldn't be surprised if he had murdered a few people.

The waiting area of Chi-Chi's was packed with Indians like the Howrah Junction Railway Station at rush hour, so they decided to wait out front. Car after car pulled up and let out a bevy of people who put their names down on the list and came back out to wait. It was a perfect evening for standing outside in a parking lot along US Route 1, warm but punctuated by a summer breeze, and the group passed the time easily by teasing Gopal about his hairline. Prem was relieved no one had asked him why he'd moved in with Beena Joshi instead of back in with them at the Singhs'.

Mohan spit something into a bush and turned to Prem. "Yaar, why did you move to Beena Joshi's instead of back with us?"

"It didn't work with Leena, so now you are trying for an older woman?" Deepak inquired.

"Ya, that is what happened," Prem responded.

"Is she as good in the bedroom as she is in the kitchen?" Lucky said. "Does she roll you like a roti?"

"Does she fry you like a pakora?"

"Does she cook you with onions and garlic and then add turmeric and garam masala?" Deepak said.

"We are losing focus," Mohan said.

"Will someone share a Tampico with me?" Gopal said. "Why American restaurants give so much of food?"

Just then, Leena emerged from a Pontiac with Falguni, Snigdha, Varsha, and four guys from Brighton Village apartments. It was unclear how they had all fit into one car; Prem did not want to think about it. He hung back, grabbed onto a high wooden beam in the architecture, and obscured his face with his arm as she and her friends came by and chatted for a minute with his group. He barely looked up, even when the conversation turned to movies, but as they were walking away, he couldn't resist. He raised his gaze; she was looking at him too, just for a second, and then she stepped into Chi-Chi's.

Prem wanted to throw up. The sight of her surrounded by those lecherous Brighton Villagers, though they were not as awful as her doctor fiancé, was too much for him. He felt he was suffocating. He began taking slow, deep breaths but had to stop and head inside when the hostess called for "Indian Studs, party of five," which was his group. Leena was not seated in the same room, but he thought he caught a glimpse of her behind a plastic cactus on his way to the bathroom. He tried to conceal himself behind an oversized sombrero in order to get a closer look at what was going on at her table, but soon realized it wasn't her and that he was just a ridiculous, sad figure lurking behind a very large hat. That night he had five margaritas—more even than Deepak—and ended up vomiting after all. In the morning, the only thing he could recall was that they had spent a lot of time arguing about how the fried ice cream was made.

The next day, he walked to Drug Fair and bought a ledger, in which he wrote the date and three questions:

1. Did you see *Tezaab*?
2. Isn't the Chi-Chi's spicy salsa and chips quite good?
3. How do you think the fried ice cream is made?

He couldn't bear the thought of all the lost conversations that Leena and he might have had, so he began keeping a log of the questions he would ask her if ever he had the chance again. He genuinely wanted to know her answers and sometimes tried to imagine what her opinions might be on certain subjects, but this could not replace his longing for the real thing. Beena came home as he was writing in the ledger at her kitchen table that first day.

"I know a question you can put. Why don't you ask if she has heard the rumors about us?" she said.

Prem put his pen down. "So people are ribbing you too?"

"Well, more they are congratulating me," she said, ruffling his hair. Then, with discernible regret she said, "Still, you probably should find a new place to stay."

Prem agreed. It would take just one day for rumors to spread through the entire apartment complex and two for them to spread to the neighboring complexes as well. This in itself did not bother him, but he did not want to damage Beena's reputation—though, actually, he seemed to be bolstering it—and he certainly did not want Leena to start thinking something untoward was going on. So he packed up his few things—his toothbrush, his Exxon jumpsuit, his ball of Leena's hair—leaving behind the VCR as a thank-you, and walked back to Building 3.

"Of course you can live with me again!" Amarleen said, throwing her arms around him.

"What, Beena Auntie broke it off with you?" Mohan asked.

"Maybe she was too much auntie for you to handle," Lucky said.

"Can you pay?" Iqbal said.

16

The Singhs' apartment was, in all likelihood, the best place for Prem to mend his broken life, as he could not possibly fall into a lonely abyss if he was never alone. There were the half-dozen people who lived there, of course, plus the friends who came over as they did in India, unannounced and all the time. King's Court was bursting at its rickety seams with immigrants, with one hundred percent of its inhabitants now from the subcontinent—one hundred and fifty if one took into account illegal paying guests and newly arrived relatives who stopped there as a first port of call before continuing on their immigration journeys. Everyone knew everyone, so addresses became relative; if anyone inquired after the location of the Singhs' apartment, they would be told, "The apartment below the tone-deaf singing chemist, Kailash Mistry, and across from the anesthesiologist janitor, Vilayat Hussain," and if anyone inquired after the Voras' apartment, they would be told, "Below the apartment of the grocery owner Hemant Engineer and his engaged but unmarried daughter, Leena," though a few years would pass before she was referred to as such. Gujarati, Hindi, Bengali, Punjabi, Urdu, Marathi, English, and Tamil were the principal languages represented there, with other Indian languages peppered in. With their tiffin picnics and Diwali fireworks, their ubiquitous blue aerograms and pirated videos, King's Court's tightly packed community boldly withstood the ravages of Westernization, which was just what Prem needed after losing everything.

On a sweltering August afternoon, the windows of 3D were thrown wide open and the boys were splayed out on their mattresses, dousing themselves with water periodically to keep cool while watching a movie they had already seen an obscene number of times. The film's lead actress, Mandakini, was singing in a wet, clinging white sari, wearing no undergarments, and frolicking rather too close to a waterfall. It was the only thing that could effectively distract them from the heat and Prem from his situation.

"Again?" Amarleen said when Iqbal and she came home from their bimonthly trip to Jackson Heights, Queens, that corner of New York which had essentially transformed itself into Delhi, drawing Indian Americans from miles around to purchase three pounds of assorted sweets followed by a visit to Sam & Raj to satisfy their discount-electronics needs. "You have watched this song 700 times, isn't it?"

"Never enough," Lucky said.

"It is timeless," Deepak said.

Iqbal plunked himself down on Prem's sopping mattress. "Is this sweat from your body?" he said, jumping up but immediately sitting back down. "No, it is no problem, it is good, fine, very good."

Everyone had been painfully nice to Prem since Leena's engagement, which made him feel doubly pathetic. The gas-station guys covered some of his shifts, and Shanta Bhatt began throwing his laundry in with hers. Even Leena's friends stopped by with cassettes and Parle-G biscuits. Prem deduced that his roommates had conspired to make sure he was never left alone by putting into place a schedule of sorts, with timeslots available from midmorning into the late-night hours. He felt he was being involuntarily babysat, which, in the end, wasn't such a bad thing.

"Okay, duffers, I need potatoes," Amarleen said. "Who is going to the store for potatoes for me?"

"I can go," Prem said.

Lucky quickly jumped in. "No, man, you stay, relax, I will go," he said.

"Fantastic," Amarleen said. "Next, bathroom is disgusting. I am not a servant here. Who is cleaning it?"

"I will clean it," Prem said.

"No, man," Lucky said. "Gopal can do it."

"I can?" Gopal said.

"I am getting the potatoes, remember?" Lucky said, widening his eyes and tilting his head in Prem's direction.

"Oh ya, no problem, I will do it," Gopal said. "Prem, you just sit, rest."

"Enough!" Prem said, in an authoritative voice even he did not recognize. He stood up to address the room. "Thank you, all of you, for helping me."

"Welcome," Deepak said.

"Mention not," Mohan said.

Prem continued, "For taking my shifts and never leaving me alone, for cleaning the bathroom and getting the potatoes and sitting in my sweat. But you can stop all of this, okay? I am fine. I will be fine. Absolutely. Hundred percent."

Though he spoke with conviction, he had none. It was as though his soul were in an in-between mode, a sort of waiting room before the next life. He couldn't leave and go back to India, nor stay and forget about her. He had decided over the previous few sleepless nights that he just had to keep moving forward, try to make something of himself, and hope that she would somehow come back to him. She wasn't married yet, and a lot could happen. Plus, her doctor fiancé could die; people died all the time. It would require tremendous forbearance, but he could wait. He had asked Leena to wait, so he should be prepared to do the same. He could not countenance the possibility that he had lost her forever, so whenever the thought entered his mind, he pushed it away and watched another movie.

"Great speech, man," Mohan said. "Since you are up, can you rewind the song?"

After the damp actress finished her number and the hero finished snapping photos of her with his enormous camera, interest in the movie began to wane. *Ram Teri Ganga Maili* was a controversial yet widely lauded film, a social commentary with echoes of Hindu sacred texts coupled with gratuitous nudity. Only Prem and Iqbal continued to watch.

"She must be cold," Iqbal said.

"Ya, those mountains get quite cold," Prem said.

Though he was broken by the events of the previous few weeks, things took a slight upturn in mid-August when two improbable events occurred. First, Kailash Mistry gave him his bike. The former Revlon chemist had secured a new job as a junior formulation chemist in the body-hygiene division at L'Oréal and concurrently decided to dedicate himself more wholly to the practice of his singing. He came home from work by six, ate with his wife and attempted to talk to his two teenage daughters, then spent two hours belting out what he believed to be scales, followed by a series of jarring renditions of Anup Jalota ghazals. This left no time for casual bike rides. Prem imagined riding around town, the wind at his back—like Dev Anand and Nutan in the song "Mana Janab Ne Pukara Nahin," in which the former pursues the standoffish latter against an obviously prerecorded green-screen backdrop of a city; or like Dev Anand and Mumtaz in the song "Hey Maine Kasam Li," in which the couple rides through the countryside on a bike with her in front, then stops to cuddle in a field of flowers, then continues to ride, this time with her in back—and he was glad to have the bike.

The second improbable thing that occurred was that he met the biggest movie star in the world at the Exxon gas station. On that steamy day in 1988, Amitabh Bachchan was in Edison briefly to discuss a potential business partnership to create an American television station with Indian programming, and his friend stopped to fill up his tank. The international superstar actually had a very pleasant experience at the Exxon that day. An earnest, somewhat nervous attendant posed an interesting question that Amitabh enjoyed mulling over. At the end of that conversation, which he feared he may have monopolized, he gave the boy a dollar to build upon, for luck moving forward in his life.

The bill imbued Prem with a redoubled sense of hope and optimism and immediately became his most prized possession other than the pile of Leena's hair. After work, he rode his bike to Drug Fair, barely registering the stifling heat, and picked out a small picture frame. When he reached the apartment, he opened the frame and positioned the dollar carefully in the center and closed it back up. Because he had no wall of his own on which to hang anything, he kept the framed dollar in his bag, where he could look at it daily and be reminded that luck was on his side. But he also thought of how Mr. Bachchan never relied on luck. His punctuality, impeccably memorized lines, and general professionalism were unparalleled in the industry. When he faced setbacks, he did not say, "I am too tall and unattractive to make it in this business." He persevered. After reaching great heights, he remained humble and diligent. These qualities made him a colossal success; luck was never part of the equation. Prem took the dollar as a call to action, as though Amitabh himself were in his duffel bag, asking him every day, "When are you going to take action?"

After his wondrous encounter with the wise screen idol, Prem decided he needed to do something big. He had to stop his petty gambling and abandon his latest idea of jumping in front of a car in a pedestrian crosswalk to collect a personal-injury settlement. The appearance of Amitabh Bachchan was like an omen, a sign that it was time to take command of his life. Later that week, he had another such sign. He received a small package from his father containing a large check along with a note saying that if this was the life he was choosing, dealing with mysterious "significant matters" across the world, then he would be cut off from all family funds after this initial money got him started. Also in the box was a six-pack of tongue scrapers.

A feeling like suffocation overcame him. He'd never had to live solely off the money he earned and was sorely underequipped for survival. Leena's father had been absolutely correct in refusing to give his blessing. He had reserved his approval for a more prosperous suitor, a man like Hemant himself who fully understood how to thrive. How did people know these things? Were they born that way, either built for self-reliance or for dependence? If he deposited the check, he would be declaring his intention to make it on his own. There would be no going back without abject humiliation, if he were allowed to come back at all. He thought then of a boy he used to see singing in front of Plaza Cinema, charming patrons for change. If he, born into those difficult circumstances, could carry himself with such strength and confidence, why couldn't Prem? The reason he could not, he realized, was that he thought he had little strength and no confidence. He decided to forge ahead.

* * *

In the waning days of that summer, King's Court erupted in jubilation upon the opening of a Pizza Hut restaurant on Oak Tree Road. The residents had not realized until then that a Pizza Hut, with its aggressively red roof and red vinyl booths, was what was missing from their lives. There was no waiting area or system for putting down one's name, so customers had to stand in an orderly line in a narrow corridor until they reached the front, which, on a Friday or Saturday night, was typically one hour later. But they did not mind. It was a place where good times were had, so they waited, chatting happily and anticipating the doughy yet crunchy crust, stretchy cheese, and red pitcher of partially flat soda.

Prem was a reluctant fan of the Hut. He was not in a state of mind to become a new fan of anything but found that he now enjoyed the taste of pizza, especially this particular style. On an unseasonably cold day in September, Abdul Rashid suggested it for lunch before they reported for their afternoon shifts.

"Last time, I ordered pepper-onion pizza," Gopal said, "but they brought the one with red circles of meat."

"You must have said 'sausage,' " Mohan said.

"Why would I say 'sausage?' " Gopal said.

"I agree," said Yogesh Cyclewala, a very short, entirely too loud new attendant with nearly connected eyebrows whose ancestors had repaired bikes. "You seem like someone who might say 'sausage.' "

"What does that mean even?" Gopal said.

"They made a mistake in the kitchen, maybe," Prem said.

"Excuse me, but I couldn't help but overhear." A sharply dressed man in his thirties, maybe forties, with hair slicked to the side elegantly and a round pair of Gandhi-looking glasses, spoke to them from the next table, where he was dining alone. In enviably smooth English, he said, "I had this problem once, with the pepper and onions. They think you are saying 'pepperoni.' Red meat circles."

"Oh, pepperoni!" they all said.

The man nodded sympathetically. "You have to say 'onion-pepper.'"

"Wow," Gopal said.

"Roopesh Ghosh," the man said, coming over and offering his hand around the table. "My friends call me Vinnie."

"Why?" Abdul Rashid said.

"I don't know," Vinnie said.

He ended up joining them in their booth and sharing his pizza with them, which was greatly appreciated since they ordinarily split one small pie amongst the five of them, resulting in Mohan and Abdul Rashid fighting over Prem's discarded crust. It turned out Vinnie knew Gopal's uncle in Calcutta and had frequented his sweets shop, though the exquisite sandesh had caused him to put on more than a few kgs. He laughed at Yogesh's joke about Indian newspapers and answered Gopal's question about why America refused to use the metric system. Overall, he was marvelously charming, the kind of guy who called people "boss" when they weren't his boss. By midway through the meal, they were all enamored of him, especially Prem, who admired everything from his pleasing personality to his gleaming shoes.

"How did you get this way?" Prem asked with wide-eyed wonderment. He thought at once that the others would taunt him for his fawning question and awkward demeanor, but they did not. They were equally intrigued.

"What way?" Vinnie inquired, dabbing one corner of his mouth with a napkin.

"You know," Prem said, "just dressing nicely and talking nicely and, you know, just doing everything nicely."

"Don't be weird," Mohan said.

Vinnie gripped the table with both hands and straightened himself up so that he seemed suddenly to be a head above everyone else. "Have you heard of Wall Street, boys?" he began. "It is a magical place where your one dollar can be multiplied to one million. I began by investing a small amount, just on the side of my regular job in engineering. But then, the investment grew and grew, and led to other investments that grew and grew, until I had so much money that I could leave my job. Now I help others manage their investments. You see, this is a country where everyone can dream of getting rich. Where the opportunity is endless. There is nothing standing in anyone's way."

The boys were mesmerized. There was an awed silence, which was broken by Gopal asking, "Which engineering company?"

"That is not the point," Mohan said, gnawing angrily on a breadstick.

"It's okay," Vinnie replied. "Assurevent Analytics. A small company."

Prem could not contain his questions. "What kind of investments? How long does it take? Do your clients also leave their jobs?"

Vinnie answered all of them in the same, amiable way, explaining everything to Prem's satisfaction. When he was done, he dug into his salad.

"So now we know why you can afford a salad!" Yogesh said too loudly.

Vinnie chuckled. "You want a salad? One more salad plate here!" Vinnie said in the direction of the waiter. "Don't worry, they don't charge me for the salad."

The manager himself came over with the plate and greeted Vinnie as though greeting a visiting dignitary. "Please, have more salad, sir, have as much as you want. Take more croutons, the croutons are the most important part."

For Prem, the crouton discussion cemented his faith in Vinnie's abilities. When Yogesh declined the salad plate, Prem asked for it and went up to the salad bar with Vinnie, who was getting more.

"How much do I have to put in?" Prem asked.

"Oh, as much as you want," Vinnie said.

"What if I just put in a little?" Prem said, "Will that still be okay?"

"I think that could be really good," Vinnie said, seeming quite enthusiastic.

"And when will I see any return on my investment?" Prem said.

"Investment? I thought we were talking about croutons." Vinnie looked at Prem carefully from the top of his Exxon jumpsuit to the bottom. "You want to invest?"

Prem began to feel self-conscious about his apparent poverty. "I have some money," he said resolutely.

"Well, you know, there is some risk," Vinnie said, dousing his salad with ranch dressing. "You have to be brave. Are you brave?"

"I am ready to be," Prem said.

To Prem's consternation, Vinnie still seemed hesitant. "You know, maybe you should think it over. I am here every Thursday for lunch. I come to the area to meet with a major player in the market. You can find me here."

"But I already know my answer," Prem said.

"Great, boss. Let's connect soon," Vinnie said.

Back at the apartment that evening, Amarleen was hosting a rowdy group of women for a card party. They had taken over the roommates' mattresses, leaving Prem to sit at the kitchen table with Iqbal, the only other person home, who was fiddling with some extremely tiny tools trying to adjust his glasses, which had been sitting crooked lately. Today's chance encounter seemed to Prem like an aerogram from God. It was the big idea he had been searching for: the stock market. It couldn't get any bigger than that. This way of making money was what America was all about. He knew with a prescient kind of certainty that this was the path, but he also did not want to be too hasty.

"Do you know anything about investing?" he asked Iqbal.

"I am thinking of investing in a light-bulb factory," Iqbal replied without looking up. "Who does not need a light bulb?"

There was a clamor of angry, vanquished voices from the card party when Shanta Bhatt took the pot. Nalini Sen cursed a surprising amount.

"Okay, ya, great, light bulbs," Prem said. "How about stocks and such?"

"Stocks?" Shanta Bhatt said on her way out the door, her pockets stuffed with cash. "Wonderful. My nephew's wife's uncle made thousands."

"The problem is," Iqbal mused, "how can I fix my glasses without wearing my glasses?"

"Stock market? Who is thinking about stock market?" Tun-Tun said. "Too much of risk. My brother's friend's neighbor lost thousands."

"Uh, okay," Prem said. "This is helpful, thanks." He helped Iqbal fix his glasses. That night, as he stared up at his onions, he gave the matter of investing a great deal more thought.

"I believe in America." Vinnie sprinkled crushed red pepper liberally on his pizza. He was at Pizza Hut on Thursday as he had said he would be and invited Prem to join him. He was certain he was going to take the leap and invest but couldn't figure out how to convey this to Vinnie, who was delivering an impassioned speech about the promise of their adopted country. "This is a place where anything is possible. For anyone," he continued.

"Ya, you said something like that last week," Prem said.

"Exactly. I don't care about any Colio Volio," Vinnie said, referring to Pat Jud Colicchio, the former mayor of Wanaque who opposed housing development because it would attract "all these Dotheads" to the area. "We cannot be scared. We have to show Americans what we are capable of, that we can contribute to the nation's greatness." He squirted hot sauce on top of the layer of red pepper and served Prem a slice.

"Ya, that's good, we should do that," Prem said.

"So, tell me," Vinnie plied.

Prem had a moment of hesitation, wondering if he should find a safer option. But time was passing quickly and he had nothing to show for himself. He had to go for it.

"I'm going for it," Prem declared.

"What telepathy, man! I knew you were going to say that!" Vinnie came around to Prem's side of the table and shook his hand heartily. "I'll have my secretary Mary draw up the papers for you to sign and then you can give me the cash you want to invest—"

"I have it here," Prem said, pulling from his jacket a large envelope full of cash, secured with a rubber band.

Vinnie was surprised but quickly recovered. "I'm going to take good care of this, don't keep any tension," he said. "I'm going to have my best associate working on this with me, John, he is my A-one guy. And call me anytime, two-oh-one, triple three, double zero, double one," he said, jotting the numbers down on a napkin. They agreed to meet again the following Thursday to sign the papers and have a celebratory onion-pepper.

17

In India, as in America, the number 420 has taken on layers of meaning associated with unlawful activity. While in the latter, it has come to be correlated in a decidedly celebratory way with the consumption of cannabis, in India, char sau bees, or four hundred twenty, refers to cheaters, liars, swindlers, and conmen: frauds conducting fraudulent activity. The origin of this association comes from Section 420 of the Indian Penal Code, which addresses cheating and dishonestly inducing delivery of property, but the usage has become much more casual, referring also to everyday dastardliness. To date, no numerologists have published any findings on how this one particular number came to have a crime-related meaning in two different languages on two different sides of the world.

On a frigid, miserable day in November 1988, Prem was thinking about the number 420 and how he had let another char sau bees so easily into his life. A week after he had handed over all of his money to a stranger, Prem sat alone for a very long time at Pizza Hut. He went home and tried calling the number Vinnie had given him but found it not to be in service. His heart pounding, he raced his bike back to the Pizza Hut, where he questioned the manager, who said he hadn't seen the man since the previous week. Prem tried to convince himself not to jump to conclusions, but even he, with all of his naïveté, knew in his heart what had happened.

As he waited for the following Thursday to arrive, Prem attempted to track Vinnie down. He looked through the phone book for Assurevent Analytics, hoping they might have some contact information for their former employee, but there was no such company. When he called the operator to find a listing for Roopesh Ghosh, he had a moment of uplift when he was given the numbers of seven different men of that name in the tristate area. He spent the afternoon calling them, some of whom were quite nice, but he did not find the Roopesh Ghosh he was looking for. It hit Prem particularly hard when he deduced there probably never was a Mary or John either.

When Thursday came around again, Prem entered the Pizza Hut with trepidation. He wasn't afraid of not finding Vinnie there; he already understood that he would most likely never see the man or the money again. What he was afraid of was the depression that he knew he was about to be plunged into when the matter became final. He walked into the dining room and found the table vacant once again. Feeling lightheaded, he pulled out a chair and sat down to catch his breath before the bike ride home. Around him, everyone was enjoying unlimited fountain soda and meat lover's pizzas, having a good time just as he and his friends had on the day they first met Vinnie. How charismatic and magnetic he had seemed. Never could Prem have imagined the level of deception that he would practice. He thought of the salad bar with the delightful croutons and felt more hapless than ever before.

In the following weeks, Prem brooded over a lot of things. He pondered whether this was punishment for his desire to make money without working, or if the tracksuit brothers from the airport were somehow involved. He would never know. He left the apartment only to do his job at Exxon and then came immediately home to sleep or listen to a depression-themed mixtape of his own design. Day after day, he immersed himself in "Din Dhal Jaaye" (*Guide*, 1965), the most hauntingly beautiful and upsetting song he had among his cassette collection, and he stopped shaving altogether. His roommates began to ask questions, and reluctantly he shared what had happened. Those who had met Vinnie were shocked to learn that the charming pizza-sharer was actually a rakish scam artist. Soon, everyone in the building and King's Court and the neighboring complexes had heard about poor Prem, and they became, again, alarmingly nice to him. Aunties brought him food and his roommates refrained from teasing him, giving him time to mentally recover. Even Amarleen, sensing his need to reflect and recuperate, desisted from flinging herself onto his mattress.

On a sunny day at the end of the month, Prem reached an even darker, lower point. Beena came to break the news to him herself, gently, before he heard it inadvertently: She had finally caught a glimpse of the medical-student suitor and could confirm that he was, unfortunately, exceedingly handsome. As if this were not enough, Beena had also learned that Mikesh Aneja, almost MD, was polished and charming and studying medicine right there in New Jersey. It was like a punch to the heart. With no money, no plan, and a highly accomplished and apparently ravishing rival close by, he felt his own failure even more acutely. He thanked Beena for her discretion and showed her out. Sunlight poured into the room and he felt somehow pressured by it. He drew the curtains, and those who were home did not question it. Prem pulled out his ledger and began a new entry. Right under "Did you hear that I met Amitabh Bachchan?" he wrote, "Did you hear that a guy ran away with all my money? Did you hear what a loser I am?"

Hemant had heard. It brought him no pleasure to hear of the boy's hardship; he felt proud, in fact, of his sympathy for Prem's plight. As he was restocking the ghee shelf, he commended himself for his great depth of feeling and for his wisdom in warding off the useless, unlucky boy from his daughter.

Things had been going well ever since the unfortunate episode. They had taken on, along with Viren Bhai, a series of new paying guests, all of whom turned out to be reliable and harmless, owing to Hemant's new policy of taking in only married couples who planned to stay just a few weeks until they found a place of their own. The grocery store, which had recently added Vicco Turmeric skin cream and Sunsilk egg-based shampoo to its wares, continued to thrive. Even Hriyan was sprouting new vines all the time.

And of course, the most splendid thing of all had occurred when he and his dear friend Sanjay Sapra had orchestrated the meeting of Leena and Sanjay's almost-endocrinologist nephew Mikesh. On a snowy December morning, when Hemant and his daughter were visiting his sister in Minnesota, he invited Sanjay Sapra's cousin Sanjana to come over for tea at his sister's house and to bring along her promising young son, who was home for the holidays.

"This is Mikesh," Sanjana said. "He is doing medical."

Hemant lit up like a Diwali diya. "Welcome, welcome, come sit!"

Leena had just stepped out to run a few errands despite Hemant's vehement protests, but it turned out well because he had a chance to learn the basics of Mikesh's history. He had just completed his first year of medical school at the prestigious UMDNJ, which Hemant knew to be a highly prolific producer of Indian American doctors. Mikesh came from a respectable Punjabi family that boasted several physicians back in India and was the first to bring his exceptional brain to America, where he was doing a stellar job of reinforcing the stereotype of the model minority.

After having tea and biscuits, the mother and son stood up to leave. Hemant practically pushed them back down in their seats and gave them more tea. They couldn't leave before Leena came home. Sanjana seemed to catch on to this plan when Hemant and his sister began frying samosas. Four cups of tea later, Leena finally returned from the store.

"Leena! Look who is here! Our dear friend Sanjay Sapra's cousin, and look who she has brought with her, her son Mikesh. Mikesh come meet Leena, she works so hard in the store, she is the reason it is even open, and now she is thinking of opening a salon. Leena, tell them about your salon idea." The excessive caffeine seemed to have hit Hemant hardest, although Mikesh appeared to be shaking considerably too.

"Uh, hello, I have a salon idea," Leena said.

"He is doing medical," Hemant said.

"Tell her, Mikesh," Sanjana said.

"I am doing medical," Mikesh said.

"You know, Sanjanaji," Hemant said, "you were going to show me that thing, that new item, frozen batata vada, in Annapurna Grocery Store, was it?" He shoved his dear friend's cousin out the door and pulled his sister along as well. Looking over his shoulder before pulling the door shut behind him, he caught a glimpse of Leena's supremely annoyed face. She will thank me later, he thought.

Twenty minutes later, when the three returned, they found Leena and Mikesh laughing together on the couch, looking already like honeymooners. "Have you seen how nice his teeth are?" Hemant said. "Also, no family history of heart disease."

Leena and Mikesh looked at each other and burst out laughing, which Hemant thought was just great.

* * *

A few weeks later, Prem realized even greater depths of despair when he saw Leena with Mikesh at Tun-Tun and Tony's New Year's Eve party. He hadn't wanted to go, but his roommates, coworkers, Beena, and assorted other friends said it would be good for him to get out. He walked over with Deepak and Lucky, whose chest hair was especially resplendent that evening. The sky looked perfectly white and blank. Prem found a relatively quiet corner at the party and sipped whiskey from a disposable cup while feeling unnecessary. Leena came in an hour later with whom he presumed to be the doctor. "Is there scope for her to get any prettier?" he overheard one guy say to another. He tried to will her to look in his direction, but she did not notice he was there.

18

Prem left the party almost immediately after that and stumbled out into the cold. There were people milling about, huddled together, drinking, celebrating, their breath appearing and disappearing before them. Still clutching his plastic cup which he'd topped off with a heavy pour, Prem sipped and struggled not to slip on the ice. Hindi music seeped out of more than one building. A light snow started to fall, and the k of the Quicker Liquor sign flickered on and off. He turned toward home but thought better of it. What comfort would he find there? His cup now empty, he threw it into a bush and plodded through the hardened snow until he came to his bike on its rusted rack. He got on, not knowing where he would go.

After pedaling a long time down Oak Tree, up Grove, and across James Street past the JFK Medical Center, he found himself on Route 27, chasing distraughtly the crumbling concrete orb of the Thomas Alva Edison Memorial Tower in the distance. The road inclined and he began to breathe heavily, the cold air sharp in his lungs, when a car swerved and nearly hit him. The bike spun out and he was thrown into a snowbank. The entire right side of his body was wet and the snow stung his cheek. In that miserable moment, he wondered what reason there was to bother getting up. What had he achieved in his life? Nothing. Was there a chance he could win back Leena? No. All was lost and he would have to live in that snowbank forever. But something—call it fate, call it frostbite—made him climb out and get back on his bike. He spotted the tower's Art Deco sphere looming up Christie Street and determined to get there.

The memorial tower was in a sad state of disrepair unfit for the man whose laboratory invented the movie camera. Nothing remained: no evidence of the labs, no sign of the machine shop. Exactly 110 years ago to the day, Christie Street had become the first street in the world to be lit up by incandescent bulbs, but on that night, it was completely silent and dark. Prem dropped his bike at the curb and plodded through the snow toward the tower, looking up at it as he approached. Coming so close to the 131-foot structure, he was overcome by his own insignificance. He fell to his knees and pleaded as if at the feet of Thomas Edison himself, not unlike Amitabh communing with Lord Krishna in *Mr. Natwarlal*, or in *Deewaar*, challenging Lord Shiva. He begged for a sign.

The only thing that happened was that Prem's knees got wet. He looked around for any indication, but everything was the same, cold and quiet. Then he did something he'd never done before: he screamed. A savage, primal scream that would have terrified anyone had anyone been there. At the end of it, spent, he saw a light coming up the road. It wasn't headlights but rather one weak shaft of light moving slowly forward. Prem rose out of the snow and turned to get a better look.

Coming up the road was a shadowy figure with a sort of old-timey lantern. Prem could make out that it was an older gentleman, the moonlight reflecting off his silver hair and wild eyebrows. He was dressed in an old-fashioned way, with a vest under a jacket and a loose bowtie. When the figure was directly across from him, he stopped and shone the light straight at Prem, who froze. Then he moved on, up Christie Street and past the tower, leaving him behind.

Forever after whenever Prem would recall that encounter, a shiver would go up his spine. He couldn't say for sure that he had seen a ghost that night, but he certainly saw something inexplicable, which was sign enough for him. He picked his bike up off the curb and started the long ride home, sobered by the encounter. He went the other way down Route 27 this time, in the direction of the Metro Park train station. At the first light, still shaken, he was happy to be around a lot of cars. Turning left past the competing Exxon, he thought about the strange turn the night had taken. As he started up the incline of Wood Avenue, he considered its meaning. He remembered reading about how Thomas Edison had pushed forward through ten thousand or so failed prototypes before building a successful electric light bulb, and he pedaled harder. As he came upon United Skates and Marshalls to the left, he reflected on how the American dream was not handed to you when you got here. It was something you had to work hard to earn a piece of. Gasping for air while passing the Chinese restaurant and Hallmark shop, he realized that to move on with his life, he had to try harder. He had been too depressed to act—lately and always. Passing now in front of the Drug Fair, he decided he would apply more vigor in accruing the curious, single-hued money of America. This would require a major shift. And though it may not bring him any closer to Leena, it wouldn't bring him any farther either. He would prove to Hemant that he could make a million and one dollars, maybe even more. He would prove it to his skeptical father and his siblings who had written him off as a clown, the friends who called him pumpwalla, and ultimately, himself. The time had come to acquire some dignity.

By the time he reached the top of the hill and rounded the corner onto Oak Tree, the car wash and defunct drive-in on the left, he made a resolution to build something from the ground up. As King's Court and the India America Grocers beyond that came in sight, he decided to start a business of his own.

It was past midnight and the parties were still carrying on, but Prem went home to his mattress. Thus he climbed out of the darkness—that night and in life—with a notion to do something big.

* * .*

That winter, all of King's Court watched a lot of Hindi movies. It used to be that they had a limited array of uncomfortable and inconvenient venues to watch their films. They squeezed into Tun-Tun and Tony's apartment with thirty others to view a shaky pirated copy with a slight rainbow on top that they'd brought with them from India; they attended a screening at John Adams Middle School, where they would sit on folding chairs and at the interval eat cold samosas in the vestibule next to a trophy case; they trekked to a theater in Jackson Heights that played a Hindi movie one Saturday per month. All of this changed when India America Grocers started renting out videos. They began with a meager offering—a few newish movies, a couple of seventies hits, some Raj Kapoor classics for good measure—but when Hemant observed their popularity, he ordered hundreds more, built shelves to house them, and raised the rate from one to two dollars. Soon, the tapes were everywhere, stacked up on the counter, piled up on the windowsill, and the windows became overwhelmed by film posters. Customers learned to pop into the store on Wednesdays when the new movies tended to arrive, and if they couldn't find what they were looking for, they would comb through the returns bin, asking, "Is this a camera copy?" and "How is the print?" As a result of Leena's brilliant business maneuver—and her ability to convince Hemant the idea was his—there was an uptick in the purchase of VCRs by King's Court residents, many of whom bought them before even buying a bed.

That year would go down as a banner year for Hindi movies. The songs from *Chandni, Ram Lakhan, Tridev,* and *Maine Pyar Kiya* were hummed and whistled on street corners throughout India and Edison, and decades later, they would still be evoked in conversations about how they don't make them like they used to. At the same time, all of India—and subsequently King's Court—was consumed by *Mahabharat*, the television series based on the Hindu epic. When it aired on the state-sponsored Doordarshan channel on Sunday mornings, the streets became deserted and businesses shut down for exactly one hour.

On New Year's Day, Iqbal Singh unveiled his new VCR. He had bought it two days prior and had picked up a video that day as well, but he decided to wait until the holiday, when everyone would be home, to debut it. Behind all his loudness and tallness, Iqbal was an insecure soul in need of validation, which he'd given up on extracting from his wife years ago. Somewhere along the way, he'd begun stuffing his apartment with as many paying guests as possible and inviting others to come by regularly. He lived for the moments when people were pleased with him and praised him, forever trying to plug a hole that could never be plugged. The reaction from his paying guests to the VCR was even bigger than he had hoped it would be. Gopal shed tears and Lucky embraced him for a very long time. Word spread through Buildings 3, 4, 5, and 11 that the Singhs had issued an open invitation for a screening of *Janbaaz*, the 1986 thriller featuring a steamy song sequence in a horse stable with excessive hay. No one in King's Court had seen it yet; Iqbal had snagged the only copy from the grocery store as soon as it arrived. An enormous crowd poured into the cramped apartment for the inaugural viewing, and by the time Uttam Jindal arrived with his wig, there was no room for anyone to enter; even the standing room–only section by the refrigerator was packed.

"Sorry, house full," Amarleen said at the door.

"But I won't take up much of space," Uttam Jindal said. "I can sit on the stove."

"On my stove where I make chicken curry? No, thank you. Why don't you buy a VCR? Go to Crazy Eddie."

"His prices are insane," Mohan called from behind.

There was much excitement as they readied to start the movie. Iqbal prolonged the anticipation, reveling in the attention and admiration. Shanta Bhatt asked, "Is someone making popcorns?" and Gopal wondered out loud, "If there are major motion pictures, are there also minor ones?" Once the movie was underway, the crowd behaved as though they were in the bench seats of a Bombay theater, hooting and hollering, talking back to the screen, having full-blown conversations with the characters. Someone even threw a cashew. At the interval, Iqbal paused the tape and everyone got up for a break. Amarleen made an enormous amount of chai, and a few brave addicts went out in the snow to smoke.

"I don't know, yaar," Yogesh said. "How can there be no other police officer available to chase Amar except for his brother Rajesh? They couldn't give the assignment to another guy?"

"You know, I think that is not really the point," Prem said, shifting in the one square foot of floor he had claimed for himself. "It's about the two very different paths that brothers from the same family can take in life. It's about decisions and consequences, you know?"

"But why would Dimple suddenly decide to sleep with Anil Kapoor in a barn," Yogesh asked, "when he has been drunk the whole time and stumbling around like a hairy clown?" He raised his voice to declare, "American movies are better. More realistic, better acting, better stories, better quality, actual kissing. There's no singing for no reason and they are not all the same dishoom-dishoom formula. What is good about Hindi movies?"

Prem had never really thought about why he loved Hindi movies; he just did. He gave the question serious thought. It was difficult to explain yet difficult to deny the movies' appeal. They crammed it all

in—romance, comedy, drama, suspense, action, international tele-
portation, song, dance—creating a glamorous spectacle, a singular
genre, "the masala film," a big, spicy mix. They celebrated Kathak's
graceful aerobic choreography and preserved an Urdu-Hindi mix of
poetic language that might otherwise fade. Even when unrealistic, they
expressed reality, transmitting the agony and ache of problematic love.
He left theaters feeling the world contained too much beauty to bear,
that the characters were larger than life—and thus he could be too.
"Everything," Prem answered.

Nearby, Dave (formerly Devinder) Reddy, a pharmaceutical sales rep
who took great pride in his spiked hair, was bragging to Falguni about
the two American concerts he had attended late last year. "You know,
it is hard to decide, was George Michael better or Michael Jackson. On
one side, there is the 'Faith' and the 'Father Figure,' on the other side is
'Bad' and the 'Smooth Criminal.' How can I say?" Three people rolled
their eyes. Dave continued, "Michael really can dance. But then, George
also has some nice moves. And Michael, I don't know, something was
looking wrong with his face."

Mohan said, "I do not believe you went to either of these shows,"
which led to a short but vigorous brawl. Dave lunged at Mohan and
they rolled around on the floor in a tangled embrace. When they
came too close to her, Beena Joshi rolled them back the other way. All
through this, Prem was oblivious. In his mind, a grand and glittering vision unfolded for an astonishing enterprise. It was a singular
light-bulb moment precipitated by *Janbaaz* combined with Dave. Prem
conceived the idea to start a company to produce lavish stage shows
featuring Hindi movie stars. What if he could get Anil Kapoor, Jackie
Shroff, Sanjay Dutt, Sunny Deol, and all the popular heroes of the
day here, to Edison? They could each perform their numbers, and it
would be bigger even than the American concerts that featured just

one megastar. When Sridevi, Madhuri Dixit, and Juhi Chawla came out, the crowd would go wild, and he could also include some of the old guard, the Kapoors and such, who would bring an element of sophistication to the event. Maybe some playback singers could come and sing their songs as the actors dance to them live on stage. There could be special effects, magnificent lighting, a screen showing scenes from the movies. Every show could have a surprise performer, someone who would make the audiences lose their minds in the best possible way. If he could pull off such a program, it would be unlike anything the Indians in America—or Indians anywhere—had ever witnessed.

Prem did not watch the second half of the movie that day. When Iqbal pressed play, he grabbed his coat and hat and slipped out of the apartment to find his bike. Later, he would be hard-pressed to tell you where he went, crisscrossing the town many times over, mulling over the possibilities, contemplating the best ways to execute this new and sudden dream.

19

Many years later when Prem would find himself enlightening a reporter for the *India Abroad* on the subject of industriousness, he would claim that from the moment of his arrival in Edison, he had been seized by the spirit of its eponym, its former wizard-in-residence from the days when our town was still Menlo Park. He would lean back in his chair at Bombay Talk (a block from Sona Jewelers, Virani Jewelers, and Kundan Jewelers, right next to Sangam Jewelers and Jewelry Treasures II), order a third cup of milky tea, and wax nostalgic about his earliest American days, when he slogged and strove, when he was fiercely single-minded, a veritable workaholic, as he had taken to describing his younger self.

That assiduousness did not kick in, however, until he went to Beena Joshi to find out how exactly one went about starting a business. She had recently expanded her catering business to include extensive buffet dinners for upscale events hosted chiefly by physicians. This shrewd decision, Prem felt, demonstrated her perspicacity and acute understanding of the doctor-party market. She would certainly have keen insights into how to get his venture off the ground.

When Beena heard Prem's impassioned speech about his vision for stage shows in America featuring Hindi movie actors, she immediately dismissed Bob the electrician, who was helping her hang picture frames, then turned to Prem excitedly. "Can you make me meet Rajesh Khanna?"

"Yes! And Amitabh and Anil Kapoor and Sanjay Dutt. You will become friends with all of them," Prem replied excitedly. "You can have lunch with Jackie Shroff, you can pick Sunny Deol up at the airport, you can ask Govinda to show you how he moves his hips like that."

"Rajesh Khanna is enough," Beena said. "Now, you find a pen and pad, I will make the chai."

Beena's apartment could barely contain Prem's feverish pacing as he threw out questions: "What kind of hall should it be in? How will I sell the tickets? Should I take an ad in the *India Abroad*?" He stumbled over a bag of almonds next to five packages of straight blades, lined up along the wall with a number of other items to be taken to India sometime next year and distributed to various family members. The assortment of face creams, suit pieces, Spanish saffron, blenders, bras, perfumes, and more ran almost the entire perimeter of the apartment. "How will I get the actors? Also, why are you taking a skateboard?"

"Okay, first, you can talk to my customer Kishan Chopra about the hall. He organized that Anup Jalota ghazals performance last year and the Jagjit Singh one the year before."

"Oh, ya, that guy," Prem said. "He has a small mustache, Charlie Chaplin–style, no?"

"Ya," Beena said. "Someone should tell him it is also Adolf Hitler–style."

"Good, I'll take his number. Next, we will need people who know about lighting and microphones and sound systems and the things on the stage, you know?"

"Yes, there is Nachiket Rao in Building 17, whose daughter is on hunger strike until she is allowed to marry a plumber. Nachiket is involved with audio and visual support in wedding functions, he will know who to call, what to do."

"His daughter is on hunger strike?"

"As if she is Gandhi fighting the British Empire."

The pair went through dozens of questions and came up with action plans for each category, filling up an entire notebook in the process. Four rounds of chai and salty snacks later, Beena summarized the key takeaway from that meeting: "Basically, you have to make lot of calls."

Prem was not looking forward to this aspect of the work. Calling the friends of Beena would be hard enough, but ringing up movie stars? Though booking Indian celebrities meant mostly talking to their secretaries—managers and agents rolled into one—it would likely require talking on the phone directly with the stars as well. A shiver went through him at the thought. Talking with complete strangers, trying to get them to do something—it wouldn't be easy. He had hated it the first time around and would hate it once again. "You can make some calls if you want. Wouldn't you like to talk to some stars?"

"Uf oh! What is so hard about making simple calls?" Beena said, slapping her forehead with her palm. "Have some confidence before I hit you with my rolling pin. Now let us have some paan."

Back at the Singhs' apartment that evening, Harbhajan Gill and his angry family were over to visit his sister. They sat at the kitchen table while the roommates huddled around the television watching an early episode of *Mahabharat*, which everyone agreed was surprisingly riveting despite the difficult vocabulary, slow pace, and religiosity. When Prem entered, he was happy that no one turned around; though he was ecstatic, he wasn't ready to talk about his new venture. He tried to slip past the dining table without attracting anyone's attention.

"Are you trying to go around us without attracting our attention?" Iqbal said.

"Oh, no, you know, I thought you were having dinner just with family, private, you know," Prem said.

"But you are in this family!" Amarleen said. "Come, sit. You can share my chair."

"What is in that journal, Pumpwalla?" Harbhajan said with a suspicious edge.

"Nothing, just, you know, addresses, phone numbers, lottery numbers. They say if you use the same numbers every time, you increase your chances."

"Something is in there," Iqbal said. "You are holding it so tight, like you would die for it. Who would die for a journal when nothing is in it?"

"I was watching the 60 Minutes program last week and they showed how a terrorist tried to make a bomb at home," Harbhajan said. "He wrote the instructions in a journal."

One of Harbhajan's kids yelled, "Show us the journal, you skinny nerd!"

Prem reluctantly laid out his plan for them.

There was silence at the dining table, then Harbhajan's wife burst out laughing. She kept laughing for a long time, at times trying to catch her breath or slapping the table. Prem looked around to see who else found his idea hilarious.

"Stars don't have time to fly to America to pretend to sing on a stage," Iqbal pointed out.

"You think Amitabh Bachchan will take your phone call?" Mohan asked from his spot in front of the TV without turning around.

"Shh," Deepak said, chomping on a donut. "*Mahabharat.*"

"Here is the problem," Harbhajan said. "People will not pay money for this. Why would we go there to see the stars dance when we can see them here?"

All of Prem's enthusiasm evaporated. "Okay, then, thank you, I guess, for the advice," he said, hanging his head and moving in the direction of his sad mattress.

"Wait, pause the show," Lucky said. He turned to face the room. "I think this is a fantastic idea."

"Really?" several people said simultaneously.

"Really!" Lucky shouted. "Imagine, you are standing in front of the stage and the music comes on and there is Madhuri Dixit, smiling, dancing, jumping. Then comes Sridevi dancing with Anil Kapoor, and in the end, the Big B himself, right in front of you on the stage."

Everyone except the Gill family began to chime in, fantasizing about their favorite stars who might come and the dances they might do. Even Amarleen briefly released her focus from Prem to envision Dharmendra on stage before her. Prem, relieved and exultant once again, smiled and tucked his journal into his bag.

Meanwhile, King's Court at large was bursting with entrepreneurial spirit. Though sections of Oak Tree Road were still what Monte Burke described in Forbes as a "cesspool of biker bars, prostitutes, and abandoned buildings," the town was beginning to show signs of what it would someday be. The ambitious residents of King's Court residents opened new businesses, supported each other's dreams by frequenting each other's little shops and maa-and-baap stores. Sujata Mehra opened her elegant jewelry emporium, and Nathan Kothari moved forward with his travel agency. Raghava Sai Shankara Subramanya established his casual South Indian restaurant, and Urmila Sahu was close to unveiling her Sari Palace, which also carried videos like her sister's store in Chicago. When the sister heard about Urmila's plan, she said, "It won't work there, it has to be in a big city where there are lot of Indians," to which Urmila replied, "Visit me in Edison sometime."

Not every tenant of King's Court met with professional success. The Ghataks in 20E bet everything they had on a small jewelry business from out of their apartment, catering to upscale customers who never came. Bhuvan Khurana in 14G tried to become an accountant but could not secure a position in his field. For several months, he toiled at Roy Rogers on Oak Tree Road, not far from Exxon, mopping floors, picking up soggy lettuce around the Fixins Bar while steeped in fried chicken and roast beef aromas until it became too much for him; he packed up his family and returned to India, broken. There were countless such stories of hardship and shattered hopes. Many an immigration story rewound back where it started, where there would still be suffering, but at least the parameters were familiar. Those who stayed and even prospered lived with the constant awareness that failure and deep shame could be just around the dingy, litter-strewn corner.

Hemant felt it his duty to prevent this sort of thing. He continued to impart his wisdom, but now it was to people who were actually listening. Many would-be entrepreneurs came to him for guidance, to whom he was delighted to offer his pearls of wisdom, such as "The man who removes a mountain begins by carrying away small stones," or "A free lunch is only found in mousetraps." He followed these aphorisms with concrete advice and was immensely pleased when the receivers of his advice opened new stores.

As all of this was happening, news of Prem's would-be venture spread through King's Court as well. Urmila Sahu heard a rumor about a business Prem wanted to start with Indian stars coming to America to perform in shows, and she mentioned it to Gitanjali Vora, who felt sad at the thought of him trying so hard to make something of himself and possibly failing. She told this to Poonam as she was hanging popular magazines like *Stardust*, *Cineblitz*, and *Femina* on a clothesline behind the counter at Poonam Video. Because she didn't have any clothespins, Poonam opened the magazines and made them straddle the line so they hung sideways, causing customers to tilt their heads to read the covers. When Nalini Sen came in with her unruly twins and tilted her head to look at Juhi Chawla on the cover of *Stardust*, Poonam

told her that Juhi would likely be coming to America soon to participate in the Superstar Entertainment show, the name of the company
having come to her as quickly as the rest of the lie.

"Juhi Chawla? Here?" Nalini said.

"Oh ya, all the stars will be coming," Poonam said, spacing out the
magazines. "Juhi, Sridevi, Madhuri—"

"Any of the heroes?"

"Oh, all of them," Uttam Jindal answered from the golden-oldies
section. "Aamir, Anil Kapoor, some of the older ones. Maybe Jitendra,
I heard Jitendra really wants to come."

"Really? That will be something!" a customer nobody knew said.

Poonam told the same story to the next person who came in and
the next one after that, and everyone who heard it repeated it to two
others. The rumor spread through the Indian American community
faster than news of a Macy's one-day sale until eventually it became
common knowledge. Some of this was the result of wishful thinking
on the part of movie fans, while the rest was due to Prem's friends'
desire to see him do well. As the weeks went forward, these friends
continued their "marketing," as they liked to think of it, embellishing
a little more each time, adding fireworks and laser lights and appear-
ances by every star they could think of, raising ticket prices and hoping
that the program Prem put together would be as grand as they were
promising it would be.

20

When the rumors inevitably reached apartment 3D, Prem was perplexed by the discovery that his company had a name. "Superstar Entertainment" had a strong, sensational quality to it—much better than the name he had come up with, Indian Movie Stage Program Productions—so he decided to keep it. For Prem, February 1989 unfolded largely on the phone in Beena's apartment, Superstar Entertainment's first headquarters. He would leave to work his shifts at Exxon or to shower and sleep at the Singhs' place, but his remaining hours were spent making calls for his new venture. First, he focused on securing a venue, figuring it would be difficult to entice any talent to come to America without any details to offer. Beena's customer Kishan Chopra directed him to a few local theaters that might have the kind of stage and capacity he was looking for. Prem actually had no idea what kind of stage or capacity he was looking for but called those places anyway. He quickly narrowed the options down to two places in nearby New Brunswick, the State Theatre and the George Street Playhouse. After visiting both several times, it came down to seats: 1,850 versus 180. "Are you stupid?" Beena said, referring to the possibility of renting a theater with so few seats. Thus it was decided that the inaugural Superstar Entertainment show would be held in the recently restored gilded halls of the State Theatre, on the entirely arbitrary date of March 10, 1990.

With the venue and date in place, Prem began, of course, to panic. He had taken a small loan from Beena to put down a deposit on the theater, and if the show failed, he would have to work at Exxon for years before he could repay her. What if he couldn't convince any stars to come? How could he hire them without money? How could he get money from sponsors and advertisers without any actors? This was the business model that Prem and Beena had formulated: the bill for putting on the event would be covered by money from sponsors and advertisers, while he would keep the revenue from the ticket sales. Beena advised lining up the talent first. "But how can I do that with no payment to offer?" Prem said.

"Are you stupid?" Beena cried. "Not you," she said then, addressing a plumber who was hanging some curtains for her. "Promise the payment to the stars and find the money later." So Prem began calling managers and agents whose numbers he still had from his days as an aspiring filmmaker in Bombay. It would not be easy to get them on the phone, but he steeled himself and prepared more chai.

* * *

"It's going to be me and you sitting in the empty State Theatre, watching the empty stage," Prem said to Beena.

"I will bring samosa," Beena said.

It was April, and they were at Raghava Sai Shankara Subramanya's Dosa Hut, which had become the hottest hut in town. On one wall was a shaky yet enthusiastic mural of Juhu Beach, and on a shelf behind the register was a large TV showing movie songs. Multicolored streamers crisscrossed the ceiling, and the pepper shakers on the tables were filled with red pepper instead of black, which Prem hailed as a stroke of genius. Beena was treating him to idli and dosa to celebrate all the hard work he had done the past two months.

"But I didn't book a single actor," Prem said. "Are we celebrating my total lack of progress?"

"Look," Beena said, "you are making progress. It is just not visible yet."

"Invisible progress, fantastic."

The super painful and upsetting song "Aa Meri Jaan" from the movie *Chandni*, which Sridevi sings to her beloved Rishi Kapoor after he is paralyzed, started on the TV. At the exact same time, Leena walked in. She was with her usual gang of friends and her frustratingly well-dressed doctor. Her hair looked about three inches shorter and was parted on the side instead of the middle, and she had on a different, pinker shade of lipstick. She glided as if on air, and when she tilted her head a certain way, it wrecked him.

Everyone exchanged hellos and waves, except for Leena and Prem.

"That's it, this is ridiculous. Why can you not talk to her and ask what happened and does she still love you?" Beena asked, pointing her hand in Leena's general direction.

Prem swatted her hand down. "She is engaged," he said, trying to lower the volume of their conversation. "It is pointless."

"Then let me ask her."

"No! There is no need."

"Fine," Beena said. "Then you need some distraction. You are spending too much of time alone, working, worrying, working, worrying. Your stress is increasing my stress. Here, meet some new girls." Beena pulled a copy of the *India Abroad* from her purse and slid the last two pages across the table to Prem.

"What do you want me to do with this?" he said.

It turned out that Beena's solution was for him to respond to the matrimonial advertisements in the classified sections of Indian American newspapers in which parents, for the most part, sought potential partners for their children by presenting and soliciting relevant statistics—biodata, as it were—such as height, age, profession, degrees, location, religion, hobbies, and precise categorization of skin tone. It was too much for Beena to hope that Prem might forget about Leena altogether, but she wanted him to at least get out and meet other people and take his mind off his all-consuming, ill-advised love. Prem looked at the pages before him:

SEEKING suitable alliance for slim, fair
MD daughter, 31/5'3", from prominent
Gujarati Jain family. Boy should be
well-settled in US (preferably in medicine),
never married, cultured, nonsmoker. Reply w/photo.

ALLIANCE invited from qualified
professionals 33–35 yrs for beautiful,
clean-hearted daughter, 33/5'2", wheatish complexion,
Ivy League grad, MBA from top school. Seeking
match with successful, handsome Hindu
vegetarian boy, caste no bar.

SIKH parents invite correspondence from
MD/MBA/JD family-oriented candidates
for their caring, very fair, 29/5'4" dentist
daughter. New Jersey resident, innocent
divorcée, traditional with modern outlook.

"These ads all are looking for doctors," Prem said, trying to ruffle the pages angrily.

"I am not saying you should marry them," Beena said. "Just meet some girls, have some fun."

"I hate this idea," Prem said.

"Okay, fine, be alone," Beena said, stuffing too much idli into her mouth.

Laughter erupted from Leena's table at the same time that the heart wrenching song "Lambi Judai" ("Long Separation") from *Hero* began, and Prem wondered how this restaurant had become a showcase for depressing song videos. They changed the topic of conversation to Isha Rao's failed hunger strike, trying to ignore the disproportionate amount of fun the other table was having. Beena paid the bill, and Prem thanked her for the kind gesture and good food. As they got up to leave, he said, "You know, you really have some bad ideas," but stuffed the pages into his pocket anyway.

Prem carried on his solitary existence on the phone at Beena's. He had started to book other vendors, such as a lighting and AV company, a security firm, and a limousine service for airport pickups and drop-offs, though there were still no stars to pick up or drop off. By May, the snow, hardened and brown at the curbside, had melted, and it started to feel like a temperature he could withstand. June saw the arrival of AC units sticking out of King's Court windows, and Prem wondered why Beena didn't install one when she could afford it.

That same month, Gopal got engaged. He had met Radha at Sanjay Sapra's daughter's graduation party at Moghul Fine Indian Cuisine, the most celebrated and formal restaurant in town, where he noticed her across the room hovering around the paneer station, a giant orange flower tucked behind one ear. Her face had a dewy glow and her plump arms were threatening to bust free from her skin-tight sari blouse. Without speaking to her, he already couldn't imagine his life without her. When he finally approached, he said, "You look like actual Radha. The one with cows." She smiled shyly, and he admired her modest nature and chin dimple. She, in turn, liked his curly, tousled hair and was impressed by his incisive questions about American culture such as "Why is Jack short for John?" which demonstrated a delicious curiosity. It wasn't long before the Singhs were hosting in their apartment a grand potluck engagement party for the couple, which quickly spilled out onto the lawn on a hot summer night. Prem stood around with his friends and watched the happy couple feeding each other coconut laddu, then boondi laddu and besan laddu. In that moment, with no one feeding him excessive laddu, Prem recognized how lonely and bored he had been these few months. He had taken to frequenting places where he thought he might see Leena—Drug Fair, Dairy Queen, the parking lot of the Mediplex building across from John F. Kennedy hospital where her gynecologist had her offices—but he never saw her this way. Only when he was least prepared for her presence did she appear, at Bradlees discount department store, at the post office, in the queue at Krauszer's. Sometimes, he positioned himself just so on a doorstep where he could sit and peer into the Engineers' store for a good long while.

That night, after the partygoers had dispersed and the apartment residents had gone to sleep, Prem took a peek at the matrimonial pages Beena had given him. It seemed ludicrous to consider responding to an ad when Leena was in the world, yet he found himself reading each one carefully and did not take long to select one:

> BENGALI Hindu parents seek match for
> well-mannered physician's assistant
> daughter, 35/5'1", issueless divorce, somewhat
> dusky complexion, slight limp, with sound values.

It seemed the most desperate and least demanding of the lot, and he liked that there was no medical expertise expected of him. He called the contact number one morning when Beena was working a shift at Drug Fair, and the girl herself answered. Her name was Suchitra and couldn't believe that someone responded to the ad.

"You don't mind the dusky complexion, slight limp, and issueless divorce?" she said.

"I would like to meet you," Prem said.

"Fantastic!" she said.

They arranged to meet at the Woodbridge Mall, which Prem knew Leena and most people from King's Court did not frequent, and he enjoyed the half hour it took to bike there on that bright morning. Suchitra was standing outside in front of Alexander's department store when he arrived, smiling and holding a yogurt container. She had on an Indian top with jeans and very elaborate gold earrings.

"Prem? This is for you," she said, handing him the yogurt container. "It is rajma. Oh, why did I bring rajma? So stupid. Who brings rajma for a date? I just thought, you know, sometimes bachelors do not eat good food and they miss our Indian dishes, so I made it for you. But now you have to carry it around. I can take it back. Give it here."

Prem was thrilled to meet someone who was more awkward than he was and pulled the yogurt container out of her reach. "Are you trying to steal my rajma?"

They had an easy, enjoyable morning together, strolling through the mall, grabbing a slice of pizza at Sbarro's, stopping at Stern's so she could buy a pair of sensible slacks. Prem carefully avoided A&S, where Gitanjali Vora worked, but other than that, he felt a refreshing ease he hadn't felt in a long time. Suchitra was as warm-hearted as the ad had stated and chattered incessantly, which was always a good situation for Prem, who preferred listening over talking.

"So I started saying the temperature in Celsius again after my divorce, you know, because I thought I will probably go back to India anyway. I came for that stupid guy, so why stay in this Fahrenheit country? That was three years back. Mum and Dad live with me now, but we will see. Today is twenty-three, twenty-four degrees outside."

Suchitra told him the story of her not-so-issueless divorce from a man who had openly cheated on her. He would call her dark and crippled and then order her to make him tea. He would berate her for having an unimpressive job, though he had lost his as a dental billing manager almost immediately after marriage. He had begun to drink during the day, and quickly his mental abuse had become physical. She called the police to have him removed from her life.

Prem's eyes welled up as he heard her story. When she was done, he put the yogurt container on the floor and turned to face her. "Your skin color is dark and beautiful, the way you walk is cute, and your divorce was a horrible nightmare you survived. All of these qualities make you superb."

Her eyes filled with tears too, and she smiled. "You know I cannot marry you, right?" she said.

"Of course not," Prem said. "I work in a gas station."

"No, no, that is not the reason. Because you are too young and too not Bengali. But let's become friends, okay? Good. Settled. Now let's go on the merry-go-round."

That night, Prem made an entry in his ledger:

I went to Woodbridge Mall with someone named Suchitra. It was nice. It did not mean anything.

21

After Salman Khan burst shirtless onto the Hindi movie scene in 1989, nothing was quite the same. His debut as a leading man in *Maine Pyar Kiya* broke all box-office records, eschewing the standard revenge-justice-long-lost-twin-brother storylines for a simple love story. Romance was the central issue rather than a side distraction, and it was exactly what India—and Guyana, Trinidad and Tobago, Peru, plus Edison—wanted. It was the story of an innocent village girl and a worldly America-return boy from a prosperous family who fall for each other when she stays with his family as a houseguest. Their forbidden love, combined with exceptionally catchy songs—one a rip-off of the theme from *Love Story*, another a full-blown antakshari session, and still another sung to a pigeon—captured the hearts of millions.

It wasn't so much that Salman Khan himself changed everything, but his movie signaled a shift in the Indian film zeitgeist. In the 1990s, movies would no longer be dominated by angry men doing angry things to get back at someone; instead, films about love, individual growth, and family relationships would predominate, often with heroines gaining (almost) equal billing with heroes. *Aashiqui*, *Dil*, and *Deewana Mujh Sa Nahin* followed *Maine Pyar Kiya*, heralding the dawn of a new, gentler Hindi movie that Prem had no trouble getting on board with.

After his date with Suchitra, Prem, embracing the romantic life-style espoused by these new movies, took out a new, slightly unwanted heroine each week. All summer long, he charmed and comforted them, making the women feel special, like a handsome, therapeutic escort, an anti-Lothario. By September, it was an open secret in Edison that Prem was the go-to guy if you wanted someone to entertain your old-maid cousin or divorced aunt. He started getting invitations from all corners of the town and the surrounding areas, and he gladly accepted them as they offered him some relief from his daily stress.

For their first meeting, twenty-nine-year-old Sayali Barve asked Prem to come by her apartment in Fords and let himself in. It was more spacious than the ones in King's Court, yet it seemed to close in on him with its overwhelming concentration of wall art. There were framed portraits of clowns, needlepoint sailboats, a gaggle of plastic ducks captured midflight. One wall was plastered with pictures of waterfalls torn from calendars. Prem counted four different "Home Sweet Home" signs as well as two owls woven from some sort of rope. He sat down on the couch in front of a coffee table plagued by too many cardboard "Alaska: The Last Frontier" coasters and waited.

"Prem? I'm coming!" Sayali finally called from what seemed to be a coat closet. When she emerged, he couldn't see her face because she came out backward and moved immediately toward a back room. "I am just hiding some jewelry," she said. "You know, with the robberies and all. I am listening, tell me some things." She was referring to a recent string of break-ins targeting Indian homes, some of which held significant stashes of twenty-four-carat gold, diamond and ruby necklaces, rings, bangles, earrings, pendants, chains, arm cuffs, toe rings, nose rings, an-klets, and waistbands. The perpetrators reportedly came equipped with metal detectors and ferreted out the jewelry, leaving the homeowners devastated and wondering why the robbers didn't take their TVs.

"So, I, uh, work in a gas station," Prem said in Sayali's direction.

"Great!" Sayali called from somewhere inside. "I like that smell, you know, from the petrol."

"Ya, it's not bad," Prem said as she stuffed something under her mattress. He was pleasantly surprised by her positive reaction to his line of work. "They give us the jumpsuit for free."

She moved over to the kitchen, but again she walked in a way that obscured her face. She pushed a chair against the fridge and stepped up on it. "Some people get bank boxes, but they cost so much of money, and also I do not trust those bank workers. They all are Indian, they know what we put in the boxes. Jyoti in First Fidelity Bank wants my emerald set."

Prem was intrigued by Sayali's long slender hands and elegant forearm, her hair that cascaded to her waist, and her sensible approach to safeguarding her valuables. "Can I help?" he said.

Tiptoeing on the chair and trying to shove a small bundle into a cabinet, she said, "No, no, I don't think Jyoti will try anything."

"I meant—" Prem began, but trailed off when Sayali disappeared into the bathroom. When she came out, she had a towel over her head.

"Can I make some chai for you?" she said, walking back to the kitchen. She stuck her head in the oven and pulled out a slim red velvet box, which she then stowed in the freezer.

Prem guessed then what she was doing and his heart sank for her. She was hiding her face for some reason, maybe bad skin or some sort of scar or deformity. But what could be so bad? She was lovely, and he felt certain they would be good friends. He went to her in the kitchen and stood directly in front of her, then lifted the towel as though lifting a veil.

A sizable birthmark, reddish in tinge, covered most of one side of her face. Yet it was nothing at all. She had averted her eyes and he saw a tear escape from one of them. "Yes, with extra sugar," he said.

Sayali looked directly at him for the first time. "I am guessing you will be going now. Okay, bye, see you."

"No, no, no, you are trying to get out of making my chai. How could you do such a thing? I like it with a lot of milk."

She smiled widely and began scurrying around collecting the ingredients for the tea. Sayali seemed to Prem what a sister should be: warm and open with kind eyes, unlike his own sister, who was distant with bloodthirsty eyes. They sipped their chai and talked for a long time on the couch, and very quickly he learned the basic facts of her immigrant experience: she was sponsored by her sister and brother-in-law to come to America, she had made the journey by boat because it was her strong belief that humans were not meant to fly, she made a robust living as a tailor, altering nearly fifty pieces per week, more around Diwali. After some time, they switched to Johnnie Walker Black, and she told him she approved of sex before marriage.

"Um, I don't think, you know, I . . ." Prem stammered.

"Oh, no, I didn't mean with you," Sayali said. "I understand you prefer the company of men. I did not mean to make you uncomfortable."

"No, no, what? I don't—"

"It is all right. I know in our community, in this world, there are many, many people who do not accept lifestyles different from their own. They are intolerant and fearful and full of hate. I am not like that. You are safe here with me."

Prem was so moved by her words of love and tolerance that he forgot he did not actually prefer men. "Thank you, dear Sayali," he said, then suggested they go out for some pizza.

"I do not go outside," she said.

"What do you mean, you do not go outside?"

"I stay inside almost all of the time."

"You never go outside?"

"That is right."

Prem was astounded by the tragedy of the situation. He looked around her apartment—the landscape pictures, the Alaska coasters, the bird knickknacks, a painting of a tree he had not previously noticed—and realized the entire motivation for her unique decorating scheme was to bring the outside in. There was a red marker in a cup of pens and pencils on the coffee table. He pulled it out and proceeded to draw on his face. Sayali looked on in astonishment. When he was done, he had a large mark on his face similar to her own.

"Now people won't stare at you," he said, "they will stare at both of us and think this is a new kind of cool tattoo."

She threw her arms around him and kissed him all over his fake new birthmark. Then she went to the bathroom and got some earrings out of a bottle of shampoo, and they went out. For the first time, she ate pizza in the place it was actually made and was elated. She confessed she wanted to be a fashion designer and maybe someday open a boutique specializing in Indian bridal attire. Prem poured out the story of his own struggle to plan an Indian star stage show, which in theory would take place in March. He had recently found a show director who would be responsible for choreography, sequencing, music selection, special effects, and such, as well as a stage manager. But whom would they be directing, what would they be managing? He was visibly distressed by the fact that he had yet to book a single actor.

"I might have some connections," she said.

* * *

That fall, after the leaves had changed color and carpeted the ground with a fun, crunchy layer, Prem was set up with a woman who was described by her friend as "mature." They arranged to meet at a park, but when he got to the appointed bench, he saw only a young Indian

American woman, much too young to be the person he was told to look for. Mrinalini Das was forty-five and charming, with a worldly wit. They walked around the pond for hours, and she recounted for him how she had dedicated all of her energy and time to her education and career as a pharmacist, and by the time she was ready to get married, she had aged out of the marriage market. He spoke to her animatedly about her gifts and beauty, he made her laugh and twirled her around a tree and took her for a pedalboat ride, which was all the rage in Edison since the release of *Maine Pyar Kiya*'s love-song-in-a-pedalboat scene on Ooty Lake. By the end of the day when they returned to their original bench, he had convinced her that she was still youthful, full of life, and poised for a future of adventure and love. She was grateful, and as they watched the sunset she turned to look at him in the same way his mother used to look at him, with love in her eyes.

"I am sorry," she said, "but you are too young for me."

"It is my bad luck for being born so late," he said.

During the course of their day together, he had told her about his business endeavor and how he was happy to have booked a set designer and security firm for his upcoming show with no stars. When they finally said goodbye and she was walking away from him at the bench, she paused and turned to him one last time.

"I might have some connections," she said.

Winter came again, and this time, Prem was less appalled by it. He found comfort in the usual sight of women in saris and snow boots, with gold jewelry and puffy jackets, pushing through a blizzard, and children kicking the snow and jumping in it because they hadn't been in America long enough to know they were supposed to make balls and angels. The only drawback was that he received fewer invitations to meet lovely and lonely women—which he had quite come to depend on for companionship and distraction—because no one wanted to go outside. He turned again to the matrimonials, where he found an ad for a "compassionate" girl who was "uneducated but an excellent cook."

"So all of these horrible men keep calling my parents, looking for a wife-cum-servant," the girl explained. Anamika Painter was a tall, somewhat angry person with a very long ponytail. She had asked to meet him at the Ved Mandir in Milltown, for which he hitched a ride with Chotubhai Charlie Patel, who preferred that faraway temple for its abundant sunlight in the prayer room. In the basement cafeteria, they sipped piping hot chai from Styrofoam cups and learned about each other.

"Mummy and Papa insist I meet each one at least one time before saying no," Anamika continued. "All are the same, no respect for me, just want me for cooking and cleaning and having the babies."

"And how do you know I am not like them?" Prem said, genuinely interested in the answer.

Anamika furrowed her brow and looked him over carefully. "You seem soft."

Most days, she worked long hours as a manager at a Speedy Mart, a thankless job, she felt, but one at which she excelled. "A bunch of idiots, teenagers mostly, work with me there and don't know how to do anything. And now also I have to hear 'Thank you, come again!' hundred times in a day because of that useless Simpson show."

"Ya, that show is a real problem for us," Prem said.

"Terrible," Anamika said.

"Ridiculous," Prem said.

"Too too much," Anamika said.

"At least we are on American TV," Prem said. He cleared his throat and changed the subject. "Why did you want to meet in the mandir?"

"Oh, I am a part-time professional funeral mourner," Anamika said. "I have to mourn someone at three."

"I see. So, uh, your last name is Painter. Do you come from a painting family?"

"No, I don't know, maybe long time back."

"So you don't paint?"

"No," she said.

Prem was having a harder time than usual forging a connection with his date and began to think it was not worth the effort. In a last, desperate attempt to interest her in some conversation, he told her about his Indian stage show business and his mounting, terrifying fear that he would have no stars for his show of stars, which did not seem to interest her at all. He gave up on that approach and tried one last thing. "I like your ponytail," he said.

She responded to this with a look of confusion, but then her face relaxed. "Actually, I play the flute."

It turned out Anamika was a talented musician who had studied with some of the best flutists in India. But her training ended abruptly when her parents dragged her to America to build a better life. They were praying for her to marry a doctor but were concerned about her lack of a college education. Prem asked her a series of in-depth, extensive questions about her music, which, it seemed, no one had ever done before. She twirled her ponytail between her fingers while she talked. By the end, Prem had convinced her of her exceptional qualities and the special value of her musical education. Maybe she even could continue it in New Jersey, he said. He asked a passerby for paper and a pen and composed a new ad for her on the spot:

SEEKING match for extremely talented musician daughter, tall and slim with beautiful long ponytail. Strong and confident with excellent managerial skills. Ideal candidate would be professional with above-average cooking skills.

Moved beyond words, she folded the paper carefully and tucked it inside her shirt. She took Prem's hands and held them on the table between them. "I do not really want to get married," she said. "To a man, I mean. Not to a woman either. I mean, I don't know." Prem understood that she had some things to figure out. He assured her it was okay and squeezed her hands in his.

"I have to go mourn now," she said. Then, after a thoughtful pause, she said, "You know, I maybe have some connections that could help you."

Thus Prem's years as a philogynist began. He spent the better part of 1989 helping emotionally distraught women feel good about themselves and, in the process, felt better himself, less lonely and more useful. But Leena was always with him. He had been in America for just over three years and loved her for two years and eight months. It was unlikely, he knew, that she would suddenly break with her fiancé and run through a field of tulips into his arms, but he couldn't say for sure that she would not. He also knew he could never be in love with anyone else. His work would have to be his avenue to happiness.

But the show was supposed to go on in three months and he had no superstars. He had no show at all. The thought of this had recently begun to induce hyperventilation and visible shaking in Prem, and, one frigid January morning, a full-on panic attack. Beena found him on the kitchen floor hugging a sack of Royal Basmati, sweaty and dizzy and mumbling about actors. She put a blanket around him and convinced him to let go of the rice. She helped him to the couch and got a cold compress for his forehead. When his breathing slowed, she tried to talk to him. "You cannot continue like this," she said gently. "There are two months left. You still have time to cancel everything without losing too much of money."

"But Hemant," Prem said, as if out of a fever. "But my father."

"What does one thing have to do with the other?" Beena said.

"They will see I have failed."

"You have to stop this," Beena said.

"But Leena," he said, repeating it until she stopped trying to reason with him. He fell asleep and was in and out of consciousness all day, even missing an Exxon shift, all the while trying to understand how he had ended up in a situation in which he wanted so badly to succeed, to stand on his own feet, and its exact opposite, to do nothing, to hide from the world, at the same time. His conflicting desires left him paralyzed on Beena's couch for two more days. On the third day, Salman Khan's secretary called.

22

Salman required home-cooked chicken biryani; his secretary was adamant on this point. Despite his international fame, Salman was a simple guy and adhered to his simple ways. He maintained his superhuman physique by eating fresh foods and limiting greasy restaurant fare. Prem assured the representative that Salman would have the best home-cooked chicken biryani New Jersey had to offer, every day for lunch and dinner and even breakfast if he desired, to which they replied that Salman required egg whites in the mornings.

Prem promised to provide everything Salman could possibly want as long as he signed the contract and fulfilled his promise to rehearse and perform in the show. The secretary said they had a deal and Salman looked forward to participating and eating American biryani. Before ending the call, Prem wanted to know one last thing: What made the secretary finally return his call? It turned out the secretary had received a call earlier that week from an extremely persuasive, chatty Bengali lady in America to whom Salman owed a long-ago debt.

Next to come on board was Govinda, whose uncontrollable hips were sure to add a certain verve to the program, followed by Sunny Deol and Jackie Shroff, all of whom signed on as a result of their agents being persuaded by single Indian women living in New Jersey. It wasn't hard for Prem to deduce the identities of his mysterious benefactors, and he thanked those dear friends that very afternoon.

After the first four agreed, it was easy to get other artists to sign on. With four men lined up, Prem turned to recruiting female stars, beginning with lovable newcomer Juhi Chawla, up-and-coming starlets Pooja Bhatt and Sonam, and finally, the crowning glory of the entire show, Madhuri Dixit. To round things out, Prem brought on legendary singer Asha Bhosle and comic actor Kader Khan. The lineup was too good for Prem to trust it. In fact, every aspect of the show was coming together too perfectly. The director and choreographer in Bombay were on track to begin rehearsals by mid-February. Posters went up all over New Jersey and New York and full-page ads ran in *India Abroad*, thanks to a rag-tag team of part-time publicists who worked for free in exchange for a promise to meet the stars. Nathan Kothari used his skill at paperwork to arrange the work permits for the actors, also in exchange for a chance to meet them. A volunteer army of Indian Americans handled the event's myriad details—airline and hotel bookings, teleprompters, press interview scheduling, airport pickups—all free of charge, in the hopes of getting some autographs. Ticket sales soared.

"Stop eating my head," Beena scolded Prem, who kept asking her to verify that the chicken biryani would be made in time. They were at Pizza Movers, right next to Ashoka, which had just added to its offerings a thin-crust, hot-and-spicy vegetarian pizza with onions, chili peppers, and a secret sauce called the "Indo-Pak Pizza," trademark pending.

"Okay, ya, sorry," Prem said. "There are just too many details. How will everything work together? How will it all happen?"

"I do not understand," Beena said, sprinkling on some extra red pepper. "I thought it was going nicely, no?"

"Ya, but you know, so many things can go wrong." He hadn't been able to sleep the past few nights, staring up at his onions, turning over and over in his head the hundreds of things that still had to be done. It was true the whole operation was moving along shockingly smoothly, yet he was in a constant state of wanting to throw up. How could he trust a team of Indian actors, crew, and support staff to get their jobs done on time when they came from a land where the word for "tomorrow" was tragically an auto-antonym, the same as the word for "yesterday"? Where IST—Indian Standard Time—meant arriving at least an hour late to everything?

"Why do you worry when there is nothing yet to worry about?" Beena said. "Have some pizza. Do you know your show will be the first show like this in the world?"

"Like what?" Prem said, using a napkin to sop up oil from his slice.

"There have been classical programs, ghazal programs, Kathak and Bharatnatyam performances, Qawwali shows, but nothing filmi," she said, using an adjective that had lately come to describe everything about mainstream Hindi cinema as well as anything marked by exuberance and rampant melodrama.

"That is just more pressure! If I mess it up, if it is a horrible disaster, I will have to jump from the King's Court roof."

"Stop your filmi dialogue before I hit you with my rolling pin," Beena said.

They ate in silence for a while, partly because of the heaviness of what Prem was feeling and partly because their mouths were on fire. Joseph Kisch, the owner of the pizzeria, had consulted with local Indian American business owners to craft his fiery recipe. It proved lucrative, bringing in a steady stream of Indian and Pakistani customers daily, but alienated some white customers who were unhappy with his coziness with his immigrant neighbors.

"Joe!" Beena called when she spotted him behind the counter. "Bring your rolling pin!" she added as she waved him over.

"Beena, my darling," Joseph said, embracing her and kissing her on both cheeks.

"Oh, Joe, superb, just superb," Beena said in a squeaky voice Prem hadn't heard before. He wasn't sure what was going on, so he excused himself and waited outside. A light snow had dusted the parked cars with white. Across the street, an abandoned bar had boarded up its windows and an auto repair shop was in a state of disrepair. But the rest of that corner of Oak Tree Road hummed with activity. Two jewelry stores, Nina and Sona, were gearing up to open, along with a casual sort of street-food eatery named Chowpatty, after the beach, to complement the more traditional Ashoka. Up the road, just before King's Court, an elegant new restaurant named Moghul had relocated from New York, giving the higher-end doctor, lawyer, and business crowd a place to kick back and enjoy their tikka masala. Prem wasn't sure why, but the thought of all those people working so hard to start their businesses made him sad.

Prem had not been entirely honest with Beena about the reasons for his hugging-the-rice-sack panic attack. Even in his feverish haze, he'd summoned the wherewithal to know he could not let her or anyone know he had entered into a hasty, misguided verbal contract with a murderous Indian gangster.

A few weeks earlier, he had started to question the viability of his plan to finance the show by relying on deep-pocketed sponsors. How could he convince Macy's, Roy Rogers, and Midlantic Bank of Edison to voluntarily pour money into a show with no stars, based on movies they knew nothing about? He began to consider alternate sources of investment: his father (not an option), his friends (they had no money), taking on additional hours at Exxon (physically impossible), selling his belongings (he had none). Then, while he was working the early shift one bleak winter afternoon, huddled in the store with too many other guys, the Tiger Mart logo caught his eye. The image rolled around in his mind until it took him back to the miserable final days of his ill-fated movie venture, when Tiger Nayak's thugs demanded money from him, threatened to hurt his heroine, and ended up killing a cat. But the thing they had really wanted all along was to make a simple show-business investment.

At first, Prem had wanted to approach an American gangster. He thought a local thug might be more accessible and the underlings might be more polished and perhaps would kill fewer domestic animals. But it occurred to him that maybe some distance between him and the gangsters would be more prudent. Also, he didn't know how to contact any American gangsters. So it would have to be T-Company. He realized he had always communicated in person or via menacing letter with the gang members, never on the phone, yet he felt certain that one of his Bombay contacts would be able to provide him with contact information. In the end, it was Brijesh, the crooked-teeth hero who couldn't memorize anything, who gave him the phone number he needed.

Brijesh had retired from acting and worked full time for T-Company, which paid very well and had a surprisingly comprehensive dental plan. "Just don't mention my name," Brijesh said. "Unless they like what you are saying. Then, please, could you mention my name?"

In the first of several surreptitious early morning calls, using a prepaid phone card at a payphone outside of Krauszer's, Prem was pleasantly surprised by the mafia family's thoughtfully organized automated phone system. After just two quick transfers, he found himself speaking with T-Company's official spokesman, a civilized and proper fellow with a fine Indian boarding-school accent.

"Sir, good evening, or should I say good morning, given your current location."

Prem was taken aback by the spokesman's excellent manners. "Ya, good morning, good evening, good morning, I mean," he said. "I am Prem Kumar."

"Sir, my name is Anthony Braganza. How may I help you today?"

"Well, you see, I had some, uh, relations with Tiger Nayak some time back, and I would like to discuss, uh, working with them again on a different, uh, project in show business."

"Oh, you are acquainted with our esteemed leader. Very good, very good. Just hold, please."

Less than a minute later, Prem was speaking with the chief investment officer, a position he had not imagined existed in such an organization. Mr. Shailesh Kamath was even more polite than the spokesman.

"I understand you have a business proposition for T-Company," Mr. Kamath said.

"Sir, yes, sir," Prem said, feeling a military tone was called for.

"A quick review of our records indicates that you were a reliable business partner, trustworthy and delivering outstanding results."

"It does?"

"Furthermore, Tiger Nayak feels that it would be in our organization's interest to do business with you again."

"Really?"

"Now, tell me about your proposal."

Prem laid out the particulars of his Superstar Entertainment plan, beginning with the excellent venue and ending with the lack of stars. "Please hold," Mr. Kamath said. Prem watched the cars lining up at the traffic light on Oak Tree, the morning rush to get to decent and respectable jobs on time. He wondered what they ate for lunch and whether or not they liked their coworkers and what time they would go home. Why couldn't he be more like them, instead of on hold with a network of criminals? When Mr. Kamath returned, it was with the news Prem had been hoping for. "Tiger Nayak would like to make a sizable investment," he said.

Prem tried to maintain his composure as they hashed out the numbers and terms of the agreement. The rupees-crore-to-hundreds-of-thousands-of-dollars-conversion conversation was at times difficult to follow, but all around exhilarating. And although icicles had formed on his eyebrows and he couldn't feel his toes, he was the happiest he had been since losing Leena.

"Very good then, the cash will be delivered to you on Tuesday evening by our man in America," Mr. Kamath said.

"Perfect, hundred percent, wait, what?" Prem said.

"This Tuesday, the cash will be delivered. Our man's name is Wristwatch and he will identify himself by exposing the T-Co tattoo on his neck."

"Wristwatch."

"He is exceptionally punctual."

"So Wristwatch with the neck tattoo will be coming. Does he have to?"

"Do not be alarmed, he is quite professional."

"Where even will I put so much cash?"

"The safe in your offices should be adequate, so long as no one knows you are in possession of such a large amount."

"The safe. In my offices," Prem repeated. "Can you just wire the money to my account like a normal investor?"

"Tiger Nayak is no ordinary investor," Mr. Kamath said, sounding agitated. "Now, would you like to move forward? Tiger Nayak will be very upset if you back out now."

Prem swallowed hard. "Do you always refer to your boss by the full name?"

"Yes."

"Good to know. Please tell Tiger Nayak that we have a deal," Prem said, hardly believing what he was saying. "Oh, and Brijesh! Uh, he said to mention his name."

"Very good, sir, I'll make a note to issue him a referral fee," Mr. Kamath replied.

As Prem began the long walk home, he was still considerably high from his long-awaited victory. How bad could it be? he asked himself. With a spokesperson, investment arm, and even a referral-rewards program, T-Company appeared quite professional, actually. But as he pushed forward against an arctic wind and thought about what had just transpired, the shine of being indebted to a ruthless criminal organiza- tion began to wear off. What would happen if he couldn't keep his end of the deal? How could he have been so shortsighted? Maybe he should have requested a formal written contract, one that specified no murder- ing. By the time he reached King's Court, a full-on panic had set in.

For the next two days, Prem had an extreme reaction to loud noises. If Iqbal dropped a frying pan, or Lucky closed the fridge too hard, or any- time he mistook anything for a pounding at the door, Prem jumped up, spilling tea, toppling canned goods, bumping into Amarleen, who was always near enough to be bumped into. When Tuesday evening finally arrived, he was bruised in several places and had burned himself twice.

He began hovering around the door in the late afternoon, leaving his post only to use the bathroom. It was during one of these breaks that the knock came, and disastrously, Iqbal answered. A very tall man, dwarfing even Iqbal, with a thick, tattooed neck and broad chest stood before him. He had on a tidy black suit and unnecessary black sun- glasses and, though no longer a young man, curiously had no laugh lines to speak of.

"Mr. Prem Kumar."

"No," Iqbal answered. He was still trying to comprehend the man's height; he had never had to look up at anyone before.

"Is Mr. Prem Kumar present?" the stranger asked, peering into the apartment. The assortment of men in the room stared shamelessly at him with their jaws dropped.

Amarleen stepped in to offer a modicum of hospitality. "Let the poor giant come inside at least," she said, shoving her husband out of the way. "Come in, Prem is just coming."

The giant man nodded at Amarleen and entered. He had with him an orange suitcase which he continued to carry as he began to pace the room, methodically examining the space as if taking inventory. The others continued to gawk until at last Deepak said, "What kind of milk did your mother feed you?" and Gopal said, "Why is your neck like that?" to which Wristwatch responded with a grunt.

"No towel in the bathroom," Prem said, emerging with dripping hands. He stopped short at the sight of the henchman, whose appearance— so serious, so enormous—was even more distressing than he'd imagined.

Wristwatch looked Prem up and down, then gave the room one more scan. "Interesting," he said.

Prem came forward and offered his hand, which Wristwatch shook. Prem was alarmed at the suitcase's similarity to one he'd once purchased. "He's, you know, my buddy, college roommate, uh, my, uh, friend," he stammered. "Let's talk in the hall," he said to the giant, leading him toward the door.

As he had done and would do again many times through the course of his quest to make something of himself, Prem put forth the outward appearance of confidence while inwardly hating himself for making yet another poor decision. The reproachful faces of those who mattered to him—his father, Leena, Hemant, the murdered cat—were watching him, he felt, judging and chastising him out the door. Wristwatch, with his sinister suitcase in tow, followed him out and pulled the door shut.

"So . . . how are you?" Prem began.

Wristwatch did not answer. Prem guessed he was not amused,

though it was difficult for him to gauge the man's frame of mind as he still wore his sunglasses.

"Wristwatch, is it?" Prem said.

There was no visible reaction from the man at all; Prem thought for a moment he'd fallen asleep. He was on his toes trying to look into the glasses for some sign of movement when Wristwatch finally spoke. "You are the one Tiger Nayak has chosen to oversee T-Company's North American operations."

"I am?" Prem said. "No, you see, it is just an investment." He jabbered on about Superstar Entertainment and actors and choreography and the challenges associated with indoor pyrotechnics until Wristwatch silenced him with a raised palm.

"Just stop."

"Sorry."

Wristwatch gave Prem another once-over. "I do not have confidence that you will do a good job."

With that, Wristwatch relinquished the suitcase to him and turned and walked away. Prem focused on getting his knees to stop shaking. He hoped against reason that he'd never again have to come in contact with that man, who seemed less like a human and more like a robot programmed to terrify with his size, condescension, and punctuality. Prem composed himself and headed over to Beena's to stash the suitcase there. He told her and all the tenants of 3D that the suitcase was a gift from his old friend who had become a suitcase salesman, which was believed by exactly zero people.

23

The stars arrived ten days before the show, and Prem actually found a moment of enjoyment in it. He met them at their hotel in New Brunswick, which was within walking distance of the theater in an almost charming part of that college town, with an attractive sort of brick mosaic border on parts of the sidewalk there. He brought Beena, who had chicken biryani with her, and though they were supposed to meet in Event Room B, the party was already underway at the lobby bar, where it appeared Govinda was trying to do a split on the countertop.

"The current economic climate in India must change," Juhi Chawla said to Pooja Bhatt while sipping her soda. "Really, if we do not put an end to this License Raj, India will be left behind."

Pooja seemed to agree entirely, shaking her head side to side as well as up and down. "We need more than a few reforms, we need a complete liberalization of the system."

Jackie Shroff poured a shot down Govinda's throat and patted him on the back. "Keep trying, you can do it," he urged, leaving the star mid-split, still several inches away from both thighs making contact with the bar top. On the other side, Salman and Sunny were locked in a tender yet robust embrace, which, if abandoned, might cause one or both of them to collapse to the floor, while Madhuri and Sonam were discussing nuclear-arms control. Comedian Kader Khan was puking in veteran singer Asha Bhosle's purse while she rubbed his back and motioned for Juhi to bring water.

Prem stood at the threshold with Beena, taking in the impossible scene. Everyone was so beautiful, as if they had walked right off the screen. Friends had warned him that the celebrities would seem less lustrous in person, like ordinary, albeit familiar-looking people, but this was false. They were glowing, burning brightly like the stars they were, and Prem had to shield his eyes from the filmi glare.

Beena gave him a little shove, and he lurched into the room and into Jackie Shroff.

"So sorry, yaar, didn't see you there," Jackie said.

"No, no," Beena blurted out, "he bumped into you!"

"Sorry, man," Prem said, "didn't mean to, um—"

"Here, have this shot." Jackie shoved a little glass into his hand. "At least if you are drunk, you have an excuse!"

Beena laughed and laughed at this as if she were already drunk and threw herself at his chest, to which Jackie responded by offering her a shot too. For the rest of that night, he seemed to have an endless supply of shots hidden somewhere in his clothes, ready to offer one to anyone in his path, and it turned out Prem was the one most often in his path. Clamorous excess and hearty claps on the back were punctuated by moments of solemn confession, Prem telling Jackie of his lost love and her inexplicably long engagement and Jackie telling Prem about his prostate.

Later in the night, he was accosted by Madhuri and Juhi, who seemed to know everything about his romantic life and asked what he thought were overly intrusive questions. "You mean you followed and watched her without her knowing?" and "How many times did you do this?" and "What do you mean 'all the time?'" but then he remembered he'd shared this information earlier with Sunny Deol, which was the same as sharing it with All India Radio, so Prem could only blame himself.

Prem would not recall everything from that night, but enough to know that he'd had a rollicking good time. There was the moment when Jackie called to Salman, "Salu Bhai! Your biryani has come!" and the moment when Govinda finally, inevitably, split his pants. He remembered the excitement that unfolded when he introduced himself as the organizer of the show and these famous, fabulous people switching to calling him "sir" and "Mr. Kumarji, sir." Salman and Sunny debated with him the recent emergence of a more muscular look among Indian actors and whether they should start lifting weights; even Asha Bhosle, simple and demure in a red sari and bindi, looked like she had been hitting the gym. Then Jackie Shroff and Sunny Deol tried to bench press her. Salman devoured his biryani and proclaimed that Beena would hereby be known as "Biryani Auntie." Madhuri and Juhi switched to drinking cosmos and discussed tensions in Kashmir while Sonam and Pooja tried to fend off their male counterparts without offending. The women were warm, kind, smart, and put-together in an unexpected way, and the men were like a bunch of hooligan children on a school bus with no parental supervision. Yet, they also were harmless, nice enough guys who maybe just drank a little too much. At some point late in the night, Salman and Sunny lifted Prem up onto their shoulders and everyone chanted his name. It was all so magical—the stars, the stories, the contest to see who could bench-press Asha Bhosle— and in the morning, after throwing up, Prem couldn't tell what had been real and what had been just a dream.

Beena and he woke up in Salman Khan's hotel room without Salman Khan. It was unclear whether the actor had even slept there that night; Beena was in one bed and Prem in the other, and neither remembered sleeping next to Salman. "Do you think he is still in the bar?" Beena asked, after she finished throwing up too.

"The bar must be closed," Prem replied. "Do you think he maybe got up early, had a shower, got ready, and went to the rehearsal?

"I think he is in Sonam's room."

They freshened up as best they could and headed downstairs. The lobby was quiet, with just a receptionist and doorman and no stray Indian celebrities. A pit formed in Prem's stomach. He was off to a terrible, unprofessional start. None of the men must have made it to the rehearsal. Even some of the ladies must not have gone as they were up so late. He'd have to ask them not to go to the bar for the rest of the week, but how could he do that? Maybe he could ask the hotel to close the bar. But how could he do that? They stopped off at the bar to see if any staff was around and to apologize for the previous night's debauchery.

The manager couldn't understand what there was to apologize about. "But I heard it was a great night! Nothing broken, nice, slightly rowdy people, tremendous tippers. Do you know they paid extra for the drinks and then left huge tips on top of the incorrect prices? I mean, even the vomit was contained nicely within an old lady's purse." Prem looked at Beena, who shrugged. "You tell them to come back tonight, okay?"

"Uh, okay," Prem answered.

Next, they went to the theater. Prem assumed the director and crew would be waiting, wondering where the performers were. It would be humiliating to stand before them and endure their judging looks. For the second time in his life, he felt betrayed by the thing he loved most, Hindi movies—or rather, the people who acted in them. He crossed the street with Beena and entered the theater, still in thrall to his own wretchedness. In the lobby, they heard music coming from within. "Tirchi Topiwale," the peppy and invigorating Gloria Estefan knockoff from *Tridev*, was on full blast, and when Prem threw open the doors, he found Salman and Sonam on stage dancing in bouncy, glorious synchrony.

Miraculously, all of the artists—Madhuri, Juhi, Jackie, even Kader Khan—had arrived on time, ready to rehearse the dances they had learned back in Bombay. Prem rushed down the aisle to the stage, and someone stopped the music. "You are all here?" Prem said.

"Sir, good morning! How you feeling?" Salman said.

"Hi, sir! Difficult night?" Sonam said.

"Kumarji, sir, is your back feeling better?" Juhi called from the wings.

Prem did not understand what she was asking.

"Because, sir," Juhi said, "you tried to lift up Asha Bhosle last night."

Prem tried to hide his embarrassment by assuming an authoritative tone: "Fine, fine, I'm great. Carry on, good work, everyone," he said.

Beena and he sat back to watch the rehearsal, Beena shaking and shimmying in the front row and Prem tense and unsettled by her side. The next number the group practiced was a multi-starrer featuring nearly all of the actors dancing to an evergreen song from the sixties. It was flawless. Everyone moved perfectly in step, forgetting nothing, laughing and enjoying while looking unreasonably attractive. How could it be that everything was going so well? The choreographer, Faiza, was disturbingly relaxed, crouched in a front corner of the stage, picking her teeth with a toothpick, occasionally waving it to direct the performers though it was not needed. Prem tried to let go and enjoy the show—all these stars, dancing to his favorite songs, right before him, because of him—but he couldn't help but wait for the thing that would go wrong.

The director of the production, Jagan Bose, was a theater man long past his prime, accomplished and revered in certain entertainment circles, who had a stilted manner of speaking and a wild shock of smoky gray hair inexplicably streaked with orange bursting forth from beneath a floppy beret. Horn-rimmed glasses and the occasional pipe gave him a professorial air consistent with his view of himself as a doyen of his craft. As he coached the Bollywood stars, he brandished his wrinkled, bony hand like a conductor's baton, as though he were directing Laurence Olivier in *King Lear*, and the actors, flattered to be taken seriously by someone so serious, did as he said.

That day, Jagan Bose was supervising the installation of a backdrop of one hundred bulbs that would shine on and off strategically during the show. At the rehearsal, when the director yelled, "Damnation!" Prem, assuming the worst was happening and the one-hundred-bulb backdrop was the beginning of the end, rushed up onstage to the director's side.

"What happened? What's wrong? Did the electrician mess up the wiring? Is the installation going to catch on fire?"

"No, no, nothing of the sort," Jagan said.

"Then what?" Prem said.

"I stepped on a nail," Jagan said. Feeling that Prem did not adequately grasp the gravity of this news, he added, "It hurt."

Prem experienced a strange sense of disappointment; he had actually wanted it to be something worse so he could stop worrying about something terrible happening. He hoped this nail issue was more serious than he realized. "Should I call an ambulance? Your foot could get infected and they might have to cut it off or you could die," he said in a hopeful sort of tone that Jagan found disconcerting.

"Just a Band-Aid will be fine."

Prem sat back down with Beena to watch the rest of the rehearsal, which was impeccable. But he was unnerved by an unshakable feeling that he was forgetting something of vital importance.

"What is wrong with your head?" Beena said. "The show is perfect and there still are few days."

"It is sold out," Prem said.

"Is that not good?" Beena said.

"Everyone is expecting so much," Prem said.

"The show is fantastic, first-class!" Beena said.

"Many things can still go wrong, Prem said.

"Uf! Let's go," Beena said, deflated by frustration. "I have to make biryani for Salman."

The week of rehearsals continued without incident, but Prem's anxiety only increased. The stars continued to party at night and report on time for work the next morning. It should have been one of the most fun weeks of his life, but instead, Prem chewed off all of his fingernails.

A full dress rehearsal was scheduled for late Friday afternoon. The show's official car service dropped Prem off in front of the theater, where the sidewalk was wet from melted snow dripping off the eaves. Though it was still cold, the setting sun felt warmer and brighter than it had in months. Looking up at the marquee, which had been updated to read "Superstar Entertainment Presents: A Night of Indian Superstars," Prem experienced a moment of calm, unfamiliar and welcome, before going in.

He had arrived early, before the actors and most of the crew, as the director wanted to go over a few things beforehand. It was completely quiet and empty inside. Prem took a seat in the front row and waited. The backdrop installation of bulbs seemed to be in place, but he still had doubts as to whether the lights would shine at the appropriate times. There was a shuffling sound backstage followed by a loud jolt. The backdrop turned on, flooding the theater with a radiant glow, its brilliance lifting Prem up out of his seat. He let his head fall back and his eyes close, enjoying the feeling of being bathed in the light of a hundred incandescent bulbs. Prem opened his eyes and thought for the first time ever about anything he had ever done: It might be good.

On Saturday night, a long line of ticketless fans stood outside the
theater. A security officer had informed them the show was sold out,
yet they refused to leave. What if someone decided to sell their ticket
or didn't show up? What if Madhuri, running late, arrived right before
their eyes? Two teenage girls began to cry. Ticket holders streamed past
and joined the gridlocked horde in the lobby. The house lights flashed
on and off, and they found their seats in the auditorium, which was
packed and crackling with energy. The show began on time with a short
word from its sponsors. Two men from Prudential in borrowed Indian
clothes spent three minutes explicating the benefits of purchasing life
insurance, both term and whole life, then shuffled offstage to a smat-
tering of applause. The lights dimmed and the crowd hummed with
anticipation. Suddenly, a booming voice announced the beginning of
the program: Juhi Chawla performing "Disco Dandia." Harbhajan Gill,
who had driven his entire angry family down in his taxi for Juhi Chawla
and Juhi Chawla alone, couldn't contain his ardor. When the number
came to a close, he stood up and inserted his thumb and forefinger
in his mouth and whistled repeatedly, stomped his feet, and clapped
vigorously. Shanta Bhatt preferred the second song, the more pensive
"Mere Rang Mein Rangne Wali," which Salman Khan performed taste-
fully with Sonam, who wore a tight-fitting sequined outfit that Deepak,
Lucky, Iqbal, and Anamika Painter all appreciated immensely. When the
first three-couple song began, the entire audience leaped to their feet
and joined in the dancing. The backdrop lights started flashing strategically and confetti rained down, and Mr. Khosla, the owner of the Exxon,
wondered if perhaps he was paying his employee too much. While the
stars changed into their flashy costumes for the final number before
intermission, the comic actor Kader Khan took the stage to entertain
the crowd and had Nalini Sen and Gitanjali Vora rolling in the aisles.

The lobby was jam-packed during intermission, with hundreds

of people vying for a limited number of samosas provided by Beena Joshi Catering. Charlie Patel, who had helped Beena bring the samosas from King's Court in his Honda Accord, elbowed Raghava Sai Shankara Subramanya, who in turn shoved Uttam Jindal, whose hairpiece shifted to an inelegant position.

Once all had returned to their seats, the fog machine came on and, as if out of a cloud, Jackie Shroff and Pooja Bhatt appeared and dazzled everyone with their sultry dance moves, which made a few of the older women—Urmila Sahu, Rachna Bajaj, Priti Sinha—uncomfortable because they liked it so much. Next was a ladies' performance, with all four leading ladies and a bevy of competent sideys shimmying and swiveling, causing a tiff between Nathan Kothari and his wife, Pratima "Pam" Kothari, who felt her husband was applauding a little too enthusiastically. All of this raciness was nicely balanced by a vocal interlude from Asha Bosle, graceful and modest with flowers in her hair, who sang three of her evergreen songs, calming everyone down except Kailash Mistry, who felt he should be up there singing with her. The superstar men performed the song "Papa Kehte Hain" and brought down the house with their energy and passionate pelvic thrusts, calling to mind for Dave Reddy the George Michael concert, which he inwardly conceded was not as fun as this one. By the penultimate *Tridev* multistarrer number, Falguni, Snigdha, Varsha in Row K, Suchitra in Row W, and Sayali in Q were all in pain from wearing heels, which they wore not realizing that they would be on their feet the entire time. They all sat down at precisely the same moment, but popped back up when the bright-eyed and stunningly beautiful Madhuri Dixit came out and offered the audience a "namaskar." Every person in the theater that night knew what her namaskar meant: "Ek Do Teen" was next and the grand finale would be everything a grand finale should be, which it was.

Prem had arranged an afterparty for the show but did not attend it. He remained in the theater long after it emptied out, the set was cleared, and the crew was gone. He paced the stage for a while, replaying the show in his mind. It had been perfect. Nothing had gone awry and he had not failed in any way. He sat at the edge of the platform, his legs dangling down, and looked out at the empty seats. In a moment of utter happiness, a golden, aching instant of bliss, he realized he had made money. Not nearly enough yet, he thought, and some of it earmarked for an organized crime syndicate—but it was a start.

He was the first one back to the apartment that night, and he collapsed onto his mattress without changing his clothes. Before falling into the deepest sleep he had had in months, he rooted around in his bag, past his Amitabh Bachchan dollar and his backup tongue scrapers, pulled out his ledger, and wrote:

41. Did you like the show? It was for you.

24

Leena's favorite part of the show was when it was over. Mikesh and she had sat in the front row thanks to Varsha, who would not name the completely obvious source of her miraculously free VIP seats. Leena found the show impressive, dazzling. But while she enjoyed seeing the stars dancing, gyrating, and pretending to sing, it was hard for her not to wonder if Prem had put in all this effort just to prove something to her and her father, and the thought of this bothered her. All the old outrage and injustice came rushing back to the surface. Plus, she was bitter that Prem got to meet his favorite, Juhi Chawla.

Hemant had also been in the audience that night, in front-row-center balcony seats that his dear friend Sanjay Sapra had acquired. The show held little interest for him; he was not much of a Hindi movie fan and his mind was preoccupied by the terrible news of a new Indian grocery store opening up on Oak Tree Road, just a little ways down from his. As if one were not enough. The new store was twice as big, with more aisles, more fridges, and three separate checkout lanes, but Hemant doubted this was the experience customers were looking for. They wanted personal attention, the feeling of coming home to India. What they didn't want was unlimited bitter gourd and economy-size cans of ghee. There was nothing to worry about really, he told himself. Besides, Hriyan was still thriving, his leaves strong, green, and crisscrossing the

ceiling, assuring him that everything would be fine. Halfway through
the show, when the fog machine kicked in, it struck Hemant that the
production values of this program were not bad at all. In fact, the whole
thing was quite a feat. It occurred to him then that Prem Kumar, that
lousy gas-station attendant who had tried to steal his daughter, might
still be trying to make the million and one dollars. Why would he do
this? Didn't he hear of her engagement to a dashing endocrinology student? What if he made the money and came after Leena again? Hemant
wasn't sure how he felt about this fresh, unforeseen possibility.

The rest of the community, however, was thrilled. The morning after
the show, Prem awoke, in his apartment full of roommates, a hero.

"Petrol! A way to go!" Iqbal said.

"Rocking time," Lucky said.

"I did not think you could do it, yaar," Mohan said.

"Ya, I also did not think so!" Deepak said, using his sleeve to wipe
crumbs from his chin. "I was thinking it will be a total flop!"

Amarleen balked. "Have some respect! Prem has turned out to be the
least useless of all of you," she said, then deposited herself next to Prem
on his mattress. "Now, tell me about Sunny Deol's muscles."

"Uh, they were very big," Prem said. Ordinarily, he shied away from
too much attention, but today and for the rest of that week, he relished
the much-needed boost to his reputation. People actually applauded
when he walked around King's Court. He was no longer just the awkward
Pumpwalla; now he was someone who knew the stars and organized a
first-class show. They wanted to know what Salman Khan and Madhuri
Dixit were like and who was coming for the next one. Suddenly, uncles
wanted to talk business with him or, rather, give him unsolicited and
unhelpful advice, such as "You should get more stars to come," and "Next
time, try adding some animals."

Midweek, he received a note from his chief backer, written neatly on the peel of an unopened banana and delivered mysteriously; he found it sitting atop a pile of pears and apples in the apartment's fruit bowl. "Tiger Nayak congratulates you on a fine show," the banana read. Prem chose not to think about how this was achieved or how Wristwatch knew he was the only one there who ate bananas and was the first to approach the bowl every morning. Instead, he focused on the surprising patience and magnanimity of his Bombay underworld financier who understood the logic of waiting for a big payout.

Financially, there was also still the goal of the million and one dollars, which Prem had decided he would keep to prove to himself—and perhaps also to Hemant, a man he had developed a hatred for but whose approval he still craved—that he was not the loser they all thought he was. He was already thinking about the next show, which he hoped would be early the following year. He would soon begin scouting locations and contacting vendors. He was in an atypically happy moment in his life, proud of himself for the first time. He even thought of calling his father to share the news of his success. But in the end, he decided against it; his achievement was still too minor to make up for the hurt he had caused him. He would just forge ahead, trying not to think about his family in India, or about Leena, who had sat next to her doctor fiancée at the show.

* * *

To make the time pass more easily during those next few years of hard work and loneliness, he spent an increasing amount of time with his unattached lady friends watching every new Hindi movie, good or lousy, that found its way to America, thus finding some everyday enjoyment for himself.

It was in Sayali's apartment that he viewed *Dil* fifteen times on fifteen consecutive evenings, until finally she declared it was time to move on. They moved on to another Aamir Khan blockbuster, *Dil Hai Ke Manta Nahin*, which they watched just seven times because, while it was quite good, it was no *Dil*. Nineteen ninety-one brought the movie *Hum* and Amitabh's entirely respectable comeback, which Prem relished at Suchitra's place along with her mother, who made some wonderfully spicy bhel. The other landmark movie of that year was *Lamhe*, which, though it did poorly at the Indian box office, enchanted Prem when he saw it one afternoon with Anamika. Sridevi mesmerized in her double role as mother and daughter, Pallavi and Pooja, and the songs were top-of-the-line, he thought. The next day, Anamika purchased the movie soundtrack for Prem, who was touched by the gesture and delighted to own his first CD, though he had nothing on which to play it.

It should have been a peaceful time—an intermission or interval, a time to rest and eat samosas until the next part of the story began—but in real, unscripted life, at the end of May, on the third night of an Anil Kapoor marathon, Lucky heard something outside. "Hey guys, did you hear that?" he said. Apartment 3D was awake much later than usual, finishing up *Kishen Kanhaiya*, a double-role, twins-separated-at-birth movie whose conclusion they could not go to sleep without seeing.

"I can tell you what I did not hear," Mohan said. "The last dialogue, because of you talking." They continued to watch the climactic fight scene, in which the long-lost brothers reunite and beat up the bad guys. After two solid minutes of top-notch movie bloodshed, there was a violent smashing sound outside, the high-pitched crackle of breaking glass. Prem pressed pause. From the window they saw five cars, some of them high-end, circling the parking lot. One car stopped in front of Building 3 and four beefy young men emerged. One was holding a baseball bat and another held a broken beer bottle. A third screamed, "Dots die!"

"Finally," Deepak said, polishing off the end of a cheeseburger. "I was thinking maybe we in King's Court were not good enough for getting harassed."

They had all heard the stories about Indian Americans being terrorized lately, windows broken, dead animals laid at doorsteps. When an Oak Tree travel agency was vandalized, the police's response was to suggest calling the insurance company. "If they are so jealous of the success of the Indians," Lucky had said, "maybe they should try being successful themselves. We saved half of New Jersey from rotting."

"*You* did not save anything," Mohan said.

Lucky sulked. "Fine, I didn't. But some other Indians did." The following week, the Lost Boys, as the gang called themselves, beat a twenty-year-old Indian boy with baseball bats, sticks, and rocks behind a convenience store, surrounding him and repeatedly striking his head, leaving a segment of New Jersey terrified and panicked.

Amarleen locked the door. "Prem, protect me, I am feeling so scared," she said, pressing herself against him at the window.

"Woman, do you not see me standing here?" Iqbal said.

Prem tugged the window shades down, but a few of the roommates continued to peek out from the sides. Outside the gang members were yelling, at times incoherently, calling on all Dotheads to come out of their homes so they could be killed. One of them, a short, dark-haired man with an incongruously thick neck, called to a man in front of another car at the far end of the property. "Yo, you didn't say anything about killing anyone. Maybe we just beat them up a little?"

"Donny's right," a guy from a third car yelled, "maybe we should just beat them until they're unconscious."

"I'm tired. Can we just tie some of them up and spit on them?"

"I don't think we have any rope!"

"Really?" Mohan said inside. "These are the duffers everyone is worried about?"

Unexpectedly, from one building over, Snigdha and Falguni hurled some filthy words from the window while one flight up Nathan Kothari lobbed a handful of cricket balls out at the young men and threatened to call the police. Suddenly, the gang members jumped in their cars and drove off. The tenants of King's Court pulled their curtains and returned to what they were doing, only a few of them noticing Beena Joshi standing in the grass in her nightgown pointing a gun.

It was all on the Channel 7 News the next evening, to which most of King's Court tuned in hoping to catch a glimpse of themselves. Paul Goldenberg, head of the state attorney general's Office of Bias Crime and Community Relations, said that fifteen of the Lost Boys' members, including an auxiliary police officer, had been arrested on various charges. When Goldenberg had asked them for a motive, they said they did it for "a thrill." The segment ended on a note of optimism, however, with an interview with "prominent community organizer" Hemant Engineer: "Isolated incidents happen," he said, "but this is still the best country to live in."

As if in defiance of the attackers, the Swaminarayan organization presented the Cultural Festival of India in Edison over four weeks that summer. Well over one million Americans, Indian and non, attended the events on the campus of Middlesex County College, where they encountered folk dances, lectures, food stands, cultural exhibits, puppet shows, daily parades, four full-size temples, and five enormous archway displays; a fifty-seven-foot-high Five Pinnacled Monument featuring three domes and twenty-two pillars topped by dancing statuettes; a five-story-tall Four-Faced Monument depicting the four faces of Brahma; an assortment of other equally colossal monuments; and a recreation of an Indian village. The diaspora put its best, most nostalgic foot forward, exhibiting a dazzling spectacle of its romanticized homeland. Prem attended three times, with three different women, each time hoping to see Leena.

The first visit, he went with Anamika, who was unimpressed. "Why do I need to see this diorama about being vegetarian? I can see that in my kitchen," she said. The next time, he took Suchitra, who was troubled by the wedding ceremonies being performed live on Saturdays and Sundays from noon to five. "Why would anyone have a wedding like this? Are they crazy?" she wondered aloud. "Anyway, it is thirty-one degrees today. Let's go back." The third time, he went with a sixty-plus-year-old widow seeking a travel companion, Usha, whose ad he answered in *India Abroad*. Though she was older than the others and had a braying laugh, she was also much more lighthearted and fun. She asked him to take a picture of her with a thirty-two-foot-tall replica of the Statue of Liberty rather than one of the Indian displays. "Why would relatives in India want to see me standing next to a giant Natraj?" she explained.

After the excitement of the festival and the horror of the racist gang wore off, Prem returned to movies, along with his ongoing work for Superstar Entertainment and Exxon, as his primary pastime. His life fell into a gentle rhythm that went on for years, and in this time of work and heartache, he was grateful for the movies that sustained him. He welcomed, in 1992, the eminently watchable *Beta* and *Jo Jeeta Wohi Sikandar* and the offbeat *Roja*, which marked the mainstream debut of composer A. R. Rahman and his haunting soundtracks. Nineteen ninety-three was significant filmically for two reasons: Madhuri Dixit created an uproar with her dance to the song "Choli Ke Peeche Kya Hai" ("What is Behind the Sari Blouse"), which for several solid months played on an endless loop in apartment 3D; and Shah Rukh Khan burst onto the scene in *Baazigar* and *Darr* and changed the face of Indian cinema forever. Shah Rukh, a.k.a. King Khan and SRK, named one of the fifty most powerful people in the world by *Newsweek*, one of the wealthiest people in the world by *Forbes*, and the world's biggest movie star by the *Los Angeles Times*, began his movie career as a villain but moved quickly to romantic hero. He became known as a gentle soul, in touch with his emotions, ready to help others, a global citizen who declared, "I sell dreams and peddle love," in his eventual, inevitable TED talk. Prem found that he related to Shah Rukh's characters, many of whom were named Rahul, more so even than Amitabh's characters, who were often named Vijay, and to Shah Rukh's mushy young man more so than Amitabh's angry young one. As Shah Rukh's stardom skyrocketed over the years, so too did Prem's affinity for him. The significance of SRK in Prem's life and in the world cannot be overestimated.

During this period, on Saturday mornings, *Cinema Cinema* was joined by the *Asian Variety Show* and *Namaste America* to provide several solid hours of Hindi movie-musical entertainment, which Prem usually enjoyed with Beena Joshi in her apartment. She was quite taken by 1994's *Hum Aapke Hain Koun..!* the villain-less, drama-less, violence-less surprise smash hit that centered around a shockingly happy, well-to-do extended family enjoying a family wedding without killing each other, and that in the process set the tone for Hindi films for the duration of the decade. Prem bought the VHS tape of it for Beena and spent many hours by her side watching it. These years of movies were punctuated by sightings of Leena—some enchanting, some devastating—and by productions of his own magnificent stage shows, for which he always found a way to give her front-row seats.

25

The New York Times
*In New Jersey, an
Importer of Indian Stars*

By ALEX STEVENSON   JUNE 11, 1994

Some weeks ago, Prem Kumar was trying to find a place to hold a meeting with some of the organizers of his upcoming show. Their usual meeting room at Dosa Dream Palace was booked, so someone suggested convening at Kumar's house. "I just laughed," he said. "How could I fit 10 people on one twin mattress?"

The mattress Kumar, 31, was referencing is on the floor of an apartment in Edison, N.J., where he lives as a paying guest along with four other men. "People think because I produce these big shows, I must be living in a big house," he said, taking a sip of chai at Dimple restaurant in Edison. He added, "I am happy on my mattress."

This is not the lifestyle people expect from a highly successful show-business entrepreneur whose company, Superstar Entertainment, has been putting on elaborate stage productions featuring Indian film stars since 1990. The flashy, Vegas-esque shows play to sold-out audiences at increasingly grand venues, the latest of which will take place on June 25 at the Nassau Coliseum.

The "Temptation Beyond Borders" show, which almost immediately sold out its 18,000 tickets, will be a four-hour song-and-dance spectacle in which the actors, along with background dancers, reenact musical sequences from their films. Also along for the ride are comedic actors, musicians, and playback singers, the largely hidden talent that supply the vocals to which the actors lip-synch.

So how will this performance distinguish itself from its predecessors? The show's organizers believe the answer lies in the addition of one major star to the lineup. "The participation of Anil Kapoor is nothing short of a miracle," said Jagan Bose, the show's director. "He brings a star power we have rarely seen."

At a recent rehearsal, Kapoor, a veteran actor with a long list of box office hits behind him, leaped off of a staircase and went straight into a 10-minute dance

[269]

routine. "It will be better on the day of the show. There will be flames erupting on both sides when I jump," he said.

By all accounts, Superstar Entertainment's productions have never been short of spectacular. The first show, at the State Theatre New Jersey, wowed audiences with its array of movie stars emerging from within simulated fog. The 1991 show at the Paramount Theater (formerly the Felt Forum) and the '92 and '93 shows at the Trump Taj Mahal Hotel and Casino in Atlantic City all drew audiences of up to 5,000 people and featured laser lights and showers of confetti.

Interspersed with these extravagant shows have been smaller, non–movie star shows centered around singers from various genres: classical, Sufi, playback, ghazal. A server at Dimple interjected on this subject, addressing a visibly embarrassed Kumar: "Excuse me? Sir? Your Kumar Sanu, Anuradha Paudwal singing program was first-class."

But it is the big shows, the ones with A-listers such as Shah Rukh Khan, Rani Mukerji, Hrithik Roshan, and Preity Zinta, that have captured the hearts of an entire immigrant population. Kumar's timing for launching his company could not have been better; with the U.S. government's 1990 establishment of the H1-B visa, which allowed highly skilled workers from other countries to come to America temporarily, India experienced a "brain drain" as many people in the tech and software industries emigrated, precipitating a huge growth in the Indian American population and,

therefore, in audiences for Kumar's shows, in New York and New Jersey.

Apart from having the numbers and the actors, it appears that Kumar's meticulous planning and Herculean work ethic are what have made the shows a success. "The guy thinks of everything," Bose said. "I do not know if he sleeps."

Nachiket Rao, whose Electric Productions manages lighting and audio-visual effects for Superstar, put it this way: "I cannot think of anyone else who could have done this. He has a vision in his head for each show and he does not rest until he has achieved it."

Yet the president and primary full-time employee of Superstar Entertainment is the exact opposite of the thing he is selling. He leads a simple, ascetic lifestyle and is deeply private, declining to discuss his personal status or his own origin story. With no evident family, one wonders what drives him. Kumar's answer is, "I guess I would have to say the movies." Faiza Khan, the company's choreographer confirmed, "The main thing about him is that he is a movie lover and knows everything about them." When questioned about whether he gets starstruck in his line of work, Kumar expressed surprise that he has not had this experience thus far. "Somehow, it is just work," he explained.

Stepping out into the bustling India-in-America business district on Edison's Oak Tree Road, Kumar added sheepishly, "If I could get Amitabh [Bachchan] to come someday, well, that would be something." He smiled as he got on his bicycle and rode away.

26

"What a program, yaar!" Tony exclaimed, giving Prem several hearty thumps on the back. Prem had just emerged from his apartment on the humid summer morning after his Nassau Coliseum show. He was heading to First Fidelity Bank to make a large deposit and then over to Exxon to give notice. He didn't think his quitting would be much of an issue as he had been spilling unreasonable amounts of gas on himself lately, annoying Mr. Khosla to no end.

A large group of AC-less people sat under a tree out front. "Best show ever," Tun-Tun called. "Anil Kapoor was too good."

A cricket-inclined neighbor lauded Prem in the lingo he knew best: "Ya, man, you really hit a sixer."

"Sixer!" someone in the parking lot concurred.

Gitanjali Vora asked the question that was on everybody's mind. "When is the next one?"

With one hand, Prem shielded his eyes from the sun. "December," he said.

"It will be a Bollywood show only, no?" Tony implored. "No more ghazals, yaar, please, no ghazals."

The term "Bollywood" had only just arrived at King's Court, and Prem hadn't yet decided how he felt about it. A cinema scholar in the 1970s had replaced the "H" of Hollywood with the "B" of Bombay, Abdul

Rashid posited, while Urmila Sahu credited the filmi magazines *Cine Blitz* and *Stardust*. Nalini Sen insisted it was derived from "Tollywood," the nickname of a studio in the Tollygunge neighborhood of Calcutta. Lucky found amusing this new word to describe something that had been around for ages, but Prem was concerned that it could imply they were a poor cousin, second best to Hollywood. Backstage, he'd heard rumblings from the actors themselves that they deplored the term. But, Shanta Bhatt held, the word was helpful in differentiating from the artistically inclined, non-mainstream, hey-this-should-win-an-Oscar Parallel Cinema movement. The entirety of Building 19 embraced the epithet as a way to capture Hindi commercial cinema's global success. Wherever they fell on the to-Bollywood-or-not-to-Bollywood spectrum, all agreed it slid off the tongue more easily than the eight-syllabled "Hindi commercial cinema" or seven-syllabled "Hindi mainstream cinema." In the interest of convenience, King's Court took up the word without getting involved in its politics. Unceremoniously, it came into the vernacular; one day it wasn't there, the next day it was.

"Yes," Prem confirmed, "it will be a Bollywood show."

27

E dison's evolving identity took a peculiar turn when architectural palimpsests became a common occurrence up and down Oak Tree Road. The Pizza Hut became Gokul Vegetarian Cuisine and later Sukhadia's, all the while boldly retaining its predecessor's overwhelming red roof. Up the street, the Dairy Queen became Dosa Corner without giving up its signature red-and-white exterior, while the Boston Market kept its black-and-white awnings and cream-colored siding as it morphed into Indian Express. Some hailed all this as a crime of design, but it was also a multilayered record, a living history of Edison's transformation from American to Indian American.

Between 1990 and 2000, the Indian population in New Jersey more than doubled to 169,180; in the same time period, the Indian population in Edison nearly tripled to almost 17,000. Moreover, they lived not only in Edison but in Metuchen, Colonia, Woodbridge, Scotch Plains, Piscataway, New Brunswick, South Plainfield, etc., and half of the Little India business district was actually in Iselin, but somehow, Edison was the name that became synonymous among expatriate Indians with a homeland in America. Local newspapers popped up, such as *Little India* and *Khabar*, catering to the Indian population there, and Congressman Frank Pallone, Jr., representing the sixth district of New Jersey, cofounded the Congressional Caucus on India and Indian Americans after studying his rapidly changing constituency.

Just when it seemed there were enough Indian American businesses on Oak Tree, more appeared. A slew of new grocery stores—Panchvati, Patel Brothers, Patel Cash and Carry, Subzi Mandi—ensured that no Edisonian would ever go without turmeric root, betel leaves, or the sweet and tangy, mouth-freshening cumin balls commonly known as jeera goli. Several music and video stores—Sangeet, Poonam Video, Patel Video, Music Box—met the town's Bollywood needs, while a proliferation of Indian clothing boutiques—Sari Emporium, Khazana, Aishwarya, Sari Bazaar, Nazranaa, Indian Couture, Sahil—still was not enough. Dozens of new restaurants opened up, banking on the supposition that Indians largely want to eat Indian food when they go out. India Sajawat, Pooja Hut, Butala Emporium, and Patel Vasan Bhandar provided Hindu religious accessories and wedding décor, and Kitab Indian Bookstore sold books. These new businesses drew thousands of people from near and far, and when they stepped out of their cars and onto the paan-stained Oak Tree sidewalks, they felt as though they had stepped through a window to their earlier lives.

Hemant Engineer inspected the progress of the commercial district one afternoon while walking down the street. In front of Gujarati Grocers, a young woman grilled samples of masala vegetable burgers; a few doors down, a man attempted to drape a sari on a mannequin in a window. There were signs everywhere—an Indian bridal expo, a $5.95 Gujarati lunch thali, dhokla made fresh daily, passport photos at a Halal meat shop, and phone cards at Smriti's Sari and Spices Center. Hemant, whose sign had started it all, viewed them with a sense of satisfaction. He was pleased to see King's Court so well represented on that stretch of road, with Gopal's sweet shop and Varsha's video store, which also carried carrom boards, the Singhs' electronics store, and Lucky's small, upscale clothing shop, The Sassy Salwar. But the main thing he came to survey were the beauty salons. It was time to get Leena's business out of his bedroom and out onto Oak Tree Road.

He spotted only two, Payal Beauty Parlor and Shangar Beauty Salon, but he knew there were others close by. Still, in this area, with its endless supply of hirsute women, Leena's expert hair-removal services would certainly develop a following. In fact, they already had. For years, she had operated an underground salon out of their apartment, ironing out their wavy tresses and threading their excess facial hair. When she was younger, she had taken a short course at the Shahnaz Hussain Beauty Institute in Delhi and learned all the requisite techniques for hair removal and blackhead extraction. She had quietly graduated from Rutgers and decided to continue on at the grocery store and help navigate it through the increased competition. When the store was on firm footing and she had more time, she started casually removing mustaches. Soon, women had standing appointments to have their lip hair removed and their eyebrows disconnected. The business grew by word of mouth, without the benefit of signs or ads. At first the customers were just from King's Court, but quickly they started coming from all over town, arriving at her door after they noticed Manju's flawless upper lip or Jaya's delicately manicured hands. They raved about Leena's ten-dollar arm waxing, five-dollar haircuts, and fifteen-dollar facials. She would squeeze them in on an overbooked day, effortlessly tending to five clients and a cantankerous father at the same time.

Leena's salon became a full-time operation. She took over Hemant's bedroom, nailed a row of mirrors to the wall, and mounted a steel rod on one side for a curtain to conceal a long, plastic-cushioned table and the women who lay down on it. He was forced to stay out of his bedroom all day, and when he could finally go in, there were broken pieces of white thread scattered all over the floor. Sometimes Leena insisted on testing out a new moisturizer or even a mud mask on him and poor Viren

Bhai, who didn't mind, it made his skin glow. There were women in the apartment all day every day using the sitting area as a waiting room, and if Hemant wanted to take a nap, he had to go to his dear friend Sanjay Sapra's or else to the back room of the store. But the worst thing about Leena's thriving business was the unending fight over the TV.

In recent years, the Dish Network satellite service provider had begun to carry channels with Indian programming—TV Asia, Zee TV, Sony, Star Plus, Sahara One—and for the first time since immigrating to America, Hemant could once again enjoy the thing he loved most: cricket. So many years had passed in which he had little involvement with the game, and the embers of his fanaticism reignited quickly. He was the first in King's Court to install a dish, drawing fans to his home at all hours, often in the middle of the night with blankets and pillows so they could watch the matches as they occurred live on the other side of the world. Even after every family had acquired a dish and the disks bloomed from the sides of King's Court's buildings like clusters of oversized flowers, people still came to his home to watch.

Just when Hemant had grown accustomed to the elegant roar of a cricket match in his apartment, Leena declared she needed the TV and VCR to play Hindi movies so her customers would not get bored while waiting. It was the first time he had ever found his daughter to be entirely unreasonable, insisting on having her way even when India was playing Pakistan in the World Cup quarterfinals. When he asked how she could preempt India-Pakistan cricket and, in the process, called into question her loyalty to game and country, she clapped back, "It is a sacrifice I must make. If the customers are relaxed and happy, their blackheads pop out with less of squeezing." Hemant found it impossible to argue with her on this point and ultimately succumbed to watching cricket only at night so she could show *Dilwale Dulhania Le Jayenge* during business hours.

For that entire year, Leena never changed the tape because that year, and for years after, everyone was crazy for *DDLJ*. The Shah Rukh Khan–Kajol starrer focused on Hindu Family Values—which became such a significant concept in political discourse that they began capitalizing it—and ushered in the era of the diaspora romance. Its plot centered on non-resident Indians, or NRIs, who affirmed Indian traditions, setting the tone for Bollywood for the rest of the decade. But for Hemant, it was always the useless movie that overrode his cricket.

After a great deal of thinking about how to solve this problem, he had the idea for his daughter to rent an actual storefront on Oak Tree Road. It would be good for both of them if she left the apartment. He was proud of how hard she worked to build a grooming empire in his bedroom, but lately, she had been especially irritable with him. He wondered if she still resented him for what had happened all those years ago with that superstar show boy, though she was now happily engaged to Mikesh. And there were plenty of others waiting in the wings if that didn't work out: Sandeep the podiatrist and Akhil the ophthalmologist, and a very eager colorectal surgeon named Harsh, all of whom had had their mothers get in touch. But he thought things with Mikesh, who had become a fixture in their apartment, would work out just fine; the two were always laughing and talking secretly together. He wondered what they were waiting for and decided he would have to ask the boy's uncle, Sanjay Sapra. Whispers were beginning to swirl—did he break it off with her? were their horoscopes incompatible?—as Leena was dangerously close to turning thirty without being married.

Fortunately, Hemant did not have to worry for long. Like all gossip in King's Court, that one died down when the next one began. The rumor that swept India and the diaspora that fall would later be referred to as the "Hindu milk miracle." Before dawn one morning, in a temple in Delhi, an offering of milk to a statue of Ganesha inexplicably disappeared. Quickly, word spread that the elephant-headed deity of good fortune had drunk the milk himself; by midmorning, Ganeshas all over the country were taking in milk, and by the afternoon, temples in America, Canada, and the United Kingdom were reporting the same. Soon, Hindu authorities declared that a full-blown, worldwide Hindu miracle was occurring. Traffic jams ensued in front of major temples and milk sales skyrocketed. Around the world, people offered their in-home Ganeshas spoonfuls of milk, some with more success than others. Before long, scientific explanations for the phenomenon and theories of mass hysteria were put forth, yet many thousands of people maintain to this day that their Ganeshas drank milk.

Leena was not one of these people. Throughout King's Court, Hindus tried to feed their statues all day, but no one could confirm a miracle occurring in their apartment. Some said their Ganeshas seemed to sort of drink a little, with most of it dribbling down the chin, but Leena felt strongly that this did not qualify. Still, she made attempts.

Hemant came home in the afternoon as Leena was making an oblation. "Maybe you should mix some sugar in it. Ganeshji likes sweets, you know."

"No one said anything about sugar," Leena said, not looking away from her unresponsive statue. "He is supposed to drink plain milk, period, end of story."

The apartment was enjoying a rare moment of quiet as Leena had given herself two hours off that day to rest. No aunties were disrobing in the waiting room or having anything removed in the salon.

"Can I sleep for some time?" Hemant said.

"I give up," Leena said, pitching the spoon of milk into the sink. "This is not drinking anything."

"Just for twenty, thirty minutes," Hemant said, heading in the direction of his room.

"You can," Leena said, "but I will be doing Mrs. Iyer's stomach waxing there in ten minutes."

"That is it!" Hemant declared, throwing a root comb applicator at a pile of dirty towels. "I cannot live like this—no naps, no cricket, no fun. Sticky wax cloths everywhere. It is time for you to move your hairy-ladies business to a proper store on Oak Tree Road."

Leena was silent, which unsettled Hemant, who was used to his daughter having an immediate and loud opinion on everything. When she finally opened her mouth, she spoke slowly and calmly. "You want to kick me out from my apartment so you can sleep and watch TV?"

"No," Hemant said uncertainly. Leena narrowed her eyes. "Okay, yes," Hemant said. "But, but, just think how good it will be—"

Leena erupted with the fury of a thousand underpaid aestheticians. She spoke at length about sacrifice and the importance of family, moved on to the virtues of small business and the primacy of keeping overhead costs to a minimum, ranted about the cost of labor, and finally concluded with a reminder about taxes.

"Never mind," Hemant said, waving his hand as if to erase the past two minutes. Mrs. Iyer came in boasting that her Ganeshji had drunk three spoonfuls and unbuttoned her blouse as if he weren't there.

"Really, something has to change," Hemant decided.

The thing that changed was that Leena moved out. She packed up and relocated the salon and herself with it. Mrs. Sneha Dhar was the first to suspect that something was afoot when she spotted Mikesh and Leena hauling boxes from his car into his condo building. Mrs. Namita Tiwari also became suspicious when she called Leena to make a waxing appointment and was told to report to a different address; the same thing happened to Mrs. Deepika Dayal the next day, though she decided to wait rather than jump to the obvious, scandalous conclusion. When they met one afternoon for their monthly kitty party along with the other nine members, all these bits of clues, along with nine more, spilled out onto the table among the potato cutlets and finger sandwiches. The ladies parsed through them until Leena's sordid new living situation came into stark focus. They went on to the next stage, which was to pronounce judgment while sucking down Bloody Marys, after which they turned to other gossip. At the end of the visit, they each threw in their monthly contributions of five hundred and one dollars for the kitty—which that month went to Hansini Mangal, two-time champion of her women's tennis league—and left with the unspoken intent to spread any unseemly news they had acquired that day.

By the time the news about Leena moving in with Mikesh had bounced around Edison and landed back at her father's doorstep, it had morphed into "grocer suffers heart attack due to unmarried daughter's pregnancy." Hemant was not surprised; this was just the way things went here. But when Mrs. Laghari came to the store for a bag of urad dal, two types of masala mixes, and nothing from the produce aisle or freezer section, he took the opportunity to set the matter straight. There was neither a scandal nor anything inappropriate going on. His daughter had simply settled down with her fiancé—who, by the way, was a doctor, did you know?—and it was actually a step to be celebrated. It just made sense given their busy schedules, et cetera, et cetera, and it was a move in the right direction with Mikesh Aneja, MD. Hemant left out the part about how he had practically driven her out with a dispute over the TV but was honest about the rest of it. Though he missed Leena terribly and the apartment had become too quiet without her and her revolving door of clients, he was happy with her new living arrangement, and he and his daughter were as close as ever. Which, in effect, brought an end to the gossip, because what was the controversy if her father approved?

Prem, who did not share Hemant's view, immediately fell down a short set of stairs upon learning the news from Beena. He had been helping her with a large catering delivery, carrying tray after aluminum tray into Hari's Event Center and Bingo Hall, and took a tumble and landed in a heap at the foot of the back stairs, lathered in a tangy green chutney and tamarind concoction. Nothing could have prepared him for the blow he felt at that moment. Since Leena and Mikesh were not yet married, he held out hope that their relationship had stalled. Maybe she'd grown tired of his thyroid-centric conversation or his Chunky Pandey looks. Prem had learned about Leena's home salon from a piece in *Desi Talk* newspaper about Edison's thriving underground beauty parlor scene. The article did not mention last names or exact locations—for the obvious prison-related reasons—but it was clear to whom "Leena, daughter of a prominent grocer, engaged to a promising young endocrinologist" was referring, so Prem tracked down the reporter to squeeze every bit out of him that he could on the subject. Through Prem's network of unknowing spies—Urmila Sahu, Nalini Sen, and assorted aunties in King's Court who could easily be nudged in the direction of giving up other people's secrets—he was able to glean the salient facts of Leena's life from afar. This was how he learned she had taken up running in Merrill Park. Her hair was longer now and she always pulled it into a ponytail right before she began, which he observed from the bench of a discreet gazebo. He didn't believe it was stalking, per se; he simply happened to like to go to the same park on the same days, at the same times, that she did. When he could, he attended events where he knew she would be present—the opening of Desi Mike's Driving School, Tun-Tun's inexplicable birthday luau—so he could be near her and remind her that he was in the world. It pained him when he heard from Gitanjali Vora, who heard it straight from Hemant, that Leena had contracted pneumonia, and it pained him just as much to admit that it was probably helpful at that time for her to be engaged to a doctor.

And now this cohabitation news. He biked past Mikesh's building multiple times that week, though it was out of the way, in Metuchen. It was so much more impressive than King's Court. How could she not want to live here in this palace, with its functioning light fixtures and its washer and dryer in every unit? The thought of it depressed him, but he kept cycling by all the same.

* * *

Many months passed during which Prem did not see Leena at all. When he finally did, it was from a great distance, in the vast chaos of the India Day Parade, and he wasn't sure it was actually her. It was a sweltering Sunday, and two men were unloading enormous speakers from a van, their TV Asia shirts sweat-soaked under the arms. To one side of the stage, a Fairfield Farms truck was parked in front of Chowpatty, and a small army of waiters transported bottles of water from the truck to the restaurant. Over ten thousand people were expected, and it seemed to Prem that five thousand were already there, though the organizers and shopkeepers were still setting up and there were no floats in sight. Prem, Mohan, Yogesh, and Lucky had found some space to stand in front of a small stage set up by Money Jet transfer services, which featured a few teenage girls in white Money Jet T-shirts on the verge of dancing. On the main stage, someone said over and over, "Mic check one, mic check, one, two, three, mic check one . . ." while the mandatory ambulance pushed its way through the crowd and parked near Sona Jewelers. Prem thought he caught a glimpse of Leena hovering around an orange cooler of Frooti mango drink boxes in front of Devi Sweets. She wore a gauzy blue kurti and was with her friends. Prem slipped into the crowd, leaving behind his own friends, and tried to cross the street to where she was. It was a gridlock situation and he had no choice but to shove an elderly lady in a patriotic orange, white, and green sari, followed by a child handing out Granite Planet flyers. He slipped between an Accord with a yellow Om bumper sticker and a Maxima with a Ganesha on the dashboard, then elbowed his way past a non-Indian woman wearing a Cleveland Indians hat selling balloons out of a shopping cart. When he reached the cooler, Leena wasn't there, but he thought he saw her up the street under a pair of flags, Indian and American, sticking out of a telephone pole near a gigantic Indian Business Association banner. He squeezed between a man with a child on his shoulders and a police barricade and weaved his way through a crowd of blue-shirted women holding Indus American Bank balloons, but when he reached Leena, it wasn't her; it was a teenager in a Sahara India cricket jersey who joined five other teenagers in Sahara India jerseys. He looked around and couldn't find Leena. A row of white-haired women on folding chairs sat behind a line of restless children sitting along the curb. A woman with henna-dyed hair used a Diamond Depot promotional postcard as a fan, and a man with a tricolored sash poured water on himself, but no sign of his love.

Prem wiped the sweat from his brow with the back of his hand. There she was again, in front of the festive red Kingfisher beer tent, next to the Society of Indo-American Engineers table. By now, the bass was pumping and the emcee was directing everyone to make some noise. Three police cars were visible at the top of the hill, approaching from the far end of Oak Tree, a row of Indian flags and a billowing float behind them. Prem turned and squinted into the distance. When he turned back around, she was gone. Immediately, he was assailed by the familiar emptiness of losing something he never had. A girl in pigtails said, "Uncle?" and offered him a heart-shaped flyer for a matchmaking service.

He didn't know what he would have done if he had reached her anyway. The marchers were coming now, along with float after float: the TV Asia display adorned with large posters of Gandhi and others; a large inflatable Jet Airways plane promoting nonstop flights to Delhi; an Air India float promoting the same thing, but without the inflatable plane; the Middlesex County Pipes and Drums band featuring white men in kilts and dark glasses; the Swamibapa Pipe Band featuring brown men in kilts and dark glasses. The Marathi Vishwa marchers struggled to hold up a banner, while the Mangalorean Catholic Association of the East Coast moved in a disturbingly synchronized goosestep. Prem watched with indifference as they passed before him. By the time the grand marshal's orange, white, and green tiered float came into view, with an Indian pageant winner waving an American flag at the top, Prem was lightheaded and dehydrated. The parade became a blur, the myriad passersby all blending into each other, until he was jolted back to coherence by the sight of Hemant Engineer towering above him on the Oak Tree Business Association float.

Prem had heard that Leena's father had become even more heavily involved with community organizing in recent months after a spate of bias incidents in the area. Indian American shops had been vandalized, swastikas scrawled across their windows—the irony of the symbol being a peaceful Hindu one centuries before it became a hateful Nazi one, lost on the perpetrators. Indian homes had been egged and mailboxes set on fire. In response, business owners became vocal, holding rallies and speaking out on local newscasts. Hemant spoke on the local news about the need for solidarity with other people of color, from whose civil-rights movement they and other Asian Americans had benefited. That same week, he put together a small demonstration outside the police station in which multiple races were represented and for which he wore what he surely considered his best protest attire, a gray Nehru vest over a white kurta pajama which he wore for the parade as well.

Seeing him up there draped in an orange sash, Prem felt a pang of sadness that he couldn't commend him on the good work he was doing. He wondered if Hemant had heard of his success and whether he experienced any regret about rejecting him. The Marlboro Hindi School passed by with their banner, as did the Sindhi Association of New Jersey with theirs, followed by a campaign float for a congressional candidate looking for Indian American votes. The humidity was suffocating, yet the marchers continued to march and the watchers continued to watch, perhaps, Prem thought, because the dense crowds and constant music, the air of masala and unbearable sun, recalled for them the clamor of the country they had left behind. When the Asian American Hotel Owners Association float went by, Prem reflected on the backbreaking work that the members of that group had undertaken since coming to this country, and inevitably his thoughts went to Leena. She must be working so hard for her business. As the Gopi All-Natural Paneer float drifted forward, close on the heels of the Korean American marching band, Prem felt the acute sting of time passing by.

28

Toward the end of that decade, when Indian American teenagers turned on the TV, they began to catch glimpses of themselves. Nupur Lala, a fourteen-year-old Tampa native, spelled "logorrhea" to win the Scripps National Spelling Bee, just one in a wave of Indian Americans who would dominate the competition for years to come. M. Night Shyamalan wrote and directed the blockbuster *The Sixth Sense*, and Kalpana Chawla became the first Indian American astronaut. Impossibly beautiful Indian supermodels began winning international pageants and dating Derek Jeter. While Kumar had not yet gone with Harold to White Castle and Aziz had not yet mastered anything and Mindy had not yet taken over everything, the browning of America had begun, with a yoga studio on every corner and Starbucks offering chai lattes, also on every corner.

This tide rising in America had already risen one hundredfold in Edison. The movie theater on Oak Tree Road began to include Bollywood films in its offerings, and soon, half the screens were showing the latest hits out of India—*Hum Dil De Chuke Sanam*, *Kuch Kuch Hota Hai* (*K2H2*), *Biwi No. 1*, *Anari No. 1*, and all of the "No. 1" movies thereafter— until they finally decided to forgo American films altogether and show only Indian ones. The Eastern Broadcasting Corporation launched a radio station featuring only Indian programming, which required purchasing a particular type of radio, on which the local Indian-owned electronics stores made a killing. Packaged Indian foods became readily available at Foodtown, ShopRite, Pathmark, and A&P, and a former toy factory was transformed into a Swaminarayan temple. In 2000, the grand and garish Royal Albert's Palace, boasting four banquet halls, a restaurant, and a twenty-one-foot-tall statue of Sardar Vallabhbhai Patel, was inaugurated by the Chief Minister of Gujarat; it would go on to host thousands of Indian American weddings, baby showers, political fundraisers, beauty pageants, and parties for birthdays, anniversaries, graduations, and one divorce. All this growth bolstered the suspicion held by many and disputed by few that Edison, New Jersey, had, by the turn of the century, the highest concentration of Indian people outside of India.

Now in his twelfth year of longing for Leena, Prem looked sadly upon his adopted home's progress as it reminded him of how long it had been since Hemant laid down his decree. And while Oak Tree Road was shiny and new, the people around him were showing signs of aging. Iqbal Singh developed a limping gait due to bursitis of the hip, and Tun-Tun was fitted for dentures. Deepak and Lucky lost most of their hair, while Beena Joshi had been sleeping a lot lately. Others, such as Sujata Mehra, Shanta Bhatt, and the Yadavs, moved on to bigger, flashier homes in other parts of Edison and in Colonia and Metuchen, and a few made it all the way to toney Watchung and Short Hills. But Prem remained through the vicissitudes of twelve years, two months, and twenty-one days as he was. Still nervous and skinny, sleeping under a basket of onions, fully entrenched in the habit of loving her.

Though Prem himself had not changed much, his reputation in King's Court had soared to great heights. He had been the most reliable name in Bollywood entertainment in New Jersey for almost a decade, producing sold-out show after sold-out show, each one more spectacular than the last. His neighbors respected and admired him, but at the same time, they wondered where all the money was going. "He has gone from zero to hero, but why he is still riding the bicycle?" they would say. They never saw him spend any money, and, in fact, a few said he was quite stingy, never treating anyone to dinner or giving away free tickets. People wondered why he continued to live in King's Court as a paying guest on someone's floor and why the office he rented was in a dilapidated former motel. Thus an aura of mystery began to surround Prem. Some said he was remitting the money to poor, sick relatives in India or funding the construction of schools in remote villages. Others claimed he was squandering it all in Atlantic City. A myth grew about the enormity of his wealth, with some speculating he had saved so much that he could buy ten Mercedes or launch his own university where he could occasionally offer guest lectures on entrepreneurship, which, of course, he would never do because of his aversion to large group discussions. People began approaching him for help with their complicated matters—negotiating with a landlord to procure parking passes for paying guests, settling a dispute between rival purveyors of kababs over the name Tikka on a Stikka—which Prem would oblige, asking only that they be prepared to return the favor if someday the need arose.

Prem's legendary status was further cemented by an unannounced visit from the Nightingale of India, the most renowned and adored of all playback singers—the hidden songbirds that constitute the backbone of the Bollywood movie industry—the preeminent Melody Queen herself, Lata Mangeshkar. She was in New Jersey rehearsing for Superstar Entertainment's upcoming *Bollywood Dreams* show at Continental Airlines Arena—the largest venue yet—and had grown homesick for moong dal khichdi. Prem offered to take her to Oak Tree Road, where she would have plenty of restaurant options, though khichdi would likely not be on any menu. The seventy-one-year-old politely rejected this plan in favor of a home-cooked meal, if possible. So he called a car and off they went to King's Court. Beena would not be home until after six, so they would have to wait in 3D for some time until he could knock on her door and announce that Lata Mangeshkar was in need of khichdi.

Prem was nervous about what Lata, who must certainly have become accustomed to luxury, would think of King's Court, but as they walked up the broken path, fragments of concrete scattered in the grass, she looked up and smiled at the modest building. "Reminds me of a home I once knew," she sighed.

He was delighted that she was not horrified. "And our laundry facilities have recently been remodeled." The loud, staggered shushing sound of dozens of pressure cookers letting out steam engulfed King's Court as it did every evening. A man on a balcony two buildings over was yelling into his cell phone to someone in India, though the days of having to yell were long gone. Lata, seemingly unfazed by the shushing and yelling, walked right up the creaky steps and into the cramped apartment, continuing to smile even after the screaming began.

"Holy fucking fuck!" Lucky was the first to recognize Prem's distinguished guest. Others had similarly offensive reactions that almost gave Prem a cardiac event.

"Stop, just stop it! I mean, come meet Lata Mangeshkar."

"Tun-Tun, Tun-Tun, come quickly," Tony yelled into a very large cell phone, "Petrol has brought Lata Mangeshkar!"

Yogesh, who had moved in a few weeks before, began hyperventilating, and Iqbal was the first to invoke God. "Hai Rabba, Lata Mangeshkar is here!"

Mohan called out the window, "Hey yaar, Lata Mangeshkar is here!"

"Shut up your face, really?" someone yelled from below.

Deepak dropped his pudding cup, picked up the home phone,

and dialed quickly. "Dolly? Lata Mangeshkar is in our drawing room. Quickly, bring everyone."

"Who is making the chai? Who is making the chai?" Iqbal panicked.

Prem had hoped no one would be home, but everyone was home, plus some people who used to live there and some he'd never seen before. One of them vacated a chair so Lata Mangeshkar could sit down. Sweet and decorous in her signature white sari with colorful border, she spoke to the room. "Namaskar, very nice to meet you all. Please, sit. Do not make any fuss for me."

Amarleen was the only one not starstruck. "I suppose you will be requiring tea," she said.

Everyone else bombarded the singer with questions and assorted compliments.

"Do you always meet the stars of the movies?"

"Who is the better singer, you or your sister?"

"I like your sari."

"Your singing is like a sweet breeze that flies over the ocean and into my ears."

"How come you never married?"

"What is your favorite song that you have sung?"

"Thank you for your glorious service to the humanity."

Then they began requesting songs, arguing among themselves over which song she should sing—"Dam Bhar Jo Udhar Munh Phere" or "Bade Aarmanon Se Rakha Hai Sanam," "Kahan Ho Tum" or "Sawan ka Mahina"—without noticing that Lata had slumped over in her chair, clutching her head.

"Didi!" Prem said, addressing her as "older sister," the term of endearment bestowed upon her by fans worldwide. "Are you going to puke?"

"No, no, just sudden headache. Can I rest here?" Lata Mangeshkar said, slouching toward Prem's mattress. This caused an enormous fracas, with Iqbal insisting on the bedroom and others frantically trying to remove the onions. "She cannot sleep under onions, it is not right," Urmila Sahu said. "She sang 'Aaj Phir Jeene Ki Tamanna Hai.'"

Prem watched all of this in horror until he realized he would have to do the thing he hated, which was to take control of the situation. "Everybody! Step back from Lata Mangeshkar."

There was an abrupt silence. Prem cleared his throat. "I will take the Nightingale of India to Beena Joshi's, where she can rest peacefully. Come, Nightingale," he said and helped Lata Mangeshkar to her feet and out the door. In the stairwell, Prem faced the most shocking turn of events he had ever encountered.

"Prem," Lata said, apparently headache-free, "your father has asked me to check on you and report to him how you are doing. Now, what am I to tell him, that you sleep on the floor under a bag of onions?"

The reality of the situation did not immediately settle in. "It is not a bag, it is a basket," Prem said.

"He is worried about you. How could you leave your family behind this way? What would your mother have said if she were still in this life?"

Prem was dumbstruck. It was not out of the realm of possibility that his father knew Lata Mangeshkar, as famous movie types and wealthy industrialists often ran in the same circles. But did she sign on to perform at the concert just to spy on him? Had other stars been double agents for his father? Did she trick him into taking her to his home? Did she even want khichdi?

"Uh, no, Didi, I think you have the wrong number, you must be thinking of some other fellow, you are tired, let us get you to a proper bed."

Lata Mangeshkar stopped in her tracks and turned to look directly at Prem. "You are the son of Ashok Ratan Kumar, head of the Kumar Group. Do these people know?"

The creaking of a floorboard in the stairwell below them drew Prem's attention away from the awkward interrogation and toward a man who was listening from downstairs. It was Harbhajan Gill, the taxi driver brother of Amarleen, who had never stopped being suspicious of Prem from a years-ago incident. It seemed he had heard everything.

* * *

In the ensuing weeks, it became clear that Harbhajan was the most incompetent blackmailer ever. At first, he didn't say anything. They had passed each other on the stairs that day without a word, not even an acknowledgment that Lata Mangeshkar was there. Later, when Harbhajan visited King's Court, he would only scowl at Prem from afar. But he began visiting more and more frequently, as if to taunt Prem, staring at him while gnawing on a stalk of sugar cane.

Prem wished Harbhajan would come speak with him like a normal human being. He supposed he could approach the man himself, but the thought of it made him anxious and sweaty. The dread of what might happen caused Prem to live in a constant state of alarm and nausea. To take his mind off of the looming revelation of his hidden past and the subsequent inevitable backlash against his years of duplicity, Prem took up speed dating.

The events he went to were the Desi kind, though the occasional stray non-Indian with an Indian fetish was always welcome. Often taking place in hotel banquet spaces or restaurant party rooms, Desi speed dating was typically limited to fifteen women and fifteen men aged forty or under, who would spend four minutes chatting with each of their dates with the hope of unearthing their life partners. Prem, of course, was not on the hunt for a life partner but enjoyed talking with the participants and supporting them in their quests.

"So, what kind of car do you drive?"

This was the first question that Prem was asked on his first date at his first speed-dating affair, which took place at the Quality Inn Edison-New Brunswick in plain and unnecessarily frigid Conference Room B. "I ride a bicycle," he said.

The girl made a note on her scorecard.

Things got easier as the evening progressed, the women more friendly and Prem more relaxed. He settled into a routine in which he stated upfront that he was there to cheer on the participants and give them a short break during the course of dating, which confused everyone at first but ultimately helped them get comfortable and feel good about themselves. He helped one woman realize that a scar on her neck gave her character and another that her awkwardness was endearing. At his next speed-dating session, he gave an uplifting pep talk to a reticent radiologist. His usual social anxiety did not come into play in this milieu because (a) he was not interested in finding a romantic partner; and (b) he didn't have to face a group of boisterous people who conversed easily with each other, but rather could speak one on one with nervous people who were obliged to speak to him as well. All social interaction should be this organized, he thought.

At his seventh such event, at Akbar Restaurant and Banquet Hall, where the lighting was particularly dim and the Desi trance music particularly entrancing, Prem was thoroughly enjoying a conversation with a petite accountant about Amitabh Bachchan's recent return to prominence, so much so that he was unaware of what was transpiring at the next table. When it came time for the men to rotate, Prem found himself seated across from Harbhajan Gill.

"Harbhajan?"

"You did not think I would find you, did you?" Harbhajan said. The driver, with his excessively unbuttoned shirt and dark glasses, struck Prem as a regular, sort of sidey guy trying to move into the role of lead villain.

"I see you every day," Prem said.

"But not like this."

"Uh, ya, you're right, not at speed dating," Prem said. He noticed the organizers glaring in their direction. "Are you looking for a girl?" he said, leaning in closer to Harbhajan. "I think you're on the wrong side, man. Wait, what happened to your angry wife?"

"She is with my angry kids," Harbhajan said. "Why you are here? Did I not tell you to find the blonde wife? Never mind, never mind, I am not here for that. You know what I am here for."

"Okay, but why did you have to follow me here and sneak into the incorrect side of speed dating? Why could we not talk in King's Court?"

"I don't know, this seemed better. Now I am going to blackmail you."

Prem braced himself for a devastating monetary value. "Just tell me, what do you want."

Harbhajan caressed a tuft of hair on his chest. "You tell me."

"You want me to tell you what you want?" Prem said.

"No, but ya, I mean, what do the blackmailers usually charge in this kind of situation?"

"Well, I think it depends on many factors. Do you want me to check with some people and get back to you?"

"Ya, ya, check, that would be good." Harbhajan narrowed his eyes and leaned in. "Don't take too much of time, Pumpwalla. I will be watching you," he warned, then stood and rotated to the next date.

Prem could hardly believe that Harbhajan had turned out to be such a diabolical taxi driver. He began popping up in increasingly odd locales, in the seat next to him at the movie theater or the ends of grocery store aisles, exacerbating Prem's already extreme anxiety. The Continental Airlines Arena show was in a few weeks, he hadn't caught a glimpse of Leena in ages, and Lata Mangeshkar was still on his back. Together, all of this made Prem's head spin faster than the inner circle of a traditional Gujarati folk dance.

These were the concerns that were on his mind as he stood on the sidelines at the Raritan Center Navratri, the largest celebration of that holiday beyond the borders of India. Traditionally a nine-day autumn festival occurring in various forms throughout India—some regions honored the goddess Durga, while others commemorated Lord Rama's victory over the demon king Ravana, and still others took an admirably feminist slant by celebrating multiple goddesses, and all versions shared the theme of good's triumph over evil—this American incarnation of Navratri took place over five consecutive weekends in an industrial park three times the size of a football field, in a heated canvas tent with metal detectors at its entrance. Here, the holiday was observed in the Gujarati manner with the production of a large-scale garba, the traditional, high-energy, percussive yet graceful folk dance performed in concentric rings of decked-out dancers spiraling and circling, gradually increasing in speed until reaching a frenzied peak. Just a decade earlier, this festival had taken place in various auditoriums, cultural centers, and school gymnasiums throughout the state, but the crowds grew every year until a massive venue accommodating ten thousand guests seemed appropriate. There had been trouble the past few years, with the township taking legal action against the organizers, citing complaints of noise pollution from the live music. But in the end, the Indian Americans won.

Chomping on a paan as he stood watching, Prem wondered if the court victory had emboldened the band to play even more vociferously. Two singers seemed to be battling for the title of most grating, and standing in the wings was Shatrughan Sinha, the Shotgun himself, aging film hero and womanizer turned politician, waiting to be honored. The mustachioed philanderer was slated to appear in Prem's *Bollywood Dreams* show, in what the actor considered a collect-two-paychecks-with-one-airline-ticket scheduling coup. Prem's usual array of roommates, former gas-station colleagues, and various others were scanning the crowd for potential young women to accost, urging him to join them as they homed in on a pack of unwitting targets. But Prem focused his attention on the opposite direction, toward the bleachers and food stalls, the sari vendors and jewelry displays. He knew Leena would not be dancing; she harbored the firm belief that only Gujaratis were qualified to participate in garba and all else should refrain. He searched for her among the cotton kurtis and the magnificent eight-armed Durga statues, but instead, he spotted Harbhajan Gill lurking behind a rack of bangles.

Prem went directly to him. "Why are you lurking again? Just come talk to me, man."

"I am not lurking, I am shopping," Harbhajan corrected. He ran a finger down a row of bangles, causing them to tinkle softly, then slid over to the somewhat-fine jewelry section. "A few gold chains would be nice . . ."

Prem immediately began to calculate how much it would set him back to buy his blackmailer a few necklaces. How had it come to this? Was the secret of his upper-class upbringing even worth this hassle? Alas, the answer was yes. After all these years of his toiling to belong, to be one of the struggling gang, what would they say if they discovered the truth of his deception? They would be outraged. They might boycott his shows and kick him out of the apartment, maybe even out of King's Court. And Leena, who already wanted nothing to do with him, would want him even less. Just then, Prem glimpsed a gigantic sunglassed man who looked a lot like Wristwatch prowling nearby. He wondered how he had come to have two ill-intentioned guys spying on him at a garba.

"I thought of something I want from you," Harbhajan said.

"I understand, you want some chains," Prem said.

"Can you make me meet Shatrughan Sinha?"

"You don't want chains?"

"I really would very much like his autograph. Please."

As they elbowed their way through the VIP dancing area toward the stage and Shatrughan Sinha, Prem had an idea. He could offer Harbhajan backstage passes for all future Superstar Entertainment shows in exchange for his silence. Thus he would not lose any money and Harbhajan would be placated, no, thrilled. Feeling quite good about this plan, Prem squeezed through the thick crowd of Desis. Just a few months back, they had faced yet more racist attacks on Oak Tree Road—a barrage of spit, BB-gun pellets, and lazy ethnic slurs—yet here they were, celebrating the festival of lights in the birthplace of the light bulb. The community's resilience was staggering.

As they approached Shatrughan Sinha, Prem spotted Leena among a friend group with too many males, all in her thrall. Her long hair tumbled down her back as she laughed and threw her head back as if everything was great.

29

Not long after that, Prem attended the *India Abroad* Prominent Desis in America gala in New York City. At first, he thought there must be some mistake when Iqbal handed him the gilded envelope. He thought perhaps the organizers wanted to extract a donation from him, but then it occurred to him that he actually was a prominent Desi.

When he entered the grand and gaudy ballroom with his gaudy and grand date, Beena Joshi, on his arm, Prem felt what an honor it was to be there. Immediately he spotted Drs. Sanjay Gupta and Deepak Chopra, presumably discussing doctorly things. Not far from them, Bhairavi Desai, activist and founder of the New York Taxi Workers Alliance, was asking M. Night Shyamalan, "So, when did you decide he would be dead the whole time?" To their left, D J Rekha commended Jhumpa Lahiri for winning the Pulitzer Prize and thereby rendering creative writing an acceptable career by Indian immigrant parents for their American children, and to the right, Fareed Zakaria gnawed on a dinner roll and asked, "Why is Western bread so hard?"

While it was an honor to be there among the stars of the Indian community in America, Prem became noticeably sweaty at the mere thought of mingling. Plus, lately, he couldn't be sure, but he thought he saw Wristwatch everywhere—at the post office, in the toothpaste aisle at Drug Fair, hovering near the open bar at this gala—and he worried that his grip on reality was becoming increasingly tenuous. At least Beena was accompanying him that evening and could help ground him.

"I was moved by your use of the child's perspective as a lens through which to view the adult horrors of partition," Beena said to acclaimed filmmaker Deepa Mehta. She was comporting herself in a surprisingly classy and dignified way, Prem thought. And why not? She belonged there as much as anyone, she worked as hard as anyone in that room, and no one had endured as much.

Wildly successful hotelier Sant Singh Chatwal added, "I completely concur! Wise choice by the book's author and beautifully translated to the screen by Ms. Mehta," then turning to Beena, "Do I know you, madam?"

While Beena charmed and regaled, Prem slouched and avoided eye contact. Anxious and drenched, he excused himself to find the men's room. Soon they would take their seats and munch on their salads, listen to speeches, and politely clap. Then he could go back to his regular things. The Atlantic City show was coming along nicely, with preparations going well for the sold-out show. A few local casinos had purchased $1,500 VIP seats as gifts for their high-roller clients, and the show was being televised for the first time by satellite TV channel Star Plus. All of this was excellent for Prem's bottom line, and though he was busier than ever and had taken to carrying two cell phones and occasionally sleeping in his office, and though he'd received a letter written in blood on official T-Company stationery—who could have guessed a crime syndicate would have its own letterhead—demanding a return on investment, it was all okay because it distracted him from the agony of unrequited love.

The dim, golden glow of the ballroom made everything float as in a watery dream, so when he entered the men's room and came upon his father at a urinal, he rubbed his eyes to make him go away. He went about his business, but soon, midstream, he realized his father was still there.

"Son," Ashok Ratan Kumar said from two urinals down. "This is not how I wanted first to see you."

Prem had trouble understanding what was happening. Here was his father, in America, at this gala, hair almost completely silver, pants unzipped. "I don't understand," he said.

"I have missed you," the Titan of Technology said. "How could you stay away so long?"

"Papa," Prem answered, "you told me to."

"When?"

"In your letter. With the tongue scrapers?"

"Oh, yes," Ashok said. "I have had some time to think since then."

Tears poured down both Kumars' faces as they zipped up. They looked at each other and then, under the sterile lights of the Times Square Marriott Marquis's sixth-floor men's room, they reached for each other and locked in a powerful embrace, a climactic Bollywood moment, the camera looking down on them from a God's-eye view, circling, spinning as a dramatic, soaring soundtrack obscured their sobs.

Three men entered the restroom, two heading to the urinals, one ducking into a stall. The father and son separated.

"What are you doing here?" Prem asked.

"Of course I came to see you," Ashok said.

"No, I don't mean in America, I mean, what are you doing here, in this men's room at this hotel?"

"Oh, oh, ya, I am presenting an award."

"You are?"

"You know, I thought I maybe could do both things in one trip."

Prem didn't know what to say, so his father kept talking. "I know how well your company, Superstar Activities—"

"Entertainment."

"Superstar Entertainment has done. It is at the height of its success.

Even in India you are known for what you have done here."

"That reminds me, how did you involve Lata Mangeshkar?"

"No one can tell Lataji what to do. She does what she wants," Ashok said. He continued, "But more than the money you must have made, I am impressed with your vision. Come home, Son. You have shown everyone what you can accomplish. There is no need to continue. Come back, join Kumar Group."

Prem felt the old familiar sadness rise and cause a lump to form in his throat. If ever he was going to say the thing he wanted to say, now was the time. His fists clenched and his heart raced. "You never had confidence in me before. You wanted me to get married to a wealthy family and stay away from your precious company."

Ashok was stunned. His mouth agape, he looked at his son with deep confusion and hurt in his eyes, straining as if seeing him from a great distance. "I believed in you. Always, I had confidence in you. The problem was you did not have confidence in yourself."

A troubling odor began to seep out from under the door of the third stall. This, combined with the turmoil in his head, caused Prem to feel a sudden suffocation. He had to leave immediately. "I am going home," he said.

"Wait, I will go with you after this award-presenting business," Ashok said.

"I have to go now, Papa."

"I will find you after. I will come to Edison to your little place."

"No, don't find me, don't do anything. Just . . ." Without finishing his thought, Prem exited the men's room.

Beena was part of a small horde of people leaning in to listen to world-renowned conductor Zubin Mehta tell a story. "And then he pulled his pants back up!" Zubin said, setting off an uproar of laughter. Prem tugged on Beena's elbow, pulling her out of the crowd.

"I'm gonna make a move," Prem said.

"What? The program has not even started as yet. And you must meet Zubin, he tells the naughtiest stories."

"The orchestra conductor? Never mind, I'll take the car and send it back for you. Stay, enjoy."

Sant Chatwal, tall and imposing in his signature red turban, interjected, "Do not worry, I will make sure she gets home."

Prem looked back and forth between them. "Uh, okay."

He made his way to street level and his driver brought around the car, which he ducked into without the usual small talk. Still reeling from the unexpected urinal reunion, Prem was silent the entire ride home. The weight of what his father had said, that he had never had confidence in himself, pressed down on him, and he realized this was because it was true. He had always placed the blame on others for pressuring him, for expecting too much. And then he had run away. His thoughts bounced between this and more pressing questions: What would he say when his father inevitably tracked him down? What did his father expect him to do? Was he really invited to the gala as a prominent Desi, or was it his father's doing? Was he prominent or not?

The apartment was uncharacteristically quiet when Prem got home. The Singhs had taken their visiting relatives to Niagara Falls for the obligatory relatives-visiting-from-India trip, US side only, while Deepak, Mohan, Yogesh, and Lucky were at a card party two buildings over. Overcome with exhaustion, Prem collapsed onto his mattress without changing his clothes and slept for two hours before being awakened by his roommates' return and the appearance of Beena and Ashok shortly after.

"Jesus," Prem's father said as he surveyed the apartment. "So these are the onions. Lataji informed me of these."

Prem sat up straight and tried to tamp his hair down. "I see you have met Beena," he said.

"Mr. Chatwal introduced us," Beena said rather proudly.

What transpired next was a scene right out of *Aakhree Raasta*, Amitabh's 1986 double-role crime drama, when father and son face each other in a graveyard and are confronted with the reality of their opposing viewpoints. Ashok made a case for why Prem should join the family business at last, going into great detail about the brilliant prescience of his son's long-ago multiplex theater idea. By moving away from the 600-seat single-theater format and allowing multiple films to play simultaneously in smaller theaters, filmmakers would be freed from the burden of having to produce mega-blockbusters in order to turn a profit. Filmmaking would flourish, audiences would enjoy greater variety, revenues would soar. They could call the enterprise Kumar BIG Pictures, which would be a subsidiary of Kumar BIG Entertainment, both of which would develop under Prem's direction. Ashok spoke of how the company still invested in concepts that served the common person, even increasing its footprint in the automatic papad-drying machine industry. He paced back and forth, clutching one elbow behind his back, and then, with some difficulty, plopped down on the mattress next to Prem and exhaled loudly through his nose. "You must take a decision," he ordered.

Beena washed the Singhs' dishes and made a pot of chai while Lucky, Deepak, Mohan, and Yogesh stared shamelessly at the Kumars in conversation. After some time, Lucky asked, "Who is this guy?"

"That's it, you four, out," Beena said to the roommates, shooing them toward the door with a spatula. "Go to my apartment, watch TV, have paan, out out, hurry up."

Prem looked down at the floor. "You see, Papa," he said, "there is a girl."

"A girl?" Ashok said. "Of course. Well, what is the problem, then? We will get you married to her, she can settle in India, end of story."

Ashok seemed so relieved, jubilant even, that Prem felt terrible ruining his moment of bliss. He told his father everything—his court-ship with Leena, Hemant's decree, the father and daughter's unaware-ness of his privileged background, Leena's and his breakup, and her subsequent engagement.

Prem went into great detail about his internal struggles with anxiety and shyness, his fear of work, and how Hemant's demand had actually been a blessing that forced him to face his fear and do something in the world. He was proud to tell his father that he was now a successful man to whom others came for help. He left out the part about the financing from the Mumbai underworld but laid bare the rest, pouring out the contents of his tormented soul, reaching for words to communicate the depth of his pain. At last, he concluded, "For a while I worked at Exxon petrol pump."

Ashok thumped his heartwrecked son on the back before turning to Beena. "Tell me, Beenaji, what in the hell is happening in this place?"

"Kumarji," Beena said, "I have been wondering the same thing."

"You have?" Prem said.

"Of course!" she said. "What is wrong with those Engineers? Why father and daughter are torturing you? Come, let us go ask them."

"What? No. Out of the question," Prem responded.

"Splendid idea!" Ashok said. "Where do they stay?"

"Oh, just here, three buildings down."

"Perfect! Come, Son, let me straighten out this rubbish for you. Why did you not tell me this years back? I could have fixed this all up right then."

"You don't, that is not the way—" Prem composed himself and started over. "No one is going anywhere. Except maybe Beena is going home and you are going to a hotel."

"Does this Leena even want to come back to you?" Ashok asked his son.

"Well, no, not really," Prem said.

"But you are living here for her," Ashok said.

"Correct."

"And she is marrying someone else."

"Most likely."

"But she has not married yet."

"Correct."

"And you think maybe she will suddenly break with her fiancé and run through a field of tulips into your arms."

"Not exactly—"

Ashok let out a frustrated harumph. "I am losing patience, Beenaji. Let us go talk to this Engineer."

"What? Why?" Prem began but quickly gave up. "Fine, go."

"Have some chai, and maybe get those buffoons out of my apartment," Beena said to Prem, pulling the door shut behind her.

He didn't fetch his friends, but he did drink three cups of tea while worrying about what was transpiring in 5F. It wasn't so much that he was worried about the meeting of the fathers, though this was not a pleasant thought by any means. What concerned him most was what Leena would think when she learned that he had hidden his past from her, that he had lied. Then again, she might not care at all. It was doubtful, though not impossible, that she was in the apartment as all of this was transpiring. And if she wasn't, it wouldn't be long before Hemant would catch her up on everything. After finishing the tea, Prem dug around for something stiff to drink.

Beena led the way through the bedraggled lawn as Ashok looked with curiosity at the place where his son had lived all these years. The buildings were squat and plain, their railings rusted, paint peeling from the window trim. Candy wrappers and cigarette butts littered the grass. Though it was well past midnight, a man was leaning precariously over a balcony, trying to make an adjustment to a satellite dish, while another man on another balcony was yelling into his cell phone. When they reached the Engineers' apartment, Viren Bhai answered the door.

"Welcome, welcome," he said, as though Beena and a strange man's late-night visit were typical.

"Hello, Viren Bhai, sorry to disturb, is Hemant at home?" Beena said.

"Yes, yes, come sit," he said.

"Why does this apartment look like a rainforest?" Ashok said, referring to Hemant's overgrown plant, whose leaves now covered every inch of ceiling and wall.

"This is Ashok Kumar, founder and chairman—chairman, no? Or is it president? CEO?—CEO of Kumar Group, and our dear Prem's father."

Viren Bhai remained serene and unflappable, as always. "Nice to make your acquaintance. I will just call Hemant. It will be one moment."

There was grunting and muffled discussion in the back room, and finally Hemant appeared in his bedtime kurta pajama, rubbing his eyes. "Is my daughter fine?"

"She is fine," Beena said. "I mean, I do not actually know if she is fine. Probably she is fine. This is Ashok Kumar, Prem's father from Delhi."

The two men sized each other up. Viren Bhai assumed the lotus pose in one corner. Hemant could not understand the connection between this well-dressed, imposing gentleman and the gas-stationwalla who had been after his daughter. "But you look so nice."

"Thank you."

"Oh, ya, this is the owner of Kumar Group Company, the highly successful and famous industrialist and very important man."

"But you said he is the father of that cheap street lafunga," Hemant said, genuinely confused.

"Did you just call my son a cheap street lafunga?"

"You really should not call his son a cheap street lafunga," Beena said turning to Hemant.

After much back and forth and some light Internet searching, Hemant was at last persuaded that Ashok Kumar was who he said he was and that Prem was his son. "Ashokji! Why did you not say so in the beginning? Come sit on this chair, it is more comfortable. I will bring you some juice. You want juice?"

The two men spoke then as though they were in-laws already, laughing yet respectful, comfortable yet cautious. Hemant, entirely forgetting that Leena was engaged to Mikesh, was ecstatic about his daughter's possible connection with the prosperous Kumar family, quickly thanking his auspicious plant under his breath. Ashok was pleased to find that Hemant was a hospitable and friendly man after all. Beena was getting quite sleepy and frustrated that no matters were being resolved.

"Now, what about this one million and one dollars?" Ashok asked.

In all his excitement, Hemant had forgotten the cause of Leena and Prem's breakup and was embarrassed at the mention of it. "Oh, no, that is nothing, you know, forget that. Let us leave the past in the past only and look forward into the bright future of these two young people."

Ashok shifted in his highly comfortable chair. "They are not so young anymore."

"Better to not waste time then!" Hemant said.

"How was it that you treated my son in this manner?" Ashok said.

Beena slapped her forehead. She turned to Viren Bhai for support, but his eyes were closed, in meditation or sleep. "You know, nothing needs to be resolved now, let us meet in the morning. I will make dosa—"

"Your son," Hemant replied, "was penniless and without prospects. I had to take a wise decision for my daughter's well-being in this country."

"I see, so your daughter is too foolish to take a wise decision on her own."

"Did you say my daughter is foolish?"

"*You* said your daughter is foolish."

In an instant, a life of luxury flashed before Hemant's eyes: private jets, top-of-the-line cars, unlimited jet skis, homes in multiple countries, designer saris, red carpets, servants and drivers, and unnecessary jewelry. But then he saw Leena's sad face after being insulted by her father-in-law. Hemant stood and pointed to the door. "No, thank you, we do not need your money or your insults or your son. Leena has found a nice doctor boy and we are very happy."

Knowing when to exit an unsuccessful negotiation was one of Ashok's strengths. He quietly left the apartment and waited outside for Beena.

"What have you done?" Beena yelled at Hemant. "Okay, okay, I can sort it all out," she sighed, shooing him back toward his room and slipping out.

Hemant could hardly contain his anger. He turned to his peaceful boarder for comfort. "Can you believe that man? Can you believe his son, hiding the truth, telling us nothing about his background and such?"

Viren Bhai slowly opened his eyes and let out a steady, soothing breath. "Oh yes, Prem is the son of Ashok Ratan Kumar, Titan of Technology, Giant of Generics, head of Kumar Group, net worth rupees 7.1 crores. You did not know?"

That night, everyone went to bed—Ashok on Beena's squeaky plastic couch—but no one slept. Beena had come by to give Prem a summary of the meeting's salient points. He was somewhat relieved knowing that Leena had not been present. Still, he couldn't sleep. At 4:31 a.m., he wrote:

198. There are some things I have to tell you about my family. Please do not mind.

199. Also, some goondas from Mumbai are after me.

30

Ashok Ratan Kumar returned to India without his son. He did not understand why Prem had initially agreed to the grocery man's orders, nor why he continued to live as a paying guest on a mattress and ride a bicycle in the snow. But he did realize, at last, why his son stayed in America. He was there for a girl, albeit one who was not there for him.

"Come back anytime, Son," Ashok had said. "Anmol will be heading Kumar BIG Entertainment now, but we can always find something else for you, perhaps on the alcohol side?"

"Sure, ya, uh . . ."

"Come for a short time, come for a long time, bring her, do not bring her," he said. "Just be in touch."

They hugged for a long time at Newark Airport. "Don't worry, Papa," Prem said. "Even on the mattress, under the onions, it is a nice life."

Ashok patted his son on the back. "She must be something."

Leena was not only something, she was everything. Every ordinary object or occurrence alluded to her: a swing in the park reminded him of the one in her father's apartment, Gold Spot on a menu recalled their first encounter. He tried to focus on work and friends, but then he would see some cassette tape, a cricket match on TV, or someone who laughed the way she did, and he was ruined all over again. He watched

DDLJ and wondered if she saw the same meaning in it that he did. The primacy of kanyadaan, the father's blessing—for any marriage, be it arranged, love, or something in between—and whether she could see his refusal to marry without it as a heroic act. It was all in the film. While Prem found comfort in the fact that she had not yet married the doctor, he had a ferocious desire to know why not. When he enlisted Mr. Satish Rajan to investigate the matter—a return favor for intervening in an ongoing mouse infestation issue at Hidden Valley Estates—the only intelligence he acquired was that she'd switched from Coats to Vanity brand thread for her salon.

When the *Bollywood Dreams* show, the biggest, showiest show yet, was mounted at the Continental Airlines Arena, Prem anonymously gave Leena premium tickets through Varsha Virani. Though twelve thousand people were in attendance, Shilpa Shetty entered from the ceiling on a trapeze lowered from the rafters, Akshay Kumar appeared from within a cloud of smoke, newcomer heartthrob Hrithik Roshan ripped his tight white undershirt from his body and performed a rigorous shirtless dance while Rani Mukerji and Kajol danced fully clothed beside him, and the finale incorporated ticker tape, jugglers with flaming torches, and a pole-vaulting Shah Rukh Khan, Prem was crushed because Leena came with Mikesh instead of Varsha.

He saw her a handful of painful times more that summer, sometimes by accident, sometimes by design. At Singas Famous Pizza, that small chain of informal restaurants with a mysteriously fanatical following among Indian Americans throughout the tristate area, she ordered pineapple topping, which was a distressing reminder of how many little things he did not know about her, of how much had changed since her strictly onion and green pepper days. Another day, as he entered Swagath Gourmet, he spotted her stepping out of Avsar Bridal Emporium, which ruined July for him. He drifted through that

summer, weary and withdrawn, beaten down by his decade-long obsession. When the India Day Parade came around again, he went with
the intention of seeing her. He'd heard that India America Grocers and
Leena's salon had entered a float this year, one third of which Hemant
had sublet to tax and accounting specialist Bansilal Patel CPA LLC. He
stood in the crowd in the sweltering August heat and searched the
horizon with the distant eyes of a man remembering a long-ago love.
When she appeared, she wore a sky-blue salwar and her hair was in a
messy ponytail, and she waved and tossed out coupons for one-dollar-
off chickpea flour, which people dove after as if for gold. Prem picked
one up from the ground. It had been stepped on and was partially
torn, but he folded it up and put it in his wallet anyway because she
had touched it. On the days he saw her with the doctor, he wondered
whether it was better to see her with him or not see her at all. He suspected others were after her as well; a young owner of a chain of motels
seemed to be hanging around her a lot on group outings, and a few
IT guys also seemed to be vying for attention. Perhaps they'd learned
she had no real interest in the doctor and thought they stood a chance,
which at once heartened and disturbed Prem. He thought about the
prevalence of love triangles in Hindi movies—*Devdas, Pyaasa, Sangam,
Muqaddar Ka Sikandar*, the list went on—and hoped he wasn't the tragic
hero who dies alone. In the deepest depth of his sadness, he questioned
what he was doing and doubted that she even remembered his name,
only to regain, in time, his hopefulness, because what choice did he
have?

Beena, irked by her friend's situation, asked Prem at the beginning
of September, "How can you keep waiting like this? How can you waste
your youth?"

He sighed. "Hindi movies can be quite long sometimes."

It was with the desire to catch a glimpse of her from across a crowded banquet hall that Prem accepted a position as a judge at the Miss India USA pageant. Over six hundred people packed the ballroom at Royal Albert's Palace to witness thirty-two of the brightest, most talented predominantly pre-med Indian American women in the country compete for the crown and a chance to represent the nation in the Miss India Worldwide pageant, to be held in Dubai in April. Prem was seated next to fellow judge and cricket legend Kapil Dev, who was in a chatty mood.

"I cannot decide, yaar, *Goblet of Fire* was good, but *Prisoner of Azkaban* was fantastic," Kapil Dev said. It was intolerably, unusually hot outside for September in New Jersey, but the massive room was overwhelmed by air conditioning. Heavily bejeweled women mingled among tables while their husbands moved on to their second Johnnie Walkers. Prem immediately spotted Leena chatting with Snigdha, her father nearby straining to catch a glimpse of Kapil Dev. She wore a maharani pink sari with simple earrings, her hair in a high bun. She was more stunning than all of the contestants taken together. If he could have, he would have awarded her every prize right then: Miss Beautiful Smile, Miss Beautiful Skin, Miss Beautiful Eyes, Miss Beautiful Hair, Miss Talented, Miss Photogenic, and Miss Well-spoken; and then he would invent five new categories—Miss Contagious Laugh, Miss Exceedingly Straight Teeth, Miss Astute Businesswoman, Miss Devoted Daughter, Miss Not-Too-Much Makeup—and bestow them upon her as well.

"Really?" Kapil Dev continued. "You have not read any of them?"

The night went on like this, with Kapil Dev whispering in his ear and Prem finding reasons to turn and glance in Leena's direction. When Miss Michigan, whose hobbies included Bharata Natyam dancing and spending time with her grandmother, lost a set of eyelashes during the Indian dress competition, Leena laughed but quickly covered her mouth with her hand to keep it in. When Miss Virginia, a fan of kung fu films and

Justin Timberlake, tried to execute a show-stopping twirl in the last leg of the evening gown segment, Leena accepted a refill of her wine. He sat through three Bollywood dances, two off-key vocalists, one tap-dancing performance, a violin solo, a poetry recital, and an inspirational talk, all the while thinking, Leena, Leena, Leena. When the interviews began and one subpar contestant after another answered the question, "How would you use the Miss India USA crown to help the world?" he had had enough.

"What is wrong? Are you okay?" Kapil Dev nudged Prem's arm gently. "I know, Miss Kentucky's answer was terrible, but really, try to hold it together, man."

Prem had buried his face in his arms on the table and begun emitting a low moan. The judge on the other side of him, model and acclaimed cookbook author Padma Lakshmi, also tried to help him rally, and onstage, the emcee paused and gawked. The entire ballroom that night thought the owner of Superstar Entertainment had been so disgusted by Miss Kentucky's incomprehensible, rambling answer about using her platform to eradicate dengue fever that he became physically ill. Only Lucky, watching from backstage, as The Sassy Salwar was the official sponsor of the Indian Dress category, saw that Prem's sudden collapse nearly coincided with Leena exiting the ballroom with a tall and handsome man. It had been years since Prem and Leena's short-lived, star-crossed romance, and Prem hadn't mentioned her name since. Not many knew what had caused the breakup, and the whole episode was soon forgotten as the community carried on with living. Prem always seemed fine; not cheerful, but certainly content. Few could have guessed.

Lucky leaped onto the stage from his place in the wings. "No need to worry, his buddy is here," he said to everyone in the ballroom and jumped down to the judges' table. "Don't worry, buddy," he whispered to Prem, "let's get out of here." He put his arm around his roommate and walked him out of the ballroom, on the way announcing, "Tummy troubles! Probably the mutton. Nobody eat any more mutton!" By the time it was announced that the Miss India USA 2001 crown went to Miss Minnesota, Nirali Nath, they were back at King's Court. They hadn't spoken at all on the car ride home. Lucky tucked Prem into his mattress and turned off all the lights. He got himself ready for bed as well and checked one last time on Prem, who was already fast asleep. All this time, Lucky thought.

LITTLE INDIA IN NEW JERSEY

Backlash in Our Backyards

BY MONA KULKARNI October 8, 2001

Page 1

Though it has been almost a month since the devastating attacks of September 11, for brown-skinned people in America, the terror has only just begun.

In the week immediately following the attack, Americans of South Asian or Middle Eastern descent faced an unprecedented number of incidents of racial bias, ranging from verbal abuse to vandalism, bullying in schools and workplace intimidation to physical assault and murder.

On September 15, Balbir Singh Sodhi, a Sikh gas-station owner in Mesa, Ariz., was shot and killed in the parking lot of his Chevron, where he had stepped outside to plant flowers. His killer, later identified as Frank Roque, was heard at a bar saying he was going to punish those responsible for September 11 by

shooting "towelheads." Sodhi, a father of five, is remembered as a generous, loving man who gave candy to children and allowed customers to pay later if short on cash. Earlier that day, he had donated the contents of his wallet—about $75— to a 9/11 victims' fund.

On September 15, admitted white supremacist Mark Anthony Stroman took revenge for the September 11 attacks by shooting Pakistani immigrant Waqar Hasan in the head while he was grilling hamburgers in his Dallas, Texas, convenience store. Six days later, Stroman shot Bangladeshi immigrant Raisuddin Bhuiyan in the face at a gas station. While Bhuiyan survived, he was left blind in one eye. Still not finished with his killing spree, Stroman shot and killed Vasudev Patel, a Hindu Indian immigrant, on October 4 at his convenience store. The killer was arrested the following day.

While the horrific killings of Sodhi, Hassan and Patel were, to an extent, covered by the national news media, the everyday insults have remained largely hidden: the Sikh cab driver from Washington state who was brutally beaten by a customer; the "Towell [sic] Heads Go-Home!" sign left outside a Salem, Ore., convenience store owned by an Indian immigrant; the threatening phone calls and rocks thrown through Sikh Americans' windows in Canfield, Ohio; the Pakistani man in Tulsa who, after being badly beaten and left with missing teeth and swollen eyes, still proclaimed his love for America; the countless South Asian and Middle Eastern Americans who were told to go back to their countries; the Indian man wiping away his tears outside a Washington mini mart after being threatened and harassed while working there. This list, compiled by South Asian American Leaders of Tomorrow (SAALT), goes on. The organization has been meticulously documenting such instances and has reported the occurrence of 645 in the first week after 9/11 alone.

Many believe there will be more.

Whatever the case, South Asian communities around the country have been organizing to stand up against racism and ignorance. Here in the Edison area, local businessman and community activist Hemant Engineer is coordinating a protest march for October 20. "We must show that we are strong and cannot be bullied. We are no longer helpless 'dots' to be easily busted," Engineer says, referencing the string of crimes perpetrated in the 1980s by the hate group Dotbusters.

"Also, we here, whether we are Hindu, Sikh, Parsi, Buddhist or Muslim, we are not terrorists, we did not attack anyone. And now we are the ones being terrorized," he continued. Mayor George Spadoro, Congressman Frank Pallone,

Jr., and local police enforcement have already confirmed their participation in the event.

South Asians in the area have also begun taking certain precautionary measures against possible bias attacks, such as displaying American flags on their lawns and U.S.A. bumper stickers on their cars to announce their allegiance to the country. Men have shaved their beards and women have donned bindis, all in an effort to show they do not share the religion of the hijackers. Others are skeptical of such tactics. With the high concentration of Indians in our area—the population of Indians in New Jersey has increased by 113% in the past 10 years, reaching 169,180 people in 2000—some are concerned that the density and visibility of Indians here will make us an easy target.

Page 2

LETTERS   October 8, 2001

Model Minorities No More

In the "Letters" section of your September 24 issue, a Mr. Kavi Bakshi exhorted Hindu Americans to "please fly your American flags, shave your beards and wear your bindis." I would just like to say that these things will not protect us. Instead of separating ourselves from other minorities in this country, now is the time to join forces with them.

We have long embraced the "model minority" label thrust upon us, which used us as a shining example of how, with hard work, any rule-abiding citizen can succeed in America. But now, we are experiencing the same widespread, blatant racism that other minority communities have always endured. We must not think we are different or better. We all are Muslims.

For more on this line of thinking, I implore you to please pick up Vijay Prashad's eye-opening "The Karma of Brownfolk" from which my opinions derive.

Hasmukh Jha
Colonia, N.J.

32

"Sir, the stars have been detained at Immigration and Customs," Prem's new, very efficient, and monotone assistant, Pankaj, informed him. It was mid-October, one day before rehearsals were to begin for *Lights, Camera, Indian!* Prem had decided the show must go on.

"Which ones?" he asked.

"Aamir, Salman, Shah Rukh," Pankaj replied.

"Jesus," Prem said. The three Khans, the show's headliners, had played leading men for many years and continued to play the role of college students well into their thirties. Three of the biggest movie stars in the world, they were not accustomed to such treatment.

"The airportwalla will not give me any information, sir—how long they will be there, what they are doing to them."

"Did you tell him these are major superstars of Indian cinema?"

"Yes, sir. He was not impressed, sir."

Prem had heard the stories of people of South Asian ancestry being pulled out of line at the airport for additional screening, the increasing occurrence of "Would you come with me, sir" directed at brown-skinned travelers. He could understand the reasons for the increased measures, but why would these three men in particular, enjoying fabulously glamorous lives of wealth, fame, unlimited creative expression, and universal adoration, take down an airplane and themselves in the process? More precise methodology was in order, Prem felt.

It was true, Aamir, Salman, and Shah Rukh were at the top of their game. With *Asoka* and *Lagaan*, Shah Rukh and Aamir, respectively, ushered in the rise of big-budget historical epics. In the same year, they heralded the era of the diasporic romance with *Kabhi Khushi Kabhie Gham (K3G)*, *Dil Chahta Hai*, and *Kal Ho Naa Ho (KHNH)*, which brought the worlds of expatriate Indians to Indian audiences. They also brought Indian actors out from their soundstages and into the open air of foreign countries, where they could shoot outdoors without being attacked by adoring mobs.

Prem was not interested in seeing Indian movies set in America about the lives of super-rich business families; he missed the classics that portrayed the lives of poor, struggling Indians fighting for justice in the mean streets of Bombay when it was still called Bombay. Yet, he had to admit he enjoyed *K3G*'s misunderstood-son-trying-to-find-himself storyline and its role in Amitabh Bachchan's triumphant white-goateed comeback, which was bolstered by his role as host of the hugely popular *Kaun Banega Crorepati*—the *Who Wants to Be a Millionaire* of India. Meanwhile, Salman, still riding the wave of his 1999 and 2000 hits *Hum Dil De Chuke Sanam*, *Hum Saath-Saath Hain*, and *Chori Chori Chupke Chupke*, was doing a solid job of remaining on top despite the encroachment of the slightly younger set, including Hrithik Roshan and new-Khan-on-the-block Saif Ali.

The bottom line was these three could not remain at the airport. Something had to be done, but what? Prem had amassed a large number of contacts over the years, but none with any political or aeronautical influence. He paced his modest office—which he'd acquired at the same time he'd acquired his modest assistant—as Pankaj stood solemnly and obediently very near the dangling leaves of a plant. The plant had been a gift from Suchitra, the kind-hearted divorcée, after his

No

last show, an offering of good luck on his continued journey to prosperity. It hung from the ceiling, and apparently, when the leaves spilled over the sides of the basket and touched the ground, he would be rich. Someone else had a plant like this, Prem remembered. He stopped pacing and turned to Pankaj amongst the greenery. "I know someone who maybe can help."

* * *

"I've been calling since a week," Hemant said into the phone in an aggravated tone. He was on with the mayor's office, according to Kailash Mistry, who answered the door and invited Prem in. The apartment was crawling with cricket fans who had come over that morning to cheer on India versus South Africa in the final of the Standard Bank Triangular tournament. Though it was not a major event, they had piled in, pillows tucked under their arms at seven on a Wednesday morning, and made themselves comfortable, sprawling out beneath the canopy of green as though sunbathing.

"Not looking good for India," Kailash said to Prem. "Maybe you can bring them luck. Come, come."

"No, you see, I—" Prem started.

"Why everything is taking so much of time?" Hemant growled at the mayor.

"You, shift," Kailash said, shooing Charlie Patel to the outer reaches of the couch to make room for Prem.

"Really, I just—"

"Now, sit. Relax," Kailash insisted.

Prem gave up and sat. He had never cared much for cricket but tried to follow along over the years because he knew it mattered to Leena. He was surprised and disappointed she was not there for the match; it was hard for her to resist this kind of scene. Though she was usually the only female in the room, she'd once told him, it was the environment in which she felt she most belonged.

Hemant ended his call and began grumbling to himself. "Always they give so much of hassle. Never getting anything done ever." Then turning to cricket and the situation in his apartment: "All out for 183? Hopeless. Where is my pillow? What is Petrol Pump doing on my sofa?"

Prem cleared his throat and began unwedging himself from between Charlie and Nathan Kothari, which was more challenging than expected. When at last he launched himself free, he tripped on two sets of legs and an arm before fully coming to an upright position before Hemant.

"Can I help you?" Hemant asked in an unhelpful tone.

Prem had not come face to face with Leena's father since 1988, when the Berlin Wall still stood and Rajiv Gandhi still lived. The man had aged accordingly. His hair was almost completely gone, though he still seemed to apply the same amount of Brylcreem to it, and his jowls had drooped to well below his jawline. Still, he had a younger man's fire in his eyes, which was directed at Prem at that moment.

"Sir, can I speak to you on the side?" Prem said.

"On the side of what?" Hemant said.

"Sorry, I meant on the other side of the room. In the kitchen."

Hemant grunted and nodded. "Be fast, my match is on."

They stepped over two more legs before reaching the kitchen. Prem remembered that Hemant now knew everything—his parentage, his family's situation, his outright deception. Best not to bring that up, he thought, his thighs quivering as in childhood after an exceptional tarriance at a squat toilet. He explained the problem of his actors spending the night in airport detention, but it was unclear whether Hemant was moved. "I believe they had to remove all their clothing and were only given French fries to eat," Prem added in an attempt to make his story more compelling.

"Is that right?" Hemant said.

Prem took a seat at the dining table to gain some control over his body, a move he instantly recognized as a mistake because Hemant was now towering over him, his jowls looming above. Prem craned his neck. "Also, they searched their suitcases and confiscated their tongue scrapers," he explained.

After a lot of heavy breathing, Hemant said, "Which actors?"

"Aamir, Salman, Shah Rukh," Prem said.

"Hmph. Was that fellow in *DDLJ*?" Hemant said.

"Which fellow?" Prem said.

"Salman," Hemant said.

"No, no, he was in *MPK*," Prem said.

"Then who was in *DDLJ*?"

"That was Shah Rukh. He also was the one in *K2H2*, *KHNH*, and *K3G*."

"Then who is Salman?"

"From *MPK* and more recently *HAHK*."

"And then this Aamir was in *1942: A Love Story*?"

"No, *1947 Earth*."

"And they are at JFK?"

"No, sir, Newark."

"Okay, then I can make a few calls," Hemant decided. "Also, I will alert the newspapers and TV stations." He was inclined to help not because of the detainees' celebrity status, but because of the gravity of the backlash toward South Asian Americans. Though more than a month had passed, things only seemed to be getting worse for his community. And he was the person in Edison and the surrounding areas to whom everyone turned for leadership—even Prem Kumar. The ugly episode with Prem's pompous yet distinguished father was still very much on his mind. He hadn't told Leena anything about it, mostly because he himself did not know what to think of the whole thing. On the one hand, Prem had been duplicitous with him and his daughter, disloyal to his own family, and had worked in a gas station for a really long time. On the other hand, he had apparently stayed true to Leena all these years, built what seemed to be a legitimate business, and, most bewilderingly, was from a well-to-do family. How wonderful it would be for Leena to marry into such comfortable circumstances. She would no longer have to clip the toenails of rude women or do whatever it was she did with their body hair. He did not know if she still thought about Prem at all or if she was really interested in marrying Mikesh. He really ought to talk to her sometime, he thought. In the end, all he wanted was for her to achieve the dream for which they had come all the way to this country. Like all loving parents, he wanted her to have more than he had had. But she was expanding her business into an eyebrow empire, and it was clear she did not need a rich husband to support her. He knew that she would be the one to choose. Funny how that happened, he thought.

But why shouldn't it have? Leena was from Edison, and the story of Edison was the story of progress. Of risk takers, path breakers, Thomas Edison, and possibility. Of Laxmikant Chakravarti, who opened Chuck's Sports Collectibles though he'd never seen a baseball before coming to the United States; of Vaishali Variyar, who converted the First Fidelity Bank into a sari shop. Of Mahatma Gandhi Plaza and Krishna Auto Repair at the Gulf station. Of the Indo-American Senior Center, taking more than a thousand nanas and nanis, ajis and ajobas from Edison on fun beach and temple outings. Of Metropark station, whose platform and stairwell billboards advertised Dish Network's Hindi Megapack and Lufthansa flights to Delhi, making Indian Americans feel right at home.

Some, however, did not view all this progress as addition, but rather as subtraction. They felt their town had become "a maze of charmless Indian strip malls" and didn't appreciate the presence of Indian immigrants because of the "amount of cologne they wear." They made light of the 1980s Dotbusters hate crimes and said they could have come up with better racist insults "for a group of people whose gods have multiple arms and an elephant nose." For a while, they had assumed all Indians were geniuses, but when "the doctors and engineers brought over their merchant cousins," they were no longer sure about that. They started "to understand why India was so damn poor." At least, this was how one particular former resident described it some years later in *Time* magazine.

Prem turned to leave, knowing a handshake was out of the realm of possibility.

"Pumpwalla, wait," Hemant called. "What were the names again?"

By that evening, the actors were released. Because of the publicity that Hemant generated during the course of the day, a massive crowd of fans gathered at baggage claim to catch a glimpse of the Khans. The stars emerged, weary and disheveled yet handsome and chiseled as ever, their five-o'clock shadows causing grown aunties to swoon. The three men smiled and waved, then put on dark shades though indoors to deflect the flashes of the cameras. No one could believe they pulled their own luggage. Flowers were offered and autographs were signed, and the next day the US ambassador to India apologized for the detentions, promising that authorities were working to ensure it would never happen again.

Lights, Camera, Indian!, mounted at the historic, newly renovated Boardwalk Hall in Atlantic City, was a tremendous success, surpassing all previous shows in grandiosity. Five-hundred-dollar tickets sold on the secondary market for one thousand, and the headliners attracted enough people to fill the 14,000 seats: Preity Zinta, Karishma Kapoor, and, for the first time on one stage, the three unrelated Khans, Shah Rukh, Salman, and Aamir, who was fresh off two hits—*Lagaan* and *Dil Chahta Hai*—and an age-defying makeover. It was widely hailed as the over-the-toppest show yet, with Shah Rukh and Malaika dancing astride a train cutting across the hall à la *Dil Se* while Preity and Aamir lip-synched and danced dangerously close to a pyrotechnical display. In a brief moment of solemnity, the special contingent from the Red Cross Gujarat Earthquake Relief Fund made a plea for donations. The only glitch of the evening occurred late in the show when Karishma Kapoor's feet began hurting and she flung her high heels at the fog-machine operator.

All of it would have taken Prem's breath away had he been in the mood to have his breath taken. The truth was that the stars, the shows, and the glamour of it all had lost their luster; it had become just a business for him. He watched from the wings as Salman took off his shirt while being doused with water, aware that he felt nothing. The crowd roared at the final number, eventually simmering down and beginning the slow stream out, heading to the Trump Taj Mahal to gamble in a gaudy, utterly un-Taj Mahal-ish environment. They would enjoy the slots and tables, have one or two scotch-and-sodas, stop by the gift shop to browse the large selection of eponymous merchandise—Trump natural spring water, Trump Success signature fragrance—then head home to somewhere in New Jersey with their loved ones.

33

The Sassy Salwar, Lucky's small but upscale boutique on Oak Tree, had quietly thrived all these years. Like Prem, Lucky chose to continue living on a mattress in a crowded apartment to save money, but also because—and he would never admit to this—he liked the company. He enjoyed the camaraderie of it, the we-are-in-this-together aspect of his unconventional living arrangement. When Mohan and Yogesh began to consider leaving their mattresses behind and moved to situations with actual beds, Lucky was deeply affected. He tried recruiting replacements—an upbeat Urban Thali waiter who might liven things up, a couple of gas-station guys out of a sense of nostalgia, a Jalal's Halal Groceries stock boy with an effervescent mango air—but they all turned him down.

Amarleen tried to comfort him. "They probably just thought you were a dirty type of desperate guy. Why would these young fellows want to sleep on the floor with a forty-year-old man?" This made sense, so Lucky looked for fulfillment beyond the apartment, frequenting bars and other people's homes, crashing graduation parties, and finagling invitations to his clients' wedding receptions. When he got tired of the usual amusements, he began manufacturing his own vehicles for entertainment, spending obscene amounts of money on hosting bowling tournaments, and chartering party buses to Atlantic City. He became known in King's Court and surrounding complexes as Lucky the Good-Time Guy or That Bengali Guy Who Pays for Everything. Everyone assumed he wasn't looking to settle down because, after all, why ruin the fun? But the truth was he chased these festive diversions to fill the wife-shaped hole in his life.

He had spent many years cultivating a reputation as a ladies' man, bragging to his roommates about the throngs of women constantly accosting him. Over the years, there had been the occasional woman who looked in his direction; a few even met him for chai and samosas at Delhi Garden, but no one lasted for any significant amount of time. Lucky attributed this to his razzling-dazzling wardrobe and overwhelming virility as showcased by his lush chest hair. They found it intimidating, he deduced. He was correct in his estimation that The Sassy Salwar would open up a whole new avenue for meeting women, but they tended to be married or on the verge. So he continued to enjoy his bachelor life until one day, the woman of his dreams walked through the Sassy doors.

"Sushila. Sushila Mukherjee, Century 21," she said and aggressively offered her card.

For years to come, Lucky would repeat the story of how, when he saw Sushila enter his store that day, the background Bollywood music surged and engulfed the entire room and Sushila's brown pantsuit metamorphosed into a sky-blue chiffon sari, the pallu billowing in the inexplicable wind.

"Oh, come on," Sushila would say whenever Lucky recounted their origin story to people. "Don't be so dramatic, my love."

"And then," Lucky would continue, "my customers suddenly became sideys, dancing on both sides of her, not with so much grace, but still knowing all the steps."

"Really, darling, they don't want to hear this."

"They do."

He loved repeating this story, which invariably ended with "she had me at 'Century 21,' " which Sushila took as her cue to distribute more cards. It wasn't long before they were inseparable, admired as the "it" couple around town, a regular real estate–women's wear super team. If pressed to name one minor, miniscule flaw in the otherwise delight-ful couple's aura of glory, friends would without hesitation point to Lucky's and Sushila's excessive public displays of affection. At social events, they found ways to continuously touch each other, even when engaged in separate conversations. During the grand opening of No More Work, Indo-American Assisted-Living Community, they buried their hands in each other's back pants pockets and began kneading, causing everyone to slowly step away from them until a four-foot-wide buffer ring surrounded the couple, who didn't notice a thing. And on a chartered bus to Six Flags Great Adventure, no one dared look in the direction of the last row, where the happy couple had claimed all four back seats.

So, when Sushila turned up pregnant a few months later, no one was surprised except her mother. They expected Mrs. Mukherjee to be furious and to throw Sushila out of the apartment, as was standard for that corner of Edison under those circumstances. Instead, when Sushila approached her, she said, "Really? Great! Now that storewalla will definitely have to marry you." Mrs. Mukherjee ordered Lucky, through Sushila, to come over the next day to formally ask for her permission to marry her daughter.

Lucky put on his best crushed-velvet shirt and even buttoned it al-most to the top, stifling his ordinarily unfettered chest hair. He had been to the apartment many times when Sushila's mother was not home and was familiar with its dismal atmosphere and lack of natural light. The drawing room was sparsely decorated, with just one woeful painting of a swan and unnecessarily heavy blue velvet drapes that were always drawn. Mrs. Mukherjee was as dreary and unappealing as her home, dressed in a gray salwar, her hair pulled back in a severe bun. Thinking back on that day, Lucky would not be able to recall Mrs. Mukherjee giving him a chance to say anything, let alone ask for her daughter's hand in marriage. After a stern lecture about responsibility and the modern man, Mrs. Mukherjee—who stated upfront that she preferred to be addressed as Mrs. Mukherjee—handed Lucky a list of demands, neatly typed and formatted.

The Path Forward: How to Marry My Sushila

By Mrs. Mukherjee

1. Marry immediately. We must avoid a scandal with Indian relatives, who shall remain uninformed of the pregnancy.

2. Pay for most of wedding.

3. Expand the Jazzy Panty store and earn more money.

4. Move to proper apartment as soon as possible.

5. Or I will beat your brain out with my rolling pin.

Lucky felt like vomiting. How could he possibly do all these things? Was she crazy? Why did she think his store was called Jazzy Panty? Had that rolling pin on the coffee table been there the entire time? Where was Sushila? He folded up the paper and put it in his back pocket, which visibly irked Mrs. Mukherjee. So he pulled it back out and unfolded it, trying to smooth it out on the table, at one point using the rolling pin, to no avail. "Perfect list, first-class, absolutely," he said. "No problem, I will take care of everything, do not take any tension. Can I talk to Sushila?"

That night, Lucky tucked the list under his mattress. He lay awake for a long time, thinking. If they had a modest wedding at the Swaminarayan temple, with no flowers and a small amount of food from Beena Joshi, he could cover much of it. He could find out tomorrow if there were any one-bedroom apartments available in King's Court, and he could find a few paying guests to help cover the rent, hopefully with more luck this time. Maybe they would trust him more with a wife and baby. But no one too noisy or too handsome; maybe a couple of those guys who unloaded trucks at Sudha and Niranjan's Grocery Emporium near his store. But they might have too big muscles. Maybe some computer guys. But expanding the store and making more money were no easy tasks. To make money, he would need money—a lot of it, quickly. No bank was going to lend him anything because of his abysmal credit rating, which had plummeted after the fifth party-bus rental. After a quick rundown of his relatives, he realized he needed wealthier relatives. At 3:00 a.m., he shook Deepak, who was fast asleep on his mattress. "Hey. Deepak. Do you have any money?"

"What? Stop shaking me. Are you crazy? I will give you five dollars in the morning."

Lucky turned then to Prem's mattress. It had been vacant for nearly two weeks as Prem worked long hours and slept in his office again in advance of the big Giants Stadium extravaganza, *Masala in the Meadowlands: An Intimate Evening in a Huge Stadium*, or something to that effect. The show had been sold out for weeks. Lucky tried to calculate how much money Prem must make from ticket sales but gave up when it came to estimating the number of VIP and VVIP tickets, floor seats, etc. But he knew the number was big. Everyone knew Prem had become a highly successful man, though it was easy to forget because of his bicycle and his mattress. He must have accumulated a gold mine. Under ordinary circumstances, Lucky would not have thought of borrowing money from friends; it was like getting a tattoo on the face or renting five party buses in one year—a bad idea. But a baby was involved, and Mrs. Mukherjee had turned out to be quite scary. In a few weeks, the show would be over. After that, he would ask.

34

"I am so sorry, sir. I cannot understand how all of these people found out," the driver said to Amitabh Bachchan. A mass of fans were assembled on that late spring afternoon in the arrivals area at Newark International to behold the biggest movie star in the world. A hundred cameras flashed and a multilingual clamor rose up in adoration at the sight of him, tall and exalted, distinguished with an air of humility. "It is quite all right," he said.

The scene was not surprising for him; it was what he encountered every day. For hours they waited, hoping, praying for just a glimpse, and he was in their debt. He rarely felt the annoyance or burden he had heard other actors complain of. The unthinkable egotism of them! Amitabh refused to lose sight of the great blessing of success in this astonishing profession.

The driver raised his arm in a weak attempt to shield him from the throng. But Amitabh approached the makeshift barricade that airport security had hurriedly erected, namaskaring and posing for pictures for nearly an hour, the driver looking on disapprovingly. At the end of the line was an elderly woman in a wheelchair. Amitabh bent down and cupped her hands in his and said something that made her smile. He waited at baggage claim for his own bags—why shouldn't he? He worked out regularly with a trainer—and after he and the driver loaded the bags onto a cart, he pushed it himself.

"What if one day the crowds went away? I mean, there is no reason they ever would go away, of course, you being who you are, but would it be strange for you if they did?" The organizer of the show, a Mr. Prem Kumar, asked this question from the front seat of the overly substantial car. The previous questions, from the driver and a fastidious assistant called Pankaj, had been the usual ones—What is your favorite film? Who is your favorite actress?—for which he had rote answers (*The Godfather*, Waheeda Rehman). But here was something new. Of course, he had pondered this question himself many times before. In his earlier years of stardom, he often wondered how it would be when it was no longer like this. But it seemed at this late age, the crowds were showing no signs of thinning but instead seemed to be swelling—though perhaps this was not a reflection of any growing popularity on his part but rather of the increased interconnectedness of people and the unremitting flow of information. Everyone knew where he was all the time. Amitabh leaned forward to get a better look at Prem.

He didn't seem like a typical producer who acted like a big shot. He was more like a postal worker or call-center manager. He kind of resembled a younger version of his dear friend and colleague Shashi Kapoor—lean and tall, with full, fluffy hair now flecked with gray, a mirror of himself almost, but handsomer. There was something nervous about him, as if a vital part of his essence remained unsettled. "If the crowds went away," Amitabh said in his rich, philosophical game-show-host voice, "I would take a very long walk."

Before leaving him at the hotel, Prem Kumar spoke with Amitabh about the rehearsal schedule, transportation, the arrivals of the other stars. It seemed he had thought of everything, including a nightly delivery of homemade dal chaaval by a woman called Beena Auntie. When people began to recognize the actor and approach for autographs in the lobby, Prem stood by and waited respectfully until they were done. He was more like a valet than a mogul, Amitabh thought.

"Americans are complaining about removing the shoes," Akshaye Khanna said. "I had to remove even my underwear!" He had arrived one day after Amitabh on the same plane as Saif Ali Khan, Bipasha Basu, and Sushmita Sen, who had not been detained or asked to remove their underwear. "Why me only?" he said.

"Because you have that look, you know, like maybe you would hide something there," Saif said.

"Ya, definitely something wrong is going on in there," Sushmita said.

The stars of the show, minor and major, were gathered together at the rehearsal space, waiting for the choreographer, who liked to make an entrance. Amitabh loved this sort of on-set, behind-the-scenes banter. He had quite enjoyed this aspect of his profession all these years and recently had taken on a more paternal role with his young colleagues. "Now, now, let us leave Mr. Khanna's underwear alone," he said.

The choreographer dervished in with a flourish, traversing the dance floor twice before striking an elaborate pose in the center, his head bowed awaiting applause.

The actors, stunned and confused, looked around at each other. A few clapped.

"Hello, beautiful ones," the choreographer began. "Please do not be intimidated."

They wasted no time that morning, immediately jumping into the opening act, a group number to the song "Maahi Ve"—from the soon-to-be-released Kal Ho Naa Ho—which included the entire cast and ended in a human pyramid. The afternoon was spent with the director mapping out the rest of the numbers and who was to perform in what and when. Amitabh loved every minute of it. When Sunil Shetty kept turning right instead of left and falling off the hypothetical stage, husband-and-wife superstars Ajay Devgan and Kajol made raucous crashing sounds, which Amitabh found highly amusing. "Young man," he said to Sunil, "turn left or you will wind up with a concussion." When newlyweds Twinkle Khanna and Akshay Kumar squabbled about who had caused their lateness that morning, Amitabh morphed into his character from the 1989 film *Toofan*, singing "Don't Worry, Be Happy," which everyone joined in on, including, eventually, Twinkle and Akshay. At three o'clock, Beena Joshi showed up with samosas and chai for the chai-samosa break. Prem was with her and quietly nodded and waved hello, taking a seat on a stool in a back corner. Such an unassuming megashow director, Amitabh thought. He seemed more like a poet.

Beena had brought Amitabh's special warm milk—he had stopped having tea, coffee, alcohol, and all manner of aerated drink in recent years—and he sipped it slowly. There was something about this Prem chap that was nagging him. He was a humble, peculiar sort of fellow, but sometimes such characters were full of surprises.

Salman Khan approached just then, eating chicken biryani out of a very large bowl.

"Salluji, come, come," Amitabh said. "How was your flight?"

"Usual, boring. Actually, from Delhi to Amsterdam there was a bombshell flight attendant. Amsterdam to Newark, no such luck."

"Tough times, Salluji, tough times," Amitabh said, thumping him on the back. "Now, tell me, what do you know about this Prem Kumar Superstar guy? You did one show with him before, correct?"

Salman shoveled biryani into his mouth. "Prem? Ya, great guy, good guy, easy to work with, professional. I don't think I have ever talked to him."

"You don't think there is something, uh, different about him?"

"Different?" Salman ate more biryani. "You mean because he maybe is gay? Amitji, all due respect, that is not a big deal anymore. We are in 2002."

"No, that is not what I—"

"I can find out more about this if that is what you need."

"No, no, that is not—"

"Anything for you, Amitji," Salman said and walked away with his large bowl.

Amitabh sipped his warm milk and glanced in Prem's direction. That's when it struck him: he had met him somewhere long ago.

"Seven, eight, nine, keep breathing, stay strong," Amitabh's personal trainer Vrinda said. Amitabh liked to keep fit even when on the road, so she often accompanied him when he traveled for work. She had just arrived for this first international assignment. He was in the middle of his second set of squatjacks in the hotel fitness center when he asked Vrinda if she remembered ever meeting Prem Kumar on one of their trips or perhaps back in India.

"He is a tall, skinny man, sort of nervous and shy," Amitabh inquired.

"You are asking me if I have ever met a tall, skinny Indian man?" Vrinda asked.

"Okay, when you meet him this week, just try to remember if you have met him before."

"Or, I have an idea, why don't you just ask him?"

"Vrindaji, how can I do that? Then he will know I have forgotten him."

"How stupid I am," Vrinda said. "Now plank."

Amitabh hated plank but had really come to appreciate the importance of core work. He assumed the position. "Maybe that time Jaya and I attended the launch of TV Asia?"

"What are we talking about? Four, five, six . . ."

"Prem Kumar," Amitabh grunted.

"Still?"

"Or when I came back to sell TV Asia to another company?" he asked, his voice straining.

"Amitji, you are fixed on this one thing only."

"I am far from my home, far from my country and the ones I love," Amitabh said, his arms quivering. "A man has to occupy himself somehow."

"Beautiful story," Vrinda countered. "Very moving, but I don't believe it for one minute."

"I do not like not knowing," Amitabh struggled to say. "It is quite unsettling."

"Always you are having to know everything," Vrinda said. "Ten more seconds, hold it."

"When you meet him"—he paused—"just inquire, was he in attendance at the 1984 Padma Shri ceremony at Rashtrapati Bhavan?" Amitabh collapsed onto his mat.

An Indian man who had been on the other side of the room on an elliptical machine came over to where they were. "Excuse me, but why you're trying to kill Amitabh Bachchan with Pilates?"

Rehearsals proceeded in a timely and efficient manner to Amitabh's satisfaction, he being an efficient and timely man. He was in four of the song-and-dance numbers, plus he agreed to deliver a dramatic monologue from one of his classic movies, which would blend seamlessly into a soliloquy that he would compose himself about life and the Hindi film industry. The monologue chosen for him was an amalgamation of the spoken parts of the song "Yeh Kahan Aa Gaye Hum," from *Silsila*, which surprised him. He would have guessed they would go with something more dramatic, oozing with pent-up rage, as in *Kaalia*, *Zanjeer*, or *Deewaar*, rather than this softer, gentler oration on loneliness and star-crossed love. When he learned that Prem himself had selected the passage, he took it as a clue to the inner workings of his mind, though it was unclear what the learning was.

On their third day of practice for the gents-only number, he chatted some more with Salman, who was again eating biryani in between learning his steps. He had uncovered some barely useful information about Prem: "I came to know he sleeps under a bag of onions." After Salman explained what this meant and elaborated on Prem's living situation, they were summoned by the choreographer to continue moving into a V-formation. Amitabh pondered the onions. Why would such a man, who had built such a company and surely accrued some wealth, still live as a paying guest in a crowded apartment? What did he do with his money? And why onions? Maybe he was a very specific variety of ascetic and they had met at an ashram long ago. Amitabh shimmied to his place at the vertex.

The next day, as they began work on a dance with three men and three women, Prem sat in on their practice session. Again he took an unassuming position in one corner and kept to himself unless someone required him to do otherwise. On the one hand, Amitabh admired him for this; Prem didn't try to strike up conversations with him or the other actors or parade them around to friends and family like trophies. Unassuming and mostly silent, he was more like a librarian than a producer. Amitabh was used to people being interested in his every move—even his breakfast preferences were well documented—but Prem seemed entirely uninterested. Why? Had they had an unpleasant incident in the past? The bulk of Amitabh's distasteful encounters had occurred when he had ventured into politics, winning a seat as Member of Parliament in the lower house. Had Prem also served as an MP in the Lok Sabha in 1987?

In the subsequent weeks of rehearsal, Amitabh continued to observe Prem closely in the hopes of jogging his memory. When Prem spoke with any of the performers about anything, Amitabh was watching. When Prem interrupted practice to make an announcement about not destroying the hotel rooms, Amitabh studied his mannerisms. And when Prem used the men's room at the practice facility, Amitabh was right there in the stall next to him.

One evening, after the day's work was done and he was in his hotel room getting ready for bed, washing his face, scraping his tongue, Amitabh studied his reflection in the mirror. His French beard was rapidly becoming mostly white and the fine lines on his face were not so fine anymore. He was considering buying a smart pair of eyeglasses to offset some of this, but the truth of the matter was staring back at him: his youth was long gone. The "angry young man" of his early career had been replaced by this gentle nana with an untrustworthy liver. It occurred to him then that all of this obsessing over where and when he had come across Prem Kumar in his past was a symptom of his fear of losing his mind. The cirrhosis, which had developed when he contracted hepatitis B during a blood transfusion following his *Coolie* accident, could potentially cause hepatic encephalopathy, or confused thinking. He had for the past nineteen years been more afraid of this than of any of the other possible complications, which he knew was curious given that they included enlarged bleeding veins and male breast enlargement. Yet there it was. He vowed to stop racking his brain for answers about Prem Kumar and leave the man alone.

He threw himself completely into the work, rededicating himself to learning his lines and hitting his marks. He took a fatherly tack with the younger actors, counseling them on their careers and inspiring them to work harder. When Akshaye and Sushmita had trouble with their salsa dance barrel rolls and the choreographer threw up his hands and declared them hopeless, Amitabh worked for hours with them until they were in sync. He came to rehearsal even for acts he was not in just to help out and keep everyone motivated. When Saif panicked when he saw the size of the stadium at the first stage rehearsal, Amitabh practiced nadi shodhana alternate-nostril breathing with him until he stopped hyperventilating.

A week before the show, Giants Stadium was abustle with people moving heavy things from one place to another, connecting and disconnecting wires, yelling into mobile phones. It was a much larger enterprise than anything Amitabh had witnessed before, and he was grateful to be a part of it. He stood at the edge of the stage one morning and took a deep breath of pure New Jersey air. It was cooler than he was used to for May, and he pulled his pashmina tighter around himself. As he took it all in—the vast sky, the enormity of the place, the seats high up from which no one would be able to see anything—he wondered, What if it rains? What will happen? A panic seized him as he thought of those thousands of fans who had paid so much and would walk such a long distance from the parking lot, stampeding toward the exits, disappointed and soggy. He spotted Prem in the distance sitting in a lower mezzanine seat while on his phone. After a minute, Prem walked up a few flights and to the left and sat down again, still on the phone. He did this over and over again, and Amitabh finally stopped Pankaj and asked what was going on.

"Oh, Mr. Bachchanji, yes, certainly, you see, Mr. Kumar is checking the view from different seats so he can advise the ticket buyers."

"Interesting. He is doing this for how many people?"

"I think fifteen, twenty have called, sir."

"And he will walk around the stadium and check seats for all of them?"

"Correct, sir."

"And is the show not sold out?"

"Secondary market, sir," Pankaj said.

"And what happens if it rains, Pankajji? Is there a plan for that?"

"Mr. Kumar has thought of everything." Pankaj cleared his throat and shifted in place uncomfortably. "Mr. Bachchanji, you are, I think, sir, the best person in the world."

Amitabh became distracted by a stray cloud in the sky. "Oh, yes, thank you, you as well," he replied. Pankaj did not know how to respond to this unintended compliment from his idol, so he nodded and bowed many times and left. Thankfully, the cloud seemed quite benign and passed quickly. And even if there had been rain, Prem Kumar could apparently handle it. Whoever this man was, he certainly had an ability to get things done. Later that day, as Amitabh drank his milk, he saw Prem speaking with the special-effects crew, and the following morning, he was occupied with making sure the hospitality suite was up to his high standards for hospitality suites. One minute he was with the parking supervisor, the next with the head of concessions, who was unhappy about the importing of off-premises samosas. Prem had everything under control and the performers were left to perform.

Three days before the show, they had a glorious full-dress rehearsal at the stadium. Amitabh could feel the electricity, the excitement, the covert Johnnie Walker in the air. They were allowed to sit in the floor seats and watch each other's performances as long as they reported backstage in time for their own turns, which proved to be a mistake as the rowdier of the young stars became quite rowdy. All of the actors sat together to watch the special guests, all-male acapella sensation Penn Masala and multilingual Indian-Californian rappers Karmacy, the latter of whom were so original and magnetic that they caused Sushmita and Bipasha to throw intimate articles of their clothing onto the stage and Akshaye and Sunil to drink heavily, alarmed that the talent before them so far exceeded their own. As the sun began to set behind what the grounds crew referred to as "the Hoffa end" of the field, Amitabh took the stage. Stagehands, electricians, wardrobe, sound, catering— everyone stopped to watch. He breathed deeply and into the pin-drop silence spoke his evergreen lines.

Mein aur meri tanhai	Me and my loneliness
Aksar yeh batein karte hain	Often they talk about this
Tum hoti to kaisa hota	Had you been here, how would it have been
Tum yeh kehti, tum wo kehti	You would have said this, you would have said that
Tum is baat pe hairaan hoti	You would have been shocked by this matter
Tum us baat pe kitni hasti	You would have laughed so much at that matter
Tum hoti to aisa hota	Had you been here, it would have been like this
Tum hoti to waisa hota	Had you been here, it would have been like that
Mein aur meri tanhai	Me and my loneliness
Aksar yeh batein karte hain	Often they talk about this

"Loneliness," he continued in his own words, "who is the one who knows loneliness best? Is it the jilted lover or the widowed wife? The parent who has lost a child or the child who has lost a parent?" They hung on his every word, and when he quietly yet firmly declared, "No," they believed him. "It is the person who lives in fear who is most alone. He could have all of the love; she could be surrounded by admirers. But the one who leads with fear is alone."

He spoke then of his parents and the beautiful influence they had on his thinking. He talked of the enduring depiction of strong mothers in Hindi cinema, which he wove into an eloquent love letter to the industry he cherished. "Our movies," he declared, "have borne endless criticism and ridicule but now provide the platform for intellectual debate. They have entered educational curricula and have become a forebearer of the nation's identity. Bollywood, as some unfortunately deem to call it, has survived almost a hundred years and is still growing. If over a billion people love and patronize Hindi cinema, it must be doing something right." These last words, a version of a foreword he had recently contributed to a book about Hindi cinema, spoke directly to the hearts of the actors before him. Hearing their life's work extolled rather than mocked, upheld by the greatest amongst them, they rose up in applause. Ajay wiped away tears, and Saif was flat-out bawling. The Penn Masala boys tried to improvise an Amitabh medley, which didn't quite cohere. Amitabh bowed and offered his thanks.

The ladies' "Jiya Jale" dance was next, then the Salman-Saif-Sunil "Koi Kahe" number. The whole rehearsal went swimmingly; Sunil even managed not to fall off the stage this time. The full-cast grand finale to "Mehendhi Laga Ke Rakhna" was flawless, but it was decided they would go over some of the trickier numbers a few more times. As day-time discipline slouched into late-night buffoonery, Amitabh called for his car. He was tired but knew he had one remaining responsibility for the day, which was to pose for pictures and sign autographs for the mob that had waited for hours outside his hotel to see him. Every evening he arrived to the same scene of mostly calm and sensible fans standing patiently in a neat line. The driver offered to bring him to a back entrance, but he refused; photos and signatures were part of the job. Many did not even want photographic or autographic evidence; they wanted to pay their respects by touching his feet. This he didn't mind. It was the more zealous ones, the ones who fully prostrated themselves before him, that he found tiresome. What was a man to do in this situation? He wasn't a guru or swami, how was he to respond? He had tried on several occasions to help the splayed-out individual back up on their feet, but this invariably resulted in an awkward lifting and pulling of limbs.

Amitabh hoped he didn't have one of those tonight. But as the car pulled up to the hotel, two men and a woman flung themselves onto the driveway and another man appeared poised to do the same. A few photographers were also present, waiting to snap a photo that would help feed their families. This was fine with him. They had a right to their living, and the air belonged to all. He recalled the episode from his childhood when he was in the blessed presence of his big-screen hero Dilip Kumar, who had been busy and couldn't sign an autograph. Such an impact that small slight had had on his younger self. Amitabh emerged from the car to great fanfare and began tending to the horizontal fans first. What an unusual, unimaginable lifetime this was.

* * *

An hour before the start of the show, Bipasha declared she couldn't go on. It was a warm evening, the first one of the year, and hordes of people—45,000, roughly—were pouring into the stadium. Ajay began aggressively biting his nails and Bipasha threw up. Even Amitabh felt a little dizzy and had to sit.

"They never told us there would be so many people. When did they tell us? Nobody told us," Bipasha said. Twinkle had been attempting to calm her down but gave up. "What did you think was going to happen in this massive stadium? A kitty party?"

Amitabh was nearby taking slow deep breaths. He was ashamed that he, too, was nervous because of the size of the crowd. Five people or five lakh people, he said to himself, the job is the same. He jumped to his feet and gathered the actors to run through the opening number one last time. "Who are we to cower?" Amitabh intoned "We are the lovers on mountaintops, the frolickers in waterfalls, the fist fighters, the motorcycle riders, the synchronized dancers, bold and bright. We reenact our nation's history, we tackle social issues, we sing on top of trains. The comedic and the star-crossed, the romantic and the dramatic, we are villains, we are heroes, we are everything at once. We are Bollywood!"

Roused by Amitabh's speech, the performers pumped their fists and cheered. Akshaye whispered, "I thought we are not supposed to use that word, 'Bollywood,'" and Kajol whispered, "It is not about that right now." Salman threw aside his biryani, and Bipasha stopped throwing up. Even the sideys—now called "supporting dancers"—were galvanized.

The show went on. No one had seen anything like it before, and they knew as they were watching they would never see its like again. The stars left everything of themselves on the stage that night, and with each roar of the wild and adoring crowd, they gave more. The ladies' sensual semiclassical performance incited the audience to a frenzy, then Amitabh's soliloquy brought them to tears. The gents nailed the gents-only number, and applause reached a fever pitch with the un-restrained rowdiness of "Koi Kahe." By the time they took their final bows, Amitabh was drenched in sweat and out of breath. As he closed his eyes and let the clapping, the whistles, the sustained growl of the audience wash over him, he felt as he did in *Muqaddar Ka Sikandar*; alive and young once more.

Backstage, the drinking began. The cast was giddy and the smok-ing rampant. VVIP audience members with their $1,500 passes were ushered in for meet-and-greets with the stars, and the sponsors from HSBC were standing by with briefcases and satisfied looks. Still feeling a bit winded, Amitabh took a seat in the hospitality suite. The room was crowded with young people, brimming with vitality despite some questionable health habits. They would reach his age one day and real-ize that no matter the size of the audiences or the horizontality of their fans, they were still mortal. No one was immune.

After the booze dwindled and the VVIPs were adequately met-and-greeted, Prem made a speech. The performers watched him struggle to find his balance atop a wobbly table. He really does not seem like a big-shot producer, Amitabh thought. He is more like a personal sec-retary. Prem kept it short, commending them for a job professionally, excellently done. The cleanup work had already begun down on the field, and Amitabh recognized the hum of motors and things being dismantled and driven away. A faint whiff of gasoline drifted through, and something in Amitabh's memory was triggered: he knew then that he had met Prem before, right here in New Jersey, long ago.

"Tell me something," Amitabh said to Prem after he came down from the table.

"Amitji," Prem began with some hesitance, "it has been the great honor of my life—"

"Yes, thank you, I also am honored, the show was a triumph, but tell me, Mr. Prem Kumar, did you by chance ever work at a petrol pump?"

A flash of surprise crossed Prem's face as he pulled an envelope from his jacket pocket and pressed it into Amitabh's hand. "Sir, I believe I owe you this."

"Oh, my manager handles—" Amitabh said, attempting to refuse it.

But Prem had already disappeared into the wild crowd. Amitabh opened the envelope and was dumbfounded. Inside was a check for the remainder of his payment, but with something he'd never before seen in this context: an extra one dollar. It all came flooding back to him—the Exxon, the extra-one conversation, the man with the too-much-henna hair—and he was relieved; his memory was just fine. No, it was great! "I knew he didn't seem like a big-shot producer," Amitabh smiled.

35

As Prem stumbled in late, exuding an objectionable whiskey stench for the third time in a week, the Singhs began to worry. Their paying guest had, in all the years he had slept on their mattress, never shown any proclivity toward alcohol or controlled substances or women or anything; in fact, in recent years, they had wondered if he ever had any fun at all. His only irresistible need appeared to be paan, which he had been consuming more avidly lately, as evidenced by the brownish-orange betel-juice drool stains on his pillow. Back when he enjoyed only the occasional paan from Beena Joshi's purse stash, he had always been particular about brushing his teeth afterward to ensure they did not stain; but these days, with paan available every ten feet on Oak Tree Road, where the sidewalks were splotched orange with paan spit, he had it all the time and seemed entirely unconcerned about his teeth.

"Twenty-four and seven he is drinking," Iqbal whispered to his wife next to him in bed.

"No, no, he is okay," Amarleen replied. "He pukes in the kitchen sink and shouts in the night, but he is okay."

"He is needing help, he needs to go in a rehabilitation program."

"You are right, I will go help him."

"No, no, no, he is just fine."

Beyond being disheveled and drunk with orange teeth, Prem was retreating further and further into himself. He hardly spent time with Lucky and Deepak and the gang anymore, and even Beena Joshi had stopped making him food. Despite his career success and the respect it garnered, he was moving to the fringes of Edison society, doing things like standing outside the skating rink for hours and petting a ball of hair. Some dismissed his eccentricities as the mark of entrepreneurial genius; others labeled him as odd. If Prem caught wind of this buzz, he didn't show it. He continued down his path of deterioration, cycling around town in his night clothes, cradling a mixtape that Leena had once made for him.

It was the end of May 2002. Prem had just produced his biggest, most ostentatious show yet. For almost a year, he had worked harder than was even required. His supererogation was fueled by the knowledge that once all of the tickets were sold; the vendors, stadium, crew, and talent were compensated; and he had paid himself, he would surpass the monetary goal that Hemant had set for him all those years ago. Though it was an empty goal now, with no heroic victory lap attached, no getting of the girl, still it would be a triumphant moment, an exceptional achievement in his life. The added bonus, of course, was that he could pay the Mumbai mobsters, who did not like to be kept waiting.

During the glorious few weeks of rehearsal that Prem got to spend in close proximity to his screen idol, he deliberately maintained a respectful distance from Amitabh. He didn't want to be like one of those boastful producers who paraded their actors around to friends and family like trophies. He contented himself with ogling the star from afar, watching in amazement as he sipped his warm milk and blew on his soup. On the night of the show, amidst the bustle and the putting out of last-minute fires, Prem took a minute to stand in the wings and watch his hero on stage. The legendary actor began his performance of "Ke Pag Ghunghroo Bandh," the opening words of which were "The elders have requested: show us you can stand on your own feet, and this world will be yours." Prem realized then that he had lived those words, and in that shining moment, he felt the lights and applause were just for him.

He reflected on Amitabh's talismanic dollar and came to the realization that he had done the thing he had set out to do, which was hardly ever the case in his life. How fitting that this second coming of Amitabh Bachchan was the thing that had put him over the top. He should try in the coming days to rest in this glory, he told himself, before resuming his usual routine of longing and despair, but he didn't have the chance to try this. The next night, a significant setback surfaced from an unexpected origin.

Lucky was behaving oddly that morning. The tenants of 3D were enjoying a lazy Sunday morning, having stayed out late after the show the night before. Amarleen was getting the chai going, and the TV was already humming with Hindi music videos. One by one, they moved in and out of the bathroom in a half-sleep state, all except for Lucky, who was inexplicably revved up and fidgeting with the CD player while chattering on about how good the show was.

"Too good," he said. "Really, who could imagine Akshay and Twinkle on the same stage? And Ajay and Kajol? And Amitabh singing? He sang well, didn't he sing well? I think he sang well. And the big dance number in the end? First class, absolutely."

"Take a breath, yaar," Deepak said.

Lucky settled in next to Prem, who was still horizontal. "Hey, man, what are you doing? Why don't you go on your own mattress?" Prem said.

"I'm so proud of you, yaar, how are you feeling today? You must be happy, are you so happy?"

"I'm tired, man," Prem said, rolling over on his other side.

"So, what are you doing today to celebrate, you know, because everything was so good?"

"Nothing. I have to go to the hotel then the office."

"Then back here?"

"Then back here. What is wrong with you?"

"Ya, that sounds good, sounds good, good, good, ya," Lucky said.

"What is wrong with you?" Prem said.

Lucky began what sounded like a request for a favor, but was cut short by Iqbal, who appeared among them with a towel at his waist and a white sleeveless undershirt, soap foaming at his chest hair. "No hot water," he said.

"No hot water?" four people chimed.

There was a knock at the door, and two of the upstairs paying guests entered. "Do you have hot water here?"

"No hot water," a different four people answered.

Amarleen started yelling about the landlord, and two more from upstairs came down and joined her. Lucky felt this might not be the optimal time to ask Prem for one hundred thousand dollars. He picked himself up and told him they could continue their talk in the evening, to which Prem replied, "Sure. Why?"

That evening, Lucky still could not find the right words or moment to make his request. This time, however, instead of prattling on, he did the opposite, staring at Prem from across the room in an intense and unsettling way. By the time he finally mustered up the courage, it was 3:00 a.m. and the apartment was asleep and quiet, except for a police siren that grew nearer and nearer then faded away. Prem stirred. "Hey," Lucky whispered from across the room. "Petrol. Can I have one hundred thousand dollars?"

Lucky had always been terrible at saving money. Prem had noticed this years ago and had urged his friend to put some money in the bank, but instead, he had squandered it all on party buses and velvet shirts.

"You see the dilemma we are in," Lucky said in the morning. He and his fiancée had asked Prem to come down to the Sassy Salwar, where they could talk freely. Lucky had just finished a highly detailed rundown of their plight, which included the "Jazzy Panty" and some very heavy drapes. At the end of the story, Sushila stepped in.

"Prem, we know this all must be hard for you," she said, looking up from where she had been straightening a rack of discounted lehengas. "Because of, you know, how you wanted to marry me when I was working in Shoe Town."

"I told you, he is okay with it," Lucky said.

"This is no time for jealousy, Prem," Sushila continued.

"Really. Very okay with it," Lucky said.

Prem shifted in his velvet-cushioned seat beside a blonde mannequin draped in pink chiffon. "Is it not possible to get an Indian mannequin?" he wondered, then cleared his throat and returned to the matter at hand. "Did you try to negotiate the terms with Mrs. Mukherjee?"

"She is not a negotiating type," Sushila said.

"She showed me the rolling pin that she would beat me with," Lucky said.

His friend needed him, Prem thought. Lucky had always been good to him. From the early Edison days to the recent Miss India USA incident, Lucky had been there for him. And now he was getting married, having a baby, and expanding his store. Any borrowed money would be spent on worthy things. Also, Prem did not want to see Lucky heartbroken and beaten by an auntie.

"Please, Petrol," Lucky said, "we will return you the money slowly over time. And if you get married ever, your wife can have free salwars."

"And I can take a reduced commission if you buy a house," Sushila said.

"And we will name the baby Prem," Lucky added.

"Really?" Prem asked.

"Really?" Sushila also asked.

The discussions continued, but Prem knew all along that the outcome was inevitable. That afternoon, he wrote a check for one hundred thousand and one dollars, then spent the rest of the day wondering what he would tell Tiger Nayak.

"You have reached Anthony Braganza, official spokesperson for the T-Company organization. How may I help you?"

"Mr. Braganza, Prem Kumar here, of Superstar Entertainment. Can I leave a message with you for Mr. Kamath?"

"Why, sir, Mr. Kamath is in the office. Shall I transfer you?"

"No! I mean, no need to disturb him. Can you just tell him there will be a slight delay with the payments that I promised—"

"Another delay, sir?"

"Yes, another delay. But no need to say 'another' when you talk to Mr. Kamath. Just 'slight delay' is fine."

"Slight delay."

"That's correct."

"I believe Mr. Kamath would like to speak to you himself about this matter."

"Oh no, a bird has come into my office! Okay, thank you, Braganza, Mr., please give him my message, okay, bye!"

Prem did not feel great about how the conversation had gone, but the deed was done, and he probably had a few days before hearing from Tiger's people. In the twelve years since he'd first secured T-Company's investment, he had returned the principal and quite a bit more above that, so they couldn't be *too* mad at him, Prem thought. Thus far, they had been reasonable partners, only once sending a message written in blood. He could count on them to be patient a little longer.

The next day, Wristwatch threw a rock through an open window of 3D, lingering on the lawn long enough for Prem to see clearly that it was him. Immediately after that, Prem began his descent into drinking and chewing too much paan and disregarding his own hygiene. In the manner of so many dispirited onscreen heroes whose lives went down the toilet, he ceased shaving entirely and cultivated a *Devdas* beard of sorrow, which became shockingly full shockingly quickly after some initial patchiness. He seldom bathed and took to walking around barefoot outside and tracking mud and occasionally blood around the apartment. Three weeks later, he threw up in the sink again and slept, inexplicably, beneath the kitchen table. In the morning, Amarleen coaxed him out from under it and forced him to shower, then yelled at Mohan and Yogesh—who had not ended up moving anywhere—and Lucky and Deepak for allowing him to drink so much the night before.

"Why you're yelling at me? I was here watching *Lajja* with you," Deepak said, stuffing a mini muffin in his mouth.

"Oh ya," Amarleen said and turned to glare at the others.

"What do you mean?" Lucky said. "I was watching *Lajja* too—remember I made that good comment about the unequal society?"

"No one remembers any equal-vequal, we do not remember you were here even," Iqbal said.

"Then who Prem is doing these things with?" Amarleen said to no one in particular.

Mostly, he was doing them alone. Without giving it much thought, one morning, he purchased a bottle of vodka from Quicker Liquor and a Gold Spot from Grocery Bazaar and hopped on his bike and headed for his office, the two bags swinging from the handlebars and clanging together. No one was there; there was no show in the works, nothing to plan or promote. He sat at his desk and opened the two bottles. First, he downed half of the orange soda. Next, he poured vodka into the soda bottle until the bottle was full again. Then he drank. Quickly, this became a sort of habit: he would wake up late, eat whatever Punjabi leftovers were in the fridge, buy a Gold Spot, and bike to his office. When, one day, he found he had run out of clean clothes, he pulled his Exxon jumpsuit out from the depths of his bag and put it on. It was wrinkled, but it felt so comfortable and somehow right that he began to wear it daily. He took frequent naps on the floor of his office, favoring a spot under the plant, which he attributed to a certain comfort he felt after years of sleeping beneath the onions. Every few days, Pankaj would appear and ask through the door if he needed any assistance, to which Prem would reply, "Not today."

After a few weeks of this, he grew tired of the monotony of his own slothfulness and decided to shake up his routine by scheduling some dates for the evenings. The landscape of dating had changed significantly in recent years, and instead of clipping matrimonial ads from papers, he found himself scrolling on shaadi.com until he found a local face that caught his attention. As before, it wasn't a pretty face or interesting profile that piqued his interest but rather a slight desperation that suggested they might have something in common. Now, however, instead of being charmed into a lifelong friendship, the women were horrified and fled the scene. Prem would show up to various locales on Oak Tree with his unkempt beard and suspicious bottle of orange soda and launch into a lamentation on the plight of star-crossed love, omitting names and details, sometimes vaguely mentioning the Mumbai mafia, crushing his dates' matrimonial dreams in the process.

One evening at Dosa Palace, where he had arranged to meet a dental hygienist with a broken engagement, he found that his date was as drunk and lovelorn as he was. Bishakha Dey was a strikingly beautiful, youngish woman with a supermodel's stature and unthinkably high cheekbones. Her hair, cut to her shoulders, bounced luxuriously as she walked, and the other customers froze mid-dosa as she glided past.

"Parking in this place is such a problem," she said. She took a seat in front of Prem at a table by the window and assumed an unexpected hunched-over posture, her elbow on the table, her hand propping up her head. "I need coffee. You think they have coffee?"

Immediately, Prem knew he could talk to her. Over the course of an hour, they shared several onion rava masala dosas, and instead of coffee, they took swigs from his Gold Spot. She recounted the sad tale of her almost husband, who at the eleventh hour left her brokenhearted and had reportedly been seen around town with the short, prettyish daughter of a wealthy property developer. Prem in turn told selected pieces of his own story: falling in love, meeting the father, her rejecting him, him trying to get his life together, her being engaged to a doctor for several years now. He left out certain key facts, such as the fact of his hidden background and his impending demise at the hands of a T-Company hitman, but on the whole, he conveyed well his total anguish and despair.

"That is bullshit," Bishakha said. "How could she just move on like that?"

"Well, you know, I didn't really ask what she wanted to do after her father's declaration. I guess I just decided things myself."

"And you didn't beg for her forgiveness?"

"No, you see, she went to Minnesota and there was the doctor . . . it is difficult to explain, it all happened very fast."

"And now you are still living here trying to make one million and one dollars for no reason."

"Not exactly—"

"I am not completely understanding the situation."

"Maybe I am not explaining right."

"It's okay, I am with you. How could she move on with the other guy so quickly? Didn't she remember the times you shared? The words of love, the glances, the caresses, the time under the bridge?"

"Under what bridge?"

"Never mind. If I were you, you know what I would tell her? I would tell her to give me answers."

Prem gave this some thought when Bishakha went to the restroom. The thing was, after all these years, if he tried to speak with her, he knew the only thing she could say to him was that his chance had passed. The thought of this was too much for him. Instead, he studied the Presidents of the United States disposable paper placemat before him, then stared out the window. Across the street, Shah Rukh Khan stared benevolently down on passersby from a poster on a video-store window. A quick-serve restaurant's grand-opening sign announced proudly that it offered "Indo-Pak-Bangla & Chinese all on one menu with strictly halal meat"; and next door, the Kathi Roll Specialists made dhoklas fresh daily. Paan, phone cards, and carrom boards were sold under one roof at Shivani's Everything Market, while Divya Jewelers sparkled like the gold and diamonds it sold inside. Two men were entering the jewelry store, and one seemed vaguely familiar, though Prem could only see the back of his head.

"That's him!" Bishakha had returned and was pointing out the window at the men entering the store.

"Are you sure? How do you know it is him?"

"He was my boyfriend for three years, of course I know."

"Your fiancé was the doctor?"

"What doctor? He is an IT engineer."

"The doctor is an IT engineer?"

"There is no doctor, are you feeling okay?"

He was feeling fine; it was Bishakha whose eyes were glassy and glazed over. He wondered if she had ingested something questionable in the bathroom. "Okay, we are talking about two different people," Prem said.

Once they had sorted out that the first man was indeed Leena's doctor fiancé and the other man was indeed Bishakha's IT engineer—that in an improbable twist of fate, the two men were acquainted and going jewelry shopping together—Prem paid the bill and they darted across the street to investigate.

"Looks like they are looking at rings," Bishakha whispered.

"No, no, we cannot be certain from this angle," Prem whispered back.

"But rings are this side, necklace-earring sets are that side."

"Maybe they are buying rings for their mothers."

"Why would they buy rings for their mothers?"

"But Leena already has a ring, I think."

"Engagement ring or wedding band? And why are we whispering when they are inside and we are outside?"

"Aaaaa!" Prem took a few steps back. "Did you see that guy?"

"Of course, is that not why we are here?"

"No, not those guys. The other guy, the gigantic one with dark sunglasses staring at us from inside."

"No."

"Oh. Never mind, then."

They continued to creep around the perimeter of the store for a few more minutes, even snapping a few pictures with a small camera Bishakha carried in her purse, before, naturally, being picked up by the cops.

* * *

It was a long night in the Woodbridge Township police station's interrogation room. Prem was questioned separately from Bishakha, but when at 4:00 a.m. he was finally released, they assured him she had also been let go. He woke up the following afternoon and didn't

call her. What would be the point? He didn't want to know if she had
learned anything more about the ring shopping. He wanted to forget
he had seen anything at all.

That evening he biked to his office, this time with his ledger instead
of his drink. At his desk he opened it up and began:

211. I will love you forever.

212. I will love you forever.

213. I will love you forever.

214. I will love you forever.

215. If by chance I suddenly am murdered, remember I will
love you forever, okay? That is all there is.

36

By June, Wristwatch had become a fixture at King's Court, skulking around the grounds, lurking behind Building 3 as threateningly as he could. He'd visited New Jersey from Mumbai several times over the years but lately had been stationed there permanently, more or less, to remind Prem to whom he was beholden. Residents had begun to recognize him, even greeting him by name on sunny mornings. "Ah, Wristwatch! Beautiful sunshine, no?" they would say, or "Good morning, Mr. Wristwatch, you're looking very smart today!" For Halloween, more than one child went dressed as him, which he was quite flattered by. But when Tun-Tun invited him to join them for dinner ("You cannot eat only the restaurant food, Wristwatchji. Not good for the digestion."), he began to worry that perhaps he was no longer eliciting the necessary panic and dread required for a man in his line of work.

But what was that work? he pondered one day, sitting in the grass among the white-kurta uncles. This certainly wasn't what he'd dreamed of as a boy. His childhood had been marked by grueling daily labor, a particularly cruel brand of urban poverty that typically did not lend itself to optimism. An only child, he had taken it upon himself by the age of nine to shoulder some of his dear parents' workload. That work was hand-embroidering complicated designs onto blouses, blankets, lehengas, saris, and ball gowns, which would be sold someplace, someday, he presumed. A serious, somewhat bored-looking man appeared once a week to pick up the completed pieces and drop off more work. Along with five other families from their tenement, in a cramped workshop on the fourth floor, the parents and son toiled for hours, stopping only when their eyes hurt and their fingers bled. The mother would tend to her son's fingers, washing them and wrapping them in scraps from their work, kissing each one twice. Wristwatch—not yet Wristwatch but Hamza still—knew it pained his mother to keep him home from school, which he attended part-time, if at all. He never complained about the work as the neighbor children did, which pained his mother all the more. He regularly assured her that there was nothing to complain about; he loved the work.

He had become enamored of the artistry of what they were doing. The type of handicraft that their particular subcontractor supplied was in the venerated Aari embroidery tradition, in which intricate patterns were painstakingly chain-stitched using a long, hooked needle into fabrics stretched tightly over a wooden frame. Young Hamza took very seriously the acquisition of his craft. He became adept at manipulating the needle, catching and pulling silk thread through fabric. His pieces were admired for their density and precision, their metallic trim shimmering like light on water. In time, the subcontractor noticed his talent and dedication and singled him out for more difficult assignments. Eventually, Hamza began making his own suggestions for new motifs they might try out in addition to the usual paisleys and peacocks, some of which were adopted (mangoes and geese) and others that were rejected (Shah Rukh Khan and potatoes). He became the go-to guy for new patterns and was taught how to transfer them onto cloth using tracing paper and chalk solution. Thus as his life progressed, so did his knowledge of the embroidery trade. And all along, he thought of himself not as a victim deprived of his innocence by the dictates of modern capitalism and its destitute masses, but as an apprentice, honing his skill, training to become the thing he most longed to become: a master craftsman.

As Hamza's technical prowess grew, so did his physique. Nimble little hands grew into nimble enormous hands, and everyone wondered how such tiny parents could yield such a mammoth child. While other laboring children suffered from stunted growth due to cramped working conditions, Hamza somehow became a gigantic young man, albeit with arthritic fingers and significant neck pain. He always stood out among the crowd of smaller, less enthusiastic embroiderers, and no one was surprised when one day he was asked to visit the subcontractor's office.

The occasion of a possible promotion called for sharp, professional attire, in the absence of which Hamza cleaned and pressed what clothing he had as best he could. His mother combed his hair and used a bit of coconut oil to keep the part smoothly in place. At 8:00 a.m., he reported to an address just a few blocks away, which would make for an easy daily commute, he thought. The building was more impressive than he'd expected for a simple garment business, with a long driveway preceded by a gate so formidable that it made Hamza feel small for the first time. Two guards with guns and angry-looking dogs watched as he ascended a set of black marble stairs.

"Who Hamza, what Hamza?" a voice from behind the appointed door barked. "Hm? Oh, ya, bring him in."

The subcontractor was nowhere to be seen; instead, Hamza found a mustached, plump, menacing sort of figure, much like the actor Amjad Khan in *Sholay* or Amjad Khan in *Laawaris* or Amjad Khan in *Kaalia*, or really Amjad Khan in mostly anything except *Yaarana*, in which he was quite a loyal friend. Also in the room were several men in dark suits—unembroidered—standing silently, their hands clasped behind

them. The Amjad Khan–ish man remained seated and looked Hamza
up and down. After issuing a few approving grunts, he whispered in
the ear of one of the suited men, who in turn nodded at another suited
man, who led Hamza out of the room.

Hamza would look back on that moment as one in which he experienced the most consequential misunderstanding of his life. "You have
been given the job," he was informed, then directed to go up another
three flights to be briefed for his new position. Though he knew he
should be elated, he felt uneasy. There was no evidence of embroidery
anywhere, no threads scattered on the floor, no garments hanging on
display. Just frightening, silent men guarding doors and attending to
other more frightening and mostly seated men. By the time he reached
the fifth floor, he was convinced he was about to be murdered.

He wasn't murdered, but murder, it turned out, would be an integral part of the job. The person who informed him of his new position
was a tiny elderly woman, sari-clad and bespectacled with her hair in
a severely tight bun. "Congratulations," she said in an unexpectedly
deep and monotone voice. "You have been selected for the position of
junior enforcer in our organization. Come. Let us get you fitted."

This seemed to Hamza like the proper juncture to ask what exactly
was going on. He'd always been a quiet boy, but when he did speak, he
did so with complete certainty. So it came as a surprise even to him
when he lost all semblance of composure. "Madam? Fitted? Why fitted?
What enforcer? Where are the threads?"

The tiny woman glared at him and cleared her throat. "Be calm. This
type of behavior is not acceptable from an employee of T-Company."

Hamza felt a tightening in his chest, then a feeling of disconnec-
tion, as though he were watching a movie of himself. Dizzy, he tried
to steady himself as he backed away slowly to the door. "I will, I think,
madam, I am happy with my current role in embroidering, so I will

just continue that only. Thank you, thank you, good day."

It became starkly clear to Hamza that he was not being offered a choice in the matter. He would have to accept his new post, or else. So, he did the only thing he could do, which was to find the tailor and get fitted. He walked down to the fourth floor, his simple rubber slippers slapping the marble with each step. How did he get here? What went haywire? he wondered. And why did starting a job as a thug require a tailor? Only the third question was answered that day.

The floor of the tailor's quarters was blanketed in broken pieces of thread, which felt familiar and comforting to Hamza. Three men were at work on sewing machines, each with a tape measure around his neck and Gandhi-type round spectacles. "Masterji," one of the tailors, evidently an apprentice, said to the head tailor. "Client has come."

The head tailor looked up and gasped. "Hamza? It cannot be," he said. The head tailor was the boy's longtime across-the-way neighbor, Shyamsundar.

"Shyamsundarji Uncle? You are here?"

"I am here, but why you are here?"

"I don't know really how I am here, but how are you here?"

Shyamsundar took the measurements himself rather than leaving it to his subordinates. "Okay, tell me what happened," he said in hushed tones as he took Hamza's inseam.

"The embroiderywalla told me to come to this office. I thought they were making me the top embroiderer or some such job."

Shyamsunder let out a heavy sigh. "I see." He continued taking measurements with an expression of deep concern on his face. "Just do as they tell you and do not make any comments or demands or loud noises."

Hamza nodded, the reality of his situation setting in. "I thought you worked in the sari store," he said.

"Your knees are shaking, boy," the tailor whispered. "You must make them stop. You are a T-Company man now."

At 5:00 p.m., Hamza was finally permitted to leave the compound. He exited through the massive gates and stepped back into the hectic street. Relieved to be returned to the oppressive heat of the outside, stagnant and familiar, he walked deliberately. He had fresh appreciation for the auto rickshaws, the beggars on the corner, the usual waft of roasted corn from the roadside vendors. Somewhere nearby, a fire burned, as always. Yet as he continued walking, the things he knew so well seemed suddenly at a remove, as though they no longer recognized him. He was in the midst of it all yet no longer part of it.

As he headed toward home, he tried to digest what had happened to him. He was tricked into joining the underworld. He was fitted for a suit by his neighbor. Then he had his first lesson in how to intimidate, harass, stalk, injure, and shoot. In the end, he was given a watch. It offered Hamza a degree of comfort, not because of any particular fondness for high-end baubles; it represented for him the one positive point about this terrible turn of events. He would make enough money to help his parents out of poverty.

When T-Company told him the amount he would be receiving every week, plus bonuses for murdering and maiming, it assuaged some of his shock and terror. Initially, to get himself out of the predicament, he had considered telling his new employers about his chronic neck pain, weak eyesight, and arthritic hands—all byproducts of the embroidery trade. He would also inform them that they'd incorrectly assumed from his height and build that he was athletic or tough, when he was neither. But then he pictured his parents, old and hunched over their stitching year after year, and he stayed silent.

What would he tell his parents? He'd asked his unassuming neighbor, the masterji to the mob, not to mention anything to them. The best thing Hamza could do for his parents was to keep them in the dark, ignorant of their only child's dangerous entanglement. He would tell them he had indeed been promoted and that going forward he would be doing his embroidering at the company's offices and workshops, which were beautiful and state-of-the-art. He would say they wanted him to focus primarily on zari work, with only pure threads—red silk, twisted with silver, dipped in twenty-two-carat gold—which would grace the likes of movie stars and the wives of major industrialists. He would be given free rein to choose his own color combinations, and they would train him to create original designs and transfer them to silks, just as he'd hoped, when in reality, he would never embroider anything again.

* * *

The ledger that Prem had kept all these years, crammed with declarations and observations for an imagined Leena, was weathered and falling apart. Its faux-leather cover was scuffed, and on the back were several overlapping circles of tea stains. Pages were crumpled and the binding was tired and worn. Still, it soldiered on.

216. I saw you going into Gurnani Restaurant and Tiffin Service. You wore a yellow dress. Who were you meeting?

217. I hiccupped today. Was that you who was thinking of me? You must be having hiccups every day. I think of you every day.

218. Did you know that Hindi movies are colorful and bright so the people with a bad print or watching in a hall with the poor projector or dirty screen can still enjoy? I learned this today from Nachiket Rao.

219. You must have liked *Lagaan*. With the cricket match and all. Songs were good, no?

220. Have you heard about this Wristwatch character? Wears a suit always and sunglasses even in the dark. If you see him, walk the other way. He is maybe not the best guy.

221. So, ya, this Wristwatch....It seems he is here to scare me. Remember, I told you before about the goondas from Mumbai? He is with them. They want some money—return on investment type of thing—but I need just a little bit more of time. This was not a good idea, getting involved with this group. But how could I not? I wanted to make money, to be successful, to impress your father and my father. Why fathers need money to be impressed? I don't know. Maybe I was trying to impress myself. This guy, Wristwatch, was spotted more than one time trying to catch a squirrel. I think he is planning to kill it and deliver it to me.

222. I don't understand why communism does not really work. Do you? Everyone is equal in communism, no? No money worries. Do the people in China not worry about money? Are the fathers all impressed?

223. So, ya, he killed the squirrel and delivered it to me.

224. Sometimes I feel afraid when I ride around on my bicycle in the dark. I can hear your voice saying, *Then stop riding around on your bicycle in the dark.* But that is my best thinking time. I think of my business and what I am doing here, still, in America, and I think of you. What good is all this success without you?

225. In the newspaper today I read that people in Norway and Denmark are very happy and not rich and not poor but just right.

226. Do you know Markandeya and Roohi? Shah? Someone told me they are very wealthy. They still stay in a one-bedroom in King's Court.

227. Your haircut looks nice.

228. I think maybe things have gotten out of hand. T-Company—that is the group of goondas after me, I know, the worst goondas of all the goondas—sent a letter. It was the second letter they ever sent. The first one was written in blood, but this one was neatly typed. They really are quite good in office management. The letter said if I do not pay immediately, they will break the nose and jaw of the pretty girl I like. Now, this could be you or it could also be not you. Not because there is any other girl! But because how would they know? Is the T-Company research department so skilled? I think probably not. So, no need to worry you, I think. Did you notice how this threat is the same threat they made in India in my filmmaking days? They couldn't think of something new? No creativity. But they ended politely: "Kindly do the needful." Also, they included this business card:

Birju's Hindu Funeral Home
WE UNDERSTAND

cremations · poojas · final rites

we can arrange shipping of body to India

compassionate treatment and fair pricing

Hindu Funerals of America Code of Ethics

Serving Hindu, Sikh, Jain

Or maybe this was a separate delivery, who knows, it was all together in the office mailbox.

* * *

Wristwatch did not actually kill a squirrel. It was true, however, that he had recently been following them around in the grass. They seemed so sweet and he just wanted to pet one's tail. This gentle, sylvan distraction came at a particularly opportune time in his involuntary career.

The latest directive from T-Company headquarters was of the variety Wristwatch most dreaded: inflicting bodily harm on an innocent. Over the years, as he rose through the ranks from Junior Thug to the coveted position of Senior International Thug, he cultivated a foreboding persona that conveyed the impression of impending violence. He never left the house in anything but an expertly tailored black suit and prescription sunglasses his employers had given him after he failed the standard eye exam. He seldom spoke, and when he did, it was in a deep, gravelly monotone. Smiling was out of the question, replaced by a constant clenching of the jaw. All of this, bolstered by his unflinchingly erect posture, lent him the air of a bloodthirsty robot. People were so terrified at the mere sight of him that they would wet themselves and then give him whatever he wanted. A urine-soaked target was all in a good day's work.

Thus in all his years with T-Company, Wristwatch never actually hurt anyone. He threatened and insinuated, stalked and terrified, but never broke any body parts, burned anyone with acid, or maimed or mutilated, though these were important aspects of his job description. But Prem was proving to be his greatest challenge yet. He showed no sign of caving, seemingly unphased by Wristwatch's murderous façade. He began to worry that he might have to follow through on the threat put forth by T-Company to break the nose and jaw of a young woman close to Prem.

This place, Edison, New Jersey, had turned out to be a peaceful place for him, away from the constant throngs, without T-Company monitoring him. He enjoyed his time sitting with the old men in the circle, especially so that June morning, as a warm, gentle breeze rustled the very green grass. Such an interesting place, this King's Court, comprised entirely of people who had come from India and people who had come from people who had come from India. Clusters of satellite dishes burst forth from sides of buildings like unexpected flowers, allowing tenants to access Sony TV, Zee TV, TV Asia, Star Plus, Sahara One. There was a Shirdi Sai temple nearby, as well as Sai Baba, Shri Krishna Vrundavana, Sai Datta Peetham, Shri Umiya Dham, and Guruji temples even nearer. A woman watering plants on her balcony called down to passersby to inquire who had won the drawing for the five-gallon pressure cooker at Apna Bazaar, and Wristwatch marveled at the mini-India that had been created here. He wished he had come under different, less homicidal circumstances, but this was his strange lot in life. Years earlier, he had considered how he might escape his employers, but every possibility led to either his or his parents' murder. For this reason, he had never married or started a family; more loved ones would just mean more to worry about. At least I got to see America, he consoled himself.

The white-kurta uncles had been sitting in silence when one of them pointed to the street. A squirrel had been run over by a car, its carcass still fresh. Wristwatch stood and walked toward it to have a closer look. The tail was still bushy and the face still intact. A profound sadness overtook him, and he sat down on the curb and wept for a long time. When he was done, the uncles had disbanded. It was getting late, and people were returning from or going to work. He picked himself up and went to the dumpster behind Building 20 in search of some old newspaper. That night, he wrapped the squirrel in *Little India* and shoved it into Prem's office mailbox along with the business card of a funeral company, which he felt added an appropriately morbid touch.

* * *

The legendary and implausible fight sequences in classic Hindi movies have been ridiculed—or celebrated, depending on whom you ask—over the years, their action defying the very laws of gravity and motion. Jackie Shroff in *Shapath* successfully evaded a barrage of bullets while running sideways on a wall; Mithun Chakraborty in the new *Kaalia* leaped from a cartwheeling airborne motorcycle onto a burning pyre; and who can forget Dharmendra in *Loha* catching a bullet with his bare hand? The list goes on. Such films eschewed mathematical accuracy, opting instead for invincible heroes fending off entire squads of goons; speeding cars, rickshaws, and trains boasting aerobatic capabilities; and all manner of absurd flipping, lifting, straddling, hanging, and exploding. An entirely new branch of science arose, lately and lovingly referred to as "Bollywood physics."

Thanks to their familiarity with Bollywood physics, no one at the intersection of Wood Avenue and Oak Tree was fazed when one day Prem was forced to stop short and was launched from his bicycle, prompting him to execute a perfect midair somersault and land effortlessly on his handlebars. He hadn't expected to be in a near-fatal bicycle catastrophe when he woke up that morning. He hadn't slept at all well, the matter of T-Company and Wristwatch and the squirrel weighing on him all night. If he just paid the sum that was past due, his erstwhile financiers would back off; they'd always been fair in that way, gangsters though they were. But paying them back now was not an option. His living expenses were modest, but the cost of running Superstar Entertainment was not insignificant. Moreover, he had a separate account into which he deposited funds to make payments to T-Company after big shows; and another for his personal savings, which he thought of as his "Hemant ultimatum" account, the money that would prove that he was finally worthy, though there was no longer anyone to whom his worthiness had to be proved. The hefty sum he'd just lent to Lucky had come from both of these last two buckets, and he refused to pull money from one bucket to fill the other. This he was very clear on. T-Company would just have to wait.

"You are telling me you would rather be harassed and maybe killed by goondas from India instead of taking some money out from this pointless Hemant Engineer pile of cash?" Beena Joshi was not at all amused by the situation Prem laid out for her. "You know what I think? I think you started losing your mind many years back, and slowly, more was lost, and now the job is complete. No mind left."

Prem sank into the couch from which Beena had finally removed the plastic. "Can I borrow your gun for some time?"

Beena scoffed in disbelief. "Really, gone. No logic remaining at all. Also, how are you knowing I have a gun?"

"Everyone knows. It's in the Swad Wheat Flour sack."

Beena did not give him her gun that day, despite Prem's surprisingly persuasive arguments and eventual begging. He left Beena's place defeated and despondent. Thinking a bike ride might help clear his head, he set out east, headed nowhere. Almost immediately, before even the Dosa Hut that was formerly Dairy Queen was out of sight, he felt eyes on him. The sensation at the back of his neck was so palpable and searing, it seemed an absolute certainty: Wristwatch was following him. Prem didn't turn around, hoping perhaps he was wrong and no one was there, or, at worst, it was just Beena. But as he approached Movie City 8, now showing *Asoka*, he couldn't shake the feeling he was being pursued by someone ill-intentioned. He pedaled faster up Oak Tree, finally looking back as he came upon the former Shoe Town, now dealing in halal meat. It was as he suspected. Wristwatch was closing in on him despite being on foot and wearing dress shoes.

Prem held out hope that Wristwatch was just out for a stroll on a pleasant afternoon, but in his heart, he knew the madman was after him. He stood out of the saddle and bore down on the pedals with his entire weight, yet still Wristwatch gained ground. Knees shaking and lungs short of breath, Prem made the rash decision to push forward through a yellow traffic light, hoping to leave Wristwatch behind to wait for green, but he had sorely miscalculated. The light turned red as he breached the intersection, and the cars on Wood Avenue sprung forward. He applied the brakes just as he was about to collide with an Oldsmobile. He was propelled into the air, soaring and tumbling forward spectacularly, landing back on his riderless bike that had continued to move forward after flipping over the hood of the car. Adhering to the laws of Bollywood physics, Prem and his bicycle emerged from the incident unscathed. No one at that corner that day—not the attendants at Exxon, nor Wristwatch stalled by the red light—questioned what they had witnessed, not even Minerva the Psychic Reader, who had seen it coming all along.

* * *

After nearly dying in front of Burger King, Prem contemplated a course correction. Approaching T-Company again to request a deadline extension did not seem viable. He could capitulate and pay them from his savings, but this would undoubtedly send him spiraling even further into depression and poor hygiene, from which he might never return. Prem considered Wristwatch. Who was this silent, large, and punctual man? Where did he come from? What were his nonmercenary interests? There had to be some humanity in him. Suddenly, it became clear—tube light!—like Amitabh in *Aakhree Raasta*, when his character, David, decides to avenge his wife's death and his own murder conviction by going after the true criminals, who are being protected by a police inspector who is actually David's unwitting son Vijay (also played by Amitabh), he would have to take matters into his own hands and unearth where that humanity lay.

* * *

Two weeks passed during which Wristwatch left Prem alone. He had put the poor guy through so much with the squirrel and the bicycle ride of death, he thought he deserved a break. Really, he felt they both deserved a break. He had terrified people for so long, and Prem had entertained them for probably just as long, all for what? Both were alone, with a lot of cash. How unfortunate it was that money, by virtue of the way humanity had structured civilization, played such a central role in any given life. He didn't know what had taken Prem down his particular path, what had landed him here, or what was keeping him from making a change. But it was clear they were both stuck.

These were the thoughts rattling around in Wristwatch's head one evening when he came home to the apartment that had been rented for him at King's Court. It was a regular one-bedroom, but it seemed spacious because it was so spare. A table and single chair by the kitchenette and a comfortable bed were the only pieces of furniture. Which was why the unexpected presence of a large wooden frame with a beautiful piece of fabric stretched over it was all the more astonishing when Wristwatch walked in that day. In neat rows along the wall were rolls of silk, spools of thread in every color, and boxes of hooked needles, beads, and stones. Tacked up on the wall were pattern samples, and, on the table, chalk and tracing paper on which he could at last create his own designs.

Hamza knew immediately that Prem was responsible for this miraculous embroidery workshop. He took off his suit jacket and folded it over the chair. Before sitting down to do the thing he loved most in the world, he looked over everything again, noting every exquisite detail. Prem was either a thoughtful, generous benefactor or a creepy, diabolical genius adept at field research. Either way, he would give the man what he wanted, which was more time. Because the gift was lovely.

37

You find yourself atop a mall-kiosk empire of your own creation and you ask yourself, How? Much earlier in your story, well before the interval, you move with your father to Edison, New Jersey, where together you open the first Indian grocery store in town. One day, a lanky yet devastatingly handsome young man, not unlike a young Shashi Kapoor, boyish with a chiseled jaw and floppy hair, crashes into your life like lightning, on his back in shattered glass. He glows from within the way special people sometimes do, soaking in your mother country's orange soda.

You go about your work, ordering Hot Mix and counting Hajmola Digestive Tablets, all the while hoping to see him again. You do not have to wait long as your father essentially tricks him into working at the store without pay for two weeks. You're thrilled and also strangely proud of your father. You peek at the young man here and there, careful not to let anyone see.

He seems a bit offbeat, this guy whose name you've learned is Prem. His friends call him synonyms for gasoline, and it appears he shaves his chest. Aunties flock to him like he's their best friend, and, in a few cases, he is. You like him. True, he sang the completely wrong song in antakshari, precipitating a bewildered silence, but he sang it so well and with style. You tell him as much from a distance as you're leaving.

His palm when you examine it at a party—after having examined several less exciting palms just to get to his—is softer than you expected for someone who works at Exxon. You pretend to read something in the life line or fate line, not revealing you have no chiromantic abilities and invented the ruse to talk to him. You ponder out loud whether you should cancel your vendor meeting for which you need to leave soon, hoping Prem will beg you to stay. Instead, he tells you to go. You are dejected until he explains: He respects you as a businesswoman. He respects your hard work. He would never advise you to do anything to jeopardize this. Go to your meeting and come back, he says. It is almost unbelievable to you that he could be this way. Wise, unselfish, exhibiting great strength of character. He's like an old man in a young Shashi Kapoor's body. You go and come back to find multiple girls flinging themselves at him, but he looks only at you.

Things move quickly from there. You begin to exchange notes in secret, leaving them in a predetermined hiding spot in the store, which is both exciting and greasy. You meet him behind the Dairy Queen, the bowling alley, until finally he moves in. It's not a real move-in but rather a scheme whereby your father takes Prem in as a paying guest, which was of course your idea.

These are magical days for you and Prem. His hands brush yours near the automatic roti maker, you steal glances as your father tacks a plant to the ceiling. You think back to these moments a few years later when *Maine Pyar Kiya* comes out and Salman Khan romances his family's houseguest Bhagyashree, calling her bedroom phone from his home-office phone when his father is in a meeting or squeezing her when his mother turns away to throw darts. You are crushed when one day your father and Prem conspire to stall your life.

One million and one dollars. How did your father come up with such a ludicrous number? You are disgusted, not just with your father but with Prem too. It's like he became a different person when the talk of money began. You spend the rest of that rainy day in your room with the door shut. You have never been so angry. Lying in bed, you go over it all again and again, dipping in and out of sleep. When the street lamps come on in the parking lot and the Quicker Liquor sign casts its dull glow, you wrest the Gits idli mix box with its gasoline scent from under the bed. The clump of oily notes inside fills you further with rage. You ball them together and flush them down the toilet, which emits a guttural glug then overflows. You do nothing about the clog or the water flooding the bathroom. Your father and the other paying guest, Viren Bhai, are standing in the kitchen when you open the door, and they can see the lavatorial destruction you've wrought. You walk past them and out of the apartment, though you feel guilty about Viren Bhai. It turns out he was the only wise man in your apartment all along.

After a maddening fight in the rain underscores the end of your relationship, you walk around irate for days, creating an uncomfortable living situation in 5F. "Did you even think of how your plan would upset me?" you accuse your father. He accuses you back, "Did you even think how you marrying a bum would upset me?" You over-order panipuri concentrate to make a point to your father, though you're not sure what that point is.

"Enough," he says, finally, in the store one day. He doesn't seem cross, just tired, leaning heavily against the checkout counter, the fight gone from his eyes. This gives you pause. You've seen this exhaustion before. During the darkest moment in your immigrant story, in the somber waiting room of a Texas hospital, your father's knees buckled. He broke his own fall by grabbing onto a chair. But he stayed on the floor like that, clutching the chair, depressing its worn upholstery with his cheek, for a long time. You'd never seen him cry before.

Your mother's life ended there in that hospital because she had chest pain in the wrong neighborhood. You, sixteen years old, and your father had driven her to the closest medical center, where they ruled out a heart attack and asked her to leave. No insurance, they said, try Harbor View for further care. An orderly who thought herself quite benevolent let you borrow a wheelchair. Somehow you got your mother in the car. She may or may not have been breathing when you reached Harbor View. Aortic dissection, they said, at time of death.

After that, your father vowed never to be poor and powerless again. He didn't state it out loud, but you knew. Every decision he made from that moment till now, though patient dumping became illegal and he secured insurance and built a thriving business, has been colored by the devastation of that day.

From behind the counter, he looks pleadingly at you by the Golden Temple wheat-flour sacks. "Okay, Papa. Enough," you say.

But what's Prem's excuse? You can't find an explanation for his bizarre life perspective. The only option left for you, obviously, is to go to Minnesota. Your bua who lives there has been urging you to visit. You do not intend to spend a full two months with your father's sister, but then you meet Mikesh. He has nice hair. You enjoy his company, and your father enjoys that you enjoy it. Together, you laugh a lot and he takes you to a bunch of lakes. By the time you return to Edison, you are done with Prem.

You pour yourself into the family business with renewed excitement for ordering Bournvita malted health drink and negotiating the bulk price of incense. You are fulfilled, happy to be making a difference in your father's life and in the lives of your customers. You work long hours in the store but make sure to spend time with friends along the way. Sometimes you go with them to Chi-Chi's Mexican restaurant to enjoy the baffling ice cream. You keep up with the latest Hindi movies, participating in the worldwide mania for *DDLJ* and witnessing the advent of the triple Khans at first with suspicion, then with applause.

In time, the store runs itself, signaling to you, fresh out of Rutgers with a degree in business administration and a GPA-padding minor in Hindi, that it has entered the growth stage of its life cycle. You must decide whether to expand or to remain stable and profitable, allowing you to partially disengage and pursue other interests.

You disengage.

You enjoyed establishing and building up India America Grocers with your father, more than you'd expected, but it is his store. It's time you created something of your own, something so big and so remarkable that generations to come would scarcely believe that such a business as this originated on this earth. Much as in *Rocky IV*, which Mikesh rented and made you watch twice and which you ended up quite liking for its motivational soundtrack and discernible real-life impact on the Cold War, you follow Rocky's example after Apollo dies and resolve to act. The action you take is steeped in hair. For years you have already been ironing ladies' tresses out of a makeshift beauty parlor in your father's bedroom, but now you expand your offerings: haircuts, hair coloring, updos, perms, every conceivable breed of waxing. The affluent auntie set, first from beyond King's Court and then beyond that, comes in droves. You set your rates so low, they forgo fancy, legitimate salons in favor of your cheap, illegitimate one. And your most in-demand service, facial-hair threading, yields the proverbial line out the door and a near-continuous logjam at the entrance to Building 5.

As all this capitalist initiative is unfolding in your father's bedroom, Sachin Tendulkar's storied cricket career is unfolding in the drawing room. Both you and your father are captivated on a semiregular basis—semi because your customers will be more patient waiting for their appointments if Shah Rukh Khan is striking his signature arms-wide-open pose on your TV screen, so you turn off Sachin and turn on

SRK, telling yourself it's okay, the matches, for the most part, aren't live anyway. Your father becomes disgruntled. You don't blame him because in his place you would feel the same. He has earned the luxury of cricket anytime, while you are just at the beginning of your entrepreneurial journey.

You pack up and move your salon and your life over to Mikesh's, where your client list grows steadily: the usual aunties, upper-crust doctor- and lawyer-types, a growing line of American-born hirsute Desi girls. One day, an unprecedented and astonishing thing happens: a white woman comes in.

The woman is not a complete stranger who made a wrong turn on Oak Tree, panicked at the variety of Gujarati grocery stores and so darted in by mistake. Hannah Abrams is the mother of Arthur Abrams, a close friend of Mikesh's who is also a doctor and a frequent caller at your apartment. You quite like him. He is well-groomed, affable, and always comes bearing Milano cookies. He takes more than a passing interest in your business, inquiring about overhead and asking you to explain in great detail the mechanics of threading while you watch old episodes of *Three's Company* and wait for Mikesh to come home.

It is Arthur who made the appointment for his mother, who, he explains, has always struggled with her mustache. "The poor thing," he says, "at one point it was practically a full handlebar!" You don't know what this is exactly but understand that it isn't good. "For years she bleached it," Arthur continues, "but that just made her mustache look blonde. She waxed for a while, but she got burned one too many times. She went through an au naturel phase, but my dad wasn't a fan, so she tried some sort of battery-operated device that kept cutting her. There was also this chemical thing that hurt, I think. Finally, she just began plucking. One hair at a time. Super painful, she says, and it comes in all stubbly now. Leena, help her, please," he said with a moving blend of desperation and drama.

"And she has never tried threading?" you asked.

"Never even heard of it, I'm sure."

"Okay, bring her here."

Hannah Abrams does indeed have a bristly upper lip. Some spots are more woolly than wiry, and this variety of textures suggests to you that the situation is dire. "I have seen worse," you say. Beginning with a hot towel, you move through the various stages—applying baby powder to absorb oil, showing the client how to push her tongue against the inside of her mouth to make the skin around her lips taut, twisting and pulling, twisting and pulling, ending with aloe vera and an ice cube. Hannah examines herself in the mirror. "Honey, you're a miracle worker!" she says. "It's all gone! And so fast!"

"The growth will be less thick next time, and it will hurt less and less until it won't hurt at all," you smile.

"You're kidding, right? Arthur, tell me she's kidding."

"And the craziest part?" Arthur crows. "It costs practically nothing."

"How much is practically nothing?"

"Seven dollars."

"You're kidding, right?"

What follows is a mother-son, all-out verbal assault on the parameters of your current business model. She is sitting on a gold mine, how can she work so hard for so little, what about expansion, doesn't she want to tap into the untapped hairy non-Indian market? When Mikesh comes home, he joins the fray. Imagine if you actually advertised, you should write a business plan, what about investors? Of course, there are taxes, licensure, and certifications to consider, but that can be handled. They list the key selling points: no chemicals, dyes, hot wax, or sharp objects; cheaper, faster, less painful than waxing; longer lasting, no damage to skin. This could be huge.

Their excitement becomes your excitement, and you realize this is the big idea you've been searching for. Mainstream threading. So simple, so obvious. Low overhead, easily scalable, and hasn't been done beyond the Indian parlors. It's time to take your hitherto underground salon out into the legitimate light of the American shopping mall.

As soon as you can, you set up a kiosk at Woodbridge Center, then another at Menlo Park. You hand out flyers explaining what threading is. You hire a publicist to get the word out. You build a strong client base and approach more malls. You assemble a network of skilled threading specialists, unearthing them at India Day parades and Diwali garbas. In time, you expand your enterprise throughout the tristate area, then to other states, sending teams to set up the booths and recruit and train local threaders. In the span of barely a decade, the Eastern seaboard plus pockets of the Midwest and Canada are brimming with Drop Thread Gorgeous kiosks, specializing in brow shaping and mustache management. You marvel at what you've accomplished without the unsolicited participation of a man, beginning with a single spool of Griffin No. 40 pure cotton thread by Coats. The idea of a lifetime, right under your nose.

Though you've lived in Edison all these years, you haven't really been there. You've been consumed by DTG, aggressively striving, meeting, traveling, grinding it out, sweating blood, or as your father puts it, overworking, overexerting. Of course, you visit him all the time at King's Court, at the store, at the restaurants up and down Oak Tree Road. But you haven't been entirely present until now. Your father is not well, and you decide finally to come home.

* * *

In the classic Hindi movie, the audience is sometimes alerted to the importance of a character's reappearance by the manner of her entrance. For instance, a dramatic, slow-motion stride with a drawn-out, purposeful gait would likely signal something momentous. The billowing of the heroine's or occasional fluffy-haired hero's mane would almost certainly portend a significant plot point, the magnitude of which could be measured by the intensity of the waft. You glide into Building 5 one gentle spring morning looking as though you just came from a dust storm.

You notice the white walls have faded to yellow and the wood floors are not what they used to be, and you wonder when this all happened. In one corner lies a *Little India* newspaper and an empty bottle of Thums Up cola. Yet as you finally stop to take it all in, the sweet simplicity of those early New Jersey days comes back to you.

Not that your own living situation is glamorous. You've been in the same basic and efficient apartment all these years, and your car is not the kind that elicits any particular admiration. Because of this and because you prefer to keep out of the limelight, seeing no need to advertise your success, your father doesn't completely grasp how big your business has grown. For him, it can't possibly be prosperous if you've never even been on the news or in the paper or in *Time* magazine. At this stage of his life and yours, and now with his illness, you want to assure him that you've done well and he does not have to worry about you. So you allow for a bit of publicity.

In the "100 Innovators" edition of *Time*, Harvard professor Molly Galvan praises how you have made DTG synonymous with accessible grooming. *Forbes* lauds your offering free threading to women seeking employment and your commitment to training survivors of domestic violence for your "hair force" of aestheticians. Your favorite is the *Fast Company* piece "Rehabilitation Through Hair Elimination," which you casually leave by your father's bedside.

38

Despite the effort Prem put into tracking Leena over the years, he was unaware of the great heights her business had reached. He knew about the home salon and mall threading but didn't feel it necessitated any ongoing research. It's not that he thought she couldn't build a massive enterprise, but that she wasn't one to crave such a thing. "Why does everything have to grow and expand and become an empire?" she used to say. So when Prem read the *Time* magazine piece about Leena's empire, he gasped.

"What happened?" Sayali said from the kitchen, where she was tacking up another picture of a waterfall while waiting for the chai to boil. Prem had been reclining on her couch, his head on an armrest, flipping through magazines. He was purposefully relaxing that week in anticipation of the considerable work ahead of him for the Bollywood Gold Awards, a show he'd invented to give audiences and participants alike something new. He and Beena had devised the list of nominees one evening over papdi chaat at Arjun's Street Snack Shack, and then, in the interest of efficiency, went ahead and picked the winners as well. Madhuri Dixit, Aishwarya Rai, and Shah Rukh Khan (essentially the cast of the recent hit *Devdas*), among others, were lured to New Jersey with the promise of a golden Gold Spot statuette—a nod to the beloved, recently discontinued soda. To add an additional dose of glitz and prestige, Prem planned to bestow upon an as-yet-undetermined Hollywood celebrity the Friend of India Award, an idea also dreamed up over papdi chaat.

When he came to Leena's page in *Time*, he sprung to an upright position. "Oh, are you reading the section on Mohini Bhardwaj?" Sayali inquired. "They say she's going to win a medal in Athens. When did you become excited for women's gymnastics?"

Prem couldn't believe what he was reading. A nationwide network, charitable partnerships, plans for expansion. It felt like a betrayal, though he wasn't sure of what or by whom. How could he not know this much of her world? Sayali set down two mugs on her Alaska: The Last Frontier coasters on the coffee table and waited for him to speak. "Gymnastics, ya, you know. I like when they jump," he said. She looked at him, puzzled. "On the beam," he added. He downed his tea, in the process scalding his tongue, and begged her forgiveness, he just remembered he had to go, he would call her soon, sorry.

Outside, it smelled of fire, though there was none, bringing Prem back to India, where there always seemed to be a suggestion of a fire nearby. He wanted to be alone. He took his bike to Oak Tree Road, hauling himself down the street looking for a spicy paan. He wanted not to think about Leena and the entire life she'd lived without him, instead seeking only to satisfy his craving. It wasn't good for him, he knew, but it was a compulsion he couldn't shake. At Once Up-Paan a Time, he ordered two, for which he was charged an inflated price, the desperation written on his face.

That same smoky May evening, Hemant Engineer was rushed to JFK hospital with chest pain. A coronary angiogram showed significant blockage in more than one artery, and he was scheduled to have bypass surgery four days later. Leena stayed by her father's side night and day, essentially moving into his room. After five excruciating hours of surgery, Hemant was wheeled out to his recovery room in surgical intensive care, and the anguish of uncertainty was past. Leena's role turned from distraught daughter to gatekeeper and part-time unintentional host.

Beena was first to visit, bearing khichdi, the Indian patient's rice-based comfort food of choice. Next came Uttam Jindal, armed with a new jet-black wig and fresh dhokla. Sanjay Sapra came late but stayed the longest, setting up camp in one corner, where he served water and refreshments to guests. Kailash Mistry offered to sing, and astrologist, palmist, and self-driving priest Tilak Upadhyaya popped by to offer his services. Leena's friend Varsha brought homemade thepla in a blue Royal Dansk Danish Butter Cookies tin, and Charlie Patel brought a DVD of *Lagaan*, the Indian cricket lover's movie of choice. By the time visiting hours were over, all of the major business leaders of the Oak Tree community had come by, as well as several prominent Indians in politics and news and most of King's Court Buildings 3 through 12.

Leena had been so busy expanding her own sphere of influence, she'd forgotten that her father's had reached unruly new heights. Just a year ago, he had been named chairman of the board of the Indian American Retailers Association, and the year before that, he'd been honored by the American National Cricket Club for his dedication to promoting the game in America. Whenever she came to the apartment, a crowd was waiting to ask for favors, pledge their support, collaborate on projects, and plan events. As she stood by his hospital bed, she felt proud that they'd both done so well, fueled by the same personal fortitude and otherworldly immigrant determination, coupled with the abiding fear of sliding backward into that life where they couldn't save her mother.

But perhaps so much activity had worn her father out. "Okay, thank you, everyone, for coming, time to go, Papa needs rest," she said to Gitanjali

Vora, Shanta Bhatt, Nalini Sen, Urmila Sahu, Lucky, Gopal, Mohan, Deepak, Iqbal, Amarleen, Tun-Tun, Tony, and others she didn't know.

Almost no one stopped talking or made any movement toward the door. Urmila asked Leena if she could come to the hospital to thread her upper lip regularly if ever she was in a coma. "Maybe twice every month?"

"Me too, I want that service too!" Shanta added.

It wasn't a terrible idea, coma contracts, and Leena tucked it away for later. "Fabulous plan, Auntie, yes, let us discuss it some other time, okay, bye, yes, bye," she said, directing her to the door, where Gopal was asking Mohan, "If there is 'understood,' why there's no 'overstood?'"

Finally, Hemant spoke, clearing his throat loudly before beginning. "My heart, although in need of repairing, feels full today. My friends, my colleagues, my community, my accountant, thank you for coming." He joined his palms and bowed his head in gratitude. "Now go," he ordered. As the crowd said their goodbyes and get-wells and shuffled out, Hemant added, "Not Prem. Prem, you stay."

Leena had not even noticed Prem there, hovering by the door with Beena, and the suddenness of his presence was jarring. So many years had passed since she'd seen him so close up. He was no longer the gangly boy in gas-station coveralls without a rupee to his name, but instead a tidy, more self-possessed man, older and full of days. He had retained his sideburns and feathery hair, as though trying to freeze himself in an oddly specific moment in time, but weariness was also evident in his face, markers of half a lifetime lived. His features were the same, though, graceful and arresting, his essential Shashi Kapoorness still intact.

She'd watched him at a distance through the years and knew about the wild success of his superstar shows. On more than one occasion, she'd observed him standing alone and off to the side and felt sorry for him. But there, in the hospital, he no longer seemed like someone to pity. The question remained, however: why was he here?

"Leena, before you leave—" Hemant started.

"Papa, no, no, I am staying," Leena said, sweeping the hair back from his forehead with her fingers.

"I need you to take care of Hriyan," Hemant said. "He needs water right away."

"Of course, Papa. I'll stop at the store first to make sure—"

"The store is just fine," Hemant interrupted. "It is Hriyan I am worried about. Are you not?"

"Of course, I am, Papa," Leena assured him. She felt suddenly like she did not understand her father at all. His obsession with the plant, his asking Prem to stay back—she really needed to spend more time with him to make sure his mind was functioning properly. "I will be back in two, three hours," she said. The last of the visitors exited, and Prem came forward directly toward her with a piercing, unnerving gaze. They didn't speak that day but exchanged nods of acknowledgment, their sleeves brushing as they passed. Leena kissed her father, gathered her things, and left, not noticing the piece of her hair Prem had picked from her sweater and tucked into his pocket.

* * *

Prem had arrived at the hospital with a degree of trepidation, knowing she would be there. He wanted to see her—of course, he always did—but he didn't know how she would react to his presence. The absurdity of wanting to visit Hemant yet being nervous about running into Leena was not lost on him. But he had to pay his respects, so he braced himself and went in.

The old man's room was full to the brim with guests, which Prem expected. Hemant had become an important person in their little world, respected and loved. After the assistance Hemant had given Prem with the detained megastars at the airport, they had continued to help each other as needed. Prem connected Hemant with his special-effects lighting guy for an upcoming fundraiser; Hemant helped Prem to buy Thums Up in bulk for a new show he was planning. Though Prem viewed Hemant as the same tightfisted shopkeeper with the choleric disposition who had caused him to wait a lifetime for love, he also discovered that he was kind of nice.

When Hemant called for him to stay back, Prem presumed it was to discuss getting an actor to appear for the grand reopening of his store's refrigerated aisle. He considered ducking behind a gurney, harkening back to his days behind the drapes in his childhood home. He had been watching Leena for ten minutes but wasn't ready for her to see him. He took a deep breath and went into the room, coming closer to her than he had in fifteen years, one month, and eleven days, during which he'd thought of her every day. Worry lines had become evident between her brows, as had a few fine lines around her eyes. Some freckles had gained prominence at the end of her nose, and flecks of gray had appeared at her temples. She was thirty-five now. She was perfect.

After that initial visit, Prem became a fixture at JFK Medical Center's Surgical ICU, room 4021. The daily visitors soon reduced in number, and by the time Hemant was transferred to inpatient rehab in the basement, Prem and Leena were the only ones left.

"Who is ready for Beena Joshi's famous veg biryani?" Prem removed the lid from a Daisy sour-cream container while Leena organized Hemant's personal items. They hadn't spoken to each other directly yet, but instead had been speaking around each other.

"I'm going to King's Court, Papa, to get your clean clothes. Anything you want from there?"

"Tongue scraper," Hemant said.

"Got it," Leena said. "You will be okay here?"

Hemant shook his head. "Ya, ya, don't worry. Prem is here."

Prem had begun spoon-feeding biryani to Hemant. Leena took in the bizarre scene and turned to go.

"Remember," Hemant called. "Water for Hriyan."

When she returned a few hours later, Prem was hard at work rubbing her father's feet.

"Enough. That was wonderful," Hemant said to Prem. "Now I will sleep for some time."

"Very good, just rest," Prem said, sliding Hemant's socks back on. "I will get the Jell-O."

Hemant looked at Prem with a softness in his eyes that Leena had thought was reserved only for her and the plant. "I never noticed before," Hemant said, "you have a very calming nice voice. Like Jagjit Singh." Prem smiled and adjusted Hemant's pillow as he fell gently asleep.

When Prem left, Leena stopped sorting and organizing and jolted her father awake. "Papa! What is happening here?"

"Huh?"

"First you said he was a useless, no-good loafer, and now he is Man of the Match?"

Hemant answered with appropriate defensiveness. "His firm and soothing tone makes me easy."

Leena was incredulous. "So, you are telling me it is because of his voice?" Her hands were in her hair now as if about to pull it out.

"Look," Hemant said in a manner signaling he was taking control. "Prem is decent and simple. Works hard, doesn't spend. Helps the community. He is a good boy." Leena couldn't believe the hypocrisy of what her father was saying. Coupled with the overarching fear of losing him, it was almost too much for her to take. She went down to the bakery near the lobby and nibbled on a scone.

It was evening when she returned to her father's room and again found Prem, who had brought back with him legendary ghazal singer Jagjit Singh, who was eating Jell-O with Hemant and comforting him in his deep, velvety way.

After the shock of Jagjit Singh being there had worn off and she had adequately greeted, praised and thanked him, Leena noticed how frail and weak her father looked in his bed, and it frightened her. Tears welled up in her eyes and she found it hard to breathe. She did not want her father or world-renowned vocalist Jagjit Singh to see, so she excused herself and went in search of soda.

Not entirely by chance, Prem happened upon her assaulting a vending machine, banging its side with an open hand. "Can I help?" he asked.

Leena flipped her hair over one shoulder, startled, her expression one of filial distress mixed with the frustration of everyone who'd ever lost a dollar trying to buy a Coke.

"Leena, look," Prem began. He hesitated, then held her by the shoulders. "Look at me. He is getting the best care possible. I checked. Dr. B. Sharma. Top of the line. Handsome also."

Leena sniffled and looked up at Prem. "Why does it matter if the doctor is handsome?"

"I don't know."

They both burst out laughing. Prem pulled out a handkerchief from his jacket and handed it to her, then turned his attention to the vending machine.

"Really, he is good?" Leena said, drying her tears.

"World-class," Prem said, retrieving a Coke from the bin. He twisted off the cap and held the bottle out to her, its soft hiss between them.

Though she still didn't understand why Prem was there, she also did not want to ask. Because truly, he was a comfort.

39

On the second day of rehab in the basement, Mahesh Bajpai of Building 13 dropped in to visit Hemant and debut his new hennaed hairstyle.

"How old do I look?" he asked father and daughter.

Leena opened her mouth but no words came out. "Orange," Hemant said. "Very orange."

"I know!" Mahesh Bajpai said. "No white, no silver, no gray. I can give you the referral if you want. Bharati will give you best price."

Prem was just returning from the cafeteria with two cups of tea. He stopped short before entering the room upon seeing what was transpiring inside.

"Oh, do you think I should—" Hemant began, cut off by Leena before he could commit to anything.

"Wonderful seeing you, Uncle," she said, steering him by the elbow to the door, "thank you for coming, visiting hours ending, yes, looking ten years younger, bye!"

Later that day, when Prem and Leena took the elevator down to lunch together, they had an easy topic of conversation teed up for them. "He is married, no? Why didn't his wife tell him?" Prem asked.

"Maybe she likes it?" Leena offered.

"No, no chance of that."

"You're right."

"Such a tragedy."

"And he was trying to infect my father too!"

"Why not dark brown hair dye?"

"I'm sad the Indian beauty industrial complex failed him so badly."

Hemant's visitors numbered only one or two a day, but it was enough to sustain Prem and Leena's casual elevator chitchat, which soon bled into other areas of the hospital. In the waiting room, they parsed the various strains of gossip divulged by Nachiket Rao centering mostly on his neighbor's not-so-innocent divorce. In the hallway, they had a good laugh over Nathan Kothari's concern that his recently skinny wife was going to run away with Nachiket Rao's neighbor. When Charlie Patel insisted that Hindus were the ultimate recyclers—millions scheduled for cremation and subsequent reincarnation, he argued—they had to agree, later in the vestibule, that it was an interesting hypothesis.

A new familiarity grew between them, one that Prem did not want to disturb with mention of their shared past or Mikesh. He had, in fact, been leaving the hospital each day at the exact late-afternoon moment Leena's fiancé visited after his rounds, thus avoiding the fact of his existence. Instead, Prem would take a ride on his bicycle to Dunkin' Donuts just at the end of James Street or around the corner to Namasté Cafe for some legitimate chai. He would then return to enjoy studying Leena's intense concentration when speaking with Hemant's doctors or eating a cup of yogurt.

They settled into a sort of routine, and Leena began working from the hospital, taking calls, doing things on a computer. Prem knew he should have been tending to the Bollywood Gold preparations, but how could he? It was all playing out like a 1990s Hindi movie fantasy, he thought, until his single and available lady friends began showing up at the hospital to visit with assorted friends and family and ruin things for Prem. Statuesque and stunning Bishakha Dey, whom Prem had not seen since the incident with the police, came first, running into Prem and Leena in the hallway on her way to see a friend.

"Can you believe that night we had?" she beamed. "Let's get together soon."

Next, Suchitra appeared in the lobby, again with rajma in a Dannon container, this time for her mother on the second floor. "Prem! I was just remembering you when I saw the merry-go-round in the mall. How many years back was that? We must go again sometime." They bumped into one in the cafeteria, another at the bakery, and still another hovering by a nurses' station, not visiting anyone, just standing around hoping to meet a doctor. By the time Sayali turned up in the commissary, Prem suspected a conspiracy might be afoot, which, had it been true, would've been a huge success. Leena was more entertained by each woman they encountered, shooting Prem a look of amused accusation every time. They never spoke of any of it, underscoring Prem and Leena's tacit rule of not asking about such things. So when Leena mysteriously left the hospital in the afternoon two days in a row, causing Prem to panic that she had a standing rendezvous with Mikesh for romantic tree circling and spontaneous highly choreographed dancing, there was only one course of action open to him: have his assistant spy on her.

Pankaj, it turned out, was an excellent spy. The next day, he followed Leena's car out to Westfield and hid in a bus shelter when she entered the Bloom Bloom Room, where she spent over half an hour but emerged with no flowers. The same thing happened at her next stop, Vaccaro's Bakery, where she stayed even longer but came out with no cookies or cannoli. Pankaj tried to piece together a theory but could only come up with the thought that she was bad at running errands. The next day, she went for a very long drive, and Pankaj wondered if she even knew where she was going. After nearly an hour, she turned into the gravel driveway of a charming and rustic ashram. A white swami in saffron robes greeted her, and together they paced a bucolic little field in back, sometimes pausing to point something out or gesture in a certain direction. Pankaj had guessed the reason Prem had wanted her followed, and it pained him to report back, his monotone voice slightly less monotoned, that she was either becoming an ascetic or planning a wedding.

Though he knew it was not the case, Prem felt deceived. All those recent moments lost their meaning, and he wondered why he had done Hemant's laundry. He decided he had to see for himself and deliberately stayed when Mikesh came by, silently observing from behind a newspaper at the far end of the room as the dashing endocrinologist checked in with Hemant. On his way out, he said, "See you back home," and patted Leena roughly on the back as if she weren't the most perfect, precious thing.

The next day, Prem resumed avoiding Mikesh, taking his usual bike ride down James Street to Dunkin' Donuts, where Wristwatch was having a cruller.

"Premji," Wristwatch said, "I have been expecting you."

Prem turned to look at a confused donut worker, then back at Wristwatch. He knew the mafia ruffian had not stalked and ambushed him for benevolent reasons, yet Prem wanted only to collapse into the gigantic man's arms, rest his head on his shoulder, and cry. Seeing someone there who knew where he was from, knew who he actually was, and knew that he owed a large sum of money to a notorious gangster made him feel less alone.

"Wristwatch," Prem said, "I did not know you liked donuts."

"I only have tried this kind," Wristwatch said, holding up his cruller. "It is nice."

"I am getting a chai. One for you?" Prem said, reaching for his wallet.

"No, thank you."

"Let me get a chai for you," Prem said. "We can make a ten-minute truce."

"No, no, it is not that," Wristwatch said. "The issue, really, it is just, it is not really chai."

Prem's face lit up. "I know!" he said, somewhat too energetically, he realized. But he continued with what he began, tearing apart the notion of a "chai latte" for its obvious contradiction in terms and its profound dissimilarity from its authentic self. He went into what he considered to be a cultural travesty, the lack of actual boiled milk and tea leaves, all of which was supplanted by a gooey syrup pumped into lukewarm, indifferent milk.

Wristwatch looked at him blankly. "At least this concoction has brought some semblance of India's culture to every corner of every big city in the world."

"Good point," Prem admitted. It was fun for a moment to be upset about something other than his own life, but he knew Wristwatch was there to discuss more pressing matters. "So, none for you?"

Prem returned with two coffees and took a seat across from Wristwatch. They sat in silence.

"Look," Wristwatch said at last. "Tiger Nayak is here."

Prem jumped out of his chair and looked around frantically.

"Not here in Dunkin' Donuts," Wristwatch said. "Here in America, in New Jersey. Edison."

"In Edison. Tiger Nayak. The international criminal mob leader."

"Well, we are not as established internationally as we'd like, but we are hoping," Wristwatch said, touching his fingers to the table, just in case. He cleared his throat. "You are expected to report for a meeting tomorrow, one o'clock, Edison Memorial Tower. Be on time."

That night, Prem barely slept. Under his onions, he lay awake for hours. He tried to breathe deliberately. Calm his racing heart. Formulate a plan. Not think about Leena. Only think about Leena. He circled through this sequence many times before drifting off, wondering how often the Singhs used their onions and switched them out for new ones.

"Yaar, someone wake up Pumpwalla."

"I tried. He maybe is dead."

"Then just roll him to the side."

"You roll him to the side."

"I'll roll your mother to the side."

This was the negotiation Prem woke up to as his roommates straightened up the apartment in preparation for a viewing of *Munna Bhai M.B.B.S.*, the new Sanjay Dutt blockbuster about the time-honored quest to impress one's parents by becoming a doctor. Apparently, fifteen to twenty other people would be coming over shortly.

Prem, enjoying the bustle and banter, soon remembered what he had to do that day and moaned, pulling the blanket over his head.

"Pumps, what's happening to you?" Mohan asked. "Move. Varsha, Falguni, Snigdha, Manaswini are coming."

"And Gopal, Radha, Abdul Rashid, Dave," Yogesh said.

"And Dolly," Deepak added, biting into an apple.

"What did Tun-Tun and Tony say? Coming?" asked Mohan.

"She is coming. He is having loose motions and has to stay with his toilet," Yogesh replied.

"Do we need some non-Desi friends?" Deepak questioned, now eating a cold rolled-up roti.

"I talk with Roberta at Drug Fair," Yogesh said. "Sometimes her hair is very high and nice and I tell her."

"Remember we interacted with those guys ten, twelve years back?"

asked Deepak. "The ones who came in many cars?"

"The racists who tried to beat us?"

"Ya, those ones."

"Should we invite Minerva the Psychic Reader to join our social circle?" Yogesh asked.

"Why you're forcing me to have non-Desi friends?" Mohan barked. "Petrol, up!"

"Leave him alone," Amarleen jumped in.

"You leave him alone," Iqbal jumped in too.

"He is under stress. See?" Amarleen tugged at Prem's blanket.

"I'm getting up, I'm getting up," Prem said.

"See?" Amarleen squished Prem's cheeks together with one hand. "Stress."

Guests were settling in for *Munna Bhai* by the time Prem dressed and left. He had considered not going to the hospital that morning but decided that would be a childish, knee-jerk reaction to recent revelations. He was determined not to be childish. But when he got to the hospital and discovered that Leena had stepped out, obviously to visit a caterer or to interview deejays, he had an internal meltdown right there in the room with her father, kicking a side table and causing a vase of flowers to tip over.

"Jesus. Let me just . . ." Prem sopped up the water dripping to the floor with a towel and righted the bouquet.

"When I met you," Hemant said from his bed, "you were also dropping things and wiping the mess just like this. Nothing much has changed!" Though Hemant was trying to say something funny, Prem took it as an accurate summation of the pathetic standstill that was his life.

"Exactly. What has changed? Nothing. Except things maybe have become worse," he responded.

Hemant sighed. "Lousy day already?"

Prem sank into a chair by the bed and hung his head. "Listen, if I die, don't forget your blood pressure medication."

"Don't take tension, Leena is there. Also, why are you dying?"

"She might become occupied with other things, other people."

Hemant looked at the boy's face and suddenly understood. He patted Prem's hand. "She is a good girl. You are a good boy," he said. "Now I will sleep for some time."

Prem wandered a long while on his bicycle before turning toward Edison's Memorial Tower. Though it was not yet summer, the sun was like the Delhi sun of his youth, blazing and relentless. Eleven days on and there was still the suggestion of smoke in the air, from what source he still didn't know. He was panting and drenched in sweat when at last he came face to face with Tiger Nayak.

She was not at all as he'd imagined. Short in stature and slight, she was more delicate than brawny. Her hair was pulled back in a tight ponytail and she wore all black leather, yet seemed unbothered by the heat. Prem had pictured the head of T-Company to be a fearsome and strapping figure, scarred, hairy, and a man. He recognized her as Tiger, however, because she was striking a relaxed pose, casually leaning back against a black Escalade while thugs of various shapes and sizes were standing at attention in T-Company-issued uniforms.

Prem parked his bike next to a tree and crossed the street.

"Well, well, Prem Kumar, son of the Titan of Technology, CEO of Superstar Entertainment, confirmed bachelor who lives under onions. Finally, we meet." She looked Prem up and down. "Wristwatch did not report that you are slightly handsome. Wristwatch!"

A rear window rolled down and the henchman said, "Sorry, madam, I did not think he was handsome." The window rolled back up.

"Come, Junior Titan," Tiger Nayak said. "Let us walk around this

Edison Memorial Tower and its scruffy, unworthy grounds."

Her words were benign but her tone was inscrutable at best. Prem could see respect tinged with terror in her subordinates' eyes. Their knees quivered as she passed.

"Tiger is proud of you," she began. "You have built something big and successful with the money Tiger so generously lent to you. And as you know, Tiger likes making dreams come true—that is what Tiger is most known for."

Her manner of speech made Prem wonder if he was mistaken in assuming this tiny woman was the cunning and ruthless mafia boss he thought she was. They kept walking.

"But you have made Tiger angry. Tiger does not like to be angry." She stopped short and gave him a bloodthirsty death glare.

Prem swallowed hard. It was definitely Tiger Nayak.

"Tiger is not an unreasonable gang leader," she went on, her hands clasped behind her back now as they turned toward the deserted back of the monument. "She understands that people make mistakes. Do you think you made a mistake?"

Several of Tiger's men, one holding a very fat stick, encircled them. Prem, trying to appear unpanicked, gave the answer she was looking for. "Uh, yes? Yes, I made a mistake."

"And?"

"And I will pay Tiger, I mean, you back as soon as possible."

Tiger closed her eyes and took a long, deep breath. The goonda with the stick took a step closer, and Tiger opened her eyes and exhaled. "You know what Tiger does when someone disappoints her?" Prem shook his head vigorously. He thought he might throw up and prayed it wouldn't land on her. "She gives her soldiers a game to play. In this game, the players compete to reach the target first. They spread out and search for them, sometimes taking days or even weeks. The winner of the game is the one who finds the target and stabs them in the eye."

"She calls it eye spy," one of her men added proudly.

"Clever, no? Eye spy." Tiger smiled and nodded in praise of herself, then reassumed her grim countenance. "One thing Tiger forgot to mention. The target is never the one who made the mistake. No. The target is a loved one of the guilty party. Often, this means a woman. T-Company has stabbed many types of women in the eye: wives, mothers, teachers, doctors. Even . . . engineers."

At this point in an archetypal Bollywood gangster film, a dramatic instrumental track blares out of nowhere, sometimes alongside a flash of lightning. Bells from five different temples toll at once, and maybe a faraway loved one, who intuitively knows the worst has come to pass drops a tray of teacups, fruit, or religious supplies and either freezes or falls to the floor herself. In Prem's case, that hideous moment was underscored by the long-long-short-long whistles of a southbound New Jersey Transit train and an Amtrak northbound train approaching Metropark station at the same time, bells clanging as they hissed and screeched to a stop. Prem's fear turned to fury, but he managed to keep his cool. Sensing it would be the wrong tack to take with a seasoned murderer like Tiger Nayak, he refrained from trying anything along the lines of "Take me, don't hurt her." But the rage was written on his face.

"Oh no, I have angered the Junior Titan," Tiger said in what Prem did not think was an especially contrite manner. She patted him on the back and recommenced the walk. "As I said before, Tiger is not unreasonable. Forget the money."

Prem gasped. Before he could say anything, Tiger continued.

"Instead," she said, "there is one thing Junior Titan must do to save the target." She paused and looked up at the memorial's giant unimpressive orb. "He must make a date for Tiger with CNN's Dr. Sanjay Gupta."

The trains' bells clanged once more as they peeled away from the station. Prem looked to the T-Company thugs for some validation of his profound stupefaction but found none. "I guess, I didn't know, I mean, what?"

Tiger made a sound close to laughing. "What can I tell you, what can I tell you, Junior Titan? I am a fan." She was an entirely ruthless and deranged character; he could see that now. There was no negotiating with her, but still he tried. "I have the money. I will give you the money."

"Look at this," she laughed to her men, "the Junior Titan is begging!"

Prem did not think he was, but the idea of it seemed to make her so happy. "Please, I am begging!" he said.

"Too bad! You should have given the money before, but you were hoarding it to buy the wife."

"Buy the wife? What? No," Prem said. He quickly considered the possibilities. "Can I get Deepak Chopra instead?"

"No."

"Fareed Zakaria?"

"Don't be absurd."

"I have it. Jagjit Singh! He may be hanging around here somewhere, I probably could even get him today."

Tiger shook her head. "Only Sanjay Gupta."

They came back around to the clearing in front of the tower, where a nursing home van had pulled up. "I can give you few weeks," Tiger said, "but do it soon as I don't come to America in winters. Okay, now I have to make a move." She gestured with her chin toward the ramshackle Menlo Park Museum. "I am going for the 1:30 tour."

The thugs dispersed and Prem returned to his bike. Its seat had become hot, so he walked with it for a while. If he just stayed calm and did the things he needed to do, it would all be okay, he told himself. He needed to produce CNN medical correspondent Dr. Sanjay Gupta. Also, he needed to hire a team of bodyguards to follow Leena around without her knowledge. He repeated this simple list in his head throughout the long trek back to King's Court that afternoon as the sun beat down on him. He would ask Pankaj to manage the guards and, when he had a chance, find out the date of Leena's wedding to Mikesh.

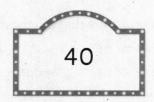

40

The New York Times

VOWS
At a Far-Flung Wedding,
a Confection Connection

Arthur Abrams had given up on love while Mikesh Aneja was living with a beard, until common friends and a love of cookies brought them together.

By STACY LEVINSON GERTEN June 8, 2003

When Dr. Mikesh Aneja and Dr. Arthur Abrams met at a wedding in Barcelona nearly eight years ago, they had no idea they were being set up. "I was on the groom's side and Arthur knew the bride, and they plotted to seat us together," Dr. Aneja said. "It was a Catalan conspiracy."

"Fortunately, they knew what they were doing," Dr. Abrams said. "We clicked immediately. And when the cookie talk began, well, it was all over."

Dr. Piya Saraiya, the bride at the Barcelona wedding, explained that she and her husband had their friends' obsessions with baked goods in mind. "We just thought, we know these two smart, kind, unsettlingly handsome guys who can't stop eating Milanos. It was a no-brainer."

"I just couldn't get over that there was another doctor who loved competing in triathlons and also eating Thin Mints," said Dr. Aneja, 38, an endocrinologist. For Dr. Abrams, it was as much the things they didn't have in common that intrigued him. "I loved that Mikesh had grown up in India and gone to high school in Minnesota," said Dr. Abrams, 37, a cardiologist. "His experience is so unique. I just wanted to know more."

When the festivities came to an end, Dr. Aneja returned to Rochester, Minn., where he was beginning an endocrinology fellowship at the Mayo Clinic, and Dr. Abrams went home to New Jersey, where he had grown up and was completing his medical residency at the University of Medicine and Dentistry of New Jersey; coincidentally, Aneja had earned his medical degree there. But neither could forget the connection they'd made in Barcelona.

It took only two weeks of talking on the phone followed by one meeting before the two began dating. For the next few years, the couple shuttled between Minnesota and New Jersey to spend time together while also establishing themselves in their respective fields. Dr. Abrams completed his cardiology fellowship and eventually joined a practice in Edison, N.J., while Dr. Aneja accepted a position at the University of Minnesota's Division of Diabetes, Endocrinology and Metabolism in Minneapolis. It was during this time that Dr. Aneja became close with the Abrams family.

"They embraced me as their son-in-law immediately, which meant the world to me," said Dr. Aneja, who had not yet come out as gay to his conservative Hindu parents. "Hannah even made rugelach, my favorite, every single time I visited."

Dr. Abrams' parents, Hannah Abrams and the Honorable Matthew Abrams, adored Dr. Aneja and were thrilled when he joined an endocrinology group in New Jersey to be closer to their son. "It was a great comfort to us to know that Mikesh was fully committed, despite the fact that he was living with a beard."

The beard in question, Leena Engineer, was happy to pretend to date Dr. Aneja, even going so far as to feign an engagement and share an apartment with him. "My father threw this big party for us, and really, we felt terrible deceiving him and everyone that way," said Engineer. "We both just needed time to figure out our lives without being set up left and right."

When the time came to talk to his parents, Dr. Aneja flew to Minneapolis to have the discussion in person. "I was terrified. I thought it might be the last time

I saw my parents." Instead, Dr. Aneja's mother, Sanjana Aneja, declared her exasperation about a related issue. "I was not mad that he was gay or that he had a boyfriend, I was mad he made me wait so long for a grandchild!"

Rohit Aneja, Dr. Aneja's father, struck a more solemn note. "I said to him, 'You are our son and we support you. We love you and we will love the person who loves you. End of story.' "

"I cried tears of relief and overwhelming love," Dr. Aneja recalled. "Then I began planning the proposal." True to their origin story, he took Dr. Abrams to a paella bar, and at the end of the night, presented him with a fortune cookie.

"We were strolling through the Village when all of a sudden he was on his knee," Dr. Abrams said. "You can guess the question that was in the cookie."

Soon after, the parents met and the wedding planning was underway. The grooms worried there would be tension between the families regarding where the wedding would take place, Minnesota or New Jersey, but were pleasantly surprised by Sanjana Aneja's position. "For a half-Indian wedding, there is no better place than Edison," she said. "It is like having the wedding in India itself!"

Though the dual ceremonies took place in Somerset, N. J., on the grounds of the Arsha Bodha Center, all the trappings of a glamorous Hindu wedding were brought in from Edison. An elegantly decorated mandap, which doubled as a chuppah, sat amid a field of native grasses and goldenrod, where the grooms were wed first by Swami Tadatmananda and then by Rabbi Edward Moskowitz, of Temple Beth Shalom of Westfield. In bespoke matching sherwanis by designer Tarun Tahiliani, their palms painted by top henna artist Neha Desai, the couple performed the Hindu and Jewish rituals before a crowd of 200 guests, after which they enjoyed a rustic South Indian lunch by Swagath Gourmet.

The party reconvened in the evening, by which time a tent aglow with candles and twinkle lights had been erected by celebrated Indian wedding decorators House of Nilam. During a family-style dinner by Moghul Fine Indian Cuisine, friends and family offered toasts that were by turns humorous and heartfelt. "I told Mik so many times to just tell his parents about Arthur," best man Parth Saxena said. "I mean, a doctor son marrying another doctor? What more could an Indian mother want?"

Sanjana Aneja did not miss a beat. "Grandkids!" she shouted from her seat.

Hannah and Matthew Abrams spoke together, wishing the newlyweds a lifetime of "love, trust, companionship and biscotti." The last to speak, Rohit Aneja brought the crowd to tears. "We Indians like to add one extra dollar when giving cash gifts," he said. "Plus-one is meant to bring luck to the recipient. Arthur is the greatest plus-one our family has ever received. Thank you, Abrams family, for this most blessed gift."

The party carried on late into the warm night, DJ Saji Saj spinning as the grooms were lifted in their chairs for the Hora. In the early-morning hours, Milano cookies and milk shots were served and guests settled into cushioned loveseats and chaises placed around the dance floor. Bleary from the revelry, Engineer reclined with her head on Dr. Aneja's shoulder. "What a love story," she sighed. "What a wedding." There was nothing cookie-cutter about it.

41

It was true, Leena loved Mikesh very much, just not like that. He was sensitive and patient, gentle, yet slightly wicked in the way he talked about people. She never tired of his company. They seemed to have a special connection, one that had begun many past lives ago, they agreed. So when he asked her to participate in an elaborate ruse with him, she had no qualms about it. The pieces fit perfectly together. He wasn't ready to talk to his family about who he was; she was unattached. Both needed time to grow into who they were without the unending onslaught of questions from aunties and uncles, friends and family about why they were still single, had they considered the future, don't they want a family, do they want to meet my accomplished and attractive offspring.

Neither party had planned for the charade to last as long as it did, but it was working so well, they were reluctant to disturb the balance. A few years into it, Leena spoke with Mikesh about the possibility of her quietly getting back out there and starting to date. They agreed she needed to move forward with her life, but also that she could do so without giving up her role as his cover. She would keep her romantic activities confined to New York City or other far-flung cities to which she might travel. No place really would be off-limits except for Edison.

After it was decided she would enter the dating pool, she had to figure

out how. Some of her friends tried to meet their soulmates at the enormous annual conventions of their respective Indian American ethnic
subgroups—Jain, Marathi, Telegu, Gujarati, et alia. A few attended the
conferences of the American Association of Physicians of Indian Origin,
with no medical degree but with the express purpose of landing a doctor. Others went to the Asian American Hotel Owners Association, with
no Super 8 franchise but with the express purpose of landing a hotelier.
The convention path was too public and risky for Leena, which was not
a disappointment to her in any way. For a while, she did the usual thing,
waiting for strangers to approach her at the airport, but this did not yield
the hero she was searching for. She then took a more proactive approach,
accosting handsome men at Penn Station, deliberately bumping into them
at Hudson News or in building elevators. A couple of suitable boys were
thus unearthed but soon proved to be cads, regular char sau beeses. There
were stretches during which she wrote off men altogether and focused on
her work, and other times when she wanted to date but had no time. And
when the era of online dating dawned, she dabbled in it, beginning with
shaadi.com, née sagaai.com, which yielded mainly duds. As her business
grew, she sometimes met interesting men that way, but they were easily
scared away by her success; one bald mogul even used the end of open
bar as an excuse to flee her. By the time she turned thirty, the age when
Bollywood actresses were historically herded into the category of "mature,"
she had accepted that finding a partner may not be in her stars.

So when she was thrown together with Prem at her father's bedside,
she was single, albeit theoretically engaged, and she wondered if the
same was true of him. At first, she was startled by his presence and
found it odd that he should be there, but after the initial uneasiness,
she saw him for what he was: a sincere, helpful friend to her father, unassuming and still attractive, with sideburns stuck in the past. She had
thought very little of him over the years, though she was generally aware

of his success and his reputation as a peculiar person hovering on the fringes of proper society. He was no longer that same boy with whom she'd had a dalliance in her youth.

Mikesh and Arthur's wedding was as much a milestone for Leena as it was for the grooms. The frequent unsolicited comments from acquaintances transitioned from "Still no wedding, Leena?" to "Poor Leena, he left you for a man?" She had broken the news to her father before the *Times* piece ran, hoping to soften the blow and also to avert a second heart attack. He had been discharged from JFK and was resting at home when she approached him. She braced herself for anger, confusion, and disbelief, but he turned out to be far less disturbed by the turn of events than she'd expected—almost too undisturbed. Maybe he was tired of waiting for progress with Mikesh, or maybe he was just tired. In any case, with the help of a small army of aunties, he spread the word that his daughter had never been engaged and look what a selfless thing she did for her persecuted friend! To the Engineers' great surprise and, they felt, to the community's credit, people were more shocked by the Leena of things than the gay of them.

And no person was more shocked or happy to hear the news of Mikesh's wedding than Prem. For him, it was even better than if the man had died. Leena had never been his at all. There was nothing like that between them. All this time.

The day he learned that Leena was unattached should have been a pivotal frame in the storyboard of his Hindi movie life, Prem thought, a radiant and resplendent panel standing apart from the rest, if only his to-do list didn't look like this:

1. Make sure beloved is not stabbed in the eye.
2. Track down CNN's Dr. Sanjay Gupta.
3. Plan extraordinary Bollywood Gold Awards program.
4. Declare undying love.

The first three were the more pressing matters. The fourth, the most important, would just have to wait. He was running errands for the show up and down Oak Tree, a job typically handled by his assistant but which Prem took upon himself as Pankaj was occupied with hiring covert-ops bodyguards. The smoky air of recent weeks had returned, accompanied now by a dull haze. Prem felt the burn of it in his throat, which reminded him again of another place. Maybe the stars, scheduled to arrive in just over a month, would find it comforting.

The usual arrangements, the ones that had been the same for *Lights! Camera! Indian!* and *Masala in the Meadowlands*, were already in place: an event space, AV, accommodations for the stars, biryani for Salman, etc., but some of the elements unique to awards shows still remained to be dealt with. A sit-down dinner was to be catered by Beena, for which the banquet hall would provide most of the infrastructure, but it was up to Prem to make it glamorous, with stage and hall décor and something called a tablescape. He would hire a company for this and a separate one for stage management and artistic direction. Apparently, a long carpet was required, and rather than renting a red one, he would commission an orange one with gold polka dots from Hayden's Impossibly Long Carpets, the best impossibly long carpet maker in the state. There was also the matter of getting the Gold Spot statuettes made and the little cards and envelopes printed with winners' names. Wine and spirits, sodas, waters, but mostly wine needed to be procured. And most bafflingly, fancy bags of free things had to be assembled for attendees, some of whom were among the wealthiest people in the world.

After he picked up one hundred fitness trackers from Crazy Aadi's Electronics, Prem headed to his office. He slept there most nights over the coming weeks, partially because the work required it and partially to avoid the constant King's Court chatter about Leena and her apocryphal engagement. Various vendors came in and out of his office daily with updates on seating charts, programs, videography, photography, movie clips, winners' acceptance music, presenters, interstitial entertainment, and Hollywood's Richard Gere. Once numbers one and three on Prem's list seemed to be coming along nicely—Pankaj having secured the best elite ex-military protection services money could buy—it was time to focus on the second item.

Dr. Sanjay Gupta of CNN proved a more elusive mark than Prem had anticipated. He tried the CNN headquarters general number and the medical desk number, both of which were dead ends. Next, he tried the CNN tip hotline but was rebuffed with extreme prejudice. After exhausting all expected CNN possibilities, he moved on to Indian ones, first contacting every Gupta he'd ever come across to uncover a relative, then digging around for Dr. Gupta's parents' numbers, both to no avail. He thought of tracking down old medical school batchmates to get to him that way and managed to get through to one, but when he had her on the line, he panicked and hung up. As a last resort, he considered inflicting some kind of medical mystery upon himself, even spending time poring through medical tomes at the library in the hopes of attracting the doctor's journalistic attention. But in the end, he couldn't figure out how.

Biking from the library to his office one evening, he stopped by India America Grocers under the pretense of inquiring about Hemant's recuperation, guessing correctly that Leena might be there in his stead. She was going through the aisles and straightening up sections that had been disturbed through the course of the day. Prem caught her smiling widely, her face lighting up when she saw him, then dimming as she regained her composure. For that moment, the whole of the week's troubles went away. They greeted each other and spoke about Hemant's health, then steered clear of topics to do with their actual lives, sticking with talk of groceries.

"When did they come out with Maaza lychee?" Prem asked, turning juice bottles so their labels faced uniformly outward.

Leena was crouching by the Punjabi biscuits, which were in a state of disarray. "There is guava now too," she answered.

"Do people buy guava over mango and lychee?"

Leena thought for a second. "No, actually, they don't."

Both smiled and kept tidying. The bell above the door, the same one that had tinkled when he first entered with his pompom hat all those years ago, announced the arrival of a customer whom Leena went to tend to. Being there again with her at the store where his life had really begun, Prem understood that this was where he wanted it to end as well.

"I see you have a new employee," the customer, a prying older auntie-type, said, eyeing Prem.

"Him? Oh ya, his Superstar business was not paying enough so he took a second job," Leena teased, holding back a smile while ringing up a price adjustment on toor dal. Prem's heart did a tiny flip. It was the first time she'd mentioned she knew anything about what he had been up to all these years.

The nosy auntie tsked disapprovingly at Leena. "See you, Prem," she said, collecting her bag of discount lentils. "Looking forward to the awards function."

Leena swept the floor and locked up soon after that, and Prem walked her to Building 5. She had moved out of the apartment she had shared for so many years with Mikesh, living now with her father to take care of him for the time being. She had offered to move him to a bigger, fancier place, she told Prem, but he had refused. "What would I do there?" he'd said.

Before Prem turned to go, he had an idea. "I forgot, I need cardamom."

"Should we go back? It's no trouble," she said.

"No, no, be with your father," Prem said. "I'll come again tomorrow."

That night, he slept on his mattress at King's Court, smelling faintly of the store's tangy garam masala aroma. To him, it was the smell of her.

* * *

The next few weeks continued like that for Prem, picking up Bollywood Gold–branded tumblers and meeting with media sponsors in the mornings, hunting Dr. Gupta in the afternoons, and stocking high shelves and organizing heavy sacks of rice for Leena in the evenings. Every night he claimed to have forgotten a different item—kidney beans, black pepper cashews, dahi vada raita masala—making sure to name only shelf-stable items so as to avoid cultivating a rotten stench in his office. They spoke easily about Iraq and the upcoming *Kal Ho Naa Ho*, the refreshingly tart and cloudy Limca, India's original lemon-lime soft drink, and, most recurrently and disgustedly, India's unforgivable recent collapse at the ICC Cricket World Cup finals. Prem told her how Giants Stadium was booked for half the summer by Bruce Springsteen, and Leena told him the Pine Barrens were on fire again.

"Again?" said Prem. "When were they before? And what are the Pine Barrens?" It turned out the veil of smoke that had shrouded New Jersey of late was coming from a wildfire to the south, in the state's wooded heartland among the highways.

"I know I shouldn't say this," Leena said, almost at a whisper, "but I like the smell of it."

Prem dropped a bag of Lay's Magic Masala potato chips and appeared horrorstruck. "How can you even think such a thing? Aren't people's houses burning down? And trees being destroyed?" Visibly appalled by her own insensitivity, Leena began to backpedal from her comment, but stopped when she noticed Prem smiling. "I like the smell too," he said.

She feigned indignance, then laughed, and he loved that it was the same laugh from before. That evening, he decided to forget a packet of mustard seeds, and the next evening, she had it ready for him at the counter. When an older couple in search of breath-freshening digestive mukhwas of the sweet fennel variety came in, Prem helped them find it, after which they tried to give him a dollar for his help.

"No, no, take it," the husband said when Prem refused the money.

Thinking she had figured out the problem, the wife interceded. "His salary must be extremely high, you know, because his boss is a millionaire." She turned to Leena at the counter. "You are a millionaire, no?"

"You are a millionaire?" the husband said, his eyebrows raised. "Then, why your dad is still selling eggplant and radish?"

Prem could see Leena was becoming irritated. "He likes selling eggplant and radish," she said.

"Fine, that's fine," the wife said. "But why are *you* here? Can't you hire ten people?"

"Miss, how many bottles of mukhwas would you like?" Prem said.

"Miss? No one calls me miss anymore, ever," the wife said, visibly delighted and returning her attention to Prem.

"That cannot be true," Prem said with exaggeratedly fake disbelief. "You look like his daughter! Are you his daughter?"

Blushing now, the woman smiled and continued eyeing Prem as her husband paid the bill. "If you still want a doctor," she said to Leena as they were leaving, "you can meet my Raju. You remember my Raju?"

Taking inventory of the refrigerated foods after the couple was gone, Leena asked Prem, "How did you do that?"

"Do what?" Prem looked down from his place removing expired Bedekar pickle bottles from a shelf.

"Get that lady off of my head."

Prem grinned. "The auntie crowd is my crowd."

They continued with their respective tasks in silence until Leena asked, "Why does everyone here always want to talk about money? Isn't it impolite?"

Prem understood the situation perfectly. "They are not talking about money, they are talking about their fear."

"Hm." Leena went back to counting boxes of frozen cocktail samosas.

Though his daytime hours were spent working under enormous stress, the time Prem got to spend with her made these days some of the happiest he'd had since 1988. One day, as they restocked the dried fruit and nuts section, she read his palm, holding his hand and peering into it for a long time before declaring she knew nothing about palm reading. They had an uproarious laugh about it, never referring to that earlier time she'd "read" his and other palms, though he was thinking of it the whole time and hoped she was too. As the Bollywood Gold Awards neared, he presented her with two premium tickets with the understanding that she would bring her father if he was able. She accepted, and they went about their dusting and tidying of the store until he felt a yawn coming on and dropped his head down to conceal it. When he looked up, she was yawning and looked away, and he knew she had been looking at him. It was the closest he'd ever come, he realized, to experiencing the sublime. That night, he brimmed with hope as he pedaled in the moonlight back to his office, which was bursting with nonperishable Indian grocery items with which he had no plans to cook.

* * *

When Prem opened his eyes in the morning, Wristwatch stood over him, unsmiling, his arms folded. "Tiger will meet you at 12:30 at the newly opened Cheesecake Factory at the Menlo Park Mall," he said and left. After he splashed his face with water and fully woke himself, Prem accepted that Wristwatch's appearance was not a dream and began to panic. He had the idea to call Pankaj to reassign half the ex-Navy SEALs guarding Leena to guard him instead, but then pictured Leena alone with the canned goods and roti and thought better of it. There was nothing he could do but go to the Cheesecake Factory.

"This shopping mall," said Tiger, already settled into an unnecessary booth with two henchmen standing guard, "is named after Thomas Edison's lab." She bit into a fried zucchini stick and motioned for Prem to sit.

"His pet name for the lab was Invention Factory," she went on. "I learned this in the tour. Excellent tour. He made four hundred inventions there. Four hundred."

Prem wasn't sure if he was meant to respond to this, and if so, how. So he did perhaps the boldest thing he'd ever done in his life: he took a zucchini stick from Tiger's plate.

Tiger looked at Prem as though he had murdered her mother. Her nostrils flared as she watched him eat and when he was done, she kept staring at him.

Prem maintained his cool outwardly and broke the terrifying silence. "You are probably wondering why I took your zucchini stick," he offered. Tiger nodded very slightly and entirely unblinkingly. The henchmen had turned to face into the booth and were glaring at Prem as well.

Prem swallowed hard. "You see, Tiger, madam, miss, is it miss?"

Tiger said nothing.

"It will be important for you," Prem said slowly and carefully, "to immediately offer your date an appetizer on Saturday."

Tiger looked at Prem as though he had resurrected her mother. "Date? You mean, really, here, Saturday?"

"Well, not here in the Cheesecake Factory," Prem said. "At the Gold Awards." He was so relieved to have pleased her that he almost believed that Sanjay Gupta would really be there.

"Oh yes, brilliant, now I will not forget to offer an appetizer to the doctor, stat." For the remainder of the meeting, Tiger ordered plate upon plate of exotic dishes for them to share, jabbering on about what to wear and what she would say and what kind of appetizers would be served. "Do one thing," she said, dipping something called a pretzel bite into a strange bowl of cheese, "give my ticket to Wristwatch next time he comes and tell him where I have to go and all."

"Can he come a normal way this time?" Prem asked.

"No, he cannot," Tiger replied, on to a quesadilla now. "What was I saying? Oh yes, magical place, this Edison. You know it was called Raritan and they changed it to Edison? Good they did that. Light bulb was invented here. The motto for Edison is 'Let There Be Light.' Is it not perfect?"

"Yes, it is perfect."

"Exactly, Junior Titan, exactly. You are a wise man, just like he was. Not just an inventor, but also a reinventor. I respect that. What did you think of the zucchini stick? I did not care for it."

Prem knew that nothing had actually been resolved there; he had, in fact, made things worse. Yet he had bought himself two days to figure out a plan. "So no need for the eye-stabbing game now, correct?"

Tiger paused mid-quesadilla and looked squarely at Prem. "We shall see on Saturday."

42

Prem went directly from the Cheesecake Factory to India America Grocers to ask Leena not to come to the show. On his way, he tried to calm himself with an illogical line of reasoning that had no relevance to the actual situation but that made sense to his frantic mind. Leena couldn't possibly die this week because she was the heroine and he was the hero. But what if he wasn't? What if Lucky was the hero? Or Beena, or Tiger? Where would that leave Leena? Then he would start again. Leena couldn't possibly die this week because she was the heroine.

When he reached the store and parked his bike, he took several slow, deep breaths with the hope of composing himself, but realized he couldn't and went in as he was. Leena was ringing up a talkative customer who wanted to discuss the smoky summer they'd been having and the imprudence of the July Fourth fireworks that had just passed. Prem lined up uncomfortably close to her and began tapping his foot, which was appreciated by no one. The Maggi Noodles packet he'd pretended to have forgotten the night before was sitting at the end of the counter.

"Goodness, she wouldn't stop talking," Leena laughed when her customer left. She picked up the Maggi packet and presented it to Prem with a flourish that made him want to cry. "No charge today, sir."

"You can't come to the show," Prem blurted out.

"What? Did you say I can't come to the show?"

"Yes, you see, it's just a terrible show. Poor lighting, unpleasant dance numbers, no chairs, cold food—"

"No chairs? And why will the food be cold?" Leena was puzzled.

This approach was not yielding the result he needed fast enough. "Actually, do you have any business trip you need to do? You should go, go to Italy or Norway, I can take care of your store and father."

"What is wrong with you? Why are you sending me to Europe?"

"You can go today even, let me check the tickets, why wait?"

Leena's confused expression turned quickly to disbelief, then disappointment, descending rapidly toward anger. She dropped a chickpeaflour bomb of condemnation upon him with fury the likes of which he hadn't seen since Sridevi's "Moments of Rage" instrumental dance in 1991's *Lamhe*. There were false accusations and intermittent foul words, tempered with huffing and the occasional stomp. "What kind of person are you?" she yelled in a way that signaled to Prem she was wrapping things up. "Falguni and Snigdha said you have become odd, and you know what I said? I said, No, he is different in a nice way. We all were wrong. What you are is unreliable."

She could have said any word in that moment and the result would have been the same. Heartbreak. "Can I be more than one thing?" he said.

"No."

Before he left, he said he forgot a Tilda Ready-to-Heat basmati-rice bag and, even though he was standing there in the store, he would come back for it much later or get it when he was taking care of the store for five or six weeks while she was in Europe.

"Here," Leena said, throwing the Maggi Noodles at him and missing, unfortunately hitting Mrs. Ambani in the produce section instead.

"Ow!"

"Take your Maggi and go."

Outside, he wandered into the parking lot without looking and stumbled on a pothole. A truck from Quicker Liquor stopped just in time to avoid hitting him, its bumper an inch from his face. Surely it would have killed him, he thought. But, then again, how could it if he had already just died?

Instead of going to his apartment or office, Prem went to Beena Joshi's and collapsed onto her sofa, as he had so many times during his American life. She was putting the finishing touches on the appetizer stations for the awards dinner, most of which had been prepared at a commercial kitchen with the help of a small but formidable staff she'd assembled. The loaded nacho-chaat bar still needed several toppings for which she was seeding pomegranates. "What happened now?" she asked.

"I have to make Dr. Sanjay Gupta from CNN come to the Bollywood Gold Awards, or else Leena will be stabbed in the eye," he moaned, lying as if on a psychiatrist's couch.

"Of course. That's it?" He sat up to look at her face, then slumped back down. "Okay, tell me, but chop these jalapeños at the same time."

Prem chopped and told, chopped and told, until the whole preposterous story was out and the jalapeños were chopped.

"So Tiger is a woman?"

"Ya, I was surprised too."

"Impressive."

"I know."

"Because, you know, they say the mafia is a man's world."

"Hundred percent."

"I would be successful in that line of work."

"Hundred percent."

"Okay, so you made Leena like you maybe, then made her hate you again. Is it 1988?" Prem was not amused. Beena continued, "She really causes lot of headaches for you, don't you think?"

"No, Tiger is the one causing the problem, not Leena."

"Yes, but if Leena was not there and Tiger was only threatening your eye and not hers, that would be better, no?"

"Yes, no, I mean, look, I would not even be having this problem if Leena did not exist. This, really, this is not the point," Prem said, growing frustrated with her lack of understanding of a simple cause-and-effect equation. He leaned against the counter and tried again. "How can I get Sanjay Gupta?"

"You cannot."

"I know." Prem buried his face in the crook of his arm. Beena stored the toppings in the drawing-room fridge and pulled out two glasses and a bottle of whiskey from the cabinet under the sink. "Let's think about it in the morning," she said.

* * *

It was the day before the show, and Prem woke up soaked in his own sweat and smelling of booze. At some point the previous evening, Beena must have put down a sheet on the couch and given him a blanket and pillow. He remembered telling her how grateful he was for their closeness, which began on his very first day in Edison—their Day One friendship, he decided to call it—and she told him she was menopausal.

She was already showered and fresh, organizing her fridges and humming a happy tune, while he felt akin to garbage. Pankaj had already left five messages at one of his phone numbers and nine at the other, but he was in no way ready to deal with them. When Beena saw he was awake, she turned the volume up on the TV, which was tuned to the news. "Beautiful morning, time to get up and face it."

Prem moaned and pulled the covers over his head.

On the news, there was a segment about female Chechen suicide bombers followed by another on a book about the eruption of Krakatoa. It cut to a commercial, but not before plugging an upcoming special report by medical correspondent Dr. Sanjay Gupta on the effects of sustained wildfire smoke inhalation on heart patients. He would be, and this next part seemed to Prem's ears much louder and slowed down, reporting from the field at a nursing home in Manalapan, New Jersey, later that day. Prem and Beena registered this information at the same time, simultaneously shushing each other and turning wide-eyed toward the TV. Neither knew where Manalapan was, but both knew that was where they'd be going as soon as Prem cleaned himself up. One could hardly approach CNN's Dr. Sanjay Gupta smelling the way he was.

Deepak, Mohan, and Yogesh were the only ones in the apartment when he got there. "Stinking like a pub, coming home in the morning and all," Yogesh said, brushing his teeth while walking around the kitchen. "Who was the lucky auntie?"

"Your mother," Prem answered, feeling rather proud of how far his "your-mother" jokes had come.

Deepak, eating spaghetti out of a leftovers container, espoused a different theory. "The stars must have arrived and you were partying all night with them. How come you never invite us for partying all night with the stars?"

"Was Aishwarya there?" inquired Yogesh. "Do not tell me Aishwarya was there and you didn't call us. Just don't."

"Why you're brushing out here, Yogesh? Go back in the bathroom, man."

The unfounded accusation (the second one, not the first) did give Prem an idea. "A few of the stars would like to go to Olive Garden after the rehearsal is finished tonight. I will be busy, but can you take them?"

"Yes!" Deepak roared.

"Which ones?" Mohan added.

"Will you be busy with romancing your auntie?" Yogesh said.

Prem gave them the details and asked Pankaj to arrange it all. They were grateful and excited, and Prem was glad he was finally able to make someone happy.

Once they were on the road to all the nursing homes in Manalapan—Beena having collected the names and necessary directions—it then occurred to Prem: Even if they were able to find Sanjay Gupta, what would they say to him?

"Maybe I can tell him the true story," Prem shrugged. "He seems like a nice guy."

"I am driving," Beena said, "but I still can hit you with my rolling pin."

"Fine. Do you have any better idea?"

Beena gave her left-turn signal and changed lanes. "Leave it to me."

Prem rummaged through the cassettes in Beena's center console, looking for an appropriate soundtrack for their uncertain adventure. Like so many in King's Court, Beena had maintained a cassette deck in her car, even when the car dealer vehemently recommended otherwise, so as to be able to play the tapes she'd lugged over from India and loved for decades. Prem picked *T-Series Mega Hit Classics* and clicked it into the slot. A classic megahit from the middle of the B-side ended as he closed his eyes. When he opened them forty-five minutes later, Beena was pulling into the lot of a place called Shady Pines. She parked and turned to inspect him. "There is drool coming out from one side of your mouth."

Prem wiped the spit with his sleeve.

"Maybe you just wait in the car," she said.

She went in and came back out just two minutes later. "Ya, he is not here," she said. Next, they tried Pine Valley Assisted Living, followed by Peaceful Pines Senior Home, then Whispering Pines Senior Residences.

·"This is a very pine-oriented place," Prem noted.

When at last they spotted a CNN news van in front of Overwhelming Pines Senior Sanctuary, he swore to Beena that in that moment he heard the soulful trumpet of a conch shell being blown, as at the start of every episode of *Mahabharata* and before many other Hindu beginnings that needed auspicious endings—the start of a show, the start of a war, the start of a grocery store, the start of a well-planned solution to a problem—symbolizing a call to duty, the opening of festivities, a cleansing away of negative energy to make room for the divine, a long primal om that only he could hear.

"Uh, no," Beena said.

"I'm telling you, I hear it in my mind."

"I also hear it." Beena pointed out the window behind Prem. "There is a man in the yard there blowing a conch."

"Oh," Prem said. Of course there would be a man in his undershirt blowing a conch in a nursing home yard, he thought. This was New Jersey, after all. Beena decided she would start by approaching the van.

"Can I come?" Prem asked.

"Do you want CNN's Dr. Sanjay Gupta to come to the Gold Awards tomorrow to meet his number-one most murderous fan, or no?"

"I do," Prem said, crossing his arms and pouting.

"Okay, then. Give me the tickets and leave it to me."

Prem watched her knock on the driver's side window of the van, then walk around to the back and disappear into it. He wondered how much room was inside, with the cameras and lighting equipment and assistants and, he hoped, Dr. Gupta. She had been in the van for over ten minutes when Prem began to worry. It shook noticeably, and he started to get out of the car, but just then Beena emerged, giggling and tossing her hair. She extended her hands and they were embraced by another pair of brown hands reaching out from within the van.

"Done," she said when she returned to the car. "Should we go to King's Court or directly to the hall?"

* * *

Shah Rukh was late for rehearsal because he had been detained by security at the airport. By now, he didn't require assistance in navigating the situation; it had become routine. Fortunately, his delayed arrival at rehearsal was not a problem since there wasn't much for him to rehearse. He and Rani Mukerji would be presenting the award for Best Actor in a Negative Role (female), after which he could just sit in the audience and enjoy. They were dressing the tables as practices went on, everything in shimmering orange and gold—linens, glasses, salad plates upon dinner plates upon charger plates, nesting Russianly one on top of the next. Name cards were carefully placed among scattered marigolds; Shah Rukh found his at Table 3. Seated to his left was director Mira Nair, and to his right was Beena Joshi, who, as far as he could tell, was someone operating at the highest levels of Superstar Entertainment. Also at Table 3 were married stars Ajay Devgan and Kajol, a person called Minerva the Psychic Reader, CNN's Dr. Sanjay Gupta, and a mystery guest signified by a blank card. Shah Rukh wondered what the thinking was behind this particular arrangement and whether the precise seat assignments were in service to some greater plan. Most likely, they had been indiscriminately positioned, he decided, and switched his card with the unnamed guest's so he would instead be flanked by Minerva and Dr. Gupta. It was a victimless sort of noncrime, he thought. He probably should have remained by Mira Nair to discuss future projects but just wasn't in the mood. He was intrigued by this Minerva, though, who might not know who he was and could therefore give an unbiased reading, untainted by his overwhelming celebrity. Plus, always opting to sit with a psychic when presented with the opportunity seemed a good rule to live by. And then there was Dr. Sanjay Gupta, whom Shah Rukh had never before met and who seemed like someone interesting with whom to converse. And if there was time, perhaps he could prevail upon the good doctor to examine his swollen ankle.

If only Dr. Gupta would show up. Prem, who was no stranger to everyday anguish, was altogether wrecked by the double anguish of thinking about his last interaction with Leena and waiting for Sanjay Gupta. "I told you he will be here, so he will be here," Beena proclaimed. It was Saturday afternoon, just a few hours before the show was to begin, and she was directing her crew as they carried in the chafing dishes. Prem sat at the edge of the stage, looking as though he'd just built it. He had slept in his office again and shown up to the event space unshaven in Exxon coveralls.

"You are very confident. Why are you very confident? What did you do in the back part of the CNN van?" he demanded to know.

Beena raised a pretend rolling pin to pretend hit him. "I simply made an offer. He could not refuse it."

"So, if really he is coming, maybe I should go back to Leena and—"

"No, stop, just no," Beena interrupted. "There is no time. Show is starting soon, Leena problem will take long time to fix and you have to brush your teeth." With that, she left to supervise the setup of the live dosa station while Prem lay down on the stage. Several of his employees looked at him then at each other, then went back to what they were doing. The hall was glittering and golden, bathed in an orange glow. He unfocused his eyes and the scene became watery and fluid, flowing and swirling in on itself, harkening back to the original puddle of orange soda that had started it all. He got up and walked around. It was much as he'd envisioned, only better, yet all he wanted to do was vomit, which was what he did, into a chafing dish.

Beena didn't witness the retching but was there for the stench of the aftermath. She rubbed Prem's back and forced a glass of water upon him. "I am sending you home in the car and calling those duffers in your apartment to help you."

Prem shook his head and hand in protest, but Beena was already on her phone.

"Hello, duffer?" Beena said to Deepak. "Wake up, it is evening almost."

"Beenaji, Beenaji, what a night we had at Olive Garden. Man, I tell you, those stars, they are wild. They drank all the wine. Not from our table only, from the whole Olive Garden! Some got out of hand, but Sridevi helped them, such an angel that Sridevi. All of them were loving the unlimited breadsticks, but then the manager—"

Beena had heard enough. "I am sending Prem home. Make him get ready, shave, shower, brush, scrape, comb, and get dressed, then put him back in the car."

"Is he drunk again?" Mohan yelled from the background.

"Can you make me sit by Aishwarya?" Yogesh yelled from the background.

* * *

By five o'clock, the unending orange-and-gold carpet had been unfurled and was crowded with reporters eager to report. Fans were lined up ten feet deep, some there since the previous night, others peddling chai and samosa—entrepreneurs recognizing an opportunity when they saw one. People stood on benches, on cars, and on each other; fans pushed other fans who bumped up against other fans who got

angry. When a rumor spread that the first star had arrived, cameras began flashing and there was shouting and shoving mixed with flowers.
Though they were all staying at the same hotel, Prem had arranged for
the stars to be picked up and delivered to the Bollywood Gold Awards
in a staggered fashion. The first to arrive was Madhuri Dixit, who
looked fresh and vibrant and generally awake, being the only one not
suffering from jet lag, having just flown in from Colorado with her
Coloradan husband.

"Madhuriji, great to see you, you're looking gorgeous!" a reporter
from *Little India* declared, to which Madhuri replied, "Ah, too sweet,
thank you," to which the reporter said, "You are nominated for *Devdas*,
which was superb, the most gorgeous and outstanding film I have
seen, so tell me, how was your experience in making the film?" to
which Madhuri said, "The experience I had in making *Devdas* was one
of the best in my career. For us, for the entire team, it will always be
extremely special, and full marks go to Sanjay and the entire unit, it
was an absolute pleasure," at which point Aishwarya emerged from a
large vehicle, and the roar of the crowd grew so loud it was difficult
for the interviewer from the *Good Weekend, Jersey Indians!* show to hear
Aishwarya's response when he asked, "Between you and me, who do
you think will win for Best Actor? Come on, I won't tell anyone, haha,"
which Aishwarya didn't really even hear and so replied, "I have been
blessed to get strong roles and work with good directors, blessed in
the sense because all of us want to make outstanding films, and what's
wonderful is—" which Salman, having just alighted upon the orange
carpet, overheard and passionately disagreed with, arguing, "Oof, the
director and role are secondary to the performances that Aish has given,
really, just mind-blowing," which startled Aishwarya, pleasantly, and
led to a warm embrace, which elicited cheers from the fans, who
seemed unable to handle this turn of events, but whose attention was

soon diverted by Ajay Devgan and Kajol, who walked the orange carpet holding hands, adorable couple that they were, giving interviews that way, about which a reporter from *India West* commented, "You are fully in love, so cute, please, can you reveal, will we be seeing you on the big screen together soon, I hope?" to which the husband responded, "I hope too! No, but seriously, ya, we are very excited to be here with so many amazing actors and filmmakers, not just with actors and film-makers, but more for the fans, America's fans are unreal—" which happened to be the exact moment a fan broke his leg jumping off his van onto what he'd hoped would be the strong and welcoming arms of the crowd but instead turned out to be the pavement, upon which another fan closer to the orange carpet fainted, causing three different people to dial 911, which ended up working out because a third person needed medical attention after she had elbowed someone who in turn attacked her eye with the pointy part of a samosa, prompting Prem to make a mental note for next year: crowd control, bleachers, first-aid tent.

By the time Sridevi and Shilpa Shetty began working their way through the press gauntlet, several police cars had arrived at the scene, circling the parking lot in anticipation of a full-blown riot. The screaming mounted and more than one person was inexplicably cry-ing. Shilpa Shetty talked with a *Stardust* reporter about the making of her latest film ("It was loads of fun. So much of attention to details as is visible in each frame, that's the main thing"). Sridevi was telling a bewildered *Star-Ledger* reporter that goodness, no, it wasn't her first time in Edison ("Many times. Every Indian in this country, and some even abroad, knows Edison. As well-known as Disneyland."), while Prem stood at the end of the carpet by the entrance to the hall, taking in the wild and glamorous scene.

Counter to his explicit instructions, three cars pulled up at the same time and three sets of megastars entered the fray. The crowd erupted in pandemonium all over again upon seeing Hrithik Roshan, Kareena Kapoor, Akshay Kumar, and Preity Zinta, and the flashing cameras became blinding. Prem spotted Wristwatch at the far end of the carpet but then lost him. Why was he there? To protect Tiger Nayak or for other, more eye-threatening reasons? He had to get to him, to assure him that Dr. Gupta was on his way and there was no need to go after Leena, who was not even coming that night. He pushed his way through the mayhem but kept getting stopped by actors, reporters, Representative Frank Pallone, Jr., of the Sixth District, there to mingle with his constituency, the Indian American vote having become crucial. He extracted himself from one conversation after another, inching forward through a blur of tuxedos and sequins. Wristwatch reappeared on the other side of the velvet ropes, towering over the fans. It made no sense that he would be over there, but then it made perfect sense—Leena was there.

Mired in a crush of people, she was trying to press ahead at the same time Wristwatch advanced the other way towards her. Prem had the sudden feeling that something was about to happen, a rumble of a disturbance to come. He forced his way forward, and everything that followed happened in slow motion with the volume on mute. The horde of fans turned hostile, clashing with each other, some getting knocked to the ground. Prem lost sight of Leena just as Wristwatch reached out his arms. The flash of a camera reflected off Wristwatch's wristwatch, catching Prem's eye at the very moment the thug swooped someone up in his arms. Prem lifted his hand to block the glare. When Wristwatch turned, it wasn't Leena he was carrying. Instead, it was the dazzling and highly educated key to taming Tiger, the handsome correspondent and neurosurgeon, CNN's Dr. Sanjay Gupta. He had come. Prem watched in awe as Wristwatch carried his precious cargo to safety, parting the crowd as he went, kicking anyone in his path, the illustrious doctor burying his face in his savior's shoulder, not unlike the singer with her bodyguard in the film *The Bodyguard*, which Lucky had once forced Prem to watch.

After that, the volume came back on and somehow the chaos subsided. The rampaging fans lost interest once the stars had shuffled into the banquet hall. Prem remained outside looking for Leena, wandering up and down the orange-and-gold carpet and among the parked cars in the lot. He couldn't see her anywhere, and he began to wonder if she'd really been there at all. But he kept searching until Beena came to drag him in. The carpet was almost completely cleared but for a few straggling producers giving unsolicited soundbites and Gopal, who had been mistaken for an actor by the American press and was giving a weird series of interrogative interviews ("Why do they call it World Series when it is only American and Canadian teams?").

Inside, the awards program began. The emcee for the evening, an up-and-coming Indian American comedian from the up-and-coming Indian American comedy scene, warmed up the crowd with some pertinent apolitical jokes while the champagne flowed freely. Prem tried to put Leena out of his mind, at least for a short time, to enjoy the product of his labor. A dance number performed by a local dance troupe came off beautifully, mashing together songs from the best-picture nominees into a high-energy triumph of synchronicity.

One by one, glamorous people disseminated awards to glamorous people, and Prem was tickled each time the phrase he'd created, "And the Gold Spot goes to..." was spoken. The winners made their way up onstage amid rounds of applause that Prem imagined were meant as much for the whole of this thing called Bollywood as much as they were for them.

And what a thing it was. He'd given himself over to it time and again—in the Delhi movie halls, at Mehboob Studios in Bombay, and, at long last, in Edison through Superstar Entertainment, forged from

nothing but his measureless worship of the films. The shows were his
ode to the genre, and he had succeeded, he felt, in honoring the movies'
magic, their grace and rowdiness, their charm and untamed emotion,
their poetry.

As Richard Gere, who had been getting quite cozy that evening with
more than one Bollywood starlet, was commended for his friendliness
toward India, Prem kept his eye on Tiger Nayak and Dr. Sanjay Gupta.
Wristwatch had deposited the doctor at Table 3 in front of the blank
place card, upsetting the entire seating arrangement to Shah Rukh
Khan's great dismay. But Shah Rukh decided not to say anything. He
saw that Dr. Gupta was engrossed in conversation with a petite and aggressively confident young woman—not an actress, but someone important all the same—so he took a seat by Minerva the Psychic Reader.
Toward the end of the show, Minerva turned to Shah Rukh. "You know,
that woman there has done some terrible things in her life," said as
she pointed to Tiger. "Terrible things."

"What does she want with CNN's Dr. Sanjay Gupta?"

"Let's see." Minerva knitted her brow in concentration. "She knows
he is married and is not interested in him in any romantic way. She
just . . . admires him."

"Hm," Shah Rukh said.

"Even murderers have their idols," Minerva shrugged.

Prem never understood what it was about Sanjay Gupta that pleased
Tiger so. Whatever it was, it was enough to placate her for a lifetime.
After that night, she stopped threatening Prem and left him to his business. It was the last he ever saw of the diminutive underworld gangster,
who thanked him outside profusely before she left, her ponytail blowing in the wind.

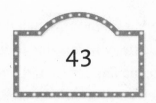

43

Prem did not typically attend the parties after his shows, but how could he refuse Sridevi and Madhuri Dixit, the most leading of all leading ladies of the post–Cold War era? They double-teamed him in the parking lot, insisting he join them at Urban Turban Bar and Grill, where a signature orange cocktail, the Mango Mojito, concocted specially for the occasion, was being doled out in tall glasses at full tilt.

"Can you believe how the fans were behaving?" Lucky mused to Mohan at the bar. "Going wild at the sight of a few stars?"

Mohan scoffed. "Yaar, you were the worst one."

In one corner, Kajol and Ajay Devgan were behaving like newlyweds, while in another, Salman Khan whispered something to Beena that elicited tears of laughter. A large mixed group congregated on sofas in the VIP lounge, with no discernible barrier to entry.

"Prem Sahib!" an actor cried.

"Kumarji!" others followed.

"Petrol!" Deepak shouted. The entire bar and grill broke out in applause upon Prem's arrival, and he couldn't help but smile. He found a cozy spot next to Shah Rukh Khan and settled in.

Shilpa Shetty resumed a story about her latest heartbreak, which involved a wealthy entrepreneur playboy and a murder-for-hire plot. "When I came to know he was planning the killing of his ex-girlfriend, he thought I would be happy. Can you imagine? So, honestly speaking, I've made some wrong choices."

Prem's assistant Pankaj followed with a devastating tale of unrequited love with his cousin, which some found disturbing and others endearing, and Kareena Kapoor shared her history of misguided romance with her onscreen romantic interests. "That is too tragic," Sridevi said, shaking her head, "too, too tragic."

Prem listened to each account with deeper and deeper depth of feeling, at the same time sinking farther and farther into the recesses of the couch. Every twist brought him back to an episode in his own sad story; every lament was a lament he'd already lamented. Beena, having dragged Salman over to join the group, recognized immediately the look on her friend's face, the everyday ache of his chronic lovesickness.

"But the longest-suffering among us," Beena said, "is our own tragic superstar, Mr. Prem Kumar." There were audible gasps and one mango-tinged projectile splatter. Richard Gere started clapping, but quickly realized his mistake and stopped.

Before sharing the saga of Leena and Prem, Beena searched her friend's eyes for permission to proceed. He responded with a blink and a nod, indicating unambiguously to Beena that he was okay with it. Though he was a secretive person, at this point, what did he have to lose? "Her name is Leena," she began.

At first, Prem listened quietly as Beena laid out the essential facts: his unfortunate immigration story, his gas-station days, the sweetness of the courtship, and the soul-crushing finality of her father's million-and-one-dollar decree. The mojitos kept coming and Prem kept drinking them, eventually loosening up. He objected to Beena's characterization of his ball of Leena's hair and later to her version of his brief entanglement with the police. When she disclosed that Tiger Nayak, the T-Company boss and underworld terror, was a woman, there was a brief digression to marvel at that revelation and then argue about who should play her in the movie. (Rani Mukerji, it was decided.) Additional uproar ensued when Beena announced that Tiger had been in attendance at the awards show that evening.

"That small person with the leather black pants?" Shah Rukh asked. "Why did you put her at my table, man?"

"Leave him alone," Hrithik Roshan shot back. "His girlfriend was almost murdered in the eye."

Prem felt compelled to clarify. "She is not my girlfriend."

"Yaar, I'm trying to help you," said Hrithik.

"Oh. Right."

After Beena reached the most recent events—Prem's romantic banning of Leena from his awards program, his heroic quest to deliver CNN's Dr. Sanjay Gupta, and of course, her own crucial role in this— there was a Q&A of sorts, during which some of Prem's life choices were questioned and a glut of irrelevant advice was proffered on how he ought to have proceeded. But overall, the crowd was sympathetic.

"Premji, do not take tension. We will create a solution for you," Akshay Kumar proclaimed.

Sridevi and Preity Zinta concurred. "We have decided. We will not go to Disney World until we solve your problem."

"I beg you, please, do not solve anything," Prem said. "You're going to Disney World?"

"Can I come?" asked Deepak.

The group debated who would play the roles of Prem and Leena in the aforementioned movie. Beena chimed in with a casting decision of her own: "I will play myself." Shilpa Shetty asked Yogesh if he had any leftover chocolate mints from the Olive Garden, and Deepak turned to Aishwarya and made an off-color joke about bottomless salad. The still-popular and ever-danceable *Koi Kahe Kehta Rahe* came on and the party moved to the dance floor.

Prem was at once unsettled and touched by the actors' outpouring of pledges of support. He decided to lie down on the couch for a minute, just until the room stopped spinning. He fell asleep watching the revelry, the bouncing and swaying, the drinks spilling and people slipping, Deepak's gold tooth intermittently gleaming in the sparkle of an overlarge disco ball.

* * *

The next day, multiple Indian actors and one American one stopped by the Engineers' store. First, Madhuri came in search of bhringraj healthy hair powder, which she used as a jumping-off point to talk about her dear friend Prem Kumar's lustrous mane. It was strange, Leena thought, that a celebrity should come in and discuss Prem's hair, but she wrote it off as one of those mysterious maneuverings of the universe and tried to enjoy the fact that Madhuri Dixit was in her store. But not long after the first internationally acclaimed actress left, another appeared, this one unclear as to why she was even there.

"Is there something I can help you find, Ms. Shetty?" Leena offered.

"Oh, you are a fan, you're *too* sweet," Shilpa Shetty said. "Then, you must be knowing Prem Kumar, whose Gold Awards I am here for?" She very quickly began to laud the producer's attention to detail, exemplary work ethic, great success, and general cuteness.

"Maybe you are looking for Ayurvedic beauty products, as Madhuriji was? They are just there," Leena said gesturing toward aisle two. Shilpa Shetty purchased a four-pound bag of red lentils, which she grabbed from the shelf absentmindedly, and soon left.

Next, Ajay Devgan and Kajol turned up, also apparently in search of nothing; a few minutes later, Sridevi, Shah Rukh Khan, and Hrithik

Roshan joined them. By early afternoon, India America Grocers had hosted a broad cross-section of Indian cinema royalty plus Richard Gere, who inquired about incense. Each visitor found a way to bring the conversation around to some aspect of Prem's evidently stellar reputation, his unwavering vision, his single-minded focus, his unrelenting loyalty. By the time Salman showed up and began praising Prem's body weight relative to his height, Leena was certain something was afoot.

A small crowd formed outside, peering into the store and trying to discern whether the rumors were true, and if so, whether they could go in. Ten or fifteen years ago, Leena might have had a similar reaction to such a swarm of celebrities, but she had lived long enough now not to be enthralled by them. But even she couldn't help being starstruck at the sight of the Nightingale of India in her store. Lata Mangeshkar had maintained a low profile the previous evening, quietly accepting the award for All-Time MVPS (Most Valuable Playback Singer) and keeping mostly to herself at the afterparty. She'd heard every word of Prem's sad love story, however, and resolved to march into India America Grocers the next day to straighten out her good friend Ashok Ratan Kumar's son's affairs.

Leena froze. At first, Lata Mangeshkar smiled sweetly, demure in her typical white sari, and approached the counter behind which Leena stood, wide-eyed. But after Leena confirmed that she indeed was Leena Engineer and she was honored to receive Lataji in her store, Lata shut down the smiling.

"You listen to me," she said. "Prem Kumar is a good boy. What did he do wrong? Nothing. So many years he has been working and working, living under the onions, for you only. He could have gone back to India and lived like a king, but no, he gave everything up. For what?"

Leena was taken aback by the Queen of Melody's wrath, and it seemed the Queen of Melody herself was also taken aback by it. She cleared her throat, causing several pretend-shoppers to move closer in case she might be getting ready to sing. Instead, she began again. "Leena, beti, I am sorry." She went on to explain that it hurt her to see two young people suffering in this way when they could be together and happy. It was especially painful, she said, because one of those people was her friend's son, who could have lived comfortably in India but subjected himself to an austere lifestyle just to be near her.

"Lataji, thank you," Leena said, "but what is this comfortable kingdom you keep mentioning? Prem is from a simple background. You must be thinking of some other family." Seeing the alarm written on Lata Mangeshkar's face, Leena understood then that it was she, not Lata, who was mistaken. The singer offered several more apologies plus a namaste, purchased all of the raisins, and hurried out of the store, leaving Leena with a tangle of questions and a few stunned customers.

The rest of the day was quiet in the store, with no further celebrities popping in. As evening approached, the sky cast a shadow over the store, the parking lot, and King's Court. Customers remarked that some rain would be a good thing for the burning trees and smoke problem, but when the rain came, customers wished it would stop. Leena turned off the lights and locked up. When she turned to walk home, Prem stood there, at a distance, wet and earnest.

"I was thinking," he called.

Leena stopped short, startled by his sudden and sopping appearance. Rain gurgled out of downspouts and dripped from awnings. A gang of pigeons descended upon a soggy samosa in the parking lot. "This is a strange place to do it," she answered.

Prem took a deep breath and blurted out his thoughts on the exhale. "You told me Falguni and Snigdha said I was odd."

"This is what you came to discuss?"

"Not exactly, but, I was wondering, why were you talking to your friends about me?"

"Huh? I can't, I just, I don't know." Leena said, her palms rising to her face in exasperation, her eyes widening in disbelief. "You're upset that I was talking about you? I really can't, I . . ." She closed her eyes briefly, then let fly a storm of indignation. "Did you forget I defended you, I said you were nice and different? Is that why you took back my tickets? No, wait, that was before. Why did you take back my tickets? Really, what type of person—"

Tony, of Tun-Tun and Tony, exited Quicker Liquor just then and offered an answer ("Who? Pumpwalla? Top of the line, five-star.") and kept walking. "Thanks, man," Prem offered, then returned to Leena and quickly spoke before she could. "If you were talking about me," he said, "that means there was something to talk about. Was there?"

Leena hesitated because it was true. She had been discussing Prem with her friends because she liked him all over again. Those days at the hospital and at the store, he was sweet and funny and more handsome even than before. And he was there for her. She relented.

"Fine, yes. Maybe."

Her admission precipitated a stunned silence. Before Prem could respond, she qualified her statement. "But then you took my tickets away, and today, I hear you are from some big, rich family in India. Did you send actors to pressure me? And why did you come to the hospital? For my father, or just to impress me?"

Nalini Sen emerged from Quicker Liquor pushing an overfull cart. "To impress you, obviously, come on," she weighed in and moved on. "For Hemantji, of course, why wouldn't he?" ghazal-singing icon Jagjit Singh countered on his way into Big Bhupinder's Divine Arts & Handicrafts, formerly a hardware store.

Prem turned for a moment to greet internationally legendary

vocalist Jagjit Singh. When he turned back to Leena, she was gone. He could see her in the distance, hurrying home to King's Court in the rain.

"Why is she yelling at you in the rain again?" Beena wanted to know.

Cash the superintendent was changing a kitchen light bulb. "Someone yelling at Prem?" he asked.

"Leena Engineer," Beena replied.

"Hemant's little girl?"

"No one was yelling," Prem clarified. "She just had a lot of questions." He was on the couch, dejected and lamenting in the same place he'd lamented for so many years. There was too much to sort out—the varied accusations, the confession of some vague level of romantic interest. What he knew for certain was that her ancient bitterness was gone, replaced by fresh, new bitterness.

"I'm going there right now for straightening out this mess," Beena said. "Don't try to stop me."

"No one is stopping you," Prem pointed out.

Lenna had also retreated to the place where she'd done so much thinking over the years. The swing in her father's apartment had developed a creak, but it comforted her all the same. The other mainstays of 5F also offered solace in their varied states of being. Hriyan had gone from remarkable feat of indoor foliage to unmanageable botanical oddity, while permanent paying guest Viren Bhai, on the balcony in Ardha Baddha Padma Vrikshasana (half-bound lotus tree pose), had stayed exactly as is. Before she could begin sorting through her manifold feelings, there was an angry knock at the door.

"Shhh," Leena said when she answered. "Papa is resting."

"Good, you are both here." Beena pushed her way in and made herself at home on the swing. "Let's have a talk."

"Beena Auntie, I have had a difficult kind of day. Can we talk some other time?" Leena kept her hand on the knob of the open door. "I can make some chai and there is a nice new masala chevda I can bring from the store, you will like it. I'll just call you—"

Beena appeared to be engaged in an entirely different conversation. "How is he doing, your father, recovering good?"

"Really, Auntie, so sweet of you to come to check up on him, but I am just too exhausted, there was some trouble at the store—"

Beena uncrossed her legs and the swing issued a giant squeak. "I know what kind of trouble you had at the store. Why do you think I have come?"

Leena closed the door and sat down. What followed was a full rundown of all of Prem's dealings with T-Company and Tiger Nayak, from the Mumbai movie debacle to the initial investment in Superstar Entertainment all the way to Wristwatch, the threat to Leena's eye, and the happy ending involving Dr. Sanjay Gupta of CNN, orchestrated largely by Beena herself, of course. It was all too much at once for Leena. She closed her eyes and rested her head on the arm of the sofa, hoping for some kind of respite. Instead, her father came out to the drawing room.

"Listen to Beenaji," he said. "She is correct, absolutely."

"You too? It's like Prem Kumar has put a spell over all of King's Court and all the Hindi movie actors. How has he done this?"

"Everything this boy does is for you only," Hemant noted.

"Exactly!" Beena clapped her hands.

"He is not a boy, he is forty," Leena said.

"And whose fault is that?" Hemant had confused even himself. "Oh yes, never mind."

"Where is that board?" Beena said to Hemant. "The one you use with the markers for your community meetings?"

It was as though Beena and Hemant had been jointly preparing the ensuing presentation for months to ensure maximum impact and results. Their backs to Leena, they worked hurriedly, creating a bullet-pointed chart the likes of which Leena hadn't seen since Drop Thread Gorgeous was debating full-frontal services. "Okay, look here," Beena resumed as Hemant propped the board up on the kitchen counter. Using a serving spoon as a pointer, she began from the top:

Reasons why Prem did weird things but is a good man

Thing he did	Why it actually is good
• Took Leena's tickets back with no explanation and told her to go to Europe	• Was protecting her from eye-murder by Mumbai mafia
• Hid wealthy industrialist family background	• Did not want people to treat him differently or try to marry him with their sisters
• Worked at Exxon	• Tried to earn on his own for first time
• Sleeping on mattress under onions for 15 years	• Is humble and simple
• Stayed in America and built successful company instead of returning to India and joining existing successful company	• Excellent work ethic, perseverance, business shrewdness, independence

• Had mental collapse during beauty pageant judging	• This maybe was not great
• Primary means of transportation is bicycle	• Forgetting now why this is good. He almost died on it, did you know?
• Visited Hemant in hospital every day even though they were kind of enemies	• Too long to write here. Will explain verbally or in separate leaflet

Sitting before the whiteboard, Leena reverted back to her school days and raised her hand when she had questions or objections, both of which she had many, including:

"Papa, you knew about his family the whole time? How? When? And you didn't tell me?"

"What sisters?"

"I told you he was simple and humble years back! Why was it bad then but good now?"

"What are these onions everyone keeps mentioning?"

Hemant explained at length his admiration of Prem's riches-to-rags-to-riches story as well as the mutual respect he and Prem had fostered by helping each other out over the years. To which Leena rejoined, "Nonsense. You only like him now because of his wealthy family." To which Hemant responded, "Wait for the leaflet."

Beena addressed Leena's alarm that Prem had sent Indian celebrities to her store to plead his case. "Nobody sent anybody. I told them the sad tale of Prem's love, and they came on their own. Their flight to Disney

World isn't until Wednesday so they had some free time."

When Leena ran out of questions and objections, she commenced sulking. Hemant flipped the board around to reveal the second part of the presentation.

Options

1. Tell Prem there is no chance
2. Marry someone else (who is not gay but maybe is still a doctor)
3. Do nothing
4. Forgive Prem and see the person he really is

"I told you don't include the doctor part, she won't like it," Beena said after Hemant wrapped up his allocution.

"But *I* like it," Hemant explained.

"Where is the eraser?"

"I lost it long time back."

"Okay, then give me an old sock."

"What old sock?"

"Any old sock!"

As her father and Beena attempted to sort out the matter, Leena pondered her options. She didn't like being pressured; at the same time, the format of the pressure appealed to her logical business side. She was lost in thought for a long time. Beena left to tend to Prem, and Hemant grew tired and returned to bed. Viren Bhai completed his outdoor yogic activities and came in.

Toward the end of certain old Hindi movies, at the exact moment that a main character most needs guidance, a spiritual figure appears—an elder, an ascetic, a priest, a yogi—and imparts profound wisdom. This divine intervention leads to what must inevitably come next. Viren Bhai went in his usual corner and sat in lotus pose on the simple mat upon which he slept. He contemplated the whiteboard and its bizarre imperatives. After a prolonged silence, he said, "I am taking a shower now, unless you need the bathroom?"

Leena shook her head. She went about cleaning the kitchen, doing the dishes as she did each evening, trying to think only of the warm water on her hands. It was basic Vedic practice: be present, just be. She pulled the curtains and straightened the cushions on the couch. On the side table was a notepad she hadn't noticed before, upon which were scribbled the words: "When you don't know what to do, get quiet so you can hear the still, small voice inside guiding you to true north."

When Viren Bhai returned, she asked him about the note. "Bhagavad Gita?"

He shook his head. "Oprah."

"Hm," she said and thought about it some more.

Two days later, Leena offered Prem her response.

* * *

The only thing Prem could think to do to avert abject hopelessness was to watch a lot of movies. He had camped out at Beena's for two days, during which time he viewed *Mere Yaar Ki Shaadi Hai*, *Zubeidaa*, *Gadar: Ek Prem Katha* (twice), and *Monsoon Wedding*, which he found a little too realistic. Beena was frequently in and out of the apartment, which Prem thought curious but not strange enough to mention. Sunday's rain had subsided, giving way to a blue sky, the clearest they'd had in weeks.

An hour into *Kaho Naa...Pyar Hai* on Tuesday evening, Prem was startled by a tap at the window. When he got up to have a look, he saw no one who might have caused the disruption. He returned to his movie as the heroine's father admonished her for her interest in a lowly bicycle-riding car salesman. The tap occurred again, louder this time. Still no one in sight, no bird pecking at the sill. The third occurrence caused more of a bang, and Prem paused the movie.

Outside, it was uncharacteristically quiet. He walked toward the front row of buildings to investigate. All seemed as it always was, but something was slightly askew. In front of Building 3, the parking lot was entirely empty, but farther down, the lot was packed with cars. The circle of white-kurta seniors had shifted to a more remote patch of grass; tenants were hanging out on the front stoops as usual. Only there were more of them, many more. At his approach, they all turned to look at him with excited stares, smiling and creepy.

A cricket match was underway in the parking lot. Prem presumed the crowd was there to watch, but the batsmen dropped their bats and the bowler tossed the ball aside and both teams came together in a line and began to bounce their hips. Some young women from the crowd jumped up and joined the line in an evenly spaced and well-coordinated manner while some older ladies—Urmila Sahu, Nalini Sen, Gitanjali Vora, Shanta Bhatt—slinked into the formation at either side. The hip-bouncing turned seamlessly to sudden, sharp jhatkas at the same time that a car with speakers jutting out of its trunk pulled up, throbbing with a vaguely familiar song. Next, Prem's roommates past and present and Leena's friends Varsha, Snighdha, and Falguni bhan-graed their way in, followed by Leena's pretend ex-fiancé, Mikesh, and his husband, Arthur. When the Indo-Pak pizza delivery boy dropped the box and gyrated into the fold, Prem began to suspect something was afoot.

The car deejay amped up the volume on what turned out to be "Bole Chudiyan" from *Kabhi Khushi Kabhie Gham*, galvanizing the growing audience, including a gaggle of kids and Cash the superintendent, who launched themselves into the performance. Someone on a ladder doing something to a gutter leaped off and grabbed a dhol from out of a bush. He hung it from his neck and thumped it at both ends, adding his raucous percussion to the already pumping bass. All the performers wore blue, Prem noticed, and when he spotted Pankaj in the audience also wearing blue, he wondered if his assistant, too, would join the dance, which he did. It was when the Bollywood stars appeared and took their places as sideys, and Beena, Tun-Tun, and Tony pulled and pushed him until he stood front and center, that Prem understood the show was for him.

Prem thought he knew what might be coming, but then, he'd been so wrong about so much in his life. Yet there was something famil-iar about this moment, as though he'd lived it a thousand times. The music, the enormous cast of color-coordinated characters, the spon-taneous and perfectly in-sync dancing with matching expressions: it was a marvel of uniformity. A film song sequence was playing out in front of him, the kind with huge production values intended to lure moviegoers to theaters for repeat viewings, not just for the spectacle but also to witness the pure expression of emotion and desire. Here, the hero and heroine could perform the things they could not say and allude to the passion they could not enact. Prem had grown up wait-ing for these songs to be released on Venus and Tips brand cassettes, produced by audio companies that had pressured filmmakers to please squeeze in a few more songs, and they were what had sustained him. The musical number was emblematic of the relationship between two people, and in this particular number, he was the hero. And so, the heroine appeared.

The supporting cast parted, revealing Leena, back and center, spark-ling in vibrant rani pink, incandescent, ravishing, at once pious and racy, flashy and demure. She was the quintessential Bollywood leading lady, his American dream girl, his one great love, and she was running toward him. The others continued their vigorous ancillary dancing as he rushed to meet her, and they were face to face, not yet embracing but searching each other's eyes, transported to a faraway land.

The sun was setting when they returned to King's Court. The choreographed routine had given way to a frenzy of whirling, swirling, kicking, and flirting as the audience joined the performers. Prem took Leena's hand at last and drew her close. The dhol and song built in intensity, and the frenetic throng spun and spun around them. Together, they all ascended to a delirious, inexorable climax until the last streak of pink sky had gone.

The party went on for hours in the lingering heat of the day. It only ended because the movie stars had an early flight and the others had to work. But Prem and Leena sat on the stoop of Building 3, looking at the sky long after the fireworks she'd arranged for had tapered out. His arm was around her and her fingers played with his at her shoulder.

"Do you think we were meant to be?" she asked. "Like soulmates set up by God?"

Prem smiled. "This isn't a Hindi movie."

"But then again," Leena said, "maybe it is."

44

They spent the next few nights in Prem's office, alone and happily cramped. It was the utter fulfillment of everything he had ever wanted, and yet something wasn't right. Before they could begin their life together, there was one thing he needed to settle. Leena was fixing her hair into a ponytail in the morning when Prem told her what it was.

"Don't be ridiculous," she said. "He doesn't want that. In fact, he would be insulted. Really, all these years later, and you know, so many things have changed. For example, I have a highly successful business and I don't need support from anyone, but if I did need support, he knows you could give it because he knows you have a successful business too. Oh, also, and you already know this, he loves you now! No more need to impress him or win him. You have won! Just leave it."

Prem had forgotten, after all these years of not talking to her, how much she talked and how much he loved it. He wanted no secrets from her, not now, not ever again, so he laid bare his plan, and eventually she surrendered. They went about their separate days, she off to the store, he to an office park three blocks away.

Three days earlier, he had quietly arranged with his wealth manager to pick up a certified check for a very large amount in the name of Hemant Engineer. The manager, Amol "Alex" Pattnayak, highly discouraged this move, but Prem insisted. Even as he handed Prem the

check that day, he recommended a long-term corporate-bond fund instead. But Prem stood firm, without explanation or apology. "Who is
this Hemant?" Alex asked. "Does he need a wealth manager?"

The check felt heavy in Prem's hand. He tucked it into his wallet,
which he tucked into his pocket, the one on the front of his shirt so
that he would see it if it fell as he cycled to King's Court. He had imagined so many times over the past decade and a half the triumphant
moment when he would present Hemant with the money he had asked
for, both of them bursting into tears and embracing under the excessive plant life of apartment 5F. Instead, Hemant looked at the check
and whacked Prem on the side of his head.

"Don't be ridiculous," Hemant said. "I do not want your money."

"But you said you wanted my money," Prem argued.

"I never said that."

"Yes—"

Hemant let out a long sigh and sat down at the kitchen table. "The
thing I said was I wanted you to earn it. I never said you had to give it
to me." Prem paused to ponder the semantics of the decree. "I know I
put you through the torture . . ." Hemant studied his check, stopping
short upon noticing an oversight. "Where is the extra one?"

Prem snapped out of his reverie and examined the check. "He forgot
to add it."

"Who?"

"Does it matter now even? Looks like you are not keeping the check?"

"No, I am not. But extra one is a very important thing. What if you
and Leena have the bad luck because of this?"

"I don't think that's how it works."

"How do you know how it works?"

"Nobody knows how it works."

"That is what I am saying!"

Prem understood he had to give his future father-in-law one dollar in order to secure his blessing and, supposedly, to avoid certain destruction. He searched his wallet, but found only two twenties and a Paan-Stop punch card. "I will be back," he said, leaving the check with Hemant.

It was the only possession he had that was unrelated to Leena and that meant anything to him. Prem raced back to his and Leena's place and rifled through his duffle bag until he found the framed dollar bill that Amitabh Bachchan had given him a lifetime ago at the Exxon gas station. In recent years, he had considered it the source of his success, a lucky charm of sorts, ascribing to it mystical powers. He would rather have parted with the million dollars than with this, but it had to be done.

He handed the talismanic dollar over to Hemant and bent down and touched his elder's feet. Hemant, in turn, placed a hand on Prem's head in blessing. "Long life," he said softly. "And the frame is included?"

"I told you," Leena chided, sliding into the bench seat next to Prem. "See? I knew he didn't want the money. You wasted the whole day for nothing."

Prem perused a menu. "Wasted? How was it wasted? I spent time with your dad. He's a cool guy."

"It's nice how you two are buddies now, but, come on, he's not a cool guy," Leena said. "He is a slightly grumpy teddy bear, but cool? No. Absolutely you wasted your time. From now on you just should do what I say, and your life will have no speed bumps."

"Is that right?"

"Of course it's right."

And this is the way all of their conversations went in the early days of their new, painless love. They pretended to bicker just so they could make up and teased each other so they could pretend to bicker. They went to a different Oak Tree Road restaurant every day, sitting on the same sides of booths. They caught each other up on their lives. He poured out the story of his privileged but lonely upbringing, his unreasonably accomplished family members, the pressure to achieve, and his desire to run away. She chronicled her journey to become a hair-removal tycoon and her life as Mikesh's beard. They were tired, both of them, from their years of slogging. But that was done now. They were together.

Pandit Vishnu Kaushik, priest, astrologer, and freelance face reader, fixed the wedding date for Friday, August 15, a most auspicious time for the couple, which also turned out to be the second day of a major northeast blackout. But Prem and Leena refused to postpone, so their team of planners transformed the nuptials at the Maharani Manor into a candlelit affair that called to mind the antakshari blackout of so many years ago. Bride and groom danced to everyone's favorite long-term relationship anthem from the movie *Jurm*, the bride draped in bespoke Wristwatch couture. Ashok Ratan Kumar was in attendance, as were Prem's siblings and their families, all of whom thoroughly enjoyed the shadowy festivities and pushed off for Niagara Falls directly afterward. Only the mothers were missed, but they were lovingly remembered and honored with garlanded portraits at the dessert table. Prem contemplated how much his mother would have loved this and how she would certainly have noted the parallels between Leena and Prem's saga and the Hindi movies of the 1990s, which extolled weddings and traditional values and romance in the context of family.

Of course, the couple's American families were all present too—the roommates, friends, colleagues, aunties and uncles, Prem's band of platonic dates, and Leena's ex-fiancé and Arthur—who together begot a rip-roaring scene on the dance floor, periodically lifting the newlyweds up on their shoulders, at times hoisting a teary-eyed Hemant, at others carrying the couple's matchmaking caterer, Beena Joshi. Even Mohan, who carried the weight of his father's untimely death with him every day, let loose and Macarenaed.

The night ended only because it was morning. Candles and torches were extinguished and the music wound down. Barefooted women toted their high heels, and everyone chugged water. Bleary and in love, Prem and Leena made their way outside, accompanied by upwards of a hundred loved ones who gave them a beautiful vidaai, their parking-lot send-off at dawn.

Traditionally, the bride's family is bereft after her departure, left with a gaping hole in their homes, unsure when they will see her next. Hemant Engineer had this experience for about two minutes the morning after his daughter's wedding, after which he went on with his day, knowing Leena and her husband would be back soon and would never be far for long. Besides, how could he be lonely in Edison, New Jersey? It had become a place where mainstream grocery stores were forced to carry Indian foods in order to compete; where voter-registration forms would soon be offered in Hindi, Gujarati, and Punjabi; where it was crucial for politicians to be familiar with "namaste" and "Jai Hind." Roughly a third of Edison's residents were of Indian descent now, and the town was allegedly home to the highest concentration of Indian American people in the United States. Despite continued racist incidents, such as school-board election flyers decrying the presence of cricket fields and Indian schools, calls for the deportation of Asian American candidates, etc., the over four hundred Indian businesses represented on that ordinary one-mile stretch of road continued to thrive. Hemant was steeped in community, with no room for loneliness even if he wanted it.

He would carry on his work with the Oak Tree Business Association and go on to establish the New Jersey Cricket League, bringing organization and funding to the local scene. Eventually, he would grow this into a full-blown, state-of-the-art academy that offered coaching, camps, and equipment, and hosted matches at both the club and youth levels, and even issued a quarterly newsletter, *The Sticky Wicket*.

He would be most proud of the academy's partnership with the US Census Bureau to lead a South Asian and Indo-Caribbean outreach effort throughout the state, mobilizing thousands to fill out their forms and make their presence known.

Prem, on the other hand, would do nothing of the sort. His interests had always lain elsewhere—with movies, with Leena—and that's where they would stay. He saw no reason to involve himself in politics or community organizing or fighting the immigrants' fight. His work trip had turned accidentally into immigration, and that was that.

The newlyweds searched for a house together and in the meantime rented their own apartment in King's Court. They opened their wedding gifts and deposited the checks, which of course were all written for amounts ending in one. Prem presented Leena with the ledger he'd been keeping for her all these years, and she read it with great interest and frequent comments ("You know, fried ice cream is not actually fried"). They made chai and unpacked their things, mostly hers, as he marveled at the sheer volume of her wardrobe. She expressed horror at the sight of his ball of her hair, which went directly in the garbage. In a cup next to the bathroom sink, they deposited their toothbrushes and tongue scrapers and went to bed, at last, on a mattress that was not on the floor.

* * *

Two months passed and Prem and Leena still lived happily in King's Court. They were walking to dinner when the snow began, and forever after, they would take snow in October as a portent of happy endings. They tilted their heads back to feel the flakes touch their faces, as if experiencing it for the first time.

"Has it ever snowed this early?" Leena wondered aloud.

"It's not even very cold out," Prem noted.

They opted to stick to their plan to eat outside. When they reached the former Dairy Queen, Prem ordered two masala dosas and paid a little extra for additional coconut chutney, because what's a dollar here or there? They sat on the same side of a rickety bench attached to a picnic table, the perplexing October snow falling around them.

"So beautiful, no?" Leena gazed at the Diwali lights strung across King's Court's balconies, their brightness muted by the snow.

"Lights were invented here, you know," Prem offered.

"What a nerd you are."

They sat like that for a long time after they were done with their food, the snow lightly dusting the table, the pavement, their hair. When they finally stood, they found they were not yet ready for home.

"How about a movie?" she asked.

"Let's do that."

They didn't know what movies were playing or what the showtimes were, but this was immaterial. The newer movies were moving away from the typical conventions in favor of more nuanced depictions of love and drama, which Prem and Leena found too realistic for their taste. They headed up the street, past Gopal's Sweets and the Sassy Salwar, past a Gujarati restaurant and a Marathi one and a Desi designer mall, past the places that had kept them from missing their original country too terribly.

They stopped at the crest of the hill to admire the view of their home. The shows would continue in the capable hands of Pankaj, the newly appointed Chief Operating Officer of Superstar Entertainment, and Drop Thread Gorgeous was poised to be sold. Prem would miss the glamour and the excitement, even the mafia intrigue, but only at times.

Leena tucked her hand in the crook of Prem's arm, and they continued their walk to the theater through the bewildering snow falling lightly over this great American town of Edison, New Jersey.

S o many thanks are in order, beginning with the team at Third State Books: Charles Kim and Stephanie Lim, my visionary editor and publishers for finding me and making me an author, and for your ferocious commitment to amplifying Asian American voices. Thank you, Mih-Ho Cha and Jeffrey Yamaguchi, for lending your wisdom and expertise to the task of putting my book in the world and for your unwavering warmth and kindness. Thanks also to Kathy Campbell for running with the idea of a vintage movie poster and designing a gorgeous book; and thanks to top-of-the-line intern Prerna Chaudhary.

I am grateful to Jafreen Uddin and the Asian American Writers' Workshop's Pages in Progress Prize; the First Pages Prize; the Jerome Foundation; the MN State Arts Board; Intermedia Arts; and the Loft Literary Center for supporting the production of this work.

For so much knowledge, I am indebted to: *Bollywood's India: Hindi Cinema as a Guide to Contemporary India* by Rachel Dwyer; *Bollywood: A Guidebook to Popular Hindi Cinema* by Tejaswini Ganti; *Bollywood: The Indian Cinema Story* by Nasreen Munni Kabir; and S. Mitra Kalita's excellent *Suburban Sahibs: Three Immigrant Families and Their Passage from India to America*.

A special thank-you to Madhavi Kavadi, Kim Richards, and Savan Sant, who did various awesome things to help me out. And for medical input, I thank the doctors: Jeff Reitsema, Meghan Shorter, and Dad. Thanks are also due to David Mura, Sandy Benitez, and Sabina Murray for guiding me at various points along the way, and to Donna Trump and Emily Freeman, my sweet, brilliant writing group.

Diivyaa Mathur, thank you for those magical Jaipur summers that did so much to inform this book. And my entire India family for welcoming me always with open arms.

For the bedrock of friendship, I thank the 5320 book club; Sonal who pointed out the funny; Molly and Stacy who made the boring days less so; my amazing Penn girls; Julie and Priya for keeping me sane; and Tiffin, my true fur love.

So much love and thanks to Aai, Baba, and my three fabulous sisters-in-law, who cheered me on even before there was anything to cheer; to my dear brother, Parth, who has been there for me and made me laugh since our days of Chips Ahoy and *Terminator 2* Rainbow on Top; to Mom and Dad, for my education, for encouraging my literary bent, for your guidance and unconditional support always; especially Mom, for taking me to lessons, nourishing my artistic inclinations, and steadfastly believing I could do this.

And most vitally, for believing in me all these years, for giving this book the time it needed, for talking it through, for reading, for contributing so many bits of Indianness, for being more excited than even I am, and for taking over everything so I could finish; for all of this and a million and one things more, all my love and thanks to Amol, without whom none of this would be possible; and to my hilarious, precious babies, Raina and Deccan, without whom none of this would matter.

—Pallavi